SACRIFICE OF ISAAC

SACRIFICE OF ISAAC

NEIL GORDON

RANDOM HOUSE NEW YORK

Library of Congress Cataloging-in-Publication Data

Gordon, Neil
Sacrifice of Isaac / Neil Gordon
p.   cm.
ISBN 0-679-43704-5
I. Title.
PS3557.O677S23 1995
813′.54—dc20   94-35370

Manufactured in the United States of America on acid-free paper

98765432

FIRST EDITION

Book design by Carole Lowenstein

To Peter Holtz and Lisa Levit Newman

In writing and publishing this novel, I received extraordinary and generous help from David Sobel, Andrew Klavan, Ellen Klavan, and Michael Drinkard; from Sheila Gordon and Harley Gordon, Roy Rappaport, and Ann Rappaport; from Richard Burbridge, Michael Greenberg, Daniel Goldin, Henry Schlesinger, Stephanie Smith, and Ingeborg von Zitzewitz. My agent and friend, Eric Simonoff, provided invaluable criticism through many, many drafts; my editor, Jonathan Karp, offered a virtual MFA in writing. Above all, I am grateful to Esin Ili Göknar, my wife.

I could not have written this book had I not had the good luck to study for nearly ten years with the brilliant and maverick Professor Shoshana Felman, under whose tutelage I was also lucky enough to attend a magnificent lecture in biblical studies by Professor Miri Kubovi. The analyses of *Sacrifice of Isaac* are drawn, much simplified, from classes that I attended with Professor David Noel Freedman nearly twenty years ago and that have remained with me ever since.

Finally, I am grateful to my employers and coworkers at *The New York Review of Books* and *The Reader's Catalog*.

|1| THIS IS what Luke told me.

That one winter he lost his much-feared father and found his long-lost brother. Then he lost his brother again. And found his father.

This is what Luke told me. That he lost his father in the bitter rain of a Jerusalem winter and found his brother in the blossoming of a Paris spring. And when he found him, on a warm dawn of a black night, he shot at him with his brother's own gun and the bullet dropped his brother like a split bag of sand to the shadows of the street.

Now Luke had killed twice. Two killings, years apart and in different countries. But as the report of the gun rolled away between the rows of houses and the neighborhood dogs began to bark, as his brother spilled to the ground and, far in the distance, sirens began to whine, Luke felt he had killed only once: a double fratricide witnessed by the same howling dogs on the same endless night.

This is what Luke told me. That then, suddenly, he was sure neither whom he had found nor whom he had lost at all.

|2| WE TALKED for an afternoon, a night, and then a morning.

Afternoon, relentlessly hot on the steerage deck of the ship moving across the Aegean, above the squint of the turquoise water stretching ahead. Luke in profile against the high Grecian sky: a beaked nose over a sharp jaw; a bony, sunburned forehead; jet black hair sweeping upward from a high line, a wound healing above one pale cheek. Eating the food I bought him, hungrily; drinking the wine. Filthy, incessantly smoking thin cigars from a blue tin as he talked.

And then night across a small table in the ship's deserted dining room. Outside the porthole the great harvest moon casting a wake of silver into the shifting fields of black.

Then a morning hotly ripening to noon, watching anxiously as Naxos, then Amorgos draw close, then pass: great bulks sleeping in the sun, on the rippling surface of blue as the ship draws to the final call.

And this is what he told me, in his low, scholar's voice, his wide mouth picking and pronouncing the German words with the practiced precision of a foreign language learned well: that looking for the brother he had murdered, he traveled south through the blooming of a European spring, from Paris, to hot Italy, and there he found the father he had lost. And that guided by a dead father, looking for a murdered son, he traveled over the Adriatic to the Ionian and on into the always strengthening sun. Always more south, always more summer, and always, always more lost.

And in the end he found me.

He told me he would never again mind being lost. For when you know where you are going, then you are your own guide. But when you are lost, really and truly lost, so lost that you no longer know even where you meant to go, then—and only then—is born the possibility that somebody will take you there.

PART ONE

The shock of being lost
as a metaphor is the discovery
that you've never been "found"
in any meaningful sense.
—Jim Harrison

1 THE NIGHT David Sayada called to tell him that he had lost his father, Luke Benami was moonlighting. Subtitling, appropriately enough, Huston's *The Dead* for its French distributor. Appropriate to the message from Dov waiting on his answering machine at home; appropriate to the snow flurrying in the neon lights of Broadway outside the studio window. He had been working for nearly thirty hours.

I see him seated next to an editing console in headphones, a keyboard under his hands and computer screen in front of his eyes. Paler than when we met, after his summer of traveling—a pale person, twenty-six years old. A single overhead light cast a descending shadow over his long face in concentration, absorbed, thoughtless, his wide mouth pursed, his black eyes, impossibly far apart, intent on the screen while he fluently typed. To his left sat a woman running the console, and Luke spoke without looking up.

"Seiko. Give me French for 'scatter.' "

The woman was Japanese, a head of black hair over a round face, a tight black T-shirt defining her slim form over black jeans; Japanese in origin, but with her perfectly pronounced French, perfectly international. *"Éparpiller."*

"No. Like leaves falling onto the ground."

She stood, stepped behind him, leaning an ear to his headphones while he rewound. Then: *"Joncher."*

"Thanks."

He kept typing while she watched, a hand on his shoulder. Perhaps it was his concentration, faultless, entirely absorbed; perhaps it was his face, entirely disarmed in his fatigue. Her expression was affectionate.

She spoke in clipped English, half Japanese accent, half New York slang: "Where you from, Luke?"

He glanced at her, then kept typing. "All over. You?"

"Kyoto, originally."

"How do you come to speak French and English so?"

"Daddy owns Sony. You?"

Still concentrating on the screen. "Me what?"

"How you come to speak French and English? You're not American."

"Yeah? How do you know? And tell me my accent's no good, you're dead."

"Nah. An American would have made a pass at me already."

He looked up now, his face still disarmed, his eyes traveling from her face to her hips. When she met his eyes, he smiled, a disarming, wide-mouthed expression that lit his face and rendered it, for the moment, as handsome as it can be: an open face that wears its emotion transparently, lit now with a rare smile.

"I'm from Oklahoma City."

She smiled back, as if against her will. "Yeah, right. I bet you've never been west of the Hudson."

"I have, too. Cinémonde took me to L.A. last spring. What say we wrap and have a drink?"

"L.A. doesn't count. I'll have a drink if you tell me where you're from."

He began shutting down the computer. "No deal. But I'll buy the drinks."

She paused, then stood and began to gather her things into her bag, her English lapsing in her frustration. "You an intense guy, Luke."

Broadway at 5:00 A.M. A step closer to home; a step closer to Dov's message. Night, a flurrying snow hazing the neon lights, the avenue empty but for cruising taxis. Wrapped in a black wool coat, he rode downtown, Seiko at a slight remove in the seat. A recorded muezzin played on the driver's tape deck, then a taped Muslim prayer interrupted every few moments by a precisely phrased translation in an upper-class British voice. Luke leaned forward to see the driver's name: Jefferson Hampton. He leaned back to the window again, the familiarity of the urgent, high-voiced prayer carrying him far away to where he was in fact from. He did not suspect how soon he was to be there again.

Thirtieth Street, a quiet club, a single bass guitar and harmonica ushering out the night on the small stage. They perched on barstools, waiting to be served. A group of dark Israelis were drunk at a table, trading war stories in Arabic-accented Hebrew, and Seiko watched Luke's face stiffen as he glanced over, then turned his back. The bartender, a tall black man in a goatee, approached with a shot and chaser for Luke, whom he greeted by name, then directed a tired, questioning glance at Seiko. She ordered Absolut on the rocks, then said, as if there had been no interruption since the studio: "I think you're Israeli."

Surprised. "And what do you base that deduction on?"

She wasn't smiling. "You're listening to those guys behind us."

He looked away at the stage, then back at her, her small body perched on its barstool, legs crossed, hips and breasts outlined in her tight black clothes, emanating a warmth, deeply seductive. A bone-deep desire passed over him; he licked his lips, drank off his bourbon, hesitated. Then: "Come on. You don't want to hear a life story at a bar at five in the morning."

"Depends who's telling."

Telling was a temptation; it always was. Had she been Lebanese, or African, or Eastern European, he might have tried. But then, had she been from those places, she would have understood. As it was, she wore her internationalism too easily; borders were an opportunity to her, not a punishment. Deeply, he wanted to be in her bed, to feel her small hands on him. Deeply, he knew that those small hands held no absolution. He said: "I'm from Galveston, Texas."

She finished her drink, pouring the clear liquid delicately between her lips, elbows raised, as if even drinking from a glass were governed by a complex Japanese ritual. Then she rose and, standing, ran a small palm down the side of his face, launching his heart into life.

"You're a nice guy, Luke, but man, are you intense. I'll see you later."

And then he was alone over a second set of drinks at the bar, feeling remorse. Just as, in his empty apartment downtown, the answering machine picked up Dov's call.

A thin snow was falling over the just-opening meat warehouses in his neighborhood next to the Hudson River when he arrived home, a thin light beginning to bleed gray into the high winter sky. Climbing wearily, drunkenly, the stairs from the street into his building, picking up yesterday's paper from the front door, walking into the apartment with no discernible pleasure at his return. He punched the answering machine, crossed to the living-room window. During the quiet, gar-bled scream of rewinding tape, he pulled up the blind and stared out at the vista of cloud and water stretching to the Maxwell House clock on the waterfront of New Jersey, thinking still in camera angles from his night's subtitling.

A low, deliberate pan, maybe nine seconds, across the liquid gray sky of lightly snowing clouds. Then cut into the field: tight on the sad eddies of snow hanging pointlessly in the foreground over the green surface of the leaden water, shifting in long, slow swells. Sound track: a message in French; *Le Journal du Dimanche* looking for a translation of a Bush press conference. A second message in English: Could he work German to English at the General Assembly that afternoon? The third in Hebrew: Dov Sayada in Jerusalem, asking him to call right away. Three languages, two foreign and one maternal, each an equal step farther into the anonymity of this cold city under the winter sky at dawn.

The radiator clanked with its steam rising in protest, and Luke turned into the dusky room. Shrugged off his coat, flipped through a Rolodex, punched the international code and Dov's office number on Mount Scopus. A secretary answered, "Good afternoon"; when Luke said it was Jules Benami calling for Professor Sayada, there was a long, distant silence, in which a crossed line clicked and an echoing voice cried the Hebrew name "Shira. Shira." Finally the secretary told him to call his father's home, and Luke hung up. He punched another number from memory, his father's. This time Dov answered, and told him his father was dead.

That he had had a heart attack and been found the previous morning in his bed.

That Dov was arranging the funeral at his father's kibbutz.

That a Benami chair of Jewish history was to be founded at the Hebrew University.

That El Al was holding the evening flight for Luke.

He hung up, the faint buzz of transatlantic distance still in his ear, mixed with the silence of the morning vista without. He felt strangely like laughing, his stomach jumping with a mirth that he did not feel. Mirth? For an instant Luke tried to name this feeling, and could not. Out of his confusion he felt back to the night before, spent awake and at work next to Seiko's warm body; remorse at her refusal of his clumsy seduction; drinking alone at the after-hours club when she had left; the return home; the three telephone messages. Calling Dov, the line clicking far and away in Jerusalem. Then, like an old machine, well used but rusty from a recent storage, a deep engine of grief sputtered into life and began to roar.

2 HIS WINTER had been busy, maniacally so. During the day he worked at the UN, a simultaneous interpreter in English, German, and French. At night he moonlighted: subtitling films, dubbing for television news, translating for magazines. The sheer volume made him known in the industry; work came constantly to him. That had seemed to be the point.

He called three employers to say he was leaving for some weeks. He did not need to say why: They had already seen the papers that he had missed. He called El Al to confirm a seat on the evening flight for General Benami's son. But after the reservations clerk had checked his ticket, her expressionless voice informed him in Hebrew that there was a diplomatic flight being held for him. Could he leave immediately? His American passport was to hand in a desk drawer; after a pause he reached in again for the blue Israeli one. He pulled a small suitcase from under the bed and packed it quickly. He put on his coat and stood in the dark hallway of his apartment, watching the stain of weak light on the dirty Manhattan windows. Already this apartment where he had lived for four years was ceasing to be his; already he was out of the familiar neighborhood, the familiar city, and into that zone of anonymity the international zone. Bitterly he felt that he had never been at home here. He locked the apartment door, pocketed the keys, carried his bag down the stairs and out of the building. It was a small bag; he did not know how long he would be gone.

3 HIS FATHER was buried in the hilltop cemetery of his kibbutz in the north of Israel. The minyan: Luke, Dov, Avishai Yerushalmi, Gilead Sharon, Isaac Wasserstein, five others; students and comrades bent over the grave. Then a huge crowd of raincoated and uniformed people standing farther back, perfectly still as Luke read a mumbled kaddish into the small, silent space under the lowering sky.

Behind the crowd, like giant mourners, memorial stones: enormous slabs of marble carved with barbed-wire patterns surrounding columns of names. In front a receding vista of dark mud under looming clouds of rain, speckled with gray steel farm buildings, extending to a horizon of fog. The Yizreel Valley. Far away in a field a red tractor sowed winter wheat against the ever-shortening odds of the season, the thin hum of its engine sputtering faintly into the noise of the kaddish.

Lunch with government people, scholars, kibbutz notables in the communal dining room on muddy floors, a wintry smell of silage pervading the air. Sitting shiva for one afternoon in Gilead's dreary little kibbutz house, the weather-beaten faces of the kibbutznikim around him, familiar from his earliest childhood: that much older, that much more weathered than when last he had seen them, some six, seven, eight years before. Watching a crew of Arab laborers outside the window, Luke thought suddenly—and surprisingly—in Hebrew: This is the first place from which I was ever exiled.

Half the traffic on the Jerusalem road that night was coming from the funeral. *Culam makirim et culam,* the Hebrew saying went—in this small country, everyone is acquainted. Dov driving, silent beside him in the dark interior of the car. His wife, Hela, in the back, crying silently, her body huge in the last months of pregnancy. In the sweep of passing headlamps, Luke watched Dov in profile, his long scholar's face, his thick black hair, a familiar mix of emotion piercing through the dullness of his grief. Feeling himself being watched, Dov shifted his head slightly right.

"What's up?"

Luke shrugged.

"That must not have been easy, Jules. That was a big event."

"I'm surprised Shamir didn't hold a goddamn press conference from the graveside." The Hebrew was slow to his mind, heavy on his tongue.

Now Dov shrugged. "Most people weren't there for politics."

"Yeah?" Luke looked at him, an expression of interest coming up, then fading on his face. "Like who?"

He watched, not listening to Dov's response—it had been so long since he'd spoken Hebrew that he was able to let the words pass, unabsorbed—feeling the familiarity of the other's face. Dov, a scholar-soldier, high in the secret world of military intelligence, the trusted assistant and colleague of Benami. Thoroughly at home in this tiny country with a harsh language and a national aesthetic of kitsch. A good place, Luke thought, turning from Dov to the car window, for a funeral. Here almost no one knew anything about the rest of the world, but everyone knew everything about death.

4 I DOUBT THAT I need to tell you who Luke's father was. General, Ambassador, Professor Benami. Hero of the Mosad le-Aliya Bet during the war, famous for his Italian Passage, the still-secret route by which he saved hundreds of Viennese Jews from extermination. Then a Hagana commander in the War of Independence and a general in the Israeli Defense Forces in the Sinai campaign. Former ambassador to France and secretary of defense in three cabinets. David Ben-Gurion Professor of Jewish History at the Hebrew University. This part of his life, everyone knows; even in my country Benami's biography was a best-seller.

Luke knew his father differently. He had grown up in New York with his mother, who had been divorced from the general for some time—eight years—before her death in '82, a suicide. Luke was the younger son. The elder, Daniel, was lost to his father in the Yom Kippur War, worse than dead, worse than disappeared: deserted, in self-imposed and anonymous exile abroad. Luke, at least, was to come to know his father somewhat: He returned to Israel for his army service. That was when his mother committed suicide.

But he knew his father only briefly. Returned to finish his service after his mother's death, he was trucked with his unit to Lebanon and assigned to policing duty in the occupation of West Beirut. After his service he left Israel permanently, and when he returned to New York to work at the UN, having studied in Paris and Geneva, he changed his name, at least his first name, and dropped Hebrew from his working roster of languages. He had still not returned when his father died.

He had returned now, of course, but it was too late. Benami had lost his wife and both his sons: one suicide, two exiles. Casualties, to Benami, of his life of service: to the war, to the endless wars. Death, for Yosef Benami, was far too familiar to hold any mystery. And as for his sons, even if their exile was so different from his own, still, Benami knew a great deal about exile.

5 MORNING IN JERUSALEM. Waking on the couch of the study, a clean, frightful understanding of his surroundings immediately in his mind. Outside the tearing window a wet rain blew in gusts of tepid wind, the empty street was covered with mud. Luke sat in the kitchen, drinking coffee and eating a salad of diced vegetables, a kibbutz breakfast Hela had left, oddly out of place in this European house from the past. The doorbell rang and Luke rose to answer. Dov and Hela had come to take Luke to his father's lawyer.

Gray Yaffo Road, the New City, crowded with splashing cars in the rain. Arab workers in kaffiyehs crouching on the sidewalks under black umbrellas, Israelis hurrying by in puffy green army-issue coats, the feel of a familiar country all around Luke like a cold blush on his face. Avishai Yerushalmi's office, through the ornate lobby of the British-built Bank Leumi, crowded with irritated customers. In the interior half-light, waving a pencil at his desk before Luke and Dov and Hela, Yerushalmi's long face. Its deep cheeks hanging from the bone, the guttural words from the front of his throat, a Russian-born Israeli speaking fluent Hebrew.

"*Nu*, there is one will, made by me after the divorce, and three changes. Each time Yosef said: 'Yerushalmi, I am an old man changing his will.' Originally the estate was to be divided between you and your brother. In 1973, emended entirely in your favor." He peered across at Luke. "You understand me? Your brother was cut out. Then again in

August of this year, reinstated. The will was returned to the original terms of the division between you and your brother, with the survivor inheriting from the deceased brother, in the event of death."

"*Achi chai?* Is my brother alive?"

Yerushalmi watched Luke for a slow moment through expressionless eyes.

"*Lama lo,* why not? You are what, twenty-six? He's a young man in his thirties."

"Is he here?"

"No." A raised stare. "Certainly not. Were he, it would be in military prison, as you know."

"Where is he?"

"Client-attorney confidence. Though the client, who gave me the address, is no longer alive to enforce it." Changing into an archaic English, as though Luke were too foreign to grasp the legal subtleties in Hebrew: "That confidence only doubtfully supersedes my obligation to report the whereabouts of a traitor. And your brother, as you know, was convicted in absentia—I have already stretched the privilege. Who knows? Your brother was protected during your father's life. But your father had enemies, as well as friends, and some of them are in the government now."

In Hebrew again: "I telegrammed Danni the day after Yosef's death and received an answer instructing me to forward his portion of the inheritance in liquid funds to him."

"Here begin the problems. The estate contains practically no liquid; who keeps cash in this inflation? To comply with your brother's instructions requires liquidation of considerable assets. Very considerable, and which can, in the short run, be expected greatly to increase their value in today's markets. Such as real estate. Antiquities. And artworks." He paused now, allowing a practiced span of silence for his information to be absorbed. And when Luke said nothing, Dov spoke.

"You advise?"

"Nothing. As executor of the will I advise nothing."

Dov: "And as Yossi's oldest friend?"

Silence. The lawyer looked at Dov with a quizzical expression, then addressed himself to Luke: "Look, you can delay this forever. You get a lawyer; you contest the will; you try to take entire possession. You won't get it, but you'll force your brother to allow the principal of the estate to remain until such time as *you* deem it correct to sell. *If* you deem it correct: Yossi's collection, as you know, is a national treasure."

This time Luke answered. "And my brother?"

"*Nu,* who knows your brother? As a boy he was wild. As a soldier he deserted during a war. As a man, who has seen him since he was, what, eighteen years old?"

"My father, apparently."

"Julie, *motek*—sweetheart—your father, all his life he went to the mountain, but only he knows what he heard. Did you know him so well you're sure he knew your brother? He knew where your brother was. He decided to reinherit him. Why? Who questions an old man changing his will? Who *ever* questioned your father?"

A silence, and the lawyer went on. "The estate is considerable, eight, maybe ten million American dollars; who knows what artwork will bring these days? Does Danni want his piece? I find it hard not to imagine so.

"So he hires a lawyer, you go to court. Maybe you win; he's a marked man in this country and cannot come back to defend himself. Then again, maybe he does not need to; there's nothing that forbids a criminal representation in a court of law. What is the legal status of a deserter in this matter? Is it the same as a criminal? Two good lawyers could argue this before the Supreme Court, and a war or two could make that take a decade. Meanwhile, the estate is in chancery, its value, already inflated, dependent on George Bush. And I'll give you dollars to dimes that he's going to give us a deep recession. That means the estate will never again be worth what it can get before the next American elections. If you sell.

"But *savlanut*—patience." He raised a hand as Luke began to speak. "Now, what if you don't sell? Then the estate is valued and death duties are imposed. But by the time the valuation is done, let's say Bush has been kicked out. So what? If you ever decided to sell, between inflation and a possible drop in the market, the entire estate would go to death duties. Danni would get nothing, but neither would you."

A silence. Then Luke: "So selling now is the only thing that makes sense."

The lawyer shrugged. "Given that Danni wants cash . . ." He

paused, shrugged again, and continued in a measured tone. "*Motek,*
I'll tell you the truth. If I've slept two hours a night since Danni's
telegram, I've been lucky. I've spoken to the best lawyers in the country, and I *am* the best lawyer in the country. It all comes down to one
point: Is Danni within his rights to ask for his inheritance in cash? The
best answer you can get without going to court? Probably. Given that,
what should you do?" He stopped, swiveled his chair to look, briefly,
through the window to the bank's lobby. Then he turned back.

"First, I'm executor of this estate. I have a fiduciary—as well as a
moral—responsibility to do what you say. Advising you is not part of
my job. Secondly, I'm your father's oldest friend. Seeing his lifetime's
work sold to strangers—it makes me ill. But thirdly, I must advise my
friend's son. How do I tell you to let a fortune slip through your
fingers? How do I tell you to miss the chance of being a rich man—a
very, very rich man—for the rest of your life? And so I have to tell you,
I don't see the choice. I think you have to sell."

There was a silence, and then the lawyer stood up.

"*Challas,* enough. It's the day after your father's funeral; you should
be sitting shiva. Think about it. Come next week, the week after, tell
me what you're thinking. There is no hurry."

6
IN THE EVENING Luke finished the half bottle of scotch he
had brought to the study the night before, Yerushalmi's
words replaying in glacier-slow movement, a geologic
process of drunken thought. For the second time since his arrival, he
ventured into the darkened living room to search the liquor cabinet by
the light of the open kitchen door, and came up with a half quart of
gin. This meant ice, so he went through to the kitchen and stood,
swaying, in front of the open fridge.

Hela had left some fruit, some yogurt, some vegetables. But the
butter, say, and the jam, Luke realized, were his father's. The ice cubes
had been placed there by his father's wrinkled hand, perhaps a stubby,
nicotine-stained finger dipping into one of the square wells of water as
he placed it on the shelf.

A line from a Hebrew novel came into his mind: "But I did not
know that there was no point in leaving a fingerprint on the surface of

water." The ice tray in hand, he moved unsteadily to the counter and began breaking squares of ice into a crystal bowl, then bent to lean his head on the counter as, with shocking intimacy, his father's face appeared in his mind.

He had not even looked Jewish. A weather-reddened, even-featured face, easy to smile, animated by bright blue eyes under a thick fall of white hair. A commanding, charismatic face; in many ways, a politician's face, with a wide-open friendliness. Behind it, Luke knew, was a zero-degree concept of survival, a wholly dogmatic simplicity of purpose, and a deeply egotistic capacity for violence that had been proved, at home and in battle, time and time again.

Gone now. That towering, distant man, the fate of a nation in his hands. Gone irrevocably, down to the very objects of his life. That Luke had, for so long, so deeply hated him seemed in no way to diminish the throbbing grief that animated him now.

But he had found his brother, a silent, grim riddle from his earliest memories. Too much older to have been a friend, and too violent, too angry. As if the very walls could speak, the noises of his brother's fights with his father sounded in the empty house around Luke's lowered head. He heard his mother when the news of Danni's disappearance from the army came in. He saw the ashen, fallen, shocked face of his father when the truth of his desertion became known. He felt a sudden sympathy for that disappointed man, now dead.

And at that surge of sympathy, the thought defined itself in Luke's mind—as if it had always been there, waiting to be discovered—that *none of this would have been the same* if his brother had not made it so. His mother's death, his own difficult, rootless, stateless life, all the way to his miserable, drunken solitude, single-handedly shouldering the burden of his father's death in a Jerusalem winter's night. *None of it would have been the same.* The day Danni decided to desert his base in the Golan he had sent not himself but all of them into exile.

Luke experienced a bitter, bitter moment of regret. He saw that if Yerushalmi was right, then he couldn't stop his brother from liquidating the estate and having his money. And more, that destroying the collection of his father's life was, for his brother, a kind of parricide.

He saw that his entire family was gone, down to the very objects of his father's life, and that from his mother's suicide to the pillage of his father's estate, it was all because of his brother. Because of his cowardice. Because of his greed.

No hurry? Weaving back toward the refrigerator, the empty ice tray in hand, Luke felt aware that there was nothing but hurry.

7 HE SLEPT. In the long, dull, muffled light of Jerusalem in winter rain spilling through the window over his father's desk. He woke, and for a long time lay, lost in hangover, reassembling the present around him. When at last he rose to the ringing of the doorbell, head aching, it was nearly evening again.

Hela was at the door, come to take him home to dinner. She drove him to Mea Shearim, Luke silent beside her, deeply withdrawn in the exhaustion of mourning. It was only after her drab, silent meal that he was able, again, to talk. Then he asked Dov, his father's prize student, then assistant, then trusted colleague, if he had known his father was in contact with his brother.

Silence. Then, unwillingly: "*Yadati,* Jules, I knew. He was here, your brother."

"How? I thought he couldn't come back."

A shrug. "Things could be arranged for your father."

"When?"

"Late last summer. For two, three days."

"Did you see him?"

"Hela did, by chance."

Hela: "I'd brought Yossi some groceries, and Danni was in the kitchen when I came in. He went upstairs like a cat caught with the roast. I swear I thought it was you, Julie. Or your twin. He looked so much like you it was crazy. I couldn't understand why you ran away. Later I realized it must have been Danni."

Dov: "Yosef never mentioned it. They spent three days closeted in the house. Then he was gone."

"Did you know him, Dov? Before the war?"

"A little. He was in Jerusalem or abroad for school; I was on the kibbutz. The surprise wasn't really that he deserted. It was that he went in the first place. The army was way too much of a group activity for Danni."

A pause for thought. Then: "What should I do?"

Hela: "I'll tell you what you should do. Let Danni go to hell. Take your father's house, and car, and come live here. Dov was more of a son to your father than Danni ever was. We're your family now."

Dov, ignoring his wife, spoke forcefully. "No. Danni will never let you be. You can buy him off with what's his anyway. By all means, come back to Jerusalem, but give him what your father meant him to have and get on with your life."

Later, when Dov had driven him home, as Luke was stepping out of the car, Dov stopped him at the open door.

"Jules. I think his address is in Yosef's papers. I think I could find it."

"Whose?"

"Danni's."

Luke was surprised. "Why would you want to?"

"I thought you might want it."

Now Luke paused, and deep in his mind a purpose continued its process of taking shape. But an instinct made him say: "What for?"

"To find him. He's your brother."

Luke shook his head no. But then, before stepping out into the street, he asked Dov: "Which papers? Where would I look?"

"Not at home, in his office. I know where to look."

"I see."

Silence. Then, awkward: "I'm sure my father wanted you to have his papers, Dov. I'm sure he meant you to carry on his work."

Looking away, Dov did not look like a hero of two wars. He looked unmasked, his dark face uneasily wearing humiliation. "You saw the will. There was no mention."

"Well, I'm mentioning." And Luke stepped out into the wet black night.

BY 2:00 A.M. the rain had peaked, and abated, and dirty white clouds drifted aimlessly in ink black sky. The Jaffa Gate floated below across the Valley of Gethsemane in a single floodlight.

Spent, Luke raised his head from the pile of letters on his father's cluttered desk in the darkened study. In a long, slow sweep, he ran his eyes over his father's desk, the countless treasures it contained, the record of a historic life. He looked up at the walls: the Chagall sketch dedicated to Benami in the painter's own hand; the framed letter from Einstein; the Rafael Soyer. He ticked off, one by one: the German expressionists on loan to the Israel Museum; the Klimt in the Metropolitan, the medieval cabbalistic texts, the correspondence with Agnon, and more. So much more than he could remember. As much as he may have hated his father, there was still a lifetime of study here. For Dov, for Dov's whole department. There was a lifetime of priceless collecting, thinking, living. He closed his eyes, and far away in a part of his mind where images, not words, play against the mind's eye, he saw drunkenly, and with tremendous clarity.

It was all to go. Objects as familiar to him as his house, as his father. Gone—a lifetime—all gone by a stranger's wish. For a moment a detailed movement of the purest contempt crossed his heart. Then it faded, and, exhausted, he rose and began the slow stumble across the room to the couch. He knew exactly what he was going to do.

Morning, sober, sitting in Yerushalmi's office, his feet wet from the flooded sidewalks outside running with the steady winter rain, he found himself still resolved.

"How long will it take to liquidate the estate?"

"A couple months. Maybe until spring. This is what you want to do?"

"Do I need to be here?"

"For much of it. And your brother?"

"Give him his, Avi. Sell it all and give him his."

Then, outside on the street under drizzling cold rain, calling Dov from a phone booth.

"Dov? Have you found it? . . . Yes? . . . Six, rue de Fleurus. Top floor . . . Yes, yes, I know, Paris six . . . Thanks, Dov."

 BENAMI'S ESTATE took three months to liquidate. Archaeological artifacts went against taxes to the Israel Museum, the books to a New York dealer, Benami's correspondence with

Scholem and Ben-Gurion to the Beinecke and with Sartre to the Bibliothèque Nationale. The artwork was auctioned in Paris, the collection of German expressionists selling to a single Japanese buyer for nearly double Yerushalmi's higher estimate of the entire estate. Two Derwatts sold in London for prices that made the front pages of the papers. Luke bought the house on Hamevasser Street and its contents back from the estate, paying, by the end—to Yerushalmi's chagrin—half the market value again in taxes and death duties.

The brooding Jerusalem winter, cold winds blowing a bitter rain before them, chilled over the muddy Judean hills, swamping the stony city in short days of gray. Luke bought some hashish in a teahouse in the Old City. Days he walked the wall, or the *shuk,* or the slummy streets leading up to Mount Scopus. Evenings he and Dov played chess, Luke aware, now, of Dov's envy: rich, young, free, in sole possession of his father's intellectual legacy. To Luke, there was nothing to envy: burdened by the inheritance, afraid of what to do, and with nowhere in the world to go.

Nights he packed the papers from his father's desk into files, sorting out unfinished correspondence for Dov to complete. The drawers contained treasures escaped from the sale: a collection of Yizkors; five letters from Golda Meir; a Roman figurine of a dancing woman in a flowing robe. Maniacally he cleared everything away. Early one morning he climbed down to the basement, came up with a hammer and chisel, and opened the lock to the last remaining drawer. Here lay ten notebooks constituting his father's private diary, written in Yiddish.

A shock passed through Luke as he realized what he had found. Could this contain the details of the Italian Passage? Now Yerushalmi, the world's greatest secret-keeper, was the only person left who knew the route. Heart beating, Luke sorted the volumes and opened the first.

But it started with Benami's arrival in Jerusalem with his new wife after the war. It was labeled "Volume 3," and the first two were nowhere to be found. Luke caught himself in the reflection that, incomplete, the diary would be worth far less to a collector. He thought: My brother has made me see my father's whole life in terms of money. He thought: My brother has robbed me even of my father's death.

Spring came in on a wet wind, warming the mud in the streets, turning the dark olive trees a lighter green. The last sale took place at the end of March; now there were only taxes to pay and the money to be shared out before checks could be issued to Luke and his brother. Luke took an advance, in cash, of ten thousand dollars. He arranged to have the rest of his money deposited in a Paris bank. He leased his father's house to Dov and Hela for a dollar, arranged for Dov to have exclusive access to his father's papers. And at the end of March he went to a travel agent with Dov and bought a ticket back to New York.

Then a last night in his father's house. A last night drinking, watching the floodlit Jaffa Gate over the falling line of rooftops in the valley, the dry desert sky beginning to warm with eastern heat. A last night sleeping under the mohair throw on the couch in the study, the rest of the house, save for the living room with the liquor cabinet and the kitchen with the ice, still unvisited country. Dov and Hela saw him off at the airport for his flight to New York. The plane mounted into the warming blue sky, and Israel lifted away, a smudge of sandy gray beside the Mediterranean.

At the airport Dov had asked: "So you will do nothing about your brother?"

"Nothing, Dov. I was going to write to him. Now I don't even want to bother."

Hela: "And in New York? What is there for you there?"

He shrugged, wondering why he did not want to tell them the truth. "Back to work, I suppose."

In a very quiet voice, Hela: "It's not right, Julie. You're sending yourself into exile. You belong here."

Belong? On the plane, staring out into the silent cosmos of blue above the sea, Luke nearly laughed. No word could more inappropriately attach to him than "belong." When the plane stopped at Orly en route to New York, carrying his luggage, Luke disembarked, passing immigration as Luke Benami on his American passport, and took a taxi into the appalling, green, obscene softness of a Paris spring.

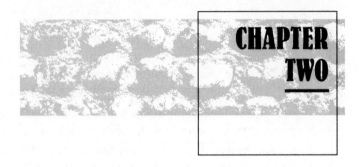

CHAPTER TWO

1 I WAS IN PARIS when Luke arrived. And I saw him there. Only I didn't know it was Luke, nor was it the first time I'd seen him. The first time was months before. And it wasn't him either.

Yes, I'll explain.

Picture the fall of 1988, the fall before Luke's springtime arrival in Paris. In the Döbling district of Vienna, on the upper floor of the house at Frederickstrasse 29, a girl sits in her room at a piano, next to the window. Not practicing, but sitting.

She's twenty-two, in her last year of college, still living at home. Medium height, blond, a Germanic face. In her attitude there are two sharply divergent strains of being. On the one hand, she is clearly used to being at home, clearly confident about her surroundings; this is a girl who's lived in the same place her whole life. On the other hand is evident a great impatience, evident in the swiftness of her movements, in the constant tic of her head, with which she flips back her hair. This is "displacement activity," and she uses a lot of it—smoking, trembling, fidgeting. She must; commensurate with her confidence is the discipline under which she's grown up, and there's not much liberty for a more—shall we say?—direct display of tension.

This is me, Natalie Hoestermann. It is late August, exactly a year before I am to meet Luke for the final time on the ferry to Astipalia. And on this day my life is going to change, entirely.

But don't be too impressed by that: I'd been waiting for it to change for a long, long time. And had it not changed the way, that day, events made it—well, I don't like to think of the various ways I might have had to change it by myself.

2 THIS DAY, watching idly out the window from my piano seat, where a brilliant autumn light spilled onto the deserted Sunday afternoon street—a silence that spoke of everything Austrian this Sunday after lunch, a desertion that oppressed me with its familiar tedium—I noticed a new element in the composition of the view from my window

It was a man, standing alone against the building across the way, watching—apparently—my family's front door. He wore a loose-cut black suit, clearly a good one, and a black cashmere overcoat. He was smoking from a pack of American cigarettes, but I didn't feel he was American.

I didn't know what he could be. His hair was black, and while he was not handsome, there was something about his face, his high, wide face, almost Arab but with pale skin, that drew my attention strongly, very strongly. More than anything, I was struck by his eyes: jet black, set so far apart on his face that for a moment I pictured him in profile as a flounder, and that made me laugh.

It's funny, that laugh. Years later I remembered it, several times, as a laugh that came from one half of my personality, a half that was not to laugh often again. You see, only a child could have laughed at that man, with the intensity of his gaze, the extreme tension of his person. Only a child could have ignored the fact that this dark, thin man, standing across the street from my family's house, could mean nothing good, nothing good at all.

I was not the only person to notice the man. I heard my mother's step on the second-floor landing, below my room, and the sound of her bedroom door clicking shut for her afternoon nap, but the next sound, the springs of her old bed taking her weight, did not come. Suddenly I sensed that my mother, too, was standing at her bedroom window, watching my father stroll across the street to greet the stranger, then turn to walk with him back into the house. And a deep feeling of sad, pitying affection for my nervous, aging mother swept through me, as if I knew this man had come to change not only my life but hers, too. All of ours.

I did not need to be told that I was not welcome downstairs at that meeting between the stranger and my father. It lasted all afternoon. Twice I passed the door to my father's study: once on my way to the kitchen; once on my way out. I walked to Wolf's house, looking to take refuge there, but when I arrived, I found myself turning to walk back, and when I returned, the study door was open. Through the doorway I could see the man standing with his back to me.

He stood by the window, gazing out, and turned slowly, as if unwillingly, when my father returned from the living room, carrying two glasses, each with a large measure of brandy—a surprisingly large one. My father, deep in thought as he approached, looked momentarily shocked to see me. Then he recovered himself and ushered me through the open door. He spoke, to my surprise, in his accented, halting French.

"Monsieur, *voyez*, this is my daughter, Natalie. My daughter speaks a much better French than I! Natalie, *ceci est Monsieur*—" My father paused, not as if he didn't know the name, but as if he didn't know which name to use. The stranger turned slowly, resting his eyes full on me before pronouncing it.

"Tueta. Monsieur Tueta, Herr Hoestermann."

I drew in my breath. I had never been looked at like that before.

3   WHAT WAS IT in the look? The high, far-apart eyes gazed at me with fathomless impassivity. The full mouth was set in an expression from which a smile was so absent that it was nearly a negative quality, a zero degree of seriousness. And in the long second that he stared at me, I saw that most painful of all was the utter, nonnegotiable lack of curiosity in his eyes.

"*Bonjour*, monsieur."

The stranger stood at polite attention, without an answer, and my father began to speak with practiced, nervous urbanity. I did not like to see him like that.

"Monsieur Tueta's interested in our house, my dear. It seems that his family once lived here, can you believe it? Now he's researching a—a family history. Lucky thing for him—he didn't know what a careful record keeper your old man is! I think"—he turned now to the stranger, and his manner changed perceptibly—"I think we've been able to give the gentleman pretty much what he came looking for, and more, *hein*, monsieur?"

There was a silence for a moment; then the other focused his gaze on my father and spoke absently, with a politeness that contained both menace and contempt. "You've been a great help, Herr Hoestermann, a great help. Still, I can't help feeling you could be a greater help yet."

"Now, monsieur." Did I know my father was scared? I suppose so. I suppose so. And yet age tells; perhaps he was scared, but he was also the elder and in many ways in control. "I think I've done quite a lot. And I think, too, that you will need to consider how far you want to go with this . . . research."

The man nodded, menace beneath his politeness more apparent. "I certainly will think about that, Herr Hoestermann. Or should I say—what was it?—*Obersturmbannführer*? And I'll let you know what I decide."

Then he was gone. My father returned from seeing him out, the lines of his face showing fatigue, and I remembered, once again, how old he was, over seventy. Too old to have a daughter my age. Too old to have a daughter like me. Someone once said that in my country we are born guilty. Some of us are guiltier than others. When my father spoke, it was as if his voice, already, came from an ever-receding point in an ever growing distance.

"*Gut, mein Liebling*, run away now. Papa needs a rest."

Liebling. How I want to hear him speak that word, just once, again, as he used to speak it, before that man came. It is like a thirst.

4 NOT LONG LATER, two or three days, I came out of classes in the early afternoon and found him waiting at the campus gate, leaning against a goldening chestnut. He wore the same impeccable black and carried a leather briefcase. I approached him, keenly aware of the distance between his proper dress and my jeans, my white blouse, my old jeans jacket. It didn't matter; absurd was the right way to feel at that age. I was not surprised to see him. It was as though we had an appointment.

He did not speak until I approached; when he did, it was with the same impassive contempt as before, and I felt the same sensation that suddenly I did not exist. Now I see that that very rudeness was a kind of acknowledgment.

"*Écoutez,* mademoiselle. Be so kind as to have a drink with me."

I nodded, and we walked in silence across the boulevard to a café. He called for a table and ordered without looking at the waiter. Like that, I saw, it was not just me. It was as if none of us existed. His eyes flat on mine, he spoke.

"I have something complicated to say to you. I'll be done in a moment. If you'd be so good as just to listen, I'd be grateful."

I nodded, and he paused, shifting his black eyes into the distance, licking his lips. Was he beautiful? I could not tell.

"Thank you." His eyes again on my face, he spoke in a measured voice.

"Your father has something that I feel should belong to me. It's worth no money, and it's of importance to no one but myself. I asked him the other night to let me see it; he said no. I threatened him; he still said no." He paused, licking his lips again as if only now becoming aware that a threat was not a common conversational item in my world. He went on.

"Now. What can I do to change his mind? I'm not about to rob his house; in fact, I'm leaving Vienna when we're done talking. I have only one weapon, and that is you. I am sorry, mademoiselle."

"I don't believe it." He was surprised to hear me speak, but I could not help myself. I have never been able to. More important, it was as if I understood, even then, what he was going to do to me. He was going to send me into exile. "I don't believe that you're sorry."

"*Je vous ai demandé d'écouter,* mademoiselle, not to speak." Shifting in his chair, he reached into his bag and withdrew a document, a faded, yellowing sheet of paper. At the top was written, in German: "*Auswanderungsvisum.*" Emigration Permit. I was not surprised to see that it bore a swastika. He let me look it over for a moment, then returned it.

"Can you remember this if you see one again?"

I nodded politely. "Not being an idiot, I think so."

He smiled for the first time, a half-smile that faded as quickly as it came, and I had the impression that under other circumstances, this man was not always as forbidding as he was now.

"Your father has a pile of these in his safe. Perhaps four hundred or so. I want them."

I nodded. "Ah."

Now he was withdrawing a business card from his pocket. "To the person who gives them to me, there's nothing I wouldn't give."

"*C'est bien rigolo, ça, puisque moi,* there's nothing I'd take. No, keep your card; I don't want it."

He pocketed the card again. "Perhaps not. But I'm going to give you something anyway."

Why didn't I get up? Why didn't I get up and leave? I wanted to, but the seconds ticked away, and I didn't move, and I didn't move. He went on now, and for the first time I felt his impassivity was beginning to wear thin.

"Here's my present to you, mademoiselle. Go up into your attic. In your house. Take a crowbar. Go to the dormer over the middle window—are you following me? The middle window. Use the crowbar to pry up the ledge under the window; you'll have to open the window first. There'll be a compartment in there between the outside and inside walls; in it you'll find something."

He stopped now. He stood up and reached into his pocket for a bill, which he dropped on the table as the waiter arrived with our drinks.

"I think you'll find it interesting, mademoiselle. Take it to your father. See what he says. Mention to the *Obersturmbannführer* that this little present, from me to you, is just the beginning of what I have to give."

I looked up. "If you're trying to tell me something about my father, I know it already."

Now a look of real contempt came onto his face, a contempt of which he did not seem the master, and I began to understand that feeling, that nothing around him really existed.

"Do you, my dear? Then I've misjudged you. Something gave me the feeling that you were not like . . ." He tossed his head, motioning around the room.

I spoke bluntly, through my shock. "My father was acquitted at

Nuremberg. He saved hundreds of Jewish lives. Read his book, you'll learn something."

But he was unfazed. "Thank you for the history lesson, Fräulein. Most informative." He stood up, and now his voice was rising. "But perhaps it's you who should do some research. Why don't you take a look? Oh, and the things you find in the hiding place? Ask Herr Hoestermann to return them to me. They belong to *my* father." And now, as if he couldn't bear to wait any longer, he walked away, leaving me alone with our drinks at the table.

And the next time I saw him was the following spring. In a tiny café on a tiny street in Paris. Only it wasn't him. And he didn't recognize me.

Yes, I'll explain.

5 THE FALL chilled and blew away on wet northern winds. Winter came in, the semesters changed, and my last months of college began, the future beyond them a sheer ascent into another world. I had made no plans: graduate school, work, nothing. It was as if I'd already known.

And still, I did nothing. I went through that winter going to classes, making love with Wolf, feeling the precious days slip away, one by one. I have even a happy memory of those last few months. But all the time I knew exactly what I was going to do. And as the winter lay over Vienna, the city of my childhood, the city in which I had spent my life, it was as if everything—my whole life—had already changed.

What a strange itinerary is our life, a story where the meanings emerge only when we are ready to understand. Now I know that I had been waiting to meet Monsieur Tueta for years. But it was not until early spring that I went up to the attic with a crowbar, opened the dormer window against the bitter winter wind, and tore the ledge from the window to reveal the hiding place below. And then, in the dark room, watching the lamplit streets below—identical, in the chill night, to the streets seen by whoever had built the hiding place—I lifted out the contents, the hidden contents under which I had slept nearly every night of my twenty-two years.

There was a heavy gold eight-armed candlestick, which I later learned was a menorah. And there was a leather-bound Torah. After I had replaced the ledge and closed the window, I read, on the inside cover of the Torah, the single word in Roman letters, alone atop a column of script that I later learned to be Yiddish, a family name. It was Neumann.

Tueta. He had meant me to take these things to my father. I put them back. But only after sitting with them for a long while, staring at the bland, blind fog of suspicion that was now my world. I did not know what these objects meant. I only knew that my life's certainty was gone.

My heroic father. A tree in the Garden of the Righteous planted for him in Yad Vashem.

What, then, did it mean that his house had once been owned by Jews? What was this man, Tueta, trying to tell me?

It had been perhaps a tenuous certainty all along.

I put the objects back, closed the hiding place, and went downstairs. Quietly. So as not to wake my parents.

Still pretending to myself that it wasn't as clear as a photograph developing, there in the fog where I hid from myself what I was planning to do.

6 AND YET what was I hiding? Nothing. I was hiding nothing. It was as if a clock had been set, and all I had to do was follow its deadlines. Winter moved into spring, my exams came and went, and while friends worried about graduate school, or planned moves and jobs, I did nothing. I played the piano in my room. I listened to Bryan Ferry while I made love to Wolf—or let him, rather, make love to me. I studied by my window next to the lengthening days, the shortening nights; I pretended that I was not sleeping in the house where the Neumanns once lived.

And it was only early on a spring morning, the morning after my graduation from college, that I took the key to his safe from its hiding place behind his desk, opened the safe, and withdrew, tied in twine, the pile of emigration permits the man had told me about. I looked at only one, in the dawn light in my room, as I packed them in with my clothes in my suitcase, with the two objects I had removed, again and for the last time, from their hiding place. Julius Michael Neumann, male, age fifty-nine. Profession: professor; address: Frederickstrasse 29, Vienna; Date: 1942. The long lines of Monsieur Tueta's face dimly evident in the faded photo of the old professor, stamped onto the document with a Third Reich stamp.

I closed the suitcase, and by the time the sun rose on Vienna, that early April day in 1989, I was on the train to Paris. That's how I was in Paris when Luke arrived.

Oh—I took two other things from my father's safe, and now, in retrospect, I see that the first prefigured a lot of things to come. I took—stole—a two-inch stack of deutsche marks. A lot of money— and still not even nearly enough to keep me until I was to see Vienna again.

And I took a business card. For Maurizio Tueta, Antiquaire, 13 rue du Faubourg-Saint-Honoré, Paris; and Piazza Santo Spirito 2, Florence.

7   NEVER WILL I be able to do justice to the strangeness of those spring days. Paris under its high blue skies, with great clouds sailing away to sea, the tulips in flower; the trees in pale green leaf, that impossible, inescapable fertility. It's a terrible city for a girl on her own. Every café, every corner, there was a man waiting to hit on me: Frenchmen, Americans, Africans. I could not even be alone picnicking on a park bench. The objects I had stolen from my father weighed on my mind, half guilt, half fear. Then I had an idea: I took my bag with the menorah and Bible and documents and checked it at the left-luggage office at the Gare de l'Est.

After that I was a bit less scared.

Every day I walked up Saint-Michel and over the Seine. Down the quai to the Tuileries, and across the garden to the rue du Faubourg-Saint-Honoré. Number 13 was a gallery, a sign of gold script on dark green reading: ANTIQUITÉS. OBJETS D'ART. Every day a steel shutter covered the window. And each time, at the sight of the closed gate, I felt panic. It was my only reason for being here.

I had come too far. And I could not go back. My father would have me back; it wasn't that. But I had come too far, and I could not go back. Not without knowing what this man knew about my father. Not without knowing if my father had lied to me all my life. Finally, in real desperation, I thought of asking at the boutique next door. Here I learned that the gallery had been closed for some months, "No, mademoiselle, the proprietor has not been back," not as far as she knew. I asked at the shoe store on the other side: same. With mounting frustration, I checked right down the block: nothing.

Until, at a little restaurant on the rue du Marché-Saint-Honoré, late on a weekday afternoon, the barman spoke to me.

"Ah, *oui*, Monsieur Tueta. He used to lunch here nearly every day. Now, oh, it's been months I haven't seen him. But now that I think, he often disappears for months; he must be on a buying trip. I believe he lives across the river. Marie!" He called through a door, and a woman came out. "Marie, didn't Monsieur Tueta tell you he lived across in the Seventh, where all the Americans live?"

"*Bonjour*, mademoiselle." The woman, after wiping her hand on her apron, shook my hand, once, lightly, with a warm palm. "*Non, chéri*, you remember Sophie's husband, Alain? He works at the café near the Jardin du Luxembourg?"

"*Ah, ouaih, ma chère*"—to me—"*ma chère femme n'oublie jamais rien, comme l'éléphant*. What was it . . . Le Fleurus, that's it. He knew Monsieur Tueta, said he lived right there."

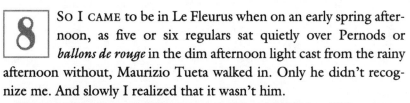

So I CAME to be in Le Fleurus when on an early spring afternoon, as five or six regulars sat quietly over Pernods or *ballons de rouge* in the dim afternoon light cast from the rainy afternoon without, Maurizio Tueta walked in. Only he didn't recognize me. And slowly I realized that it wasn't him.

The man I had met in Vienna was in his mid-thirties. This one was in his mid-twenties. Otherwise, they were nearly identical. Around five feet ten, thin, with broad shoulders and a hesitant grace, a diffidence about his movement. He hesitated, then walked, somewhat stiffly, through the glass front door into the café. It wasn't him. But as he entered, the barman called out: "*Bonjour*, Monsieur Tueta."

Evidently surprised, he looked around at the few habitués, as if wondering to whom the barman could be speaking, and in the instant he turned his head around the room, the extreme angularity of his face could be observed from a number of vantages: the sharp, high cheek-bones, the beaked nose, the high forehead under his hairline, and the eyes set so widely apart on his head. Was it him? I rose to greet him, then his eye fell on me with no recognition whatsoever, and I sat again. Finally he approached the barman, who continued to address him with a familiarity that belied the angular man's diffidence. They exchanged some words as they drank, each, a small, long-stemmed glass of red wine, but it was almost as if the man were an amnesiac returning to his home, for before the barman's familiarity he was, clearly, increasingly confused. Then another customer entered the door, and the barman moved off. Without paying, the angular man walked out, paused, turned along the building, and entered, hesitantly, the porte cochère to the courtyard of the building.

What would have changed had I spoken to this man who was the man I was looking for and yet wasn't?

Perhaps nothing would have changed had Luke and I met that day—or perhaps everything would have. Everything. Certainly two people would not have died; two murders would not have taken place, and an amount of suffering, untold, would have been averted.

As someone once said: In my country we are all born guilty.

1

THE TAXI FROM Orly Airport drew to a stop in front of 6, rue de Fleurus, its wheels skidding slightly along the wet surface of the street. There was a café in the ground level, Le Fleurus, and Luke climbed out. He stood looking at its green-and-white awning, its zinc counter and dim interior visible through the window. The view filled him with a sense of uncanniness, deeply familiar, enormously strange; it was four years since last he had been in Paris. He turned and, in the lightly falling rain, carrying his small bag, walked to the end of the street, where it gave onto the Jardin du Luxembourg, and stepped through the open gate.

The delicate warmth of the city in the first moments of spring; the hazed, resonant light; the trimmed chestnuts in new leaf stopping, then gently dropping a fine fall of rain onto the sidewalk from the leaden gray of the sky. What was his brother? He tried to picture him, and could not, and he suddenly felt a thin terror as his mind, like a flat rock skipping on the surface of a calm lake, touched upon fear after fear. He searched again in his memory for a sense of him, and felt only mystery: the dim remembrance of fear, of fright at his brother's temper. The endless fights between him and his father. The strange, flat mourning of his disappearance; his mother's crying night after night after night. Hela had said their resemblance to each other was remarkable, but presumably she meant their physical resemblance only. What was his occupation? How had he come, after fleeing Israel as a state traitor, to live now in the quiet, luxurious streets of the Sixth Arrondissement of Paris? And what would be his reaction when Luke showed up? Suddenly his army lessons in hand-to-hand fighting came fresh to Luke's mind. He walked a few steps into the park, stopped, and walked back, feeling a nervousness that was, he imagined, what actors felt before a performance. For the first time in years he felt the desire to smoke.

No one in the world knew he was there, he thought. Dov, Yerushalmi, all assumed him to be back in New York, and yet his few friends in that city had no idea where he was. For a moment an acute sense of how utterly without ties he was came over him: a lone man in a foreign city, without a country, and connected to no one in this world. How enviable he once would have thought such freedom to be.

Now what had seemed so strange, so frightening—finding his brother—suddenly was easier than allowing his life to remain as it was for a single second longer. Straightening, he set off in long strides back down the street.

But in front of number 6, his heart faltered again. And thinking to dry himself slightly and to compose himself before facing his brother, Luke went into the café.

And then something very strange took place.

2 INSIDE, in the dim afternoon light, a barman stood behind the curving zinc counter, and a few early-evening habitués sat at the small tables. The barman called out a greeting, and Luke paused and looked back at the door, in expectation of an answer. There was none. Luke turned back, and at a table in the back a girl stood, as if to greet him; he glanced at her face and she sat down again. Feeling confused, he turned to the barman, who, smiling across the counter, addressed himself unmistakably to him.

"Eh, M'sieu est enfin de retour!"

"Pardon?"

"Home again!" The barman extended a soft dishwasher's hand, then drew two *ballons* from under the bar and began to fill them from an unlabeled green liter bottle of wine.

"Tout va bien? I just saw *la belle Nicole* going up with the groceries. *Merde,* she'll be surprised to see you! Lucky her lover isn't with her, eh? Eh? *Allez, à la tienne!"*

Luke drank off his little glass of wine, watching the smiling barman over the rim, then wiped his mouth while the barman filled the glasses again. Confused, he felt that he should say something and after a moment found himself responding with the barman's same familiarity.

"And you? How are you doing?"

"Eh, ça va, quoi." He retreated a step toward a newly arrived customer. *"Allez,* Nicole'll kill me if I keep you any longer. Welcome home!" He did not seem to want any payment for the wine. Luke shook the barman's soft hand again and left the café. Now he had no choice but to enter the porte cochère into the building, which he did, hesitantly, aware of being watched from within the café.

He found himself in a hushed courtyard, shaded by the rise of the building around him. Upward an occasional window shutter jutted out against the darkening sky. Luke felt now not immediate anxiety, but rather a vivid awareness, a great visual acuity. A cat ran away through a doorway; a girl watched from a second-story window; high above, a pigeon fluttered noisily from the eaves of the roof into the air. A doorway led into the building on his left, and Luke entered. Here, in the sudden darkness, he found the button of a *minuterie* and clicked on the lights.

A bank of wooden mailboxes was against the wall, and Luke read their labels, stepping back to hit the button of the *minuterie* when its timer turned off the lights. None read "Daniel Benami," and he paused in confusion, until he remembered the name the barman had used. Looking again, he found a box belonging to Nicole Japrisot, apartment number 6A.

There were six flights to the top, each pausing at a landing of dark, highly polished oak, with doors to apartments at either end. Luke's footsteps shuffled against the smooth wood of the steps as if on a surface of flour. The *minuterie* closed the light at the fourth floor. On the top landing he paused in the darkness, then hit the light again and gazed at the two doors. An adrenaline buzz of clarity filled his ears; his mind was pure perception. Now that he had arrived, he was no longer scared, but eager: eager to face his brother, and be done, and to get on with whatever was next.

But what was next? Finally he turned, walked lightly down the hallway, and knocked on one of the doors. A stage wait. The light clicked off again, and the hall fell into murky darkness. Then a lock clicked, and the door opened on a wall of light, against whose glare not a man but a woman appeared as a slim silhouette. For a second, as her eyes adjusted to the gloom in the hallway, she stood stock-still. Then, with a sudden jerk, she stepped forward into his arms and, with a gasp of warm breath, pressed her open mouth against his.

3   SHE HELD the length of her warm body against his for a moment, her arms around his neck, her open mouth against his closed one. She drew her head away and looked into his face with a wide smile.

And then, suddenly, the smile stopped. She tensed and stepped back into the doorway, drawing him not into the apartment but into the light. She wiped her wide mouth slowly with the back of her hand, staring at him with confusion, and finally spoke.

"Daniel?" Her pronunciation was French, her voice deep, her intonation wondering.

"*Non.*"

"*Nom de Dieu,* who are you?"

"His brother."

"Daniel doesn't have a brother."

"Yes, he does."

She was taller than Luke by an inch, perhaps a decade older. Her short-cropped red hair was brushed severely back from her pale face, which suddenly flushed a deep shade.

"Impossible."

"Is Danni here?"

"What? Is he here? Who *are* you?"

Luke paused. "You can see for yourself."

Now she paused. "I don't understand."

"I'm Jules Benami. Surely my brother has spoken of me."

"Never." Fear suddenly replacing anger in her face, she stepped back into the doorway and extended a hand to the doorknob. Now, in full light, Luke saw the outline of her breasts under her shirt, her flat stomach, and the fall of a cotton skirt to her bare feet on the polished wooden floor. For a moment it seemed she was going to shut the door, and Luke's mind began to spin. Then she paused, and from nowhere a memory came to Luke.

"Danni has a scar on his throat, like this." He motioned with his forefinger. "An accident when he was a boy. He must have told you. Anyway, look at me. The barman downstairs took me for him. You did, too." From the breast pocket of his raincoat Luke withdrew his passport and offered it to her, only too late realizing it was his American one.

She turned to examine the picture in the light.

"Who is Luke?"

"Me. I changed my name. Years ago. See, it says here I was born in Israel."

"Why would you have an American passport?"

"I grew up there. With my mother. We were naturalized."

"How is it you speak French?"

"I've lived here. For two years. Four or five years ago—you can check the visas in there."

"Why didn't you look for your brother then?"

This made Luke pause.

"I had no idea he was alive. My father never told me."

"Non?" She gazed at Luke from the doorway for a long minute, examining his face, his hair, his hands at his sides. And as she looked with her hard gaze, judgment suspended, Luke felt a shift.

He felt a shift and knew suddenly what he had come for, and why. In the pause before he spoke, he gazed into the future that would be his if she denied him. He saw himself standing in the lightly falling rain of the Jardin du Luxembourg, alone, the whole of Europe radiating out around him, a solitary point in the middle of nothing. Had he come to his brother for revenge? Before him rose a future of utter anonymity in a world of strangers, an impossible future. His voice sounded loudly against his will as he said, nearly shouted: "Madame. Listen. I have nowhere else to go."

She hesitated visibly. Then stepped back and away from the door.

"Merde. Venez donc. Entrez."

And so a reprieve was granted, a *sursis* from utter exile, but still only a reprieve, and Luke followed the woman through the doorway and into the light within.

CHAPTER FOUR

1 BEFORE LUKE, in the light of the apartment, her green eyes betrayed wariness.

After a moment she motioned him a step farther in and, with practiced movements, closed the door, turning the key on an elaborate lock, then punched a code into a burglar alarm—what kind of life did this woman share with his brother?

Sitting, separated by a coffee table, they examined each other as if the strange circumstances of their meeting allowed an exceptionally long suspension of politeness.

She wore a sleeveless black leotard that showed shoulders sloping from a fine, long neck; small, round breasts; a firm stomach above womanly—not girlish—hips. Her round face was of a sensuality, a healthiness that for a moment shocked him: green eyes set under fine white brows; high cheeks of fair, lightly freckled skin; a full mouth. Her light red hair, short-cropped and brushed back, seemed deliberately intended to downplay her beauty. As such, it succeeded only partially, for if it did in fact work against the regularity of her features, it also imparted an air of modesty that was achingly beautiful. She wore no makeup.

There was a pack of Marlboros on the coffee table, and without a thought, Luke leaned forward, took one, and lit the first cigarette he had smoked in years. At the first lungful his mind swirled suddenly, and he waited a few seconds for it to calm. Then he said: "You must be my brother's wife."

"*Non.*" There was a silence.

"Is he here?"

"Non."

"Where is he?"

She didn't answer.

"When will he be back?"

Now she reacted. "When will he be back?" she repeated, her voice rising and growing slightly louder, her face going blank, the quiet, cold tone in which she answered as if opening a whole new window onto her personality.

"Écoutez, mon petit lapin. I've kissed you welcome, invited you in, given you a cigarette. Now, don't you think it might be in order to tell me, oh, I don't know. Who you are? How you got my address? Where you're from? Oh, yeah, also: What the hell you want?"

2 So LUKE EXPLAINED, an abbreviated, and largely honest, version of his winter. And when he finished, Nicole, sitting cross-legged on the chair opposite him, shook her head and clicked her tongue twice.

"Makes no sense. Why would he make you sell the estate?"

"For the cash."

"Cash?" She swept an arm away from her body, inviting Luke to witness the opulent surroundings: The large living room spoke, in its furnishings and especially in its sweeping view of Paris from the wide French doors, of a good deal of money indeed. "It looks like he needs cash? Artwork, maybe."

Luke considered, but not for too long; he felt a quick answer was required.

"Artwork was exactly what he could have had. He's the one who wanted cash."

"Bullshit. He didn't want anything at all from your father."

"Madame. He *telegrammed* my father's lawyer."

"Nonsense. And don't call me madame."

Luke stopped.

"Then why did he go to Jerusalem?"

Pause. The woman said: "Daniel isn't allowed to go to Jerusalem."

"But he did."

She faltered. "Look, he went to see his father. Not to get anything. He didn't need anything from him. He didn't *want* anything from him."

Luke: "Well he's getting something."

Nicole, again in control: "You may say so, but I haven't seen him take it yet." She bent forward—a graceful movement from the waist— and reached a cigarette from the pack on the coffee table. "Anyway, that doesn't explain what you want. If everything you've said is true, which I doubt, it still doesn't explain why you spring up out of the blue to find your long-lost brother."

Luke didn't answer, and for a moment they regarded each other in silence. Then he said: "Maybe it would be easiest if I spoke to Danni himself about this."

"You can't. He's not in Paris."

"Why won't you tell me where he is?"

"I will tell you. He's traveling."

"And when might he be back?"

"Can't say. He travels a lot. On business. Sometimes he's gone for months."

Unable to keep the exasperation from his voice, Luke asked: "What kind of business keeps you traveling for months?"

She shook her head, once. "I'm sorry. I'm not going to be interrogated by you. And I'm not going to discuss Daniel's business with you."

Again, for a long moment, Luke thought, watching her openly.

"Do you at least believe I'm Danni's brother?"

She hesitated now, drawing on her cigarette again, and then exhaled smoke as she spoke. "I don't know. I suppose you must be. It's not like you all were sending him birthday cards every year, for God's sake."

Luke held up his hands, palms upward. "I didn't even know where he was until a few months ago."

"Yeah. Right." She put her cigarette out and suddenly leaned her face into her hands. Then, just as suddenly, she rose in a fluid movement. "Yes, I believe you're his brother. I just don't believe you're sitting here. I just don't believe it." And with this she walked out of the living room into an adjoining corridor.

. . .

Perhaps a quarter hour passed. She returned in an oversize leather jacket over a black evening gown, carrying a violin case. Standing, she pocketed the pack of cigarettes from the table. Luke stood, too, and they faced each other across the coffee table. He noticed that now her face was made up.

"Where are you staying?"

Luke motioned to his bag. "Nowhere yet."

"I have to go to work now. Just for a few hours. You can wait here if you want. Otherwise you can come back. I'll be back around eleven. Or you can go away altogether. Really, the choice is yours." She waited, a faint glimmer of hope in her eyes, Luke thought, that he might take the last choice.

"Thanks a lot. I'll wait."

"Yeah, I thought you might." She paused, watching him, and fleetingly Luke felt something contradictory in her expression: an unwilling, barely acknowledged relief that he had decided to stay. "You can't disable the burglar alarm without a key, and I don't have an extra. So you'll have to stay in. Maybe there's something to eat in the kitchen."

"Thank you. I'm not hungry." He hesitated. "I could use a couple cigarettes."

She nodded, reached for her pack of Marlboros, and dropped it on the table.

"I'll be back about eleven." She went to the door, deactivated the alarm with a code, and turned the big brass handle of the lock. This time Luke saw that the door and the frame were steel, and as she turned the handle, four well-oiled heavy bars on each side of the door withdrew from their housings into the frame, more like the door to a bank vault than to a residential apartment. Then she paused and turned back to him, the vivacity of her made-up face taking him aback afresh.

"Let's say that everything you've told me is true. That still doesn't explain what the hell you want here."

As he stood by the couch, something turned in Luke's stomach; he answered quickly and regretted it instantly: "You won't give me an inch, will you?"

But she nodded, calmly, unoffended. "I'll be back at eleven. We'll talk more then."

3 A BLINKING MOTION SENSOR mounted over the front door endorsed her warning about the alarm, as had the complex Fichet lock. Luke stood and looked around the room as Nicole's footsteps descended the stairs.

The walls were covered with glass cases of the sort that might have housed a lawyer's Napoleonic Code in a story by Balzac but that showcased, instead, a variety of small objects: a polyurethane-cased page of illuminated manuscript, an alabaster swallow, a copper kohl vial on which Luke recognized the fluid curves of Arabic script. A small fragment attracted his attention, and, approaching, he saw it was a marble baby's hand, cut off at the wrist, its lines and curves sculpted in exquisite detail, a powerful and—Luke slowly realized—possibly unique piece of antiquity. The remaining wall was filled by a set of French doors that gave onto a patio, flooded in thick evening sun. In a corner, outclassing even the baby's hand, a pockmarked bust of a helmeted Greek soldier sat on a pedestal, the one surviving eye, a white marble orb, gazing forth impassively.

To the right a hallway ran past a small, clean kitchen, a bathroom, and into a bedroom where a glass door gave out onto the same patio as the living room. He retreated now, crossed the living room again, and went into the other hallway. Here he found himself entering a small book-lined study, windowless, and with a heavy country desk in the middle. Built into the side of the desk was a large combination safe.

Here, too, the blinking eye of a motion sensor. A set of bookshelves housed a library of art catalogs and art historical references. Another set held archaeological references. He turned and was leaving the room when a book in a high corner caught his eye. After crossing again, he found, to his surprise, a complete *Encyclopaedia Judaica,* in Hebrew, and a set of *The Encyclopedia of the Holocaust.* These seemed the only books that extended the library's collection from that of an art collector until, in another corner, he found a complete Freud, in French; a few of Lacan's seminars; and the white spine, familiar to him from years ago in his mother's office library, of *Vocabulaire de la psychanalyse* by Laplanche and Pontalis.

Strangely disturbed, he returned to the living room, where he crossed to the French doors and examined their locks for a hookup to the alarm system. Finding nothing visible, he opened them hesitantly and, when no alarm sounded, stepped out into the evening.

The rain had stopped, and a late sun cast long shadows from the chimney pots and antennas onto the extended plane of lead gray rooftops. Beyond, the crowns of the trees in the Luxembourg Gardens swayed against the backdrop of the gray façades of Saint-Michel, close enough to sense the rustle of their wet leaves in the slow breeze. A bird was singing a long, melodic line. He realized that it was that of a nightingale, and lifting his face to the European sun, he closed his eyes while his body suffused with a physical sense of comfort. He had been granted a reprieve. He was no longer alone.

After a time he went inside again. In the muted light it was cool, and sitting on the couch, he removed his shoes and lay back in the soft breeze carrying distant noises through the open French doors. Then he fell into the deepest sleep he had known since Dov Sayada called him in New York so many months before.

Night air carried a scent of rain through the open doors when Luke woke. Nicole leaned against the French doors, a shadowy aura of booze and tobacco. It was much later than eleven, and she had clearly not come straight home from work. Luke sat up on the couch.

"Go back to sleep." She made no motion to leave.

Luke nodded.

"You know you look amazingly like your brother?"

Luke coughed and swung his legs off the couch.

"Like him ten years ago. He was stronger, a little thinner. Women loved him. Women love you?"

He knew now she was drunk. He ran his hands over his face and through his hair, trying to wake.

"Do they?"

"What?"

"Love you."

"No."

"Bullshit." There was a pause, and she went on in the same tone. "You really don't know where he is, do you?"

Luke spoke hoarsely. "I really don't. Do you?"

She pushed away from the French doors and walked unsteadily to the hall. "I'm going to bed now." But Luke stopped her.

"Nicole." She stopped but did not turn.

"Why is it so strange to you that I should want to know my brother?"

She paused for a long time, and when she turned her face to him in the darkened room, perhaps he imagined that it had softened.

"I'm sorry. It's not your fault. Just sleep now. We'll talk in the morning."

"Okay."

A pause while she watched him.

"You going to be able to sleep?"

She was a slim outline in the dark. Luke shrugged. She said: "Danni says hell is insomnia in a foreign country."

"I know."

"How would you know he says that?"

"I mean, I know that's what hell is."

The darkness swallowed her up, and Luke fell back into his heavy sleep in the cool night air.

4 MORNING. He woke on the couch in the living room in a shaft of morning light. He turned his head and saw, through the French doors on the patio, Nicole sitting at the table reading a newspaper, outlined against the vast blue of sky. He sat up, then walked to the bathroom, in his T-shirt and jeans and bare feet.

When he stepped, washed, out onto the patio, she turned her head up to him, her arms stationary in an arc supporting the newspaper. Her short-cropped hair was wet, held back with a green band, her eyes a swimming green in the sunlight. At her motioned invitation, Luke sat across from her and gratefully poured coffee from an aluminum espresso pot into a cup, then spoke as if in continuation of their conversation from the night.

"Where did you go last night?"

The question seemed to take her unawares, and she gazed at him for a short moment before answering.

"Work."

"I mean after."

She didn't answer. Then she said, suddenly and surprisingly: "To a bar. To avoid you."

He nodded and was quiet for a moment. "What do you do?"

"I'm a musician." She answered slowly.

"A musician?"

"I'm in the orchestra at the Opéra." A shadow seemed to pass over the light of her eyes, as if a cloud had passed far above.

"Ah. A violinist."

Now her face darkened. "And how do you know that?"

Taken aback: "I saw your violin case last night. When you said you were going to work, I weighed the evidence, I reached my conclusion."

She watched him without amusement while he talked.

"So what is it you do." It wasn't a question.

"I'm a translator."

"What do you translate?"

"Anything. Simultaneous interpretation—politicians, diplomats. Movies. I've done two novels."

"I meant, what languages?"

"Oh, if I don't know it, I'll learn it in a few months. Like an idiot savant."

She squinted at him in the rising sun, her expression shifting. "That true?"

"Almost. Only the first three are hard."

There was a silence during which he felt he was waiting, although for what he was unsure. Then she seemed to have made a decision and said: "You said you lived in Paris."

"Uh-huh."

"When?"

Luke thought. "Four, five years ago. For a couple of years. I studied here. After I left Israel."

"I thought you said you grew up in New York."

"I did. I moved there with my mother after they were divorced. My parents, I mean. I was twelve. I went back to Israel after high school. For the army."

"They were divorced when?"

This surprised him. "After the war. I mean, the '73 War. After Danni . . . left."

"So when you went back to Israel, this was . . ."

Luke answered shortly. " 'Eighty."

She considered. "Then you missed the war."

"Sort of. I was in Lebanon, but of course, that was a 'policing action,' not a war. A tour of Beirut and the Bekaa Valley. And free: The army's wonderful."

This interested her. "You were in the, what, occupation?"

"You mean, Operation Peace for Galilee?"

"Yeah, right."

"Yes." He took in the sensation that they had just understood each other. "Afterward I came to Paris. I went to college here, then went to Geneva to the UN school, then went back to New York."

"I see. Three years in the army, then you were in Paris from, what, '83 to '86 for a what, a *licence*?"

" 'Eighty-five. I did the degree in two years." Abruptly: "Was Danni here then?"

Her eyes seemed to move into shade; her face—normally so animated—hardened. She answered coldly. "Off and on."

"He travels a lot?"

Silence. He rose and stood by the railing at the edge of the patio. In the soft morning breeze, billowy white clouds sailed over, paper white now in the risen sun. The nightingale was singing, and Luke stood, his back to the woman, unable to ignore the bird's hesitant ecstasy. When she spoke next, it was quietly, almost kindly, and she used the *tu* for the first time.

"*Écoute. Il va falloir que tu me dises ce que tu cherches.* You're going to have to tell what you're looking for."

He observed with interest that she had looked away as she spoke. Beyond her quiet confidence, beyond the remove in which she kept herself, he felt her anxiety. For a moment he was silent, absorbing this impression. Then, as he considered her question itself, she turned to face him, and an answer came of itself.

"It doesn't seem to me to need that much explanation."

"How's that?"

Still not looking at her, he answered shortly. "Danni and I have business to settle." There was a silence, and then an instinct made Luke go on.

"Or I think we do. I don't know. I don't know. I don't know what I'm supposed to do now. I'm not going back to Jerusalem again. Or

New York—being there only made sense while my father was alive. I'm younger than Danni, but I'm not a child. I know that my father's dead, and my mother's dead, and I have to get on with my life. But I don't know what to do, and—" He stopped, then said very slowly: "Do you have any family?"

She shook her head.

"Well then, you understand."

She shifted her focus—but not her head.

"You don't think my brother is going to be very happy to see me."

"I'm afraid I can be pretty sure of that." When he didn't answer, she continued. "I'm sorry. It's just not that simple. I know a lot about your family. Danni never spoke about you."

Luke lit a cigarette from the pack on the table, feeling something like hurt. "So what, you want me to go?"

"N-no." She drew the word out. "But I don't see how I can help you."

"All I'm asking is that you tell me where my brother is."

She regarded him, smoking, and then spoke deliberately. "Forgive me. I don't know you, do I? I don't really know anything about you except that, from all Danni's ever told me, you don't exist. And now, here you are, with this story about an inheritance." She was silent a moment. "It's not that I have anything against you. The opposite. I feel for you. It's just not my business to tell Danni's brother something he hasn't chosen to tell you himself."

Luke nodded slowly, as if unwillingly. "I was a child when he last saw me."

And now she spoke very slowly, her eyes focused on nothing and her face losing a measure of its animation. "That's the thing. Now you're an adult. Only, I don't know how much of one." Her focus switched slowly to him now.

"If you're staying in Paris, I'll do what I can for you. But you should be ready for a long visit. Danni's work takes him far away, and I just can't say when he'll be back. You might want to rent an apartment."

Suffused with a feeling that he had had an emergency and that it was over, Luke watched her.

"*Merci.*"

She nodded, once. "*Je vous en prie*—I'm not sure for what."

5 "WHEN DID YOU last see Danni then?"
When he had left her that afternoon, he passed in front of
Le Fleurus, where I was waiting. I followed him down the
rue de Fleurus, feeling foolish. But it was easy. Utterly absorbed, he
had no awareness whatever of my presence. He walked confidently,
clearly familiar with the streets, into a hotel on the rue Cassette where
he must have rented a room, for he spent the rest of the afternoon
there. I waited, sometimes in the lobby, sometimes in the street, and,
when he came out again, followed him back to the Place Saint-Sulpice,
where Nicole was waiting by the fountain. Now, in the early evening,
they sat at a café table, the sun's long shadow from the façade of the
Église Saint-Sulpice neatly bisecting the small group of tables on the
sidewalk in front of the café.

Nicole sat easily back in her chair, her legs crossed ankle to knee, a
cigarette between two long fingers. She wore very tight French jeans,
a white silk shirt, and the leather jacket. Only after a long silence,
during which she seemed to be marshaling her thoughts, did she begin
to speak.

Luke forced his attention to the question at hand. For a moment he
couldn't remember. Then a picture, precise and clear, flashed before
his eyes.

"It was when he went to the war."

There was a silence while Luke wondered why he had told her that.
He had spoken to no one about it, ever, as far as his memory could
reach, and he had no ready kind of speech in which to go on. Was there
any reason to continue?

No, and yet this woman seemed to have a claim to know. Tied to his
family—perhaps oddly so, but still, the only person outside Israel who
really was.

Tied to his family perhaps, even, more than himself, given that her
claim was one of love.

"I remember him standing in fatigues in the kitchen. Carrying a
gun—I suppose on leave—he was right at the beginning of his service.
He was what—eighteen?" He paused to look at Nicole; she calculated
and gave him a short nod. "My parents had had a fight. My mother
had wanted him to put off his service until after college. Certain professions, you can do that—medicine, for example. My father had said no.

He had been in the army his whole fucking life. And my mother was beside herself." He stopped talking.

"And Danni?"

Luke laughed, a little. "Danni stood up, turned around, and walked out. That sound like him?"

She didn't answer. "And then?"

"Then, Christ, then it was the war." He stopped again and watched her fine, lightly freckled face in pensive profile as she waited for him to go on. "They told me he had been killed in the Golan. I was what, twelve years old. But after the war *Ma'ariv* reported that the son of the great Benami had deserted and fled the country. I can't think of one other case of that happening."

Nicole was facing him now. "And your father?"

"*Ma'ariv* retracted the story. Seemed he'd been killed in action after all."

"No, I mean, how did your father react?"

"Well, you have to understand how those people are." He paused, then asked, in an odd tone: "You're not Jewish, are you?" She shook her head, and he went on. "There'd been so much damage, so much death in his life. Nothing touched him. His studies, his government work—I swear, if it was a choice between leaving his son dying in a gutter and serving Zion . . . or, for Christ's sake, even getting some piece of Aramaic garbage out of the ground . . . there'd have been no contest."

Nicole greeted this with a strange expression. For a moment it seemed she was about to talk. When she didn't, Luke continued.

"It wasn't about my father, really; it was about my mother. I mean, on the one hand, she was the same. She had been in the camps, and Israel was everything to her. But when Danni . . . ran away, suddenly it was like she had lost her Zionism." He paused and looked at her. "I don't know if I can make you understand what that means. For one thing, it broke up their marriage. That's why she moved to New York. And that's why she took me—so I wouldn't have to go to the army."

She nodded. "But you did."

"Yeah." Enough of that, Luke thought. "I had the great honor of serving my country. Tell me, does my brother speak Arabic?"

She looked surprised. "Why?"

"Because that must be how he deserted. Across the Golan and through Syria. Is it?"

She shook her head. "You'll have to ask him."

6   A NIGHT in the hotel; a day, and then night. Little glimpses of Luke as he passed from the rue de Fleurus to his hotel, and back; occasional views of them walking together, always absorbed, always talking. By now my frequent—nearly constant—presence at Le Fleurus was accepted; the bartender greeted me on my arrival, called a musical good-bye when I left.

Night. Luke watched the lights of the city from the patio, waiting for Nicole to change after work. Odéon, Châtelet, far away, the white shadow of Sacré-Coeur. It had rained, a brief spring shower; the nightingale was silent, the air cooling behind the darkness. Nicole came into the living room in jeans and a white T-shirt, carrying a bottle of bourbon and two glasses.

Luke came in and closed the French doors against the chill of the night, accepted his drink, and sat down on the couch.

"Tell me something."

"Yes."

"Where was my brother when my mother died?"

She sat down and then, to his surprise, answered: "Here. With me." She paused. "It was in the morning papers. In the afternoon we went out walking. He stopped in a telephone booth and called Israel."

"He called my father?" Luke's tone was incredulous.

"I think so. I don't know for sure. It was in Hebrew or Yiddish. I had never heard him speak it before."

"What"—Luke stopped, thought, and then continued—"was his tone of voice?"

"Factual. Short. My impression has always been that was his first contact with your father." She was silent, and Luke felt somehow that his liberty to question her was over.

"And you?"

Luke felt obliged to answer.

"I was in the army. We were on orders to Lebanon two days after she died. They let me go to New York for the burial, but then the call-up came, and I went back."

"You had to?"

This time Luke saw that she was planning to pursue the point, and he paused.

"I don't know. Probably. I never really asked."

She considered. "So you were in a war."

"Yeah." He waited for the question, wondering what he would answer. But then he was surprised by what she asked next.

"And after?"

Relieved, he answered quickly. "I came to Paris. Did a *licence* in French letters. I was older than the others, and I had all those languages. . . . I finished fast. Then a UN training in Geneva. Then went to New York. And stayed there till last December. When my father died."

"I see." She stopped, leaned forward and lit a cigarette, pondered, and then went on. "To answer your question, it's hard to explain how Danni reacted. It was the first contact he had with Israel for many years. It started a whole series of events that led to his going there years later. So it's hard to say. How did he react? By changing."

Luke was emboldened to pursue the question a step further. "I meant his emotional reaction."

Nicole leaned forward again, poured a short shot of bourbon, and drank it off. "So did I."

Early morning. The French doors to the patio a black mirror reflecting the lights within. The bottle almost empty, Luke's throat raw from so much talk and smoke.

Nicole, cross-legged in her chair: her bare foot extending from her jeans, the white shirt of worn cotton stretched over the curve of breasts seeming to emanate great warmth. Her face was unsuffering from lack of sleep, from an evening's performance, from a night of drinking.

"So all the time you were in Paris you never looked for your brother?"

Luke, tired, almost irritated: "I didn't know he was here. I wasn't in contact with my father. And Danni never tried to contact me."

"I would have thought you'd have been curious."

He thought and lit a cigarette, feeling drunk.

"I—I wasn't. Curious. It wasn't a time to be curious for me."

"You must have had some idea he was here."

Luke shrugged.

"I see." She considered, seemingly unaffected by all she had drunk. "Then why do you want to find him now, when you didn't even think about it then?"

"I did think about it." A vast weariness was washing over him. "First of all, I was barely in my right mind. I'd been at a funeral, in a war, on the front—whatever the fuck they called it, that was a war. I wasn't thinking about my brother." He glanced at her and found no sympathy in her face.

"And I didn't know where he was. And when I thought of looking for him, it was like—" He stopped short, then went on.

"You know what it was like? It was like when you're touring, and you know you really should go to see some famous sight, or a nearby city, but you're just too tired. Just too sick of traveling, and sick of looking for things, and you know you're missing something you should see, but you think: Fuck it, I'll go there some other time. I mean . . . you've lost your chance, but there are losses that are better to do nothing about than to try to make up. God, you don't have enough time for remorse about the opportunities you didn't miss. So you say fuck it. And you go on somewhere else. You see what I'm saying?"

She nodded, and in that unsteady movement Luke saw that after all, she, too, was drunk. "Only, you mean *easier*."

"What?"

"You mean there are losses that are *easier* to do nothing about."

"No, I don't think I do."

"I do." She nodded her head, dismissively. "Anyhow, it doesn't really work that way, does it?"

"Traveling? Sure it does."

"No, I mean family. Family doesn't work that way. You can't just take a train to another one. And most times you can't do anything about the losses." Now she leveled her gaze at him.

"You could have found him. But it was *easier* not to."

7 "WHAT WAS your mother like?"

From deep in his mind flashed a picture of a serious young woman, thin in a black dress, pretty under the wide brim of a summer hat, holding a baby—Luke? Danni?—in her lap. Did she mean that? Or later, when he was in high school: the graying woman, an eminent psychoanalyst, eyes sunken like dark bruises above sharp cheekbones; the slow pace of her mood; her distant responses. Did she mean that? He said, finally: "She was a complicated person. She'd been in the camps, in the war of '48, lost a son; her husband had left her."

He paused, searching, then said: "You know what she was like? Even just before the end you could tell she had been a happy child. Before the war. The youngest of a big Jewish merchant family. Even after all that had happened, you could tell that once she'd been happy."

"Why did she move to New York?"

"Why? Her husband had dumped her for a graduate student. She couldn't wait to get out of Israel. New York is where Israelis go when they leave."

"And you? What about you?"

Luke nearly smiled. "If you mean, how did I like New York, I really can't tell you. It could have been anywhere; all I did when I was a child was study. That's why I speak French; my mother put me in the Lycée Français. I had to learn English on my own. After school other kids went to get high in the park; I had a tutor, at home, in Latin and Greek. Oh, yeah, and German. Yiddish was my maternal language, so she had me turn it into German."

She frowned. "Why?"

"I don't know. She couldn't bear even the sound of the language. Maybe she wanted me to be at home anywhere. Instead of, as it happened, nowhere. Know what I didn't have when I got out of high school? Any friends. Know what I did have? Full scholarships to Columbia, Harvard, Berkeley, and the University of Chicago."

She pursed her lips to whistle and then said the most revealing thing yet about Danni: "Danni would have given his eyeteeth to go to any one of those. And what do you do? You go back to Israel."

Luke shrugged.

"Why'd you go?"

There was a long silence.

"How'd she kill herself?"

"Prescribed herself a bunch of pills." He looked up. "Why didn't he show up then? Maybe he couldn't go to Israel, but he could have come to New York anytime. Why didn't he show up then?"

Nicole didn't answer. Then she said: "You're a funny one to ask that."

"What's that mean?"

"I mean, don't you guess he figured he'd take the loss on that one? Stay on the train and come back some other time?" A pause. "Not that that would have been *easier*, of course."

8   "TELL ME about your father."

"My father, my father." He was drunk. "Everyone wants to know about my father. You know, while I was in Israel, how many requests I had for interviews about my father? Dozens. Seems I'm the only person in the world doesn't give a fuck about my father, but I'm the person they ask. I can't believe they weren't here asking you and Danni for interviews." He looked at her across the red-and-white checkered tablecloth of the restaurant table at which they sat, her face swimming in and out of focus, and spoke with exaggerated care.

"What would you care to know about my father?"

She answered softly, her age showing in the sweet, sudden sympathy of her face, the first he had ever seen her offer, and Luke wondered if she, too, was drunk.

"Why don't you start at the beginning?"

And so he told her. How Benami had, alone in his family, escaped Nazi Austria, running away to Palestine in the thirties at sixteen years old. About how, during the war, he was smuggled back into occupied Europe by the Mosad le-Aliya Bet. About his heroic rescue work, culminating in the Italian Passage, the famous secret rescue route, so celebrated in Israel under the "heroism" rubric of the national religion of "Holocaust and Heroism" in which, working with a renegade SS officer, he had saved hundreds of Viennese Jews and brought them to Palestine.

Then he told her more. How, after the war's end, working for the Briha in the Italian refugee camps, he had met a tubercular girl from Vienna, just out of Dachau. It was she who told of his family's extermination in Theresienstadt, not just his immediate family, everyone. He took her not to Palestine but to Turkey, where, while he fought the Arabs, she recovered in the dry, hot air of a hospital in Istanbul, and when the war was won, he married her and took her to the kibbutz in the Yizreel Valley.

How by the time Judi Benami became pregnant Benami was a general in the IDF and a young professor in Jerusalem, building the Hebrew University's department of Jewish history. She, having gone from the sanitarium straight to medical school in Turkey, then in Jerusalem, was a psychoanalyst, training under Max Eitingon. And with his frequent sorties, state and university, to Europe, and her modernist, metropolitan eye, they had begun to amass a serious representation of the century's art, the fruits of a life spent in the righteous defense of the Jews.

That is what Luke told her. What he did not tell her, he suspected she understood anyway.

He did not tell her that the Benami treasure—the artwork, the antiquities—had always struck him as somewhat incongruous, and he suspected that Danni had felt that even more strongly. Incongruous, these beautiful objects, to the labor that had earned them: a labor of war, a life of death. How many people had died at his father's hands? Hundreds? Or by his orders? Thousands? These killings were held to be justified: Arab soldiers killed in wars of national defense; Nazis in the desperate bid to save Jews. No doubt, Luke thought, the treasure was deserved; no doubt, in their contexts there had been meaning to those killings, meaning to Benami's sacrifice of his wife, his children, and all his humanity to his ideals. But those contexts, so simple in the past, had grown steadily more complex, while Benami's conviction had remained unswervingly simple.

In any case, Luke told her how, until the day Danni deserted his post in the Golan, their lives had been exemplars of Zionism—real European, internationalist Zionism—models of the promise Israel had held for the Jews. Until Danni brought it all crashing down.

And while he spoke and drank further into the bottle of wine that stood between them, a long, slow train of thought crystallized in his mind. When he finished, precariously drunk, he asked her: "Is that what you wanted to know?"

She shrugged.

"Then tell me something. Tell me just one thing. Why weren't they?"

Her eyes lost their focus as she thought. But even when she asked him what he was talking about, he felt that she understood.

"Why weren't they asking Danni for interviews, too? Why has a reporter never found him? Why has Israeli intelligence never found him?"

Nicole shook her head. "I don't want you to ask me that."

"I'm asking. Just tell me this one thing. Why did no one ever find Danni in Paris?"

Was it an important enough point to lose her sympathy over? To see her face, even in drunkenness, turn so cold? She was silent for a long moment, an expression of bitterness on her face, as if he had grossly disappointed her. Then, finally, tired, annoyed: "Luke, if you were wanted in Israel for high treason, do you think you'd live under your own name? Don't you think you'd have the common sense to get a new one? There's no one in the whole world but your father who would have given you Danni's address. No one." She paused.

"And since you ask, let me ask you this: What do you think it's like? To have to spend your whole life under a made-up name?" She motioned for the waiter. "Let's go now. We've both drunk too much."

 AND YET, days later, sitting in the apartment on the rue de Fleurus, the night spilling through the open French doors, they were drinking again.

"What about when your parents divorced?"

"What about it?"

She cast a withering glance at him. "How about you start at why?"

Why? What was he to tell her? How after Danni's desertion the meaning of Benami's accomplished life had no longer seemed clear to his mother either. His parents had both survived the war, his mother four years in Dachau, entering at fourteen, leaving at eighteen. They had lost their families and lived day after day with the most atrocious of deaths, and yet they shared nothing.

Everything had been a fight for them, from the raising of their children to their deepest intellectual beliefs. From far in his memory came the sounds of a fight about the central idea of his father's most famous book. For a moment his mind blanked; then the title came: *Sacrifice and Symbolism*. They had argued, bitterly, about Benami's reading of a biblical story—the sacrifice of Isaac—and clear in his ear he heard his mother's full-throated voice sounding: "Ach, Yossi, how can you be such a fool?", her Yiddish filling the kitchen, reaching up the stairs to his attic room, where he slept next to his brother's abandoned one. "Your own son has left you, and you think it's a story about the Jews. Your son is gone. Your son is gone. Where is the fucking symbolism?"

He said: "They were always fighting. My father, to him everything was history, and history was an object lesson on the survival of the Jews. I mean, he was a hero. Heroes always win, right? And if you know you're always going to come out all right in the end, well then, whatever you suffer, it's just drama, right? My mother, she didn't see much drama in anything, anything at all, and no heroism. No one came out all right, everyone was damned, and everyone's suffering was"—he paused, remembering the fight in the kitchen in Jerusalem—"unmitigated. The suffering was unmitigated, and nothing, nothing could ennoble it in any way. Do you see?"

She shook her head, and he went on.

"I mean like my father's great book on the sacrifice of Isaac. To my father, it was a parable on how the Jews made this revolutionary step of substituting a symbol—the ram—for a pagan human sacrifice. To my father it was the single move at the basis of Jewish—and that means Western—civilization. But to my mother the whole setup—the whole historical, cultural framework—was an expression of something else, a justification, an excuse. Of the very desire to kill someone else for some farfetched religious reason.

"You see? Why would Abraham want to kill his fucking son in the first place? After all, she was a shrink. That's what—what killed her. Because if you can't stand the very existence of such a desire, then you substitute a ram or a lamb or whatever; it doesn't make any fucking difference."

Silence. Then Nicole: "It does make a difference, though, doesn't it?"

Luke, deep in his thoughts: "What does?"

"What you *want* to do and what you do in reality. And then there are justifications. Historical ones."

Silence. He saw bullets, short, controlled bursts, just as he had been taught. A projectile knife in the air, slicing a body almost in half, at the waist, against the splintering wall of the hut. A laugh sounding from somewhere, someone taking his foot and pulling him to the ground. Then silence as the boy hung, poised like a scarecrow, then crumpled to the ground.

It was a leap, what she had said, a leap between two worlds. He followed her—exactly.

"Does it? Does it, Nicole? I don't know. I don't know about that."

She nodded, slowly, as if he had just confirmed something she had long been thinking about. And then she said: "You know, the more I know you, the less you look like Danni. But I swear to God, what you just said, it could have been him talking."

10 NICOLE. I see her as I saw her from my discreet distance: on her back in green grass, watching the tall white clouds crossing the immaculate sky like pirate vessels of old. Her cheekbones sharp under the pull of gravity. Her eyes perfect sloping ovals around each sky-lit iris of green.

Nicole, I imagine the woman Luke saw, night after night as that spring stepped surely toward its end: cross-legged in her armchair in a bathrobe after work: cradling a brandy glass in her strong musician's hands, drunk enough not to notice the expanse of thigh her robe let show, or the hint of full breast.

Luke not wanting to see the warmth, the deep promise of comfort, in the shape of that breast, in the texture of her skin.

Nicole, always listening, never speaking. While Luke spoke, he watched. And while he watched, he wondered: What kind of a man was it that this woman loved?

"Where'd you live in Paris?"

"Down in the Fifteenth. I had an illegal sublet on the rue Jobbé-

Duval. Got it from a Moroccan woman, a total fucking junkie. She kicked me out, I got a converted *chambre de bonne* over on Félix-Faure, then found a place down a little street called Sébastien-Mercier. If you want to see copies of the leases, I could write to the *préfecture de police,* but it might take some time."

She gave him a contemptuous look.

"Then you went back to New York?"

Luke sighed, and began, again, to speak.

"I had an inheritance from my mother. I bought an apartment on the West Side. It's called the Meat Market because all the meat-packaging plants are there. You should see it; it's like Les Halles used to be. Every morning trucks come in with carcasses; every morning they leave with bones. Kind of a bovine Auschwitz, I always thought—not that I let it bother me, of course. I didn't know what to do, so I worked. At the UN during the day, moonlighting at night. I did it for a couple years. Then my father died."

She considered. "When did you see your father? When you were living in New York?"

He looked up in surprise. "I didn't."

"Never? Not once?"

"No, no, you don't understand. I haven't seen my father since I got out of the army."

Nights, returned to his hotel, he'd lie in his darkened room and watch the clouds traversing the warming skies. Days, when he was not with Nicole, he'd read in an armchair pulled over to the same window next to the bed, books he had not read in years, Folio editions he'd buy at the FNAC on the rue de Rennes: *Un long dimanche de fiançailles, La Passion des femmes;* or at the Deutsche Haus: *Die Angst des Tormanns beim Elfmeter, Der Kurze Brief zum langen Abschied;* or at W. H. Smith on the rue de Rivoli: *Strangers on a Train, The Tremor of Forgery.*

Nicole regarding him as they walked the Quai de Grenelle. "You were decorated in the army."

He stopped, stock-still. "How the fuck would you know that?"

She shrugged. "The Bibliothèque Nationale keeps the *Jerusalem Post* on microfiche. I read English."

"Did it say I refused the medal?"

"No. What'd you do to get it?"

He started walking, and after a few steps she was beside him again. He answered her now: "Just followed orders."

 11 "SO YOU WENT BACK to Israel for the funeral and then decided to come find your brother."

"Yeah."

It was late night, and Luke answered tiredly. They had been sitting up, as had become their habit, drinking brandy and talking after Nicole's return from work. Spring had deepened a long step toward summer outside the French doors. Nicole had changed into a nightdress and sat, legs up on her chair, nursing the brandy glass between her palms and staring into its depths. And Luke, watching her, allowed for the first time a wave of desire to sweep over him, a wave of impossible desire that left him, in its wake, drained.

"Why now?" She spoke as if mechanically, staring into her glass.

Luke's attention was high. "What's that mean?"

"I mean, don't you think he would have found you if he wanted to know you?"

Luke thought, and answered: "It wasn't really a question of what he wants."

She laughed, absently, her wide lips spreading in a smile that contained no mirth. "You don't know Danni, do you?"

"No, I don't." His heart beginning to pound. "And, Nicole?"

"Yeah?"

"Fuck you."

She stopped laughing. Settled into her seat, her face growing cold. For a second Luke felt fright, deep fright. In a word everything had changed.

And in another second everything came clear.

Where did the understanding come from? He never would be able to say. A calculus of tiny things. Her anxiety. Her reticence. A thousand things she should have known and didn't know; a thousand questions she asked him. And when the understanding came, for a moment he could not speak. Then, lighting a cigarette, he said coldly, softly, deliberately: "Do you?"

"Do I what?"

It was as if she were beginning to crumble, and her cold face now was a last, hopeless defense.

"Know him. You didn't know about me. You didn't know about the estate. Everything I've told you about my family has been news to you."

"Not everything."

"No, but a lot." He waited for a reply, but she had turned her gaze back to her glass and sat in a silence that seemed to Luke scared. It scared him. Speaking gently now: "You don't know where Danni is either, do you?"

She didn't answer, staring into her glass. Then she said: "I thought it didn't matter."

She said: "I thought I knew what mattered."

She said: "Maybe I never knew him at all."

In a Paris dawn. The brutality of her composure falling apart. The enormous dignity of a woman, an adult, in pain.

"After your mother died, he began corresponding with your father. Not often. Once, twice a year. Then more. He went to Israel a year ago in the fall. He came back; then he left again last spring. He always traveled. Two, three months at a time. I never knew where he was. Now it's been eight months. I haven't heard from him, haven't heard of him. For all I know he's rotting in an Israeli military prison; now that Benami's dead, no one's going to protect him. When you came, I thought you were him. Then I thought you'd know where he is. I'm sorry, Luke. I'm so sorry. I can't help you with anything. I can't help you with anything. And neither can you help me."

CHAPTER FIVE

1 SHOULD I BE ASHAMED to admit that I watched them?

At first confusion kept me from approaching him; after all, I didn't know who he was. And then a kind of shyness set in, a strong sense of the inviolability of this man's itinerary.

Seeing him see me in Le Fleurus that day, I felt—as I had with his brother, for I now knew it was his brother I had met in Vienna—that I didn't exist, so absent was any recognition from his face.

At first I meant only to watch for a time. To gather my wits, think about this man who wasn't Monsieur Tueta and yet who was. To consider how these scenes I was witnessing, this love story, fitted into the loveless drama I was living. Sooner or later, I thought, I would approach him, him and this beautiful woman he had not come to see and whom he evidently hadn't known.

And then, as the days slipped by, and the intense concentration of their rapport established itself—a concentration on each other that seemed to exclude everyone else in the world—it became steadily more impossible to do anything except watch.

And impossible not to watch.

And now I wonder to what degree that watching was implicated in that horribly lush spring as, moving from leaf to flower, it moved toward something none of us, none of us, imagined.

2 THIS IS what Nicole told Luke, after her long interrogation was done.

This is what she told that stranger, so precisely like her

lover of so many years. Not only his sharp-featured face, his black, expressionless gaze, his long, thin body, but also in the very theme of his thoughts. As if she had known him before she met him.

This is what she told him when his story was at an end and it was time either for hers to begin or for him to leave. For by then leaving was impossible. And so this is what she told him when she had no other choice.

She told him that some twelve years before, on a summer's evening in Marseilles, she had met his brother. She was twenty-three, vacationing with her family during the long August holiday, the first time she had been back to Marseilles in five years.

She had gone to Paris at sixteen to study violin at the Conservatoire Nationale. Success had come early: a debut at the Salle Pleyel at nineteen, a European tour, a recital at Alice Tully Hall, and then a return to Paris to record Mozart's Fourth Violin Concerto with the Orchestre de Paris.

During which she fell in love with the conductor.

He had understood her, perfectly; his was the same life: the unremitting discipline, the constant competition. He had understood perfectly the wire-thin temper, the deep slides into depression, the incommunicable elation of her practice and performance. For the first time, in that bottomless private world in which a performer inevitably lives, she was no longer alone. At first the relief, the fulfillment were exquisite.

Who was worse to whom? He was, she felt sure, for his understanding did not extend, as had hers, to empathy. Perhaps he was right in his appreciation of her gift; whatever he understood, however, he was not able to leave it alone. Sometimes he was ambitious for her, and sometimes coolly destructive, cruelly. In the former mode he partook of a world she was increasingly inclined to avoid: the world of performance, of competition. In the latter he was a force of weird, unaccountable aggression, one that she had never before experienced. Perhaps she had led a sheltered life. Their parting, after two years, had been of an acrimony, a violence unbelievable to her.

And at twenty-three she found herself again in Marseilles, alone.

An evening. Walking home, late, through the shuttered streets of the old city, turning corners at random in search of shortcuts dimly remembered from her earliest youth. In a tiny street, almost an alley, a noise sounded in the darkness; she lifted her eyes absently from the ground and stopped.

Two men were standing close together, talking, then falling quiet at her approach. She hesitated, looking up the otherwise empty alley, then, almost against her will, continued, the first signs of fright in the clenching of her stomach. Nothing happened, and for a moment, relief. Then, as she heard behind her a rapid, whispering step like a straw broom beating against the ground, panic rose in a rush.

An arm was encircling her waist, a body pushing her hard, and she found herself, face to a stone wall, feeling breath against her neck, smelling sweat, and curry, and then a metallic panic surged as she realized that this cold against her throat was a knife.

Surged, but did not quite surface, and through her panic she heard guttural sounds of a language she recognized as Arabic. The two men talking, as if a negotiation were going on, and then an intake of breath from one man as the other pulled him off.

She turned and watched the two step back. She could see them now: a tall dark man, holding the smaller man around the neck, whispering furiously. While he talked, the tall one reached into the other's pocket, withdrew a small object. He talked some more. Then he pushed him away, and the smaller man turned quickly and ran up the street, his sandaled feet whisking against the cobblestones. The other stood straight, stuffing the object into a money belt he wore under his T-shirt, above the waist of jeans, tight, worn nearly through at his ass, nearly black with grease. Then he turned to her, and she had her first view of Daniel Benami's face.

Above his filthy jeans, over a wiry body, he wore a white T-shirt. Below them were canvas sandals with rope soles like those of the Arab who had just run away. His black hair was pulled tight around his high forehead in a ponytail. His eyes, large and wide set; angular cheekbones that framed a thick-lipped mouth. He stood about even to Nicole's five-ten.

For a moment they watched each other. Then, suddenly exhibiting an incongruous, winning smile, he gestured up the street with an arm and spoke in a fast, lightly accented street French, that of an Arab immigrant, using the *tu* from the beginning.

"*T'es cinglée, quoi, se balader toute seule par ici*—what, are you crazy, wandering around here alone? That little bastard could have killed us both." Panting slightly, he pulled up his T-shirt to wipe his sweating face, and she saw the hard muscles of his stomach and the outline of his ribs around the thin line of black hair that ran up from his navel. Tucking his shirt back in, he looked at her face. And after a moment, suddenly said, in a different French altogether: "Well, I don't guess he's going to stop running till he gets onto his ship, which I happen to know is sailing tonight for the gulf. Come on, I'll walk you a bit. Are you going far?"

"Not so far." She was recovering from the shock, more at the intensity of the little man's aggression than at the danger she may have been in. "And I don't need an escort."

He looked at her face again, with new curiosity. "*Eh, non?* You have, I guess, a gun? No. Anyway"—his tone changed—"I do wish you'd let me walk with you a bit. *Sans blague*—no kidding. I haven't spoken proper French in God knows how long, and you have no idea where they're sending me next."

"Where?"

"Djibouti, for God's sake. No kidding. We sail at dawn."

She began to walk up the black street, and he padded next to her on slightly bent knees, a slow, long-legged deck walk, reverting to the slangy French that rushed from him in fast, short sentences.

"*Sans blague*—I had a feeling about that little man there. He was planning to slit my throat for damned sure. Before you distracted him."

She spoke with indifference. "What was that all about?"

This time he answered in heavily accented English. "Business, my dear." Then in French again, as if she were an old friend: "Like Count Mippipopolous? With his arrow wounds?"

It happened she had read *The Sun Also Rises* and remembered the count well.

It was very late when they reached Nicole's house. While they walked, he had talked constantly, asking her dozens of questions—questions about France and, when she told him she lived there, about Paris. He wanted to know how much it cost to live there, what were the best neighborhoods, where were the art galleries, shops. There was a strange curiosity about him, a gentle inquisitiveness, and against her will she felt herself feeling drawn to him. This solitary man, his foolishly correct French emerging from his dirty sailor's clothes. Djibouti. What business did he have in Djibouti? Now, approaching home, she saw her parents standing at the door, then walking toward her with anxious expressions. Danni stopped, leveled a brief look at them, turned to her.

"Can I ask your name?"

She told him.

Now he paused, his face twisting.

"I don't guess, if I ever came to Paris, there's any way I could find you?"

She stared at him, his face against the night. His funny scholar's French. The odd reference to Hemingway. Djibouti. His thin, wiry body. It was very cold, the hollow in her he touched, from which she now answered.

"You could go to the Opéra. But probably I'd have the *huissiers* kick your ass down the rue de la Paix and into the fucking Seine."

Now his face relaxed, and he laughed. "*Sans blague? À un de ces jours*, Nicole Japrisot—see you later."

Then he was gone, padding into the night on that loping, bent-legged gait, his canvas sandals whisking away against the cobbled street as she went inside with her parents.

3

IT WAS WINTER before he showed up in Paris. In an oversize leather jacket and what may well have been the same jeans and T-shirt he had worn in Marseilles. Standing, hands in pockets, outside the stage door on a bitter cold night. With an air of amiable ease as much as if he had just strolled over from his pied-à-terre on the Champs.

"So do me a favor. Just tell me to fuck off. No kidding, it's too damn cold to get thrown into the Seine."

She stopped in front of him. He was unshaved, his eyes bruised with exhaustion, shivering in the cold, deeply tanned.

"I might just. What did you have in mind?"

"A bite of dinner. Six drinks. Maybe seven. Shit, this is a cold fucking country."

She hesitated. "It's awful late. Are you free tomorrow?"

His face fell. "Yes, insofar as someone sailing for Aden can be described as free."

"When did you get in?"

"This afternoon."

"And when do you leave?"

He shrugged, looked around. "There's a four A.M. train to Marseilles. You know what? I've never been to Paris before." He looked back at her. "No kidding."

She took him to the Sélect in Montparnasse. He sat gazing around him with an air of repose that was entirely at odds with his menacing appearance, his filthy clothes. He ate with massive appetite, drank two bottles of Gamay, and paid from a thick wad of bills from the inside pocket of his dirty jacket, which he declined to take off. He spoke hardly at all, seeming content just to be in her presence, answering her comments with monosyllables that discouraged further questioning. Finally, watching the waiter regretfully as he removed the empty plates, he withdrew a blue tin of short cigars from his jacket, lit one, and, exhaling a cloud of smoke, leaned back in his chair. It seemed to her license to ask a question.

"What was your business in Djibouti?"

He looked confused, and she went on.

"Or Aden?"

His expression cleared. "Oh, I see. Well, what you have to understand is I'm in the merchant marine."

"Oh." She thought. "Which?"

"Which what? Flag?" He looked away, then back. "Lebanese just now."

"Are you Lebanese?" When he didn't answer, she asked again. "Are you Lebanese?"

"No. Now let me ask you a question."

"Okay."

"If we get a taxi, can you take me somewhere before I get my train?"

Shit. At last he had said something banal. "I'm too tired for a midnight jaunt to the Eiffel Tower; get a tour bus tomorrow."

His face fell in disappointment, and she asked, heart sinking, where he wanted to go. His answer surprised her.

"The Pont Mirabeau."

They found a taxi, and she directed the driver down the boulevard to the river, then south to the Pont Mirabeau, where the taxi waited while they walked to the middle of the bridge. She watched him watching the black water run under the sculpted copper figures along the side. In profile, as he leaned over the parapet, his long face was absorbed in the view below. Watching, she quoted the Apollinaire poem that was the only possible reason to visit this unremarkable bridge:

> *L'amour s'en va comme cette eau courante*
> *L'amour s'en va*
> *Comme la vie est lente*
> *Et comme l'Espérance est violente*

There was a silence. Then he said, without looking up, and softly: "He got it ass-backward, of course."

"What do you mean?" Such a small voice in the night over the river.

Now he looked at her. "Hope is the one that's slow. It's life that's violent."

She refused his offer of a ride home but accompanied him in the taxi to the Gare du Sud for his train. Approaching the station in the early-morning cold through deserted streets, she spoke for the first time since they were on the bridge.

"So is Paris what you expected?"

"Oh, my God, yes. I read somewhere Apollinaire used to spend whole days just wandering around the city, and everywhere he went, people knew him. You think that's true?"

"Uh-huh."

"No kidding? God, I'd like to be like that."

"Not much chance for a sailor to get to Paris."

"Oh, I don't plan to be a sailor that much longer."

There was a pause. Then he said: "If I had your phone number, next time I came I could give you a call."

She wrote it for him on a slip of paper as the taxi stopped in front of the station. Withdrawing his wad of bills, he peeled off two hundred-franc notes for the driver and folded the slip of paper in with the rest of his money. He climbed out and motioned for her to open the car window.

"May I call you in the spring?"

"Spring's a long way off."

He nodded, and not for the first time she felt his vulnerability, so unexpected in this competent, forbidding person. It scared her.

"Oh, I forgot." He reached into his jacket pocket and withdrew an object wrapped in crumpled newspaper, then leaned in and pressed it into her hand. Straightening up, he walked away. By the main door to the station two figures in headdresses and white sailor's pants squatted. As the cab did a U-turn, she watched Danni approach them, saw them rise, and the three walked into the station toward the quai.

In the dark of the car she unwrapped the paper, the Arabic print dirtying her hands, and found, sculpted in marble, a tiny hand—a baby's hand. Curling inward from the smallest finger. Broken off at the wrist from the arm that once owned it, the break worn nearly smooth. And as she lifted it to the light from a streetlamp through the taxi's window, she felt a few grains of sand fall into her hand from the intricately curved lines of the tiny palm.

THROUGH THE long winter Nicole moved her body, as if automatically, through the punishing routines of her art: the orchestra's rehearsal and performance, her twice-weekly lessons, her three hours of afternoon practice. With a chamber group she began rehearsing the late quartets for a Deutsche Grammophon recording, and those endlessly involved meditations on death, in which whatever slim hope the music contained was reserved for the deep underscoring of the cello and the high voice of her violin carried the most abstruse pitch of despair, colored all that she did. Isolated in the emotional pitch of the work, she rarely felt her solitude. Still, the more she played, the more attractive—because less demanding—seemed a job in the Opéra orchestra, and the less did she want, as her agent urged, to tour or to record.

She wore her red hair shoulder length at the time; it fell over her pale bare shoulders in the black evening dress of her performances. Her green eyes lost in the music, her slim-hipped body long and pliant in the simple line of the dress. She could have been a star in that firmament of musicians, that strange, self-absorbed, egotistical firmament.

So her agent told her. Her talent, her enormous capacity for work, her beauty and presence onstage—the only thing she lacked was ambition. During that winter she practiced less and less. She walked in the wet streets under a pissing European rain. She went to movies, alone. Or read in her tiny apartment in Montmartre, its icy windows dripping water condensed from the hot air of the gas fire.

But she had always been a solitary person. And it was that period, in her mid-twenties, when one's vision of romance, forged in the teens, begins to fall away and, still not replaced with an adult's command of reality, renders the world all the more lonely, more challenging, and harsh. It is a bitter time, a time perhaps with less comfort than any other point of life. Nicole could not have found a harder way to pass it.

When she found Danni waiting in front of the Opéra one night in the early spring, a solitary figure reclining on his elbows against the stone steps, he seemed perhaps the person, in his rootlessness, his diffidence, who might complement, but not invade, the solitude that had become dear to her. She changed course to approach him and, when he did not rise, sat next to him on the steps.

"You lose my number?"

"Certainly not." Gazing at her steadily in the streetlight, his face holding hope and fear: and a gambler's happiness. He pulled the scrap of paper on which he had written it from the inside pocket of his jacket and held it up between two nicotine-stained fingers.

"Why didn't you call?"

Her voice rose at the end of the question with the pitch of real curiosity, not complaint.

"Well . . ." He took a breath, exhaled, and his face hardened.

"How long you here for?"

"Till tomorrow night."

They were silent, watching the crowds in the night air outside the Café de la Paix. A silence in which something important seemed to hang on what she said next. Finally she asked: "You hungry?"

He smiled. Evidently in relief. "I could eat. Say, a medium-size horse."

She didn't smile. "I thought that might be the case."

. . .

Danni seemed to know Paris remarkably well for a person on his second visit. He took her to the Porte de Clignancourt, the taxi drawing through the night streets, deserted now, of the Puces—the flea market—and directed the driver to a restaurant on a tiny, run-down street. There, in the unexpected warmth of the room, crowded with what she soon realized were real Gypsies, the waiters and the barman greeted Danni with a respectful nod. Two men played plangent jazz guitar to an appreciative crowd. They ate a stew at a communal table and drank young red wine from the carafes that everybody seemed to share. When two hulking men in brightly colored Gypsy shirts approached, Danni invited them to sit and poured them each a glass. Nicole noticed that behind their familiarity, these big men were wary of Danni, and that indeed, watching him watching them with a level, attentive gaze, she was a bit scared of him herself. When they had finished their wine, Danni excused himself and stepped out into the street with them, returning in a few moments with a satisfied air. As he sat down, Nicole said wryly: "Business again?"

He feigned surprise, raising his eyebrows. "Certainly not. Close personal friends."

"Sans blague?" It was hard to invest sarcasm into her tone, her voice raised above the guitars.

He grinned. *"Sans blague."*

Close to dawn, in a taxi, they drew to a stop in front of her building on the rue Gabrielle. They climbed out and paused in front of the door; then, without talking, she walked up the street toward the vast white bulk of Sacré-Coeur.

He caught up with her down the block, and she stopped, arms crossed. "Look. What you do is your business. I don't want to see you again if you're going to lie."

His eyes widened in real surprise.

"How long have you been in Paris that you know it so well?"

He hesitated, then said softly: "A week."

"Why didn't you call me?"

He thought, for a long moment, then spoke slowly, unwillingly. "I had some things to sort out."

"Is everything okay now?"

"Perfectly."

"Is that true, or is someone going to knife me walking down the street with you?"

He answered the question seriously. "No, everything's in order now. A week ago I wouldn't say."

She pushed it one more step. "Can you undertake not to lie to me again?"

Now there was a long pause. He examined her face slowly, his eyes moving from her hairline to her mouth, then to her eyes. She saw his small teeth emerge briefly to bite the corner of his lower lip. Finally he spoke. "Yes and no. Depends what you ask me."

It was an offer, of sorts. She watched his face for another moment, then nodded once, turned, and walked back, her shadow long in front of her from the lights of the church. In front of her apartment again, she stopped and asked: "Why did you want to go to the Pont Mirabeau last time you were here?"

He replied without hesitation. "The Apollinaire poem." Then he paused and, after a time, went on more slowly. "Sometimes it seems to me the whole world is . . . business. If you're a businessman yourself, then sometimes . . . *Tu peux croire que ça soit ringard.* You may think it's corny, but the way I live, there's not much scope for such pretty emotion."

He stopped, and when he didn't seem to want to say more, she said softly: "Okay. You'd better go now."

Without hesitation, obediently, he began to walk away. And into the cavernous silence of the street, she spoke to his retreating back: "Will I see you again?"

He turned. "If it's okay with you."

"It's okay." He turned again, first his body, then his head, his eyes resting on her for a last second, and walked off into the dark of night.

5   HIS RETURN in early summer was heralded by a phone call at five in the morning from the Gare du Sud. At six he arrived in his jeans and T-shirt, a duffel bag over his shoulder. His olive-tanned face. His wide, darting eyes. His black hair tied back from his forehead. She met him in her nightdress at the door of her tiny

apartment, half asleep. She brought him in and showed him the bathroom, where he showered. When he came out, wrapped in a towel, she led him into the bedroom, where dawn lit the window apocalyptic pink, and pulled him, his thin, taut frame, his dark face, toward her and onto the bed.

Later, wrapped in her silk bathrobe, he ate four eggs and an entire baguette. Sat at the kitchen table, drinking coffee and smoking one of his short cigars. While she watched, leaning against the counter.

"When do you sail?"

"Well, not immediately." He looked away, then up again. "In point of fact, never. I've given it up."

She lit a cigarette, too. "You're staying then?"

"Well, not quite that either. I'll be doing some traveling. But not quite yet."

"And where do you plan to stay?"

"Well, I thought maybe I could keep a few things here. I'll be traveling quite a bit. If that's okay." He gazed at her anxiously.

"Do you plan to work?"

"Oh, yes." He laughed. "That I do."

"At what?"

He replied blandly. "Import-export."

"Of what?"

He stopped laughing. Squinted slightly and watched her for a second.

"I'd like to set up a little gallery selling antiquities." Then he added, as if an afterthought: "Though, of course, most of my sales will be private."

She thought it over.

"Legally acquired?"

"The pieces on display, absolutely."

"And the others?"

"Well, I'll need to hope the question never actually comes up."

She thought some more.

"Where are you from?"

He paused and then spoke slowly. As if, even having decided to tell her, he still found it hard to pronounce the words.

"Israel originally. Though that's been quite some time. And if you want to know the truth, I wouldn't want some of my business partners to know I'm a Jew."

She thought, then asked: "How good are you?"

"Not that good, I don't guess. I haven't had much practice."

She blanked for a moment, then blushed lightly when she saw him smiling.

"I mean, at your work?"

"Very good. Very good indeed."

She considered, deliberately drawing it out, watching him watching her anxiously.

"You swear it's not drugs?"

And now he grinned happily, acknowledging a decision she had not yet announced. "No kidding, recreational use only."

"Well, let's see how it goes then."

Already she was beginning to talk like him.

6 FOR THE next few years Danni was in and out of Paris, a month here, two months there. He bought a big Triumph motorbike, and his departures and arrivals were heralded by the roar of the engine up or down the rue Gabrielle. He opened a small gallery on the rue du Faubourg Saint-Honoré, staffed by an enigmatic Corsican with a pockmarked face, but they did little to attract business, and those transactions seemed to have little to do with the pieces that passed, occasionally, through Nicole's little apartment. An Egyptian scarab. A hammered gold tughra, signature of an Ottoman sultan. Roman coins, figurines, tiles from a magnificent Byzantine fresco, about whose theft in Cyprus she had read in *Le Monde*. Later there was more variety. A folio of signed Cartier-Bressons. A Vermeer.

At the end of the fifth year in Paris he brought Nicole one day to the apartment on the rue de Fleurus and, when she approved it, transferred to her account the money to buy it in her own name. Its renovation, which he directed with exacting impatience and a scrupulous, even obsessive eye to design, was the longest period he had ever stayed with her. When it was complete, he moved her in and then disappeared for three months.

Did she come to know him? Little by little, and more by the shadow that his secrecy cast than by what he revealed. She learned he had wanted to study archaeology—his passion—but that his studies had, for tragic reasons, been interrupted. That he had a voluminous knowledge of art history, knew the Louvre from its first gallery to its very last, had a faultless eye. That he cooked, loved to eat, and set great store by his status as a regular in a number of cafés in Paris and elsewhere. That he kept a World War II Luger in the safe in his study and a small Beretta on his person. That she was, not counting working women, his first lover.

In the quiet moments she learned, little by little, more. That when he left on his Triumph for the airport, if sometimes he went to Turkey, to North Africa, to Iraq, usually he went no farther than Florence, where he kept an office and had a partner. She learned that he had spoken Yiddish and Hebrew at home, that his father had sent him to boarding school in Switzerland to learn French, that on his own in Jerusalem he had acquired the Arabic that stood him in such good stead in his business. Then she learned to question him, or he allowed her to, and early one morning he told her of the army service his father had made him do in the notorious Maccabee Tank Corps. And he told her of the Yom Kippur War and his desertion.

He told her once and never referred to it again. How he had been sent out to hold a road along with four other tanks. How in doing so, he had run down a Syrian soldier under the treads of his World War II surplus Sherman tank. The Syrian had already landed a shell on his turret, killing his gunner and captain; now under the heavy bazooka the Syrian could not run, as his partner already had, and was aiming a second shell. Still, he had tried to run as the treads of the tank spun toward him with thousands of pounds of torque.

After that Danni had run, too. He deserted not, as Luke guessed, across the Syrian border in a stolen uniform but in a Turkish tanker during a two-day pass after the war; the captain dealt in Roman coins in a small way, and Danni had already done some little work for him. It was surprisingly easy to get out of Israel, no matter how hard to get in. The tanker landed him in Beirut. A contact of the Turkish captain provided papers and a commission as an able hand. In return, he was to provide messengering services between the ports of call of a Beiruti container vessel, on which he would work. Danni's ability to carry out this assignment was something in which all three felt confident, and within a week he had shipped out in the merchant carrier *Le Cèdre du Liban*.

So from Nicole Luke learned that his brother, too, had killed an Arab.

They traveled—he on an Italian passport under the name Maurizio Tueta—to Italy, to the Swiss Alps, to Prague, to Madrid. Never to Germany, never to Austria. As the years passed, Danni kept his hair shorter, abandoned his jeans for dark Armani or Ungaro suits, traded his motorcycle in for a Range Rover. The gallery, it would appear, prospered.

His trips fell into a regular pattern, three months in Paris followed by one or two away, and when he was no farther than Florence, he would occasionally call—always, Nicole noted, from a public phone. After a time he gave her a Florence number for emergencies, and a name: Peter Chevejon, his partner, whom she never met. Twice she used the number from a pay phone across the *jardin* in Saint-Michel: once when her mother died, again when her father died. Each time a quiet voice answered: "Pronto?," listened to her message, and then told her in unaccented French that if Danni could not be there tomorrow, he would come himself.

Each time Danni was there tomorrow.

7   NICOLE KNEW by then that her lover's business was criminal. That seemed somehow irrelevant to their lives together. Because the basis of their harmony was not—as Luke had assumed—her willingness not to inquire into his business, to allow him his entire, unquestioned privacy. It was *his* willingness to allow *her* that. As if she, not he, were the criminal.

It was not that she was not in love; she was, deeply. With the quiet, calm, determined man who seemed to her to have suffered and, in his own solitary way, to have mastered his suffering. She was aware of the depth of damage his life had held—hard use at the hand of historical accident, very hard use. She was aware of the continuing effort it took him to handle his suffering now. But he handled it alone, and for her that was of the first importance.

She was in love. But she had for so long been used to a routine of privacy, so long considered the real adventure of life to be an interior one. And she knew the perverse, inbred pain of attempting to share that adventure, to communicate the deep self-doubt, the precipitous emotion, the hypochondria, the depression, that she had committed herself to as the complement of her violin's voice. To share them, she knew, she must never again try. Nor, she knew, was she ever again going to try to go too deeply into the mind of another; the distance that she wished to preserve around herself she would allow Danni, too. Perhaps this was why she never judged the criminality of his life. It was too useful to her—the necessary secrecy of his illegal affairs was too useful in allowing her a reciprocal privacy.

But if, at the outset, such privacy was exactly what Danni required, as their ménage—for neither ever suggested marriage—was sanctified by the passage of time, she began to be aware of something else.

She began to see Danni's frustration at her uninterest in the part of his life he so carefully guarded. To see that after his long years of secrecy, the time had come when he needed to talk. To tell her. About his business, his strange life in a criminal world that ran under Europe like an alternate reality. And about more.

For Danni was changing. From the day when, after his mother's suicide, he called his father in Jerusalem from a phone booth in the Fourteenth, Danni was changing.

She saw it in his correspondence, first occasional, then regular, with his father, a correspondence that revealed to her that he had given his address to his father and that occupied, as the months passed, more and more of his attention. She saw it in the change of his intellectual interests, his reading in Jewish history, in philosophy, in psychoanalysis, all the books that were so to surprise Luke when he saw them on Danni's shelves. And she saw it in the change of his business: Where once the apartment in the rue de Fleurus had housed an ever-changing assortment of antiquities, fine paintings, coins, and sculptures, now she found on his desk strange memorabilia: yellow cloth Stars of David, threads of the clothes to which they had been sewn clinging to their edges; daggers, crosses, and medals from the Wehrmacht; a can of

Zyklon B. And documents: residence permits, passports, ration books, a "Nansen Ausweis" passport.

As if he had cast a net over Europe and were reeling in every remnant of the Second World War he could find.

Mornings, returning from the studio in the Marais where she recorded, she sometimes saw him leaving the synagogue on the rue Pavée.

As his interests shifted, so did Danni's frustration grow. These objects, the nights of reading, she felt his invitation to share them as a physical force. And as that frustration came clearer and clearer to her, so did her determination not to accept that invitation. She knew, she was convinced, that the intimacy to which he was inviting her was a mistake. The profound, interior lives of lovers—to share them was destruction.

She saw his growing frustration, but it was, she learned with relief, a frustration that his rather chivalrous courtesy did not allow him to express. That she allowed him this courteous silence she would later recognize as a mistake—a fatal one.

Until then, in this strange ménage, she prospered.

8   IN HER EARLY THIRTIES Nicole toured again for two seasons, then returned to the Opéra with some relief. She left the chamber group and its lucrative contract with Deutsche Grammophon, not needing the money and finding, as she grew older, her pleasure increasingly lay in playing alone. When Danni was there, she was drawn into the peace of his absolute, uninterrupted absorption in her, for she was femininity incarnate for that strangely naïve man. When he left, she settled calmly into the comfort of her solitude, the easy routine of her life in this quiet corner of the Sixth, happily anticipating his return. The years of their life piled up, one by one, like the saucers in a prewar French café, each representing not a drink taken but a time passed, in ease, in well-being, in the promise of another of the same.

But like the saucers in a prewar café, each also represented a debt to the barman that would be paid.

She told Luke the fault was hers. With grim remorse in the center of her awareness, she knew the fault had been hers. For years before, when his mother had killed herself, and Danni had taken her on a walk into the Fourteenth Arrondissement, far from their house, and called his father from a pay phone in an obscure Arab bar, it had all been there for her to read.

Now she knew, those years before, he had invited her to inquire into his past just as he had those few times invited her to inquire into his business. And not just about his past, but about his present. About his being; about his very identity and all that—his childhood in Israel, his years of exile at sea, his life under an assumed identity in Paris— all that he suffered.

It was more than an invitation; it was an appeal. And she, absorbed in her wounds of love, convinced that at the center of being was pain and that pain was not to be shared, had chosen not to hear that appeal; she had turned him down. As the years passed, as his letters to and from his father became more frequent, as he so evidently prepared to travel, one day, into his past, she had turned away from the reality before her and chosen to file that central, living, growing part of his life with the part in which, secret, she did not have to be involved.

Eight months before Luke's arrival, the bill had come due. And even then, she had refused to acknowledge her debt, which, as the months passed and the time lengthened without Danni's return, she had had time to consider with ever-increasing remorse.

Eight months before Luke's arrival, in the fall, Danni returned from a trip a different person. His quiet confidence changed to thin anxiety, his equanimity to temper. She learned that he had crossed the border from Lebanon to Israel under the protection of military intelligence, had traveled south to Jerusalem and seen his father. This much she learned, but so deeply ingrained was their practice of privacy that what had happened when he saw his father, she never asked and never knew. Whatever it was had changed him entirely. He closed the gallery, gave up his studio, and for two weeks paced the apartment, drinking, smoking, silent.

After two weeks a package arrived, and it seemed this is what he had been looking for all this time. Its contents, she saw briefly on his desk, were papers: a pile of Third Reich documents, each showing a face from the past in a small photograph. Danni spent a day and a night in his study, then packed for his departure. He did not need to tell her this was more than a business trip.

They stood facing each other in the living room while an uncertain autumn wind blew across the rooftops and over the patio, shaking the French doors in their frames and sending a chill through the glass. Patiently, seriously, Danni went over the preparations he had made for his absence. He gave her the combination to his safe and the key to a safe-deposit box—in themselves, unprecedented acts that scared her. And in her dread Nicole felt a new truth: that her ease in her solitude, her quiet, independent privacy had always been predicated upon her complete assurance that Danni would always travel and always return. Now that she wanted to know where he was going—now that the routine of ten years was falling apart—it was too late to ask.

"You told me ten years ago you would never lie to me."

"And I never have."

"Where are you going?"

"You've never asked me that before."

"I've never been so sure I'd never see you again."

He turned his thin body to the window, paused, then enunciated, very slowly: "I don't blame you. After all, I made the rules. Perhaps they're the right rules. I can't blame you for following them. Only . . ." He turned to her briefly, then back. "We might have changed the rules if you had been willing."

With his back to her, he went on.

"I'm going to Vienna. If I find what I'm looking for, I'll be back soon. If not, I'll have to find it another way, and it will take some time. I don't know when I'll be back. I love you. And the only reason I'd ever not come back to you is if the person I become no longer can."

So Danni left. And eight months of steadily growing remorse, and fear, closed in on Nicole.

9 THAT IS WHAT Nicole told Luke.

In the dark living room. The Paris dawn turning to morning, the morning to noon, the day to a blustery spring dusk, a wet, warm wind battering the glass doors from the patio.

Nicole, slumped in her armchair, her face showing now the drink, the lack of sleep.

"I called Peter Chevejon in Florence, but the phone just rang and rang. I haven't seen Danni in eight months. I was close to calling your father. Then he died. Then I thought there was no one to call. I'm afraid that he's dead. I'm afraid that he's alive, but the person he's become can't love me because . . . I never loved him well enough. Because I never let him . . . oh, it sounds so banal, but I never let him open his heart. I'm afraid that now your father's dead, Danni's rotting in an Israeli prison. Or assassinated by some Mossad hit team."

She shook her head as if to drive away the thought, and then stood up.

"You came, and I thought you would know. I thought you were part of it all. I couldn't believe that your whole life you could have known him, and you didn't. I didn't mean to lie to you. I just needed to know. I needed to know so much. I'm sorry."

She turned now and walked to the bedroom, and in that silent living room Luke was left alone. Shocked at what he had learned about Nicole. At the glimpse he had had, so revealing, into his brother. A strange, forbidden glimpse into a stranger, into his life, his heart. And shocked, in turn, by what it meant to him.

He saw now it had all been a dream, a fantasy, to think that he had been granted a reprieve. When he thought that he had a choice. That he had found, so improbably, a connection to Nicole. And, through her, to his brother. His brother was a man too complex for him ever to understand. That connection, so tenuous, had been a delusion.

He saw now that from the moment his father had died he had been exactly what he had just witnessed Nicole to be: abandoned. Shamefully, irredeemably, alone.

And then, suddenly, he saw something else.

He rose and walked away from the bedroom into the study, for the first time since his arrival in the apartment. He leaned on Danni's desk, he looked down at the safe on the floor. He felt the impassive surface of the desk as if it alone could accord him some kind of advice. He left the room, entered the living room, stood by the French doors, watching the rooftops under a gray sky swimming in the downward motion of rain. He crouched on the floor and held his head in his hands for a long time. Then he rose and crossed the living room to the bedroom. Nicole was standing by the window. For a moment everything froze. Then she turned toward him.

Her wet face against his neck.

A long moment of sobbing, then in the whirling dizziness of something impossible becoming true, her lips against his mouth.

The sunset pale outside the bedroom window. At last exhausted, at last sober.

Sleeping, that baby's first defense from a strange new world.

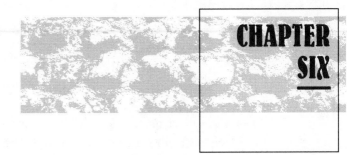

CHAPTER SIX

1 LUKE WOKE in an early silence, supine under a white ceiling, flooded in sun. He shifted his vision to its source, the clear sky out the window, its swimming blue depths timeless, stretching from Spain to Sweden. For a long time, thoughtless, entirely at sea, he watched this light. Then he turned his head to see Nicole's face beside him.

She slept in great peace, her head abandoned against the pillow, an athletic, strong body under the cool sheet, stirring with rhythmic, perfectly relaxed breath.

Returning his eyes to her face, he saw what Danni saw, on his return from his travels.

What he smelled on the surface of that warm skin.

And felt, long and slim and alive against the length of his body.

What he knew to be waiting while he traded for stolen goods on the outskirts of archaeological digs, in Turkish towns, in Cyprus cafés, in the bustle of the Rome flea market.

Nicole's eyes opened, and expressionless, she stared at him for a long moment. Then her full lips widened into a smile, and she turned toward him. Her expression changing to quizzical when Luke stopped her, a hand against her chest.

"It's not Danni."

Her face grew serious.

"I know."

And her body continued its warm roll into his arms. And her strong warmth was against him under the thin sheets.

And outside the window the nightingale measured the pure blue distance of the Paris sky with its unending, ponderous song.

2   LATER the sun rising to noon height, another reality—the yang of Nicole's yin—introduced itself. An object lesson, it seemed to Luke. For that day, too, was the day an Israeli courier arrived for Danni, carrying Yerushalmi's check.

Luke answered the door to see the courier checking his face against a photograph, then without a moment's pause, handing over the envelope. And a surge of adrenaline ripped through his sternum at the sight of the Bank Leumi envelope, its return address printed in Hebrew, Arabic, and English; at the brute fact of Danni's Italian pseudonym, Maurizio Tueta, in the address.

Then, before that envelope's brute reality and that of the world from which it came, he knew that Danni must come back. He knew it in exquisite detail. What he could not imagine was what his brother would do.

And Nicole? I can only guess what went on in her mind that day that Luke became her lover. I can only guess, and yet I feel more confident sometimes in what I know of Nicole than even in what I know of Luke.

But that afternoon, when they had risen from her bed and walked through the rising heat to the Jardin du Luxembourg, she received a shock. Sitting with the papers on a bench near the fountain, watching a lunchtime crowd circle the fountain, children plying model boats across the water, then racing to retrieve them, sending pigeons scattering toward the sky. And Luke said, suddenly: "What when my brother comes back?"

I imagine Nicole looking at him, at his beak-nosed profile in sunglasses gazing sedulously ahead, in utter surprise.

For she knew, I feel sure, that was not the question. As surely as if she had seen the future, the near future, she knew that Danni might be dead, or he might be alive, but wherever he had gone she was never to see him again.

There flowed in her a quiet river, from her childhood in Marseilles to the very moment of the present, in which the events of her life were carried from *then* to *now* in an even, measured pace; but there was no such thing in either of these men, so troubled, so fractured, so exiled from their origins.

She knew that Danni had put a foot back where he swore he never would step again, and now all that he'd done—all the life he'd built to keep the past at bay—would never again be the same and never again be enough.

Origins. She remembered then a dream Danni had when they were buying the apartment on the rue de Fleurus. He had told her, laughing, how he had dreamed that the seller had told him that he could not live there until he had a certificate from a Doctor Origins. And even while he had laughed over the transparent dream, she had known with certainty that Danni was not really buying the place in which they were to live—no matter how much money changed hands or what papers were signed. It would always be a rental, and though the lease they were signing might have a long term, the title belonged to Doctor Origins.

These boys, too sensitive to be sons of a hero. She could almost laugh at the trick history had played on them, so clearly did the standard against which they measured their failure belong to a world that no longer existed. Anyone—any woman—would have seen that their vision of what they should be—should have been—belonged to a world where good men killed Nazis. Yet they lived in a world where good boys were sent to occupy refugee camps in Lebanon or round up teenagers in the West Bank. How simple had been Benami's historical justifications. Yet how complex they became—and how quickly they faded—before the tasks these boys were sent by their elders to carry out.

A trafficker of stolen antiquities; a translator—what strange subspecialties of their father's towering life these two had chosen. Did they see that the common denominator lay in their father's life? Could they see past their shared predilection, probably unconscious, for the forced internationalism, their tie to their father? She did not think so. Nor, she thought, could they see the very Benami-esque courage they carried into their strange rebellions.

When Danni comes back? I cannot know, of course, but I think that Nicole believed only that she had for a time bound Danni's wounds with her nonjudgmental intelligence, her physical beauty, her discerning acknowledgment of his individuality, and her willingness to be loved. I think that Nicole believed that in the end her healing had not been enough.

And that now for Luke, she was doing the same. And that when he was even slightly recovered, he would be ready to go.

In fact, she was mistaken, to a degree that she would never understand, and of this I am absolutely sure. Danni loved Nicole with all the single-mindedness of which he was capable. Loved her not just as a refuge from his past, for her simple Celtic and Gallic rootedness in Europe, but for everything she was and hoped to be.

And so did Luke.

But she was never to know this, and when, that day in the *jardin*, two or three weeks into the time in which they were lovers, Luke asked her: "What when my brother comes back?", I imagine Nicole staring at him in surprise while she appreciated, for the first time, just how harsh was his state of mind. And thinking, for a long time, how to respond before saying to him quietly, patiently, as if explaining something self-evident to a child: "That's not the right question, Luke. The question you should be asking yourself is: 'Where do I go when I leave Nicole?' "

He turned to her, surprised. And relenting immediately, she put her hand on his shoulder, a gesture more of a friend than a lover.

"Look, right now we're here. Let's try to worry about doing that right."

3 AND SO POWERFUL was her belief, so used was he to being led by her calm wisdom that that day in the Luxembourg Garden Luke relaxed. Into intimacy. Into her assurance that this was not to change. Into the still midsummer day, perfect, timeless. Into the astounding reality of her body, next to him on the bench.

And as if answering confidence for confidence, Luke told now a dimension of his experience that her questioning had failed to bring out. As if a ceremony of confession, that day in the *jardin*, he began to speak of his past.

. . .

He told her of his return from New York to Israel to enter the army and how, a few days after the end of basic training, his staff sergeant— a brute, wearing his uncharacteristic kindness badly—had come to Luke's tent. He had ordered the others who slept there to leave and, sitting across from him on a cot, told him of his mother's suicide. They hurried Luke out of the camp to Lod, flew him to New York still in uniform. His-father had not come, but when he arrived in New York, a staff member from the embassy had met him with a suitcase of clothes, sent on the same plane by his father. The clothes, Luke remembered, had been for summer rather than fall, and few had fitted.

He had stayed with the parents of a high school friend, alone, for it was term time and the friend was away at college. The same friend's parents, he remembered, had arranged the cremation and the memorial, attended largely by his mother's colleagues. The friend's father, a doctor, had been very good to Luke. Had told him he needn't go back, that he could pull some strings, have Luke's admission to Columbia reactivated for the winter semester, and that Luke could stay with them. Had he considered it? He couldn't remember. But he remembered being notified of his call-up by the embassy one morning during breakfast, and thirty hours later he was in the Bekaa Valley. Now Luke could not even remember the name of his friend's parents who had been so kind; he had never contacted them again.

Later, in a restaurant for dinner, he told her about Paris, two harsh years of living in a foreign city, his mourning always present, never fading. At dinners, out with acquaintances, studying—it was always there, and in time, feeling it—simply feeling it—had become so major an activity in life that there was no time for anything else.

He told her of his return to New York, years of working, automatonlike, day and night, the succession of meaningless assignments, the social routine of their acquisition, keeping all thought at bay. He told her of the short affairs with women from the UN, the strange immigrant world of foreigners temporarily in New York, how sometimes days would pass without speaking English in this city in which he had grown up.

Then he was surprised when, from across the little table, she asked him softly: "How could you not mourn her, Luke?"

He stopped short, and while he still did not look at her, a long silence passed.

Then, in a rushed voice, he told her about Beirut.

Evening of that epochal day. Nicole stood now, smoking in front of the bedroom window, a dark silhouette outlined against the last light in the sky.

All that Luke had just told her, she felt, had passed into her, become a part of her, just as Danni's story had, and for a moment she was overwhelmed by the pain of these two suffering men.

And then she felt, as she had felt before, that she had not the luxury of despair, she with her simple, comfortable past. Their abuse at the hands of forces they could not even begin to control—historical forces, with origins before their birth—she had to bear it. She turned to him.

"You know the quote *Le passé est un pays étranger?*"

He nodded. *"Et on y fait des choses autrement."*

The past is a foreign country, and people do things differently there.

She went on softly. "In many ways you're lucky. You're not a Palestinian living with all this in a refugee camp. You're not a Lebanese Maronite exiled to Paris. You're a rich, grown man. You can do anything you want in the world. That doesn't only mean buying a villa on the Riviera. It also means reading, writing, thinking. Lucky Luke—" She pronounced it, in French, "Looky Luke," the name of a cartoon character, smiling, but kindly. "Most people never get what you have. A chance to grow up."

He turned away, still lying on the bed. Was that true? His mind blanked at the thought, as if to give up his mourning were to commit another kind of murder.

But now her body, chill from the evening breeze, was against him, and in the passion that, unexpected, sprang suddenly in him, anything seemed possible.

Possible to find out what kind of person he was in happiness. Possible no longer to regard this time as a reprieve in a punishment to which he had been sentenced, or a pause in a journey toward isolation. Possible that this was the place toward which his fractured life had been leading all along. And as he turned into her arms, he saw that he no longer expected it to end.

Certainly not to end the way it did.

Which was strange. For in the event it ended very much in the way he always feared it would.

Later, late that night, she slept.

As if having withdrawn her sensuous affection into herself, complete, a narcissistic totality in her sleep.

Luke rose, quietly, and walked out into the living room, then onto the patio, his damp body drying in the breeze.

What he had told Nicole he had never imagined possible to tell. And in the wake of his confession he found a comfort unimaginable, a whole new vista of happiness. The night, hot, still, resounded around him with enormous distances; a clarity flooded his mind, a boundless energy spread through his body.

Inside, he could not sit still, did not want to drink. There were no cigarettes. Moving quietly, he returned to the bedroom to dress, then threw on a jacket and shoes. At the door he realized he did not have his key, but in this benign night he knew no harm could come. Deactivating the alarm, he let himself out and down the stairs.

4 OH, THE NIGHT LIGHT. The undulating canopy of sky above. The stone maze of streets winding through receding distances ahead, like paths through a medieval forest, laced with the burning lamps of streetlights. He stepped into the pool of light spilling onto the sidewalk from Le Fleurus and, before the café's wide window, paused, absorbed in the vignette within: the barman deep in conversation with a group of regulars over a racing form, the plastic values of the bar's yellows and reds. As if sensing his presence, the barman turned and waved; Luke stepped back out of the light, turning his head to the street where the darkness turned colors to shades of gray. He walked to the corner, turned right at the rue d'Assas, then right up the rue de Vaugirard toward Le Drugstore Saint-Germain. He went in, waited in line in front of the *tabac* counter, moving slowly as the late-night customers stocked up in this, the only all-night *tabac* on the Left Bank. Through the open door to the street he watched a taxi let out its passengers, then wait, looking for a new fare in the milling crowds. And suddenly, without a pause, he left the line, walked out, stepped into the taxi, and directed the driver to the Pont Mirabeau.

5 WHILE THE TAXI waited, he stepped out to the middle of the bridge and rested, his arms on the parapet, watching the rushing black water below.

And now, wholly unexpected, wholly and purely painful, he found himself seeing nothing, his entire being leaned into a wave of grief. He had never before spoken, to anyone, of his mother's death, even less of his service in Beirut. Now the black water of the Seine rushing a pattern of light underneath the bridge, the night an infinite universe of darkness around him, so known, so familiar, it was as if the past were at hand to touch. New York, the fall semester under way, students rushing to class in pairs, in groups, under the ripening leaves of autumn. Luke, in the hot, dry Bekaa, had never had time to mourn his mother. He had gone from victim to executioner in a few short days, and before he had started to grieve, his right to do so was lost forever. Now gasping shudders of tears came over his face, an impossibly strong emotion, and he knew he had no right, but he could not stop, and he leaned his whole being into the comfort of grief.

For a long time he cried, seeing nothing, huddled over the parapet at the middle of the bridge. When at last, through the blur of his tears, he saw a long barge, gray with a load of gravel, slide low under the bridge and climb up the river, he sighed deeply. The majestic sculptures of the bridge swam into focus, straightened. Wiped his eyes. Reached for his cigarettes, found his pockets empty, and came back to the present. He thought: Danni was wrong, Apollinaire was right. Hope, too, is violent. Now, Luke knew, there was hope for him, too, and in the deep fatigue following his unexpected tears, he felt he might have the courage to take it.

 THE WAITING TAXI took him back to Le Drugstore again, and inside, Luke bought two packs of Marlboros, one for himself, one for Nicole. Then, red-eyed and sniffing, he crossed to the bar and ordered in quick succession two large scotches and then two beers. Over a third pair he began to feel the alcohol chasing out the aftereffects of his grief, and relaxation spread through his frame. Now a deep calmness was settling on him, and for a time he watched the lights of the pinball machine mindlessly. He thought of the apartment on the rue de Fleurus, of Nicole, in all the exposure, the honesty of her nakedness, her voice pronouncing, "You have a chance to grow up," and felt gratitude; his loneliness, his grief were moving on like the black waters of the river under the bridge. He shook his head, feeling his hair swinging against the back of his neck like a mane, and a massive sense of liberty swept through him. A clock on the wall called it one o'clock. Perhaps Nicole would have woken, found him gone. He paid, in big ten-franc pieces, and went out into the night.

7 A SHORT WALK through benign night to the rue de Fleurus. Arriving, Luke leaned his head back to stare at the great dome of sky, exhaustion, exhilaration, relief suffusing his body. The barman was closing the café. Luke called a greeting on his way to the porte cochère. The barman turned to see who had spoken, then said something. Luke considered not answering, then said: "Pardon?"

"Back already? Did you forget the salt?"

"The salt?"

"Or did Madame send you back down to buy cigarettes?" He turned from the padlock at the café's front door. "I can open up again, if you want, *mais on n'a que de brunes*. We have only Gauloises."

Confused, but too tired to care, Luke shook his head, called good night, and opened the door to number 6. He crossed the silent courtyard and began the climb up the stairs. Halfway up, a possible sense of the barman's meaning dawned on him. He paused, then shook his head and continued climbing. He owed it to her to grow up. Danni was not coming back; he no longer cared about Danni, no longer even remembered why he had wanted to find him. Nicole—the fascination of her wise, subtle mind and mysterious talent, her beauty—was real. Everything else was a delusion. Tired, suddenly very drunk, he had to pause again, to lean against the wall of the stairwell. Above him a glimmer of light shone through the open door of Nicole's apartment, just as he had left it, warm and welcoming. He finished the climb, pushed the door open wider into the brightly lit familiar living room.

Nicole was not in the bedroom. He walked unsteadily out, stopping to kick off his shoes and unbutton his shirt. She was not in the bathroom or bedroom, and he crossed again into the living room and walked to the doors to the patio. By the closed French doors he paused, lingering in a state of drunken suspension, thinking nothing. He turned, taking off his shirt and unbuckling his belt, started for the bedroom, then changed direction across the room to the hallway to the study. Perhaps there was a message on the machine. Down the short hallway he peered into the study; in the dark the light on the machine on the far side of the big desk glowed a solid red: no calls.

He turned to leave, and something caught his eye in the shaft of light from the hall: There was something on the floor, and in the light of the lamp as he turned it on, he saw it was Danni's big, black Luger. Only now did the meaning of the open door begin to pierce through his drunkenness. He bent to pick it up and as he did so, noticed something else. He rose, rounded the desk and, where its chair should have been, saw a person. Sprawled on its side, next to the open door of the safe. Its head on a black stain on the kilim rug, the color of blood in a tiny hole at the center of a burned circle above the slack jaw. A white, white face, tongue slightly extended, open eyes staring at nothing. And it was not until a full five seconds had passed that Luke realized that this body, it had once been Nicole.

CHAPTER SEVEN

1 I DID NOT know what had happened that night in Paris until I met Luke. For by the night of Nicole's death I had already left. Been made to leave.

And so it was not until much later that I understood what I had done.

By then nearly a month had passed. A month of eating alone in restaurants; of fighting off the advances of what seemed, sometimes, like every man in Paris; of watching these two strangers fall in love.

It came as a surprise to me, when I learned it, that Luke and Nicole had not realized that they were falling in love. To me, as I had watched them, it was crystal clear.

Anyone could have told. It was obvious in the way that they talked, as if no longer sparring with each other, but as if in complicity. The way they had started to smile, a humor that sat naturally on her face, less so on his. As if only now, for the first time, he were learning to laugh.

Perhaps it was that conviction, the strong awareness of their love, that had kept me from speaking to them.

But more than that, Paris, as summer set in, was seductive in a way I had never seen before, as was my solitude. Perhaps more than anything else, I was absorbed in that solitude. It was like practice for what my future would hold. I knew already that what I had found in our attic—in our warm attic, where my mother had stored my childhood toys—meant that I could never go back to that house. And what I suspected about my father, what I so desperately wished to understand—on that hinged the possibility of my ever seeing him again.

My father. His dear, lined face, which I had watched grow from middle to old age, his deep, throaty voice, his big, dry hands. I missed him with an intensity I could taste. I missed him with a mourning that filled my days like a wave rushing into a tidal pool. I talked to him constantly, in my mind, wandering the streets, trying to sleep. In my mind I screamed at him, and on my face were real tears of rage. *Mein lieber Vater.* Never to see him again: It was an act of love.

And so I practiced my solitude in my little room, on the streets of Paris. I practiced being someone other than Natalie Hoestermann from Frederickstrasse 29, Wien. I practiced not being my father's daughter.

And when I could, I watched. I sat in Le Fleurus, I trudged through the streets of the Sixth, each day I checked to see if the man I had met in my father's study had returned, and each day I caught glimpses of those two people. Each day I prayed for Maurizio Tueta to show up. To explain who these people were. To relieve me of my bag, still languishing in the left-luggage office at the Gare de l'Est. To tell me the truth and then to allow me to go on. Who knew where.

And as the month passed, as I began to despair of that ever happening, I determined to speak to them.

Had I, everything would have changed.

Because then I learned that I was not the only person watching them.

2

IT WAS A BRILLIANT DAY, the sky like water, the sun throwing shifting shadows through the trees onto the street. I had come to Le Fleurus to wait for them, and on my way in, I noticed a man waiting outside, tall and dark, with a scholar's serious face. I noticed him again as, when I saw Luke and Nicole come out of the building and head toward the Luxembourg Gardens, I came out after them. That was when the man approached me.

Perhaps it was his kindly face, an obvious intellectual. When it became clear that he was going to talk to me, I felt sorry for him, sorry that with his hopes high, he should be hitting on me now, when the last thing in the world that could interest me was his nicely rehearsed pickup line. I turned from him, hoping I could show my uninterest, and found myself face-to-face with two other men, watching me. Confused, I turned again, and now the intellectual guy was before me, talking in accented French.

"*Venez avec moi,* Mademoiselle Hoestermann. *Il faut qu'on parle*— we need to talk."

I did a quarter turn, instinctively, and tried to push past him. But he blocked my way, and now, behind, I felt the other two pressing against me.

"Please don't make a scene." He spoke with perfect calm, but now, as I watched him full face, I saw him sweat. "We won't hurt you. But we are going to talk with you."

Somewhere I found my voice. "About what?"

"About those two. About your father. And what you stole from him."

Trapped, utterly trapped, I answered at random. "Where?"

He inclined his head. "Come with us."

"No." It was a courage born of panic; I was not going anywhere inside with them. "Outside. In the café there. Or you can kill me, I don't care."

He nodded, as if I had just said the most reasonable thing in the world. "A café then. But not this one. Let's take a walk."

We crossed the street, the intellectual holding my arm on the right, one of the men on the other side, and the third behind. Then we were at the rue de Rennes, then across, and I was being seated at a table in the interior of a large café, far from the crowded terrace tables. The three men ordered coffees, and nothing for me. When the waiter had gone, the intellectual began to speak, and in his affectless voice, his clumsy French, his attractiveness quickly faded.

"Where are the papers you stole from your father?"

I stared at him. Were these men from my father? In German, I asked: *"Wer sind Sie?"*

He shook his head, a kind of smirk of distaste on his mouth. "I don't speak German."

I said nothing, and he asked again: "Where are the papers you stole from your father? Did you give them to him?"

"To whom?"

"To Danni Benami. Please don't waste my time."

"I don't know what you're talking about." Part of it, at least, was true; I had never heard the name before.

"To Maurizio Tueta."

Blood really does, I discovered then, run cold. I said nothing.

"Where is he?"

I tried to answer something, anything. "I don't know."

"I think you do."

"Who are you?" I looked now at the two others for a clue. One was short with a thick unshaved beard high up his cheeks and curly blond hair. The other was darker than the first with a thin olive-skinned face.

The first one spoke without smiling. "I don't think you appreciate the danger you are in, mademoiselle. I don't think you understand the importance of the documents you stole."

But my courage was returning as the cold of the adrenaline rush passed.

Or should I say, my courage was being born, for I had never known the feeling of which I was slowly coming aware?

Danger? Whatever danger he might mean, it seemed if not trivial, then at least bearable. I felt a kind of affront: Was it because I was young, and a woman, that he thought I could be so easily scared? Did he think me so shallow, my purpose in Paris so whimsical that I could be so easily frightened off?

It was a courage born of sheer ignorance. And so, after a pause for thought, I spoke defiantly. "Then you've made a serious mistake. He already has them."

He looked momentarily shocked. "You're lying."

Of course I was. But how could he know that?

"I am not. I gave them to him nearly a month ago. If you want to bully someone, go find him."

"When did you see him?"

"Almost a month ago, when I got here."

"Where?"

"At his gallery, rue du Faubourg-Saint-Honoré."

"It's closed." He seemed to think he had scored a point.

"So what? I had an arrangement to meet him there from last fall. You think I'm an idiot?"

"I won't tell you what I think you are, mademoiselle." There was real contempt in his voice—a contempt, to my surprise, I found reminiscent of the man in Vienna. After a pause he went on.

"Where did he go from there?"

"I don't know."

"Why are you following those two?" He inclined his head to the street, as if they were sitting on the terrace.

"Because." Now I looked down at the table.

"Go on."

Silence. Then: "He told me he'd make copies and give me back the originals. But"—real tears were coming to my eyes, as if I believed myself—"he missed our next appointment. There was no one in the gallery. So I asked around the neighborhood, and finally someone in a café around the corner told me he lived in the Sixth, by the Café Le Fleurus. So—"

He interrupted. "Which café?"

I looked at him, my eyes swimming. "What the fuck does that matter?"

"Which café? It matters." He was unmoved by my tears.

"I don't remember. It had barrels in front, and a sign saying VINS DIRECTE DE LA CAMPAGNE." This was actually true.

He nodded. "Go on."

"So I came down here. And then this guy"—now I leaned my head to the street—"came. And I thought it was him. Then I saw it wasn't. And I wanted to find him. So I didn't know what to do. I can't go back to Vienna without those papers. What am I supposed to do?"

A long silence while the man thought it over and I cried. Finally he asked, in a different tone: "You act like you were in love with him."

I sniffed. "You bastard."

"How long was he in Vienna?"

"Oh, God. A few weeks."

"I see." He retreated again into thought, from which he emerged to ask: "Is he in Paris?"

"How am I supposed to know?"

He exchanged a glance with the others, then spoke. "Come now. We're leaving."

"Where?"

"You're going back to Vienna." He stood up.

. . .

I paused now, my courage deserting me. A family, two parents and two children, were sitting down at a table near us. The father was big, and wore, I saw, a rosette on his lapel. When I spoke again, it was with the first words that came into my mind, and loudly.

"*Écoutez*, monsieur. I'm staying right here, at this table, while you leave. And you try to take me with you, I swear to you, I'm going to scream so loud that everyone in this café is going to know what you're doing to me."

It worked. He hushed me and sat down again, while the family at the neighboring table stared. He thought for a long moment, looking around the café, as if evaluating his chances of forcing me out. Then he reached a decision. Speaking softly: "Calm yourself. Now listen, here's a ticket for Vienna. Seven forty-three this evening; arrives nine twenty-five tomorrow morning. Your father will be waiting for you. Now listen."

He held up a finger as I started to speak. "I know where you live. I know who you are. And I'll know whether you take that train or not, and if not, your father is coming to Paris. Do you understand?"

I nodded now and took the ticket.

Then they were gone, and the man from the next table, leaning across, was asking if I was all right. If I wanted him to call the police.

3 THAT IS HOW my month in Paris—my bid for freedom—came to an end. In failure. My father always said I was stubborn. It was a failure I did not intend to accept.

I'm almost done now. I have only to tell you that I was on that train to Vienna. It left at 7:43 from the Gare de l'Est, the same station that held my other bag in the left-luggage office. I left it there. The train rolled through the suburbs of Paris into the countryside, and blackness filled the window beside me.

Pretending to sleep, I listened to the stops passing, and in the very early morning, as the train slowed to a stop in Munich, I rose, without looking around me, took my single bag, and climbed down.

To this day I cannot tell you if they had followed me. On the platform I ran as fast as I could for the exit, where, as I approached, I called to the ticket taker, in German, to help: There was a man harassing me. Without a word he lifted a phone, and in moments the police were there.

Did I see someone climb back onto the train just as it pulled out of the station? I don't know. No one left the station after me. The police let me sit in their office until morning; *das hübsche Fräulein,* the pretty Fräulein, could not be left alone in the big station. In the morning I took a bus into Munich and, at a pawnshop, sold the little jewelry I had brought with me. Then I went back to the station.

The man in Vienna had given me two addresses: the one in Paris and one in Florence. There was a 9:30 train, direct to Florence. And as it carried me toward the Italian border, tired as I was, I could have laughed. I was free now, really free. Those fools. *Das hübsche Fräulein* had made fools of them.

And it was not until much later, when Luke told me what happened after I left, that I realized, with horror, what *das hübsche Fräulein* had done.

And there was still another murder, brutal, senseless, to come.

CHAPTER EIGHT

1 AND WHILE I was waiting for my train in the Munich station, Luke, after a long night awake in the rue de Fleurus, was calling the police.

He hung up the living-room phone, there was a stage wait, then the Doppler plaint of a European police siren emerged faintly from the distance. From the patio he watched a convoy of small Citroëns draw up, in thin blue light under a sky of gray. A warm, wet wind blew in from the north. Luke shivered in his shirt, damp with sweat.

Inside, in the shadows of the living room lit only by the light from the French doors, he listened to the slip of their feet climbing the polished stairs. He gave the room a last glance, like a party giver checking his house. In the corner, where he'd moved it from Nicole's room, his bag sat half open, clothes spilling out around it onto the floor. On the couch was a bed of tousled sheets he had just finished making, then disarranging. Then he opened the door and turned to greet his guests.

The person in charge, a Detective Lecéreur, was looking down at Luke from his extreme height and speaking in a soothing voice. And at the sight of his kind, round face, so different from what he had expected, Luke, feeling himself suddenly sag at the knees, sat down. His night of preparations seeming suddenly a transparent deceit. And yet he was aware that the deceit was aided by his collapse.

When he could, he stood up to show Lecéreur and some of the men through to the study. Then he was escorted by a man who introduced himself as Monsieur Benichou back to the living room and seated on the couch. Five or six men, some in uniforms, some in dark suits, fanned out through the apartment. When it became evident that he was not needed, Luke went into the kitchen, followed by his escort, and loaded the Krups coffee machine. At the familiar rumbling of water beginning to percolate into the filter, Luke's legs gave out again, and he leaned heavily against the counter. The policeman helped him back into the living room.

For a time there was a blur in Luke's perception. Had he fainted? Or, for the first time in many hours, not required to act while the police conducted their opening inspection, had his mind simply shut down? When he returned to awareness, her bagged body was being removed on a stretcher. Lecéreur was returning from the study and conferring with two of the suited men on the patio. Then he went through the French doors.

All but Lecéreur and Benichou then repaired to the kitchen, where Luke heard them chattering as they helped themselves to coffee. Lecéreur seated himself beside Luke on the couch; Benichou sat on the unmade bed in the bedroom and talked on the phone, occasionally sending notes through to his boss in the living room. Lecéreur held in his hand Luke's passports and airplane ticket. He spoke in a precise, soothing manner.

"First, let me tell you what I know. Then I'll ask some questions. I know that you are Luke Benami, an American citizen, in France en route from Israel to New York. You also hold an Israeli passport under the name Julius Benami. I'm presuming that's your original name. I'm presuming that makes you the son of General Joseph Benami. Is this correct?"

Luke nodded.

"Then we'll be wanting to contact both my Department of State and the Israeli Embassy." He scribbled a note on a pad, double-underlining one word. Calling a uniformed cop from the coffee klatch in the kitchen, he sent it through to Benichou. He paused, passing a hand over his thin hair, assembling his thoughts. "This apartment belongs to a Nicole Japrisot, deceased with a presumption of murder. You stated earlier to Benichou that you spent the evening with Madame Japrisot."

It was, Luke realized, like instantaneous interpretation: Your emotions shut down while you work, and your mind is razor-sharp. He nodded.

Lecéreur went on, as if automatically. "At about one o'clock you walked up to Le Drugstore on Saint-Germain to buy cigarettes. Once you were there, you realized that you had forgotten your money, came back, then left again. When you returned, you found Madame Japrisot as we found her. You understood at this time that she had been shot through the temple and that she was beyond resuscitation. You were able to make this determination because of your training in the Israeli army. At five in the morning, you called the police. Is all that correct?"

Luke nodded. Thinking: Lecéreur would have to find the cabdriver who took him to the Pont Mirabeau and back to disprove that. Then he would have to make an even bigger leap of the imagination to understand that the person the bartender had seen coming up the stairs was not him but Danni. He wondered if this man could go that far.

2   "WHAT DID YOU do in between the time you found her and the time you called us?"

Luke put his head in his hands, then looked up. He did not need to try to make his voice hoarse.

"Nothing. I didn't think that much time had passed. She was . . . I was very shocked."

"You moved nothing?"

"I moved nothing."

"You removed nothing from the safe?"

Luke shook his head. "I told you. There was nothing in it."

"You found no weapon?"

"None."

"This woman was your lover?"

"My brother's. I've been staying here, waiting for my brother to return from a business trip."

"How long has he been away?"

Luke shrugged. "Months."

"When do you expect him back?"

"I don't know. He travels for business. She didn't know when he was coming back."

"His business?"

"An art dealer. He had a gallery on the rue du Faubourg-Saint-Honoré, until recently."

"I see." Lecéreur thought for a moment. "Did you see anyone you knew during your walk to Le Drugstore?"

"The barman, from the café downstairs."

"You spoke to him?"

"Yes."

"Don't they sell cigarettes at the café?"

"Gauloises. Gitanes—*brunes, quoi.* I wanted Marlboros."

"I see in your passport that you lived in Paris before, some years ago. You knew Madame Japrisot then?"

Luke shook his head. There was a long pause. Then Lecéreur said, to Luke's surprise: "Then why did the barman at the café downstairs say you've lived here, with Madame Japrisot, for years?"

At this Luke looked up. It had not occurred to him before that the barman still thought he was Danni. But of course, no one had ever explained it to him.

"He thinks I'm my brother."

"Ah." The tall man frowned and dipped a hand into his jacket pocket for a pack of Gauloises. "This you're going to have to explain."

When he finished, it was midmorning. One of the policemen had brought up breakfast from the café, and Lecéreur had eaten hungrily, all the while watching Luke through his round glasses with a mild expression. His face was extraordinarily pink, clean-shaven, and almost perfectly round over his thin, long body. He lit another Gauloise and considered Luke's story.

"Why did your brother not handle the sale of your father's estate?"

"He was already away. I couldn't contact him, and I had no idea when he'd be back."

"Where do you think he is?"

"I have no idea. Until recently I didn't even know he was alive. He travels very widely. And secretively. I suppose, to protect his sources."

Lecéreur considered. "What do you think happened?"

"After I left, someone must have come up. Nicole would have assumed it was me and opened the door. Someone must have waited a very long time for a chance to get past the alarm."

"What was in the safe?"

"Some objects from my brother's old gallery."

"She knew the combination?"

"Yes." He lied readily. "She had opened it before. To show me things."

"Can you describe the contents?"

"Not precisely. There were some small canvases, some photographs, some jewelry, and a number of objects."

"All gone when you . . . found Madame Japrisot."

"All gone."

"So you believe this was a robbery."

Luke looked up into his eyes. "What else could it have been?"

Lecéreur nodded and continued. "Do you think that this art gallery was your brother's entire occupation?"

"I have no idea."

"Because it's a funny thing. There's no record of anyone called Daniel Benami's ever being in France."

Luke shrugged. "If I was wanted in Israel for desertion, I don't guess I'd use my own name very long."

Lecéreur nodded thoughtfully and added: "In point of fact, you don't use your own name, do you?"

It was early afternoon when they left. Lecéreur stood at the door, shrugging his overcoat onto his wide shoulders, gazing at Luke.

"I'm leaving Benichou here"—he inclined his head toward the hallway—"outside your door and a couple more men downstairs. You'd best stay in for the present. If you need anything, tell Benichou; he'll send for it. I'll be calling soon." He stood silent for a moment, considering Luke. "You're taking this all quite calmly."

Luke thought for a moment. "How do you know?"

Lecéreur raised his eyebrows. "I suppose I don't. You've seen the dead before?"

Luke shrugged and looked away.

"When were you in the army?"

"Early eighties."

"Ah, I see. Which service?"

"Infantry."

"I see. Tell me, how did you find your brother?"

Luke lied with ready confidence. "My father gave me his address. Just before he died."

"And why did you buy a ticket to New York when you left Jerusalem?"

Luke shrugged. "I live in New York. I didn't plan to stay here. Just enough to see my brother about the estate."

"I see." He paused a moment longer. "I read about the auction of your father's collection. You did very well."

Luke shrugged again.

"Some marvelous canvases."

"So I'm told."

"What made you decide to sell?"

This was the one point Luke had not been able to decide. Lecéreur was sure to check with the Israeli police and so come to Yerushalmi. If he told the truth—how Danni had forced the sale of the estate against his wishes—Lecéreur would have to consider Luke a suspect. If he lied, Yerushalmi might tell the truth. The latter—that Yerushalmi might tell the truth—seemed unlikely. He said simply: "I preferred the cash."

3   ALONE IN THE APARTMENT, Luke did not dare close the Fichet lock. He waited for a few minutes nervously, then crossed into the kitchen and gazed out the window at the rooftops. He could see no one watching, so he knelt by the oven and opened the broiler. He withdrew the broiler pan and lifted its cover. From where he had hidden them early that morning, he extracted the Luger, an American passport, and the empty Israeli envelope that had once held Danni's check for his share of his father's estate.

Was it really only the next morning? Already it felt as if it all had happened to another person. After he'd found Nicole, he had sat beside her for a long time. Grief had crept up like an old friend, a familiar sinking into guilt, failure, as if into a viscous liquid, his natural element. He bowed to it. That she had been killed seemed so right, so correct, that for a time he did not even consider it a crime. It was what he deserved.

Only in the very early morning did it occur to him that it was not what *she* deserved. Then the emotion, as it rose up, engulfing, took a turn unexpected: This was not the well-worn grief with which he had lived for so long, the default state of his consciousness. Nicole had been taken from him with the sudden violence, the senselessness of a street robbery, a tabloid murder story. Then searing anger replaced grief.

And when he articulated who had killed her—articulated, for he had known it from the moment he saw her, so surely that he had no need to think it consciously—then fear had joined anger, and panic was born.

Danni, he saw through his rising fear, must have seen how transparently the stage was set for a play he could script and cast in one single move. He had simply walked into a way where his old agenda—his inheritance, in liquid cash—and his new agenda—his revenge on Nicole and Luke—became abruptly one. Now the script called for Luke to be jailed for Nicole's murder and for Danni to come into the entire estate.

There was no time for grief.

Sitting in the study, next to Nicole's corpse, he had thought for a long time before he rose. Then, tentatively, fighting through his panic, he set to work.

In his hand, since he had recovered it from its position on the carpet, was his brother's Luger, which Nicole had told him about. The shelves of the open safe held a collection of particularly valuable objects, maybe a dozen in all. There were some jewels, some drawings, some small artifacts. On the bottom shelf was a box of small-bore bullets, presumably for the Beretta his brother carried with him, and a collection of passports, all bearing Danni's picture under names and nationalities that ranged from Lebanese to American. Luke rose and stepped over the corpse to stand in front of the desk. A search turned up the envelope Yerushalmi's check had arrived in, empty. That was all, evidently, Danni had been interested in taking; he must have reasoned that if he took anything else, it would look like a robbery. What mattered was that Luke be arrested for the murder. At the thought a wave of heat swept over Luke's body, and he sat down again next to the corpse. He allowed a few moments to calm himself. He tried to visualize, for a last time, Nicole's living warmth in the gelid whitening of the corpse's face. Even in death the grace of her body inhabited the abandon with which she lay. And in her face there was peace, as if after all, death had not been that harsh. His vision blurred, and he found that tears were dropping from his eyes like a leaking tap. Then he started to work again.

His brother had not wanted his lover's murder to look like a robbery. Clearly, Luke saw, his job was now to make sure that it looked just like that. He gathered the objects from the safe, and the jewels, and brought them into the kitchen. He was able to crush the powdery stone of the artifacts, worn by centuries of burial, then flush the dust down the sink. The jewels, and some objects of gold, he pushed into the dough of a half baguette, then buried the bread in the garbage pail and covered it with grounds from the coffee Nicole had made that morning. The drawings he burned in the sink. Then he began to burn the passports but stopped, thought for a time. Finally he withdrew the most recent—an American passport bearing the name Louis Joseph Peterson—and put it aside while he burned the rest.

That left the gun. Reflexively, he checked the clip—there were five rounds inside. After consideration, he hid it in the broiler pan with the American passport. He went back to the study with a dishrag, avoided looking at the corpse, and wiped the safe and desk wherever he might have touched them. He replaced the dishrag and went to sit in the living room to smoke and to think. After a time he rose, found the remains of the hashish he had left in his jacket pocket, and flushed it down the toilet. He returned to the living room and thought it all through, a last time. For the moment his fear had subsided, and his thoughts came in clear, concise steps, one after the other. At five o'clock he called the police.

Now, Lecéreur come and gone, he reassembled the broiler pan, closed the oven, and crossed through to his brother's study, walking quickly and softly, aware of Benichou's presence on the landing outside. He put the gun and the passport in a drawer of his brother's desk that the police had already searched and sealed, replacing the plastic tape with care. He went through to the living room, stepped to the French doors, and repeated his inspection of the rooftops. He went into the bathroom and, from the medicine chest, took Nicole's box of Valium Roche, then went back to the living room. He took one of the little blue pills, ten milligrams, with a glass of bourbon, then another, then another. He walked to the bedroom door and leaned against the frame, watching the unmade bed. He lay for a moment on Nicole's side, his face deep in the pillow, inhaling in long breaths for a hint of her perfume. Then he left the room, closing the door behind him, crossed to the French doors, and pulled the curtains closed. He lay on the couch and stared at the ceiling.

If Yerushalmi said nothing about his brother, he had a chance. And probably, he thought, Yerushalmi would say as little as possible before speaking to him. For the moment, in any case, he could do nothing more. He turned on his side and drew up his knees.

When his eyes closed, he was visited by the image of his first apartment in Paris, a tiny room high up in the black bulk of an apartment building on a maze of dark, winding streets. A swirl of the booze and Valium drifted into his mind, and he saw the winter view of the Hudson under a cover of thin snow cloud from his apartment in New York. A degree deeper into oblivion, and he saw winter rains driving against the window of his father's study on a bitter afternoon. As he sank into sleep, his mother's voice pronounced, very clearly: "Jules. It's time. Now." Luke jerked awake and through wide eyes witnessed the glowing living room, rich in sun hitting the red curtains over the French doors. He closed his eyes and saw Nicole, her face, her bright green eyes, the slope of her shoulders, and the freckled rounding of her bare arms. Slowly, as the drug lowered him into blankness, the image dissolved to black and white. His arms and legs trembled gently at first; then his entire body began to shake. After a long while he slept.

 LECÉREUR called in the evening. "Does the name Maurizio Tueta mean anything to you?"

"Nothing."

Benichou brought a *steak-frites* up from the café.

A long, drunken night, the oblivion of Valium and bourbon. The violence of a bright dawn outside the French doors, closed and curtained.

The stage manager called from the Opéra.

. . .

A midday silence reigning throughout the hot apartment on the rue de Fleurus. A summer night outside the patio, gusty, hot wind blowing the deep green crowns of trees in the *jardin* like waving heads of hair, this way, then that. Night again. A day. Then night again.

Not until some days after did the papers report a murder in the Sixth. Motive: robbery. Suspects: none. No names were mentioned: Benichou reported that the Foreign Ministry, as a diplomatic favor, had classified the investigation and gagged the papers. Lecéreur came, in the company of two suited men: one from the State Department, one from the Israeli Embassy. They sat, again on the couch. And slowly Luke began to realize that it had worked.

"We've had confirmation of what you've told us from a Mr. Yerushalmi, through the Jerusalem police, and from the UN in New York. Mr. Yerushalmi asks that you be in touch with him right away. So does the Israeli Embassy Foreign Office. For the time being, I'm obliged to take your passport and to ask you to stay in Paris. It might be a long stay."

Luke nodded and immediately fetched his two passports from his bag, all the while congratulating himself on guessing Yerushalmi's response right and keeping Danni's forged American passport. That passport—it was his only hope. Lecéreur gave him a folder of papers.

"Fill these out and take them to the *préfecture de police,* third floor. Ask for Pierre Atar. He'll arrange a temporary *carte de séjour* for you. He expects you tomorrow at nine A.M."

Luke nodded. The two men in suits shook his hand and left silently, as if Luke had somehow disappointed them. Lecéreur saw them to the door, then returned to the couch.

"Madame Japrisot had no family. Will you be making funeral arrangements?"

Luke shook his head no.

There was a silence. Unsure of the wisdom of what he was about to say, he asked: "Will you be trying to find my brother?"

Lecéreur almost smiled. "That we will. Trying, that is. I can't find any proof that he even exists. I don't find a *carte de séjour,* a driver's license, a bank account, nothing. The apartment is in the name of Madame Japrisot, the gallery registered to a Corsican owner. If it weren't for you and the barman downstairs, I'd think someone had made him up."

"Someone has to tell him . . . she's dead."

"I suppose if he comes back, you'll be that person."

"If he comes back."

"Right." Lecéreur rose and held out his hand. "I'll leave you now. Be in touch if there's anything I can do. And of course, you have the Israeli Embassy."

Luke rose, too, ignoring the proffered hand. "So I'm a suspect?"

The other paused. "Yes, in the technical sense. But we don't have any motive, and we have support of your story from the barman downstairs. He saw you leave, saw you return after, then saw you go out again and return again. And believe it or not, we have confirmation that you were at Le Drugstore twice; there's a security camera installed at the cigarette counter. You waited in line, realized you had forgotten your money, left, and returned a half hour later. You bought two packs of Marlboros." Lecéreur smiled and shook his head. "I guess you could have committed a murder somewhere in there, but it's rather a bizarre way to go about it. But as I said, you're not to leave Paris."

Now Luke shook his hand, saw him out, closed the door behind him. Registering what he'd said. He wondered why they hadn't realized that the person the barman saw come in, then go out again, was the person who'd killed Nicole. Of course, the barman had thought that person was Luke—but then he thought Luke was Danni in the first place. And of course, Danni hadn't stopped to chat. It was a strange coincidence, their physical resemblance that, oddly, had helped Danni that night as much as now it helped Luke. Did Danni realize it? But none of that mattered; it was done. What mattered now was to get out of Paris. Quickly. Before Danni found him.

5   WHEN GRIEF pierced through the focus of his resolve, it was unlike any he had known before.

Not the seething, visceral pain of his mother, not the searing remorse of Beirut, not the dull, senseless throb of his father.

It was a wild longing, a hysteria. The compulsion to hold an object of Nicole's. A fetish, a perversion. To press her dirty clothes to his face. To hurt himself. An emptiness interior to everything he thought himself to be. Moments passed like long hours. When hunger pushed through his pain, he ate. Wondering why he was bothering.

While the police were watching him, he was safe. Danni would wait, and watch, or have someone else watch. He'd want to know that the police weren't doing the same. So in the afternoons Luke walked, north from the rue de Fleurus, over the Seine, and through the wide reaches of the Jardin des Tuileries, watching to see who followed.

The police were there. Easy to recognize, they did little to hide themselves. That guaranteed his safety, he thought, but it also kept him from leaving Paris. He did not feel they would be hard to elude.

But they were stupid: Twice, walking casually behind them, he saw his brother.

Once in the Tuileries Garden, as he looked back suddenly, a dark-suited figure a hundred yards or so behind the two policemen altered his course. He was too far off to see his face. Luke turned and forced himself to walk on slowly, heading at a tangent to the rue de Rivoli, his mind clouding with panic. When he turned again, lighting a cigarette at the exit from the gardens, the man was still behind him, this time walking with professional calm at a different angle from Luke's path. Again, he was too far to see his face, and in the heat of noon the park was filled with a lunchtime crowd that obscured the figure at each few steps. His cigarette lit, squinting anxiously into the sun, Luke took a few steps toward the man, trying to make out his face. But the man swerved in his path and headed toward the Louvre. Now, suddenly, it was Luke following, for a time gaining a few yards as, in reverse procession, they crossed the park, the two policemen, chatting, following unawares behind. After a while the man glanced back, and Luke had a glimpse of sallow skin in dark glasses; then the man broke into a run toward the doors of the glass pyramid in the courtyard of the Louvre, disappearing into the crowds. Heart thumping, Luke stopped, then turned and walked away.

The police had noticed nothing. With a sinking feeling Luke realized that they did not protect him; they only prevented him from leaving.

Now he took to carrying Danni's Luger in the deep pocket of Nicole's leather coat, despite the heat.

The second time was in the wide plaza in front of the Hôtel de Ville in the late afternoon. This time Luke had crossed the plaza and, at the edge, turned in time to see the dark-suited figure approaching him purposefully through a break in the crowd. Suddenly panicked, Luke turned down the rue de Rivoli, pushing through the busy sidewalk; in these crowded streets Danni could be next to him before anyone noticed.

When he turned back again, at the Fontaine du Châtelet, he made out Danni passing at an angle in front of the Sarah Bernhardt Café; he had taken his jacket off, his hand screening his face, but the dull black hair—as dull and black as his own—was unmistakable. The two cops were nowhere to be seen. Now it was Luke who set off at a trot, toward Les Halles, his hand on the gun in the jacket pocket, his stomach alive with apprehension. The crowds were thick here. Trying to move fast, he pushed through to the escalator down to the underground shopping center. On the escalator itself there was no room for maneuver; he went down feeling trapped, exposed in the machine's slow descent, sweating heavily in the leather jacket. At the bottom he turned left and forced his way through the line to get on the steps moving up. Almost immediately, looking over to the other escalator, he saw Danni's white shirt and black hair descending toward him from the sunlight in the street. He crouched down, entirely hidden in the press of people around him, waited, then rose and looked back. Below him he saw the back of his brother's head as it anxiously scanned the crowds below in the mezzanine of the shopping center. In the sunlight again Luke turned, ran to the metro station, and made his way home.

The two cops were waiting in front of Le Fleurus, joined by two more. They turned away as he passed, but not quickly enough to hide their visible relief.

6 HOW LONG could he wait? Clearly Lecéreur had not found Danni; clearly the police were going to watch him until they did. His diplomatic status was a curse: It did not offer enough protection to keep Danni away; it offered too much for him simply to leave. Still, he did not doubt that he could get away from the police. It was what happened afterward that he did not understand.

But he must go. Sooner or later Lecéreur would learn about the details of his father's will. Then he would have his precious motive: Luke's animosity toward his brother. And then he would cease to be fooled by Luke's clumsy deception. He had to go.

And there was nowhere to go where his brother would not find him. It was a problem to be afraid of, and when fear ebbed, it took with it all but one solution, an impossible one.

And so Luke, slowly, prepared for the impossible.

Ten days after Nicole's death, Luke walked over to the rue de Rennes and down to the FNAC, where he bought a sleek halogen flashlight. He went back to the apartment, by way of the butcher and the green-grocer. Upstairs, sitting in the living room with Nicole's sewing kit and her oversize leather jacket over his knees, he cut pieces from a cotton shirt and stitched a pocket under each armpit of the jacket. He put on the jacket and in the right-hand pocket placed the halogen flashlight, in the left, the Luger, not quite believing what he was doing. He rose and walked loosely around the apartment, his hands shaking.

For nearly an hour, he stood in front of the bathroom mirror and practiced: With his left arm he reached over and drew out the flash-light, his thumb on the switch; with his right the Luger, his thumb moving the safety.

Evening fell, and he laced on a pair of sneakers and slipped into the jacket, carefully balancing the weight of the flashlight and gun on his shoulders. Leaving the jacket open, he checked himself in the mirror one last time: There was added weight, but the jacket was oversize anyway, and it was going to be dark. He took the American passport, all the money he could find, and a few small objects from Danni's shelves; later, if he needed to, he could sell them. Then he went out onto the landing, locked the Fichet lock, and punched the code to acti-vate the alarm. Downstairs he began to walk north at a leisurely pace, stopping in cafés for coffees.

As if there were no hurry.

And perhaps there wasn't: It was only ten o'clock, and he had a long way to go.

7 THE CITY where his brother was: a deserted stand of Napoleonic monuments at the Place Vendôme, silent against locked office buildings. A wide stretch of empty boulevard along which hurried an occasional foreigner, crossing against the anonymous rush of cars. Grim prostitutes on the rue Saint-Denis eyeing the passing crowds of Arab workmen with the contempt of an entrepreneur in a seller's market. He did not check on the cops, waiting for his chance.

The night wet, and hot, the tail of spring turning to summer. Luke stopped to drink a demi panaché at the bar of a café on the rue Saint-Denis, sweating heavily in Nicole's heavy jacket. Were the police there? He forced himself not to look and continued up the street.

In front of the Folies-Bergère, he found what he was looking for: a taxi letting out its well-heeled customers in front of the club. He slowed his pace now as he approached, waiting for a tuxedoed man to settle the bill. Then, before the man closed his door, Luke stepped up and into the taxi, extending a five-hundred-franc note to the driver and slamming the door. The driver took the bill wordlessly, and as he drew away, Luke saw, behind them, the two policemen running, then falling off.

A half hour later the taxi left him at the Gare du Nord, and when Luke entered, approaching the big board listing that night's trains, he stopped short. A crowd of policemen stood in front of the ticket counter, perhaps ten of them, checking identification. Could they possibly be there for him? For a long moment he hesitated. Then his courage faltered, and turning, he walked into the street.

Now he was exposed, entirely, without even the slim protection of the police. Perhaps he had fooled the police by unexpectedly jumping into a taxi. He doubted he had fooled his brother.

For a time he walked aimlessly north, panic flaring, then calming. In the very absence of options there was a measure of comfort. Somehow he was going to have to leave Paris, perhaps simply walk out past the Périphérique and hitchhike to a border. Leaving France over a provincial border with an American passport could not be that hard; the authorities couldn't have his—or Danni's—picture at every crossing. Now he looked up, taking his bearings, and guessed which way was north. If Danni found him . . . then he was going to have to try to use the gun. He had, he reminded himself, used guns before.

Of course, so had Danni.

But then, he had planned for that.

At midnight Luke crossed the neighborhood of transvestite clubs by the boulevard de Clichy and directed himself into the deserted streets, anonymous, sinister, leading to the north. Padding softly on his sneakers through the maze of tiny streets, listening for steps behind. Sometimes he thought he heard them, but he did not look back. Sometimes he heard nothing but felt, deep in his stomach, that they would soon be there.

On the boulevard de Clignancourt occasional cafés revealed groups of Arab men playing dominoes in dim lights, looking up suspiciously as he passed. Luke turned north on the rue Lepic. He crossed the Périphérique on a bridge over the crowded traffic and found himself in the deserted acreage of the Puces de Clignancourt—the flea market—where aisles of wooden displays stood empty, waiting for dawn.

If it were going to happen, he knew, it would be here.

Or a place like here. And a time like now.

He walked for a time through the deserted stalls, the maze of shadows in the market, keeping his eyes straight ahead. Nothing happened. Now he was in a neighborhood of low, ancient houses on narrow streets winding under antiquated streetlamps. Under the yellow light his exposure was heightened; he crossed a street at a trot to keep in the shadows, the sides of the houses close on his left.

Nothing happened, and for the first time letting his guard down, he walked on, fighting to keep his sense of direction; this forgotten neighborhood of surreally winding streets was from a film by Cocteau. Finally on a side street he saw lights spilling out of a restaurant and heard the sound of a jazz guitar. He paused now, exhausted, and suddenly weak with hunger. It was going to be a long night, he thought, unless it was a very short one, and at the thought he nearly laughed with a light hysteria. Luke approached the restaurant slowly. He turned, looked behind him down the empty street, then turned again and went in.

8 INSIDE, a dark young man on a guitar and a white-haired man on a violin picked out a manic melody. A mixed crowd sat around long communal tables: here some sleek, well-dressed men of uncertain race, there some T-shirted Argentinians, and everywhere dark Gypsy men. Luke paused at the doorway before this suddenly lively scene in the deserted night. A waiter was watching him; he nodded casually and received a nod in return. He crossed the room to the bar and ordered a beer and a sandwich, then turned, watching the musicians impassively.

This careless, crazy melody to a Godard film—it swirled around him with unbearable pathos, its harmonies lost, the sound track to a story of death. Gazing around him, he watched the tables of diners eating hungrily, all drinking out of communal carafes of wine, and a realization dawned. Surely this was the Gypsy restaurant Danni had taken Nicole to, years and years ago, during his second visit to Paris? He looked to the window and, reading backward, made out the name lettered on its window in a jazzy script: La Cygane.

Now he knew he could not stay, and yet he felt a nostalgia that made him unwilling to move: nostalgia not for the past but for the present, for the tiny, pearlish moments that were slipping irrecoverably by. Yet he could not wait, he could not wait, and he paid for his order and walked slowly out, the jazz melody retreating as he moved down the sidewalk.

9 HE NO LONGER paid attention to where he was going. Just made sure to head north, keeping on the left side of the sidewalk and crossing the intersections at a run. All his consciousness concentrated in his ears, listening through the water running through the gutters for tiny sounds, and at every sound he heard, or thought he heard, he had to fight an urge to run. Ahead the street opened again into the empty flea market, and as the end of the street approached, his temples tingled, his eyes began to water, and his legs felt rubbery. It was the feeling of fear that he had known night after night on patrol in Beirut, the sureness that he was about to find what he did not want to be looking for. It was a feeling one learned to manage.

But one is never really prepared. When the shot came and the bullet buried itself low in his left calf, he dropped to his knees in surprise, then scrambled on hands and knees into a doorway to his left as another bullet threw up chips from the pavement. Then there was silence.

Luke edged himself to a standing position in the doorway, panting mouth open, listening with animal alertness. A childlike feeling of being caught in a tiny space flashed through his mind, and he panicked badly. He had started out that evening with so many choices. One by one they had fallen away, bringing him to this. Then slowly, keeping himself behind the stone of the doorway, he turned to the direction from which the shot had come, his nose to the stone casing. His left hand was folded around the flashlight in the right pocket, his right hand around the gun in his left. He took a deep breath, then another.

Then in a wide step sideways he was on the sidewalk, pulling the flashlight from the pocket, holding it up to his chest, and then the street was flooded in bright halogen light. Two more shots sounded immediately, one hitting the wall behind him on his left, the other on his right—a standard army-inculcated response to the ambush. He stepped now, a full step to the right while extending his arm to hold the flashlight still, and a bullet smashed the light, carrying it out of his left hand with a punishing jolt. But now his right hand came up, and he fired the five bullets remaining in the gun that had killed Nicole into the afterimage of a figure that had flashed briefly some yards in front of him. The deep boom of the big gun's bullets stepped like thunder down the street, and as his eyes adjusted again to the dark, he saw that figure, like a split bag of sand, sink against the side of a building, first to its knees, then, after a tiny pause, fold over onto its face, while the barking of dogs broke out in the neighborhood, as if a sound descended from the sky. A savage feeling, of triumph, of hatred, flared and faded away while for a moment he stood still. There was something wrong. Dazed, he looked at the gun in his hand and saw a strange pistol rather than a Galil rifle. Dazed, he looked around him and saw the shadowy streets of a northern Paris neighborhood, not the crumbling, bombed vista of West Beirut. Then in the distance a police siren began to howl, the dogs barked louder, a window banged open, and he came violently back to himself. Stuffing the Luger into the jacket's deep pocket, cradling his limp left hand against his stomach, stumbling from the pain of his shot leg, he began to run, away from the body, into the shadows of the flea market.

He thought he was undone by the injury. But come to earth under one of the empty wooden carts in the maze of the deserted market, far from any navigable street, he lit a match and saw it was a flesh wound, clean and oozing a slow flow of blood from both sides of his calf. In the tiny space under the cart, he wriggled out of his jacket and shirt. After ripping off a sleeve of the shirt with his teeth, he bandaged the wound tightly. He dressed again and shifted himself to the center of the space, listening. Down the street he heard sirens, then more sirens as what he guessed was an ambulance arrived. He felt searingly cold and realized that he was trembling violently.

He had no plan for what to do now; he had never thought this far. Briefly he put the long barrel of the Luger against his mouth. Did he remember that there were no more rounds? Later he was never sure. More sirens sounded; he heard voices, close, then far.

The night crept past. Afraid to smoke, his hand aching, unaccountably far worse than his leg, as if it still felt the violence of the bullet striking the flashlight from his grasp. He never heard the police leave, but in the hours before dawn the flea market began to come alive. Vans drew in, and the muffled voices of the first merchants began to sound above him. By dawn the crowds of buyers and sellers were growing thick, and when Luke looked out from under the cart, he saw a jungle of passing legs. When it had grown quite light, he shifted to his hands and knees and backed out from under the cart, toward the customers' side. He rose, practically unnoticed, into the moving crowd, briefly facing the surprised merchant from under whose cart he had emerged, then moved on stiff legs away with the flow of people toward the metro. He rode to Châtelet and, crossing to the Île de la Cité in the pearly, fresh morning, dropped the Luger into the water. Then he caught a cab to the rue de Fleurus.

10 SO IT WAS that Luke lost his much-feared father. In the bitter rain of a Jerusalem winter. And found his long-lost brother in a blossoming French spring.

So it was that he shot at his brother with his brother's own gun and the bullet dropped his brother like a split bag of sand into the shadows of the street.

So it was that Luke had killed twice—two killings, years apart and in different countries. But as the report of the gun rolled away between the shadowy rows of houses and the neighborhood dogs began to bark, as his brother spilled to the ground and, far in the distance, sirens began to whine, Luke felt he had killed only once. A double fratricide witnessed by the same howling dogs on the same summer's night.

Luke meant that to be the end of his story. And perhaps it would have been. Perhaps, in the quiet days that followed, as he waited in the apartment on the rue de Fleurus, waited to die of his festering wound or to be arrested for the murder of his brother, perhaps he was really hoping for the time to come when his own life would end.

It doesn't matter. A week after the killing in the Puces de Clignancourt one morning's mail, slipped under the door, brought a letter that changed everything. A letter addressed to Nicole in a spidery hand, postmarked in Florence, two days after the murder. Inside, a note and another, sealed envelope. The note read, "Forwarded at the request of our friend," and was signed "Chevejon."

Luke, in amazement, opened the letter, a thin airmail envelope with no return address. It was dated only days before. He read:

Ma chère Nicole,

Chevejon has had no letters from you again. I am beginning to believe what I never thought possible. That I am not to be forgiven, this time, for leaving you.

How am I to respond? How am I to envision the end of our years together? I wish we had been married. I wish I had been able to tell you all the things I've only been able to tell you this past year, and only in letters. I wish I had had the courage.

So much time has been wasted. So much petty crime, so much danger, so much running away. Now, when I see the time when it will all be over, I must see this time without you. And this is a vision so bleak.

For years I did not tell you where I traveled because I would not. Now, when I long to tell you, I cannot, for you will not respond.

I cannot come back to Europe. Business is closed, and there are many, many places I cannot show myself without opening it again. Please let me see you. Please give me a chance to tell you all the things I was too stupid, too cowardly to tell you before. I long to tell you everything, everything that has happened to me this year. But to do so, you must come to me.

I must believe that you will. I cannot believe that you have understood what I've written to you this year past without coming to me. Unless you have simply thrown my letters away, unread, then you know where I am going to finish my trip, and when. You know that I always have and always will

Love you,

D.

And so it was that Luke was not sure whom he had killed at all.

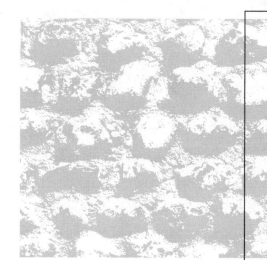

PART TWO

The question is not:
do we believe in God? but rather:
does God believe in us?
And the answer is: only an
unbeliever could have created
our image of God; and only a
false God could be satisfied with it.
—KENNETH PATCHEN, 1941

CHAPTER NINE

1 IT WAS NOT until much later that Peter Chevejon was to tell me a part of Luke's story—and mine—that neither of us could have known that long night on the ferry to Astipálaia, and by then we were all different people. But there was a profound way in which Chevejon was, when I met him in July of 1989, shortly after my arrival in Florence, the same person he had been for some fifteen years. This was the way in which he was profoundly a creation of Danni Benami.

In that July of 1989 when I arrived in Florence, having escaped my three would-be pursuers, Chevejon—for he was known universally by his last name—had just turned thirty-eight. He had lived in Florence for ten years, since some two or three years after going into partnership with Danni. He was a short man, perhaps five feet seven; his bulk gave an impression of strength, his light, graceful movements, of speed. His face, like his accent, was impossible to classify: black, slightly slanted eyes under a heavy fall of thick, sculpted black hair; a smooth, hairless chin—it all could have been Japanese. Or, with its high cheeks and broad, smiling mouth, Russian. With its laughter in his glistening eye, Italian; with its lips pursed, French. This was a handsome face, disarmingly so, and it radiated an amusement, a vivacious good humor, that I can imagine no one resisting for long.

When he talked, you believed that the language he was speaking was his native tongue: Italian, it was with every inflection of a Florentine by birth; French, of a Parisian born and bred; English, of either an American or an Englishman, as he chose. And when I tell you that he could write Greek and speak—*speak*—Latin, then you'll understand how wide was his choice of venues in which to be at home.

He addressed you with an attention, an earnestness that were impossible at first to trust; he was too smooth, too kind, too friendly for any of it possibly to be sincere. And yet he never slipped up. Whatever you told him, he remembered; whatever he promised, he did. If it was a dinner, say, in a Florence restaurant, where half the people in the room were vying for his attention, you'd never catch him in the slightest transgression of good manners, the slightest glance toward another acquaintance; he would be all yours, all the while he paid court to the people around. Then he would seem a dilettantish, rather slick Florentine art dealer.

But if you knew anything about him, if you had the slightest hint of what lay below his façade, then you knew that if he gave the impression of a facile, Eurotrash bon vivant, that was intentional. That this was, beyond the façade, a man whom it was possible to know and to know well—if he wanted you to: serious, inquisitive, highly intelligent. And that at the very base of his real identity lay a single, entirely steadfast purpose: to be faultlessly true to Danni Benami.

To complete the picture, he dressed like a movie star, in impeccable Armani suits and topcoats, Comme des Garçons shirts, Hugo Boss jackets, Bally shoes. In fact, everything Danni came to know about how to dress in the time after he'd acquired the apartment on the rue de Fleurus for Nicole, he'd learned from Chevejon. Lastly, I only once saw him angry, and then, as that lively, amused face turned to a mask of the gravest, most barren anonymity, I hoped I would never see it again. As did, I clearly saw, the man to whom it was directed, and he, even I could see, was not an unpowerful man himself.

2 I DID NOT feel safe in Florence. The card I had stolen from my father need not have been his only record of this address, and if it were, he very possibly could have remembered it entirely; there was little that my father forgot. When I had not arrived in Vienna, he could very easily have sent the three men, or come himself, to this city.

Not until much later did I learn that those men had another matter to occupy their attention, one that they considered more important.

And that my father was not about to involve himself too closely with the forces that were swirling around me that summer.

So it was not until several days had passed that I went to the address on Maurizio Tueta's card and found there not Tueta but Peter Chevejon.

Perhaps I was unwilling to follow the card to its address because I knew that afterward, I had nowhere left to go. Or perhaps the opposite: Perhaps I believed that there I would find the end of my journey. In the end I delayed until all my money ran out. I watched it as it fell to exactly the amount it would have cost to have my bag, containing the gold menorah—the last thing I had to sell—sent from Paris; I watched it as the diminishing total fell below that amount. Then I crossed to *l'altro Arno,* late in an afternoon, and climbed the stairs up to the third floor of number 2 Piazza Santo Spirito and rang the bell.

3 THERE WAS an elaborate security arrangement. A video camera peered at my face, and after a long pause I heard an interior door open, then the beeping of an alarm being deactivated, then the massive Fedeli lock on the front door turning, and the door opened to my first view of the man who was to change my life.

While he gazed at me with polite curiosity, I asked in my bad Italian if I could see Signore Tueta; he responded pleasantly, as if my request were the most usual thing in the world, no, but Maurizio was his close associate, could he help me? Would I come in? I did so, but as he closed the front door, releasing an automatic lock on the interior one, designed so that both doors could not be held open at the same time, my confidence began to waver. He was wearing a white silk shirt tucked into tweed suit pants. I watched him move into the office, and his strength, suddenly evident, was ominous. He seated me on a black sofa and offered me a drink. My hands were shaking slightly as I accepted.

I did not need to wonder how to go on. He began politely to question me, switching into smooth German after hearing the accent of my halting Italian; all I had to do was answer. In my mother tongue at that. Oddly enough, he began not by asking what I wanted, but by asking where I had gotten the address. I showed him the card Tueta had given me. And when did we meet? Last fall.

There was a shift in his face, very faint, behind its handsome, welcoming urbanity.

Where? Vienna. The man stood abruptly, walked across the wooden floor to a window, and lit a cigarette. Or so I thought. When he turned again, toward me, I saw it was a small black cigar that he smoked like a cigarette, exhaling lungfuls of gray smoke into the afternoon light. What, precisely, did the Fräulein want? Herr Tueta had asked me to send some things; I was passing through Florence and thought to bring them myself. He looked at my bag, which I had with me, having spent my last money on my hotel room the night before.

What were those things? I hesitated, then shook off my fear as best I could: I would prefer to speak to Mr. Tueta directly, as it was a personal matter. Did I have them with me? No, I had them somewhere safe. Where? There was a pause. Was I proposing—forgive me, Fräulein—to *sell* these things to Herr Tueta? No, it was a matter of . . . objects, belonging . . . to his family.

"We are far from understanding each other, Fräulein."

I didn't know what to answer.

He looked out the window, and when he turned and approached me, he was once again all amiability. Whatever the Fräulein had, it must be of some importance; it looked to him as if I had traveled far to bring it. And—he hoped I would forgive him—he would guess that I didn't have much money? No. Well then, he had a proposal.

He explained to me that Herr Tueta was away on business but was sure to be back shortly, in a day or two. Would I like him to recommend a *pensione* where I might relax and enjoy Florence while I waited for his return? As his guest, of course; Maurizio would want no less. The *pensione* was just around the corner; it had a first-rate kitchen. He'd like to invite me to dinner there that very evening, after I'd had time to refresh myself.

He seemed aware that I did not have many options, aware of that before I was. Because it was just as I was processing the realization that he asked, offhandedly, what was my name, and before I could think, I answered automatically. When I looked up, there was the slightest of smiles in his eyes. Too easy. As if he felt sorry for me, lost in a man's world.

4 THAT HE DID NOT further interrogate me during dinner seemed less an acceptance of what I had said than a smug assurance that what I could tell I would, and he could wait. Of course, he was right. The *pensione* was on a tiny street, past the Pitti Palace, overlooking the Boboli Gardens; the diners were all Italian, and they all seemed to know him. The splendid dinner—the first good meal I'd had since leaving Vienna—was served in a vined courtyard. To eat in another's company, a man's—not to have to catch the waiter myself, not to have to struggle with the currency—was deeply seductive. As was Chevejon; his charm, which gave the impression of being entirely sincere, was practically irresistible. It was a continuous effort to tell him no more of myself, to keep myself an anonymous presence, without past, without personality. That I was able to do it seemed of no concern to him; it seemed even to amuse him.

Of course, I realized, knowing that I was Natalie Hoestermann from Vienna was enough to learn a great deal about me. I couldn't help that. And it didn't seem to matter; I doubted that Maurizio Tueta was returning in a few days, and I knew—and knew that he knew—that I had no choice but to tell him everything he could want to know. Only, that first night in his company I was not about to tell him. I'd at least make him wait. When, after the long dinner, he escorted me back to my room, I half expected him to invite himself in. And I half expected to accept. His small, strong body. His beautiful, mocking, compassionate face. He, too, seemed—as much as you could tell anything about him that he didn't wish to communicate—to hesitate. Then he shook my hand and wished me a good night's sleep. He said he'd call for me tomorrow, after breakfast.

And so my first days in Florence passed. Chevejon's polite attentiveness isolated me completely. He called for me in the morning, deposited me back at the *pensione* in the afternoon, and returned in the evening. Once I tried to leave on my own. A polite, large man appeared at my side and requested that I return to the hotel. In Italian. Turning me gently, he escorted me back into the courtyard and inquired if there was anything that he could fetch for me. After that I noticed from my window that he was never far from the front door, in the street.

It was a splendid isolation; that I knew it was a forced one did not diminish its pleasure, although perhaps that is because I never seriously encountered its boundaries. Chevejon conducted me through Florence, escorted me to meals, and asked nothing. It was almost possible to enjoy his company, his boundless charm, but for that ineffable sense of danger, of threat. As it was, I found myself disinclined to—determined not to—ask him anything.

If it was a contest, it was a new one to me. But I did not see that that meant I should play to lose.

After all, it seemed to me that he, too, needed me.

Still, the contest was unequal, and I eventually would have to give in; he had the ability to constrict my liberty. So I did not see Luke in Florence. But then, for Luke's first day or two there, nor did my host.

5 | IN PARIS a brilliant, clear, dry summer had settled outside the curtained French doors in Nicole's living room. Luke slept fifteen, seventeen hours a day, setting the alarm to wake him for the news broadcasts. His few waking hours he sat on the couch in a state of nothingness, his thoughts like a pool of spilled honey. The news broadcasts reported once, twice on the shooting in the Puces de Clignancourt, thought by the police to be drug-related. Then there was nothing.

Lecéreur had called once. Where had Luke been that night when he escaped his guards? Not caring, Luke had lied effortlessly: He had spent the evening in Montmartre, alone. He was tired of being followed. Lecéreur hesitated, then protested that police were there for his protection, and behind his politeness Luke heard the fear of the Israeli Embassy, of an international incident. Luke said nothing.

He hung up, thinking with uninterest that Lecéreur's suspicions were light: The murder had taken place in a closed world, of silent Gypsy men in La Cygane, of enigmatic foreigners, of buyers and sellers of stolen art, of thieves. It was an underworld in which the guilty killed the guilty; the police were not going to risk their lives to solve the murder. He was probably not going to be caught. With faint surprise, he noted that that realization bought him no relief.

The day after that Danni's letter arrived.

THE POSTMARK on the letter from Chevejon postdated the night he had killed Danni. That proved nothing. The letter could be an elaborate blind, planned to explain Danni's unexpectedly long absence to the police. The letter could be from somebody who wanted Luke to think Danni was still alive. But its tone, the terrible pathos of longing: Who could have falsified that?

Nicole was dead, and only Danni could have killed her. That much was true. But then, who was the letter from?

Its arrival brought everything else down, like a house of cards collapsed not by a physical shock but by a passing breeze of doubt that blurred the horizon between "know" and "believe." Who was the letter from; and the corollary question that made a pulse beat deep in his stomach: Who was it he had killed?

The scene passed in front of his eyes with cinematic precision. Why had he run instead of looking at the person he had killed? He had never planned to evade capture, never thought that far, never cared. But after the shooting an animal urge had taken over, and in the barking of the dogs he had found himself running.

He rose, hurried through the living room to the bathroom, and vomited. He sat back on the bathroom floor, his head buried between his knees. In the silence, the unidimensional anonymity of the summer afternoon, he felt something like despair, like real despair, overwhelm him.

Somehow the night passed, a blur of consciousness. And yet, when he woke, something was not quite the same.

He rose, took Danni's letter from its shelf, and smoothed it out on the coffee table next to the couch. "Chevejon has had no letters from you again. I am beginning to believe what I never thought possible. That I am not to be forgiven, this time, for leaving you." And: "I cannot believe that you have understood what I've written to you this year past without coming to me. Unless you have simply thrown my letters away, unread, then you know where I am going to finish my trip, and when."

Why had Nicole not written to him? Why had she not told Luke about his letters? And where were the letters? Nothing could make him believe that Nicole had lied—nothing. And yet how had she not received the letters?

Yerushalmi had received a letter from Danni—or a telegram. Avi had said Danni had written. How had Danni been informed of his father's death? Where had Yerushalmi written to him, and from where had he answered? From his office in Florence—had not Nicole said he had an office and a partner there? For a moment he wondered where Dov had gotten the rue de Fleurus address, then remembered: his father's office files. He could not call Yerushalmi; the lawyer was sure to be looking for him. But it occurred to him Dov might know, and he could trust Dov.

 IF YOU COULD telephone the past, Luke thought, it would feel like this. The telephone rang with the short double rings of the Israeli system, crossed lines chattering unintelligibly. Then, with a sinking feeling, he heard Hela's voice.

"Julie! Are you okay?"

"*Hacol beseder,* Hela, everything's fine. Can I speak to Dov?"

"Dov's not here. He's in Europe again. Warsaw, at a conference."

"When will he be back?"

"I don't know." Her voice undulated in and out of clarity on the humming line. "I expected him last week, but you know how he is. He must have gone off somewhere." A silence, implicitly referring to Dov's work in intelligence. "I should make a chart one day; I bet he spent more time in Europe than at home this past year. You know he's trying to finish Yossi's book on the ghetto?"

"I didn't know."

"Are you at home? He'll call when he gets back. Why haven't you answered our letters?"

"That's okay, Hela." He ignored the last question. "I'll call again."

Luke tried for a moment to remember if she'd have had her baby or not. How pregnant was she when he left? That she could still be in her pregnancy, that so little time had really passed, seemed incredible. Unable to remember, he said good-bye and hung up.

8

IF IT WERE Danni he had killed, then it was Danni who had killed Nicole. That murder he would never regret.

If it were not . . . then Danni was alive, somewhere in the world, and nothing had happened since Luke had left Israel except that he had caused Nicole's death.

For a long time blankness, an annihilation of thought.

Then he thought of going to Florence.

Florence was small, or so he imagined, for he had never been to Italy. Sooner or later, he thought with growing conviction, someone would be sure to take him for Danni. At worst nothing would happen—or someone would try to kill him again. At best . . . at best he would find this partner Nicole had spoken about.

In any case he had to get away, and where else was he to go? At least in Florence there was a connection with his brother—a slim straw, perhaps, but all he had. He called the Gare du Sud.

There was a 4:00 A.M. train to Marseilles with a connection to Nice and then across the Italian border. Now there was an immediate problem to solve: getting out of France. Again he congratulated himself humorlessly on keeping Danni's American passport. But then, how to get out of Paris?

He walked the rooms of the apartment. Was there anything he should take? The now-familiar objects around him glared like hostile guests at a stranger's party. He lay on Nicole's bed, buried his face in the sheets that he had not changed since before her death, seeking in their stale smell a last hint of her. Then he put on Nicole's jacket and sat down to wait. At two in the morning he began to let himself out the front door. A thought struck him, and he paused, then crossed the room to take Danni's letter from the coffee table. In the bathroom he burned the letter, holding it over the toilet till only a tiny corner between his thumb and forefinger remained. Then he dropped it in and flushed the toilet. He walked back to the living room, stopping to fit a bottle of scotch into a deep pocket of the jacket, stepped out onto the landing, locked the Fichet lock, and set the alarm. On the landing he wondered what to do with the keys and remembered, with cinematic exactitude, the day Nicole had had them made for him. He held them in his hand as he went down the stairs.

He had no plan for how to deal with his baby-sitters from the police, other than the vague idea of losing them in a taxi. Peering out to the street from the porte cochère, he saw that wouldn't work; the two men sat in a Citroën a few steps down the street. He ducked back into the archway, trying to think, and, after a minute, looked out again. Now, his eyes adjusted to the darkness, he saw more clearly: One, his head leaning against the passenger window, was clearly asleep; the other, at the wheel, had a newspaper open in front of him. Of course. Luke was not under serious suspicion. Why should they be more careful? Luke waited until the driver was turning a page, then slipped out the door and walked slowly in the direction opposite from that which the car was facing, hugging the façade of the closed café Le Fleurus on his right. At the corner he paused to look back: The car was still there; there was no one on the street. He turned, stopped to drop the keys to Nicole's apartment into the sewer, then, looking for a taxi, began heading toward the Gare du Sud.

Only later, hours later, as he boarded the train in the empty vastness of the station, did he realize that now, if there were any more letters— supposedly—from Danni, he would have no way to get into the apartment to get them. And that, somewhere in Nicole's apartment, she must have written Chevejon's phone number. And as regret at his stupidity seared through his stomach, it was then that he realized that this was the exact train Danni had caught, those many years before, returning to Marseilles after his first visit to Paris.

9 A LONG LURCH, a tunnel, a deserted suburb, a stretch of fields in which the compartment window against the darkness turned to a mirror. Soon the window held sleeping towns flashing by, a series of freeze-frames under shooting lights. A house, roofed in red tile, a deserted intersection under yellow streetlamps, the terrace of a closed station-side café, empty plastic chairs turned over on their tables in front, country-style. Then countryside again, and against the dark of the night the window reversed again, the dimly lit interior of the deserted train compartment filling its frame, the occasional light, rocketing out of the French countryside and passing with relentless speed into that black country beyond. Night.

This was the train Danni had taken, those years ago, the 4:00 A.M. to Marseilles; this was the train in which Danni had returned from his fly trip to see Nicole in Paris, the first time. In Marseilles he had joined his ship, crossed the Mediterranean to the Suez Canal, through the Red Sea to Aden. Against that black mirror, night, Luke saw him standing on a container ship's deck, hugging himself against the Mediterranean wind, watching the coast of Israel pass, the shadows of Haifa and Tel Aviv black against the glowing blue of the sea. A strange Moses. Danni turns from the view; that shore is closed to him, but there is another now opening, beckoning across the ocean with the promise of a new life. France. Nicole.

In the hazy, smoke-filled compartment, hurtling south across France, Luke hugged himself, searched in his mind for an image of Nicole, and found nothing. It was as he had known it would be. Of his departure from Paris, hours before, nothing remained, and he had once again failed to mourn what he had so quickly, so stupidly lost.

10 HE HAD NEVER crossed a border on a false passport before. It was a trivial crime compared with what he had committed; still, it carried its own hazard. Such as the thought that if he were not able to do it, then he was no longer able to continue his journey. Of course, it was barely a border, a cursory examination between EEC countries. But it was worth the minimal preparations necessary to getting across safely. In Nice he booked a first-class sleeper to Florence on that evening's train, then walked into town. At a Banque de Paris he withdrew a thousand dollars in French francs, knowing he was leaving a trace of his passage, not caring. Then, at a series of small stores he bought some T-shirts, some jeans and underclothes, a good sports jacket, and two small suitcases. In one, he packed Nicole's leather

jacket and deposited it in the left-luggage office of the train station: It was sweltering hot, and he could not bear to throw it away.

At Ventimiglia, while night was beginning to fall, the train stopped for customs. A long wait while three Italian border guards wended their way down the aisle. The inspector glanced at his passport, glanced at his face, and handed it back without a word.

And as the train started into a country he had never visited, the taut anxiety of his trip began to lift. He felt his passage through customs, the anonymity of his entrance into this unvisited country, expand through him as a feeling of relief. The train wheels thrashed below the mirror of the window curtained in the neat little sleeper; Luke lay down on his bunk, listening to that music, and as France fell away and the train pushed into Italy, there was a moment of peace—a frontier between states of mind—and Luke slept.

11 AND LUKE SLEPT. While the train moved along the Italian coast, drawing to a slow stop on screeching brakes at local stations: San Remo, Genoa, La Spezia, Pisa. Nighttime stations lit by high lights casting long shadows across platforms. Lurching to a start and then plunging, again, into the night. Luke slept, and his train moved, steadily into the Italian summer.

I see him, lying on his back on the little compartment bed, an arm crossed over his eyes, passing lights flashing split seconds of clarity over his face, his mind blanketed by a dull nothingness. Perhaps under the lids of those long black eyes, dreams pass over his pupils like reflections of clouds on the surface of water. A maze of Paris streets, wandering, lost, hopelessly confused. A little boy floating in the clear blue water of Lake Kinneret, held in the arms of his mother. An enormous house of rooms, each doorway giving onto a vista of hallways, other rooms glimpsed through half-open doors and a vast, panoramic view of the floodlit Jaffa Gate always without.

When the train draws into the early light filtering through the vaulted ceilings of the Stazione di Santa Maria Novella in the early morning of a brilliant Florentine day, he will remember nothing. He'll wake with a start, realizing he is no longer moving, collect his things into his bag—quickly, for he has unpacked little—and open the little plastic door, light on its hinges, to the corridor. He'll step out of the train into the rising heat of the day, blinking in the sunlight, and, taking his bearings, head off into the cavernous interior of the station. He'll hear the rushed sounds of Italian around him, like an argument in song, and with a shock he'll realize that he does not understand.

And with this thought his heart will, for the slightest of moments, lift.

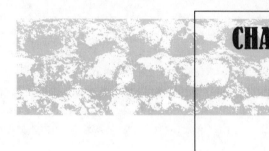

CHAPTER TEN

1 THERE WERE strange things happening in Peter Chevejon's quiet world, many strange things, and he didn't like any of them.

First was the appearance of this child from Austria. Looking, for God's sake, for Maurizio Tueta. Not that in herself she was unwelcome: She was a beauty, fresh and lovely, filled with curiosity and fight. It was confusing at first: This wasn't Danni's thing at all, a girl like this; anyway, he had Nicole Japrisot in an apartment in Paris. No, she couldn't be a girlfriend. And she would not explain who she was.

Secondly, someone had been asking questions about Maurizio Tueta. He'd almost have thought he was imagining it, except that three people had mentioned it: Jack Lazar in Paris, Willy Staso in Hamburg, and, worst of all, Max Holtz in Rome. Each had been approached by a stranger asking how to find a certain Signore Tueta. Each, thank God, had held firm, but how long could they be expected to continue? This strange Freemasonry, it fell apart the second someone showed some green; if he'd seen it once, he'd seen it a hundred times.

Thirdly—and perhaps unrelated, though he doubted that—there was the letter from the Ministry of Taxation in reference to unreported income for 1988. Chevejon didn't like that. The minister of finance had five Roman coins of his from Bergama, not one of them clean. His minions shouldn't be writing letters like that to Signore Chevejon.

As for the girl, his first instinct was to seduce her. Then that same instinct told him that wouldn't work. Next was to threaten her, but that, too, he doubted would do it. There was something stubborn about her, something determined, and he felt that determination motivated by something deeper than he was going to be able to touch. Christ, it was easier dealing with people you could buy and sell; this child, he had to make her *trust* him.

In the end he explained that Tueta was away, on business, but that he would be back shortly—a complete lie that he doubted she believed. Was she in a hurry? No, well then, might he recommend a *pensione?*—as his guest, of course, he added at the look of fright in her eyes; this girl couldn't have much money. Why didn't she relax and enjoy Florence until Tueta returned? He'd be happy to show her around. After all, Danni had given her his addresses. There must be some reason he had done that. He gave her a moment to figure out that she didn't have very many choices, while he made a mental note to get Paolo to watch her, then asked casually, what was her name? Natalie Hoestermann, she answered automatically, then looked shocked. Too easy. He felt a little sorry for her, lost in a man's world.

It wouldn't take long to get her talking, he was fairly sure of that. But this, he was honest enough to admit to himself, was due to the girl's strength more than his powers of persuasion; she realized, he thought, that her options were limited and that she was eventually going to have to take a chance and talk to him. Meanwhile, thanks to her slipup, he was able to institute some inquiries.

The results they yielded were interesting—interesting and scary. She came from a bourgeois section of Vienna; her father was well known, the head of a large, highly successful manufacturer of kitchen appliances and small electronics. Something rang a bell about that, and for a few days, after she had been safely settled in her *pensione,* he mused over it. Then, just fishing, he went up to Danni's library in the villa in Fiesole, thumbed through the indexes of a few books, and he had it: a mid-level Nazi in Vienna, in the Bureau of Jewish Emigration. Tried at one of the smaller hearings at Nuremberg. Acquitted on the testimony of an Israeli with whom he had run an escape route out of Vienna that had saved hundreds of Viennese Jews.

Bingo—the Americanism came from as far in his forgotten past as anything he could think of. The Israeli? General Yosef Benami. He put down the book, stunned, and said again, out loud: "Bingo."

This was getting seriously unfunny. What in God's name was Danni up to?

Strange things were happening in Peter Chevejon's quiet world, but he didn't guess it was any time to complain. What was clear, rising above all the local disturbances, was that strange forces were gathering around Danni Benami, and no matter what the cost, it was time to deal with them.

After all, Danni and he, they'd been lucky enough to be in the kitchen for a very long time. Small wonder that finally they were going to have to take some heat.

It was lucky he saw it that way. Because in Peter Chevejon's quiet world something even stranger was about to occur.

2 IN LATE JULY, perhaps a week after I had arrived in Florence, Paolo Cavalari came into Chevejon's office on the top floor of a house in *l'altro Arno*, above the Piazza Santo Spirito. He let himself into his boss's office with a weighty key, turning the complex Fedeli lock that shot twelve steel bolts back from their housings in the doorframe, retracting them into a thick steel door that dwarfed even Paolo, a hefty, dangerous-looking man, clearly nothing if not a bodyguard. He stepped inside the door and stopped the soft warning beep of the alarm by punching a code into a keypad on the wall, then locked the door again from the inside, reset the alarm with another code, and, turning, crossed in two small steps of his colossal legs the small dark antechamber, unfurnished save for a Turkish prayer rug on the worn marble floor and a few plants resting on odd-size fragments of marble columns. A single closed door led out of the antechamber, with a video camera mounted above. Paolo waited, presenting his face to the camera until a buzz sounded, then pushed his way through the door.

The office itself was flooded with afternoon light, spilling in through four tall windows in which the top of Santo Spirito and a small patch of its façade could be seen. An overstuffed low leather couch and two matching chairs by Le Corbusier surrounded a glass coffee table; along the far wall a series of oak-and-glass display cases held an artfully arranged collection of leather-bound books, glassware, bottles, and objects. On inspection, the books were a complete Balzac in the Pléiade edition, the glassware Waterford, the bottles various single malts with numbered labels, the objects archaeological artifacts of a value that was not immediately evident, so clearly were they fragments of pieces impossible to reconstruct.

Chevejon was seated before a wide expanse of mahogany desk next to the windows, under a massive unframed canvas hung on the walls that appeared to be a Botticelli, although this, of course, was impossible. Angled to his left on the desk, an oversize computer screen was divided into three windows: One showed a view of the front door from the camera mounted in the antechamber, one held text, and on the last was a three-dimensional rendering of a piece of pottery. Before him, in a shallow wooden tray, were a number of terra-cotta fragments, caked with dry white earth. While Paolo waited, Chevejon continued his gentle cleaning of one of these with a soft toothbrush. He turned, searched for something in the text on the computer screen, then entered a short series of commands on the keyboard that caused the image to be replaced by a different, apparently identical one. At last, his task completed, he looked up, his expression graduating from concentration to polite attention.

"Ah, Paolo. *Come stai?*"

"*Bene.*"

Paolo, it was clear, was increasingly nervous.

"What's new?"

"Maurizio Tueta is in town."

And this, I imagine, is where his expression would have changed. The half-smile dropping from his lips. His eyes, lizardlike, growing very blank. All in a way that made you suddenly sure that it was this— this closed, cold mask—that was his face's natural cast. That the lively, curious, friendly expression he habitually wore was a fake, a long-established, well-maintained fake.

CHEVEJON was on his feet. "Is he hurt?"

"Hurt? Not that I could see. He was reading a paper at the Rivoire."

"Tueta?" He was practically on top of Paolo, and though nearly a foot shorter and fifty pounds lighter, he seemed the larger of the two. "What the fuck are you talking about?"

"Chevejon, take it easy. I stopped in for a coffee, and Vittorio, the barman, says, 'Signore Tueta is outside.' So I look, and I see him there on the terrace, reading a paper."

"You speak to him?"

"No."

"Why?"

"Why? 'Cause he saw me going in and didn't say anything. I guessed he had something going on, and I didn't want to queer it. That's why."

Chevejon paused. He turned from Paolo—to the latter's considerable relief—and walked to the window. But when he turned back, Paolo saw with clear dismay that his face still held that flat, impenetrable expression.

"What paper was he reading?"

"Something in English."

"What was he wearing?"

Paolo thought hard. "Jeans. A red T-shirt. Green cotton jacket, not bad, maybe Ungaro's."

"How'd he look?"

Paolo hesitated. "Odd. Thin. A little pale."

"Jesus, Paolo." Chevejon sat at his desk, facing the windows. When he turned back, his expression was considerably softened. "You're an idiot, you know that? Tueta, in the middle of Florence, in jeans and a T-shirt, reading a *Herald-Tribune?* You mistake some hick American tourist for Maurizio?"

"I swear to you, Chevejon, that was him. Even Vittorio said so. Go see for yourself."

Chevejon paused, uncertain. Then he said slowly, "You wait here."

Twenty minutes later Chevejon was back, panting slightly from his run up the stairs. Paolo was sitting now, boxed in with every appearance of discomfort on the low leather couch. Chevejon walked through the office and sat heavily at his desk.

"I apologize: You're not an idiot. But you're no Rhodes scholar either. Where's Gianlucca?"

"Watching the girl. Why?"

"Because that's not Tueta. Can we get someone else to watch Natalie? What about that cousin of yours, Giorgio? Call Giorgio, then go back to the Rivoire, I'll send Gianluc to you. I want you two to watch that man like you thought he was fucking your sister every time you turned your back. You understand me? I want to know where he's staying, where he goes, what he does. Get extra help if you need it. And you see him carrying a suitcase or going within a half klick of the train station, you bring him in. Understand? You bring him in. Otherwise, just watch. And Paolo, don't speak to him."

4   THIRTEEN YEARS BEFORE, Chevejon's name had been Peter Luria. An American, one of the youngest and most promising graduate students in the classics department at UC Berkeley. Since arriving there, at sixteen, from somewhere in the Midwest, he'd won every Greek and Latin prize his department offered, taken a summa cum laude B.A., started a Ph.D., and, digging at Sardis in his summers, already unearthed and documented some of that famous site's most interesting finds.

A strange, slight, somewhat Asian-looking boy, withdrawn and unconnected to what went on around him. Perhaps if, the summer of 1976, he had gone back to Berkeley, turned on and tuned out, instead of staying on for the fall semester in Turkey, he would have dropped out in a more conventional manner than he did. As it was, he did stay on in Turkey, and though he did in fact drop out, this was Maurizio Tueta's—Danni Benami's—doing.

Peter had come back to Istanbul, at the end of that summer, a few days before his flight home, to work in the university library. A site contemporaneous to Sardis—long since looted—had been discovered and briefly explored by a group of clergymen traveling in Turkey in 1801. The gentlemen had unfortunately been beheaded by an overzealous bey, but their unpublished journals had somehow ended up in the university library and had guided Peter in his surprisingly lucky work at the site for three summers. It was a mystery to him that no one had ever found the journals before; that he had never thought to share his lucky discovery with his professors was, in hindsight, a sign of things to come.

His days in Istanbul were full: He arrived at the library early in the morning and left when they kicked him out in the evenings. Nights, for most of us, would have been hard: alone in a very foreign city, dinner a formidable challenge. But Peter combined a scholar's ease in solitude with an American's blind self-confidence; he'd settle happily at a table at the restaurant in his hotel and eat whatever the waiter brought him with utter indifference while he read a monograph "borrowed" from the library; the library's security, or rather, transparent lack of it, never ceased to surprise him. It was during such a dinner that Daniel Benami introduced himself.

Danni had sat down uninvited at his table the last night Peter was to be in Istanbul until the following summer brought him back to the dig. Peter looked up to see someone in principle not that different from himself. Both were in their early twenties. Both wore T-shirts, jeans, and sneakers, both were less than perfectly washed. One had thick, shoulder-length hair, the style at home; the other wore his greasy hair pulled tight back around his skull in a clubbed ponytail—a bit strange to Peter, but not actually outrageous. That one was a graduate student in classical archaeology from a prestigious university, the other a merchant sailor out of a Lebanese cargo ship, was not immediately apparent—neither from their appearance nor from the conversation that Danni started in accented English, the language of the monograph Peter was reading.

"So, you from the dig?"

Peter looked at his uninvited guest with surprise. "How'd you know?"

"Just guessing. All the archaeologists stay at the Pera. And you're reading Hanfmann. I heard they found an electrum refinery down there. Is it true?"

Peter wondered how he knew. "Yeah . . . yes. I mean, the Harvard people actually found it. I'd guess there are samples in the States for dating already."

"What I'd give to see that. What's the site like? No kidding, I'd give anything to go there."

To UNDERSTAND how naturally this conversation—and the long night that followed—evolved, two things should be explained.

For the first, Peter had never actually had any friends and was all but estranged from his family. His father, a German physicist, emigrated to America before the war and, after being blacklisted by McCarthy, had died young. His mother, a faded and more than somewhat batty housewife, had been far more concerned with his much younger sister than with him.

The second is that his studies, from the tiny public library in the Michigan town where he grew up to the vast holdings of the university in Berkeley, had been his life not necessarily by avocation but by default; he had stumbled into archaeology by chance and, having no other center to his life, had made it that. The importance of this fact cannot be understated. For it was not a strong inner tie that united Peter Luria with classical archaeology; it could have been anything: engineering, computers, mathematics. Any of these would have provided the deep, analytic concentration to which at an early age he had become addicted, much as an athlete is to endorphins. That it was the grammatical arcana of Greek and Latin—and then their real embodiment in the painstaking rituals of excavation—that had so early caught his imagination was the purest of chance.

These two needs—for a friend, for a passion of the mind—together explain, in part, what happened to Peter Luria that night. These, and the fact of his profound, almost innate lack of honesty. For it's important to reflect, in understanding what was about to occur to Peter, that a mind deeply involved in a formalism—or even an aesthetic—with no moral connection is a dangerous thing. Dangerous, because such a concentration that has no compelling tie to its object can skip from one purpose to another. As easily as the laser of a CD player can skip, say, from a Verdi aria to Liberace, in an absolute, nonjudgmental microsecond.

That night Peter saw a new—to him—side of Istanbul. Danni took him to the famous Pudding Café, where they sat at tables with outdated hippies for whom Istanbul was the staging point for the Magic Bus trips on the overland route to Thailand. The Jackson Five were playing on a scratchy hi-fi; young men and women spilled out the doors and into the kind late-summer night. They smoked hash under a plane tree in the Gülhane Park, then sat, far into the night, on the steps of the Blue Mosque, watching the vast white shape of Hagia Sophia floating against the ink-blue sky. It was a view that Peter, who could have extemporaneously lectured for an hour on the history of the Byzantine church, had never before seen, a view of superdetailed clarity of the mosque with its towering minarets majestic against the deep midnight. Perhaps the key to the building was in understanding its past, but in the buzzing clarity of the strong hashish, Peter experienced it for the first time as an aesthetic event, immediately and synchronically in the present. And he saw that without apprehending that aesthetic, he had understood nothing.

Much happened that night that he had never before experienced: stoned, awestruck under a canopy of lambent blue sky, night in the East, the dry wind blowing off the desert. Suddenly everything around him was as strange as the past, but there, entire, to be touched with the hand and seen by the eye, not just reconstructed by the mind. Danni took him to pick up two Turkish girls—whores, Peter correctly supposed—and together they went on a tour of an Istanbul he had never guessed existed. They crouched on the banks of the black Bosporus under the Galata Bridge, watching the little Bodrum barques put out for the night's fishing, skirting the monolithic bulks of Russian tankers moving cautiously home to the Black Sea. They sipped raki on the terrace of a little café in Taksim, the innocuous licorice taste running to Peter's head like a series of tiny, lovely explosions. Danni guided them through a maze of little streets back to the girls' place of employ, where in two little rooms they earned whatever Danni had paid them. And early in the first light of the next day Danni and Peter walked together back down to the Pera Palace.

6 FOR ALL that he was to come to own Peter, Danni never really understood how it was that night he had bought him. Probably he had seen himself as at the beginning of a process of seduction, a long, slow process in which he would, over time, open the studious young man's eyes to a new set of possibilities, insinuate

himself into his trust, and use him for a short time as a source. He assumed that he, Danni, was the only exception to what held true for his father: that a scholar's intellect was necessarily matched by a deep moral commitment to the truth. No doubt this is sometimes the case, but perhaps, had Danni gone into the academic career he longed for, he would have seen how rarely.

But it was not so for Peter Luria, no more than it was so for Danni himself, and at the heart of Peter lay the possibility of a terrible corruption.

Danni should have understood this. Should have understood that there was another path to where he himself had arrived, other than his own conscious decision to turn his intelligence to a criminal employment of his intellectual passion, since history had denied him a legitimate—better, a legal—involvement. What he did understand, however, as he moved Peter through the various beguilements of that night, was the other point about him: that within this thin, studious, abstract young man, about whom he had heard from his connections among the local laborers at Sardis, was a deep need for a dedication to a single person. Later Danni would learn about Peter's own lost father; at the time, however, if he understood that this need was going to be his capital in his use of Peter, he still underestimated Peter's clear understanding of what was happening to him. So, as they made their way under the pink sky of dawning morning that summer's day in Istanbul, Danni was guilty of overkill in his sales pitch.

"What gets me is, this stuff from the dig is of universal importance, you know? To think of its being locked up here, I can't stand it. Take the Dead Sea Scrolls. A fucking cabal, literally a cabal, gets their hands on them, and the rest of the world is deprived. And you know, this stuff doesn't actually have to stay here. I mean, it's surely wrong to steal from archaeological sites, it's a terrible crime. But no kidding, when I think that at least some of those pieces might turn up in a year or two at the Metropolitan or the Louvre, where anyone with a couple of dollars can see them without traveling all the way to Istanbul, I wonder—how bad really is it?"

Peter, who had been listening silently, spoke up now. And what he said dashed Danni's hopes on the spot.

"Uh-huh. Or a collector's apartment in Rome, for example."

Danni, stupidly, feigned innocence.

"Well, that, of course, is another story."

But Chevejon went on. "Sure. It would be like if, say, next time I'm working alone and I unearth, I don't know, a coin, a vase, I slip it into my pocket rather than register it with the dig. Or say, hide it for one of your connections to sneak out at night. Then you sold it to a museum. That would be liberating it, right?"

Danni was a good, subtle corrupter, with many successes to his name. But he knew sarcasm when he heard it, and he knew when he was beaten. Or thought he did. He stopped, ready to turn and melt off into the narrow Istanbul streets.

"Well, I'm still glad I met you. It was a good night."

But Peter was not done. In a fluent shift that caused him not the slightest hesitation, without a conscious thought, he had changed the axis of his existence.

"What would work great is if I went back to the site instead of to the States. I'm supposed to teach next semester, but they'll let me stay; I still have two years guaranteed on my fellowship. Especially this winter and spring, if I could get in there—after spring plowing. If you can set up a way past the guards, I could pass a museum's worth of pieces out of there. Can you do that?"

"What, get past the guards?" Danni was having trouble keeping up with the suddenness of the other's comprehension. "Fuck the guards, I could move the temple of Artemis under their noses."

"Good. Then what?"

Danni spoke blandly. "I pay cash, on delivery."

And at this Peter stopped. He looked, for a long minute, at the taller man—boy, really—in front of him. His face so seductive, his body alert with excited energy, his manner powered by an authoritative calm. He couldn't identify quite what it was, but he knew that something vital had just gone wrong. And still without understanding, he said: "No, forget it then."

Danni, surprised: "Why?"

For a time he didn't answer. "I—I was thinking of . . . some sort of partnership."

Now there was an even longer silence while Danni inspected him with curiosity. Twice now in his attempted corruption he had been derailed, both in ways he never would have imagined. Yet without being able to put it precisely into words, he knew exactly what was being asked of him. It was an unexpected, strangely attractive proposition, a graceless, charming seduction. Lighting a cigarette, he reviewed his night's observation of the other, wishing he had assumed less and examined more. He had underestimated this person, and he did not often do that. Finally he spoke in a new tone of voice.

"Honor among thieves—that sort of thing?"

"Uh-huh."

"I see." They turned again and walked in silence for a few minutes, each busy with similar thoughts. At the door to the Pera Palace, they faced each other again, and Danni made his decision.

"Fifty-fifty on what you give me. My other business is my business."

"Fine."

"I'll have a man speak to you at the site. He's called Seyhan Gücum—you'll recognize him; he works there. He'll bring whatever you have out, but once it's out, you'll have to get it to Istanbul and store it. Can you do that?"

"Yes."

"Do you speak any Turkish?"

"A few words."

"Then he'll bring an interpreter. I dock in Istanbul seven, eight times a year. Seyhan will tell you when to be here."

"Got it."

"Start slow and be careful. Take only what a half-wit will recognize as valuable; then you can bet a collector will. If you find an inscription that proves the Lydians invented the Cuisinart, let your fucking professor take it; we can't give writing away. And no fragments—I don't care if you find a piece of Christ's jockstrap. If you can't see it on a rich man's shelf, don't bother with it—or rather, take it for yourself. Don't speak to Seyhan on the site, and make sure he brings you every piece you told him to take. You got that? If there's a fucking grain of sand missing, no kidding, you tell him his ass is mine. And stay away from dope, anything that might get you into trouble. If we get caught, it's got to be for this, not for something else."

"I understand."

Danni looked at him, appraisingly, for a long minute. Then: "This might just work. But listen now, Peter. I didn't get to go to grad school. I didn't get the chance to work on a dig. I'm an able hand on a Lebanese boat. This is all I have, and anyone fucks it up—you,

Seyhan, I don't care who—I'll have them hurt. No kidding, I mean that."

There was another silence while Peter considered what he had just heard. Words far away from the world he knew. Then he said: "What a way to speak to your partner."

And Danni, suddenly, laughed. Then, his smile fading slowly, he spoke a last time, with real diffidence. "Oh, and, if you wouldn't mind, if you find anything really superb, would you document the context? Just as a favor."

Surprised, Peter answered: "We going to try to publish monographs before we sell these things?"

"No, no. Only, before we pass them on, no one says we can't learn something ourselves, do they? I can even get dating done—I know a guy in the lab at Cornell."

"Sure." Peter watched his new—his first—friend curiously. "Sure. I can document context."

He thought for a moment that Danni was about to blush.

7　PETER SPENT two years at the site before the university began to doubt that he was going to complete his Ph.D. By then a sizable number of small pieces had been taken, transferred to Danni in Istanbul, and moved, in the scant baggage of a few merchant marine sailors, to Ancona, to Marseilles, to Lisbon, to Hong Kong, to New York. Moreover, he had not stopped there. Displaying an initiative that surprised even himself, he made a number of contacts in the Istanbul Covered Market and, bankrolled by their joint profits from the dig, made a number of impressive purchases from other sites that in turn became some of their most profitable sales.

When they met, in Peter's university-funded room at the Pera Palace, they'd go over their take like children with baseball cards. And in the perfect marriage of several passions, their excitement over the objects themselves was fueled by their appreciation of the small fortune they were making.

The years passed with dreamy rapidity. Peter's previous visits to Sardis had always been for two, three months, a reprieve from the quotidian and slightly demeaning routine of graduate school, but too short to acquire a rhythm properly of their own. Now the months merged, one into the other. Time was measured in seasons rather than semesters, and the dig, rather than a vacation, was a way of life. That the ultimate aim of his efforts had changed radically altered in no way his practically mystical concentration on his work, and were it not for the periodic meetings with Danni, time would have lost all meaning for him. As it was, he came to measure his life by Danni's visits, to pace his work by their schedule, and to anticipate, more and more keenly, their arrival.

Seyhan would inform Peter some days before Danni was to dock. Peter would be sure, always, to be on hand as the tanker berthed and the hands were ferried ashore in a speeding Zodiac. Danni was always in the first boat, and Peter would recognize the familiar sheen of his hair, tied back in a ponytail, the cast of his bony, broad shoulders, the upturned squint of his gaze as he scoured the dock for his friend. They'd walk, Danni's gait wide-legged and jerky on land, up to the Pera. Danni would shower and change and, once installed in the restaurant, begin to eat hugely, more so than Peter had ever seen. And through the days and nights of his stay, while he was happy to talk, to go over his take, to count their shared money, to talk to tourists at the Pudding Café or hire whores on Beyoğlu Avenue, what Peter liked the most was simply to sit and watch. Watch his friend's complex, subtle face as he ate, as he talked, as he smoked, as he laughed. The vivaciousness of that face—it acquired for him the familiarity of a family member, a long-known, much-watched visage, too familiar even to acknowledge his love.

Danni. His vast, polymath knowledge, unfettered by any institutional restraints, his gift for languages, his singular experience. He listened to the tales of Danni's travels and life at sea like bedtime stories, fantastic, unimaginable, and while he listened, he watched the expressions animating his friend's face with a feeling of untold affection. Danni embodied, for Peter, unparalleled freedom from the mundane, the depressing, the sad—the first such real freedom, apart from the study of ancient objects, he had ever encountered. Once he suggested to Danni—only once—that he leave with him, that he, too, come to lead this life of adventure, and Danni, his face frowning in true incomprehension, said: "My God. Why would you want to do *that*? Anyway, I need you here. Hang on. Another few trips, and we'll be able to rethink this whole thing."

8 WHEN, after two years of happy partnership, Peter's fellowship ended and he was dropped from his doctoral program, his only concern was the loss of his access to the site. He waited with real foreboding to break the news to Danni. But when they met at the small hotel near the Golden Horn where, having lost his room at the Pera Palace, Peter was staying, Danni was unfazed.

"Good, it's about time. I think we're both ready to move on. Subcontract the dirty work. Diversify. Tell me, you ever think of living in Florence?"

"Why Florence?"

"It's a beautiful city. There's a first-rate archaeological museum. And I'm using Ancona Harbor for just about everything we bring into Europe."

"And you?"

Danni spoke as if to himself. "I'm moving to Paris. I got my eye on a storefront on the rue du Faubourg Saint-Honoré. The way I see it, we use that as a front for sales and centralize an office for you in Florence for import and storage. Why supply Minot anymore? Fuck him, he's making four, five times what he pays us, and we take all the risk. Let's do our own selling; we can figure out how. Plus, the boat's limiting me; I have more contacts than I can get to from our dockings. I can get more product just traveling alone."

Peter thought. "Go out on our own, you mean."

"Right. And also, I wouldn't mind the chance to live with some of these things before passing them on."

"Yes," said Peter, nodding his head absently, his eyes unfocused. As if looking into the future. "Yes, I'd like that, too. Would you see being in Florence often?"

"All the time—I got an Italian passport and an Italian name already. I'll be there every few months, at the least, for a month or so. There'll be a lot—a lot—of work."

"Okay. I'm in."

"Good. And, Peter, I think it's time you get a new name. I got a clean Italian birth certificate in the name of Chevejon. Peter Chevejon, I like it."

"Okay." Peter focused now on Danni. "I like it, too."

9 AND SO, as Danni had transformed Peter Luria, overnight, from a promising graduate student into a *tomberolo,* a foreigner in dirty jeans smuggling stolen antiquities from an archaeological dig to his partner, so was Chevejon transformed from a child playing a game of crime into a young businessman, quite well off, with all of Europe at his feet.

The first year in Florence Danni was never long gone, and a new equality characterized their relationship, for if the conception of their business was Danni's, both were equally at sea about how to live the new lives before them. In one way, Danni learned fast; in the other, Chevejon. Danni learned how to set up the business, the surest routes of supply, how to move his goods around the strange underworld of Europe without the benefit of his constant movement by sea, how to launder the profits. But Chevejon, surprisingly, learned where to locate the office, how to dress to fit their new personas, where to find and how to sell to those anonymous collectors, acquisition curators, investors—the greedy, ostentatious, and pretentious—who were to be their customers. In that first year he changed his glasses for contact lenses, cut his hair, began to dress like the elegantly garbed figures who thronged the evening streets outside the Florence boutiques. After he met Danni's couriers—the predecessors to Paolo and Gianlucca, enormous Southern Italians with dark, nasty faces—he enrolled in a local judo school and began to build the strong, lithe body that he was so carefully to maintain in the future. And as he accrued experience in receiving shipments and making sales, he began to develop the blank, impenetrable, formidable manner that was so effective in controlling the former, and the urbane, witty, altogether seductive amiability that he used, to such good effect, for the latter.

All this, of course, took years, as it had taken years for Danni to evolve into the man he'd become before he left Nicole on his last trip. But there was a difference. For where Danni was developing, given his circumstances, as a living, learning human whose passion could find expression only in a criminal underworld, Chevejon was learning, with the same meticulous, painstaking care with which once he had extracted fragile ceramics from baked-hard earth, to be what Danni needed him to be. And that was, pure and simple, a dealer of illegally acquired antiquities. It could have been drugs, arms, pornography. In the end, for Chevejon, all that mattered was Danni.

So it was that paramount for Peter Chevejon among the pleasures, the attainments of the last twelve years—the money, the beautiful women, the independence, and the freedom—had been his service, soon irreplaceable, to Danni Benami. In time Danni brought all his interests to the partnership, and Chevejon added some of his own. It was he, for example, who was approached by the agent of the son of an important Nazi who had, rolled and stored in a closet in Berlin, the Vermeer canvas that Nicole had later seen in Paris. It was he who arranged the buy of twelve signed prewar Cartier-Bresson prints. And even Danni did not know where Chevejon had acquired the entirely unsellable canvas that could not possibly be a Botticelli that hung in his office, for which a Japanese businessman had unsuccessfully offered him an amount measured in eight figures, of which the first, Chevejon admitted wryly, was not one, or two, or again three. If he took pleasure in these deals for his own sake, it was more for Danni's evident admiration that he worked. Like a gosling imprinting on a passing stranger, Chevejon had, those years before in Istanbul, come into his own as Danni's man, and nothing Danni could ever do could cause him to hesitate in a devotion that was as necessary to him as it became, too, to Danni. An unquestioning devotion that was, as is more often the case between men than between men and women, utterly straightforward and, without any personal interest, impossible to diminish.

Perhaps, it seemed to me as Chevejon, long after Luke's story was finished, told me his, perhaps this devotion was, to Danni, the complement of Nicole's more complicated and, in the end, less reciprocal one. Perhaps, it seemed to me, such a devotion cannot exist between men and women. For then the agendas are so much more involved, circuitous, and harder to acknowledge.

10 WHEN, on the midsummer's day in 1989, Paolo Cavalari told Chevejon that Danni Benami was in Florence, Chevejon knew, deep in his gut, that something in their long-standing, perfectly working business had gone wrong.

In the many months since Danni had suspended operations and

virtually disappeared, Chevejon had been confident that this was a hiatus after which, eventually, all would return to usual. At Danni's insistence they had closed their Paris shop and Chevejon had transformed their Florence office into his personal study with perfect confidence in Danni's eventual return, planning to enjoy what was, he felt, a well-earned year of leisure. Their stock sold, their money safely invested, Chevejon turned to his own collection of arcana—esoteric fragments, indecipherable scripts—for a period of quiet, reflective indulgence in concentration, his old addiction. At home, a villa in Fiesole, a progression of gorgeous women—French students, American travelers, Dutch professors—kept his house and his bed. Of course, he knew everyone in Florence, as well as in Rome and Milan, and he welcomed the chance to travel in his adopted country as a tourist rather than as a businessman. And if he missed his meetings with Danni—often intensely—he still was able, in his confidence of Danni's eventual return, to enjoy the fruits of their years of hard work.

True, Chevejon did not really know where his partner was. But Danni had never told him, any more than he had told Nicole, where he went on his travels. And usually it was only by the provenance of articles arriving through the port of Ancona that he was able to infer his partner's whereabouts, and only through a coded ad in the *Herald-Tribune* classifieds that he was able to contact him.

Anyway, for some time he had been aware that Danni's attention to their affairs was growing thin. For several years he had traveled less and less frequently, spending more and more of his time in his rooms in Chevejon's villa, acquiring and reading an extensive collection of books that had nothing to do with archaeology. His mother's works, his father's works, and a host of ancillary sources about those writings. Chevejon hadn't cared. Danni's extended periods in Florence had been the purest of pleasure, even as his mood had grown increasingly withdrawn. He hadn't minded the withdrawal, nor did he mind his absence. And he had remained unconcerned even when Danni started using their extensive European network for the acquisition of the oddest of objects: Nazi memorabilia, wartime diaries, documents, and photographs; an actual yellow Star of David from the Lodz ghetto— valuable, in their own right, but far from their usual run of goods. He trusted that there was a profit in it, and if that was not to be measured in strictly financial terms, well, it had been a long time since they had

had to worry too much about money. For what had taken Nicole, as his lover, nearly a decade to know about Danni—and still she had not wanted to understand—Chevejon had learned in the first few years of their partnership, and his confidence in him was perfect. Wherever Danni was, it was worth being there, Chevejon felt sure. And he would come back.

11 HE WOULD NOT, however, do so without telling him, would not take a terrace table at Florence's most visible café and read an English newspaper. Beside any of the other myriad reasons why he would not, he was known in Florence as Maurizio Tueta, an Italian born and bred, whose putative ignorance of English had helped them in more deals than they could count. So when Paolo announced that this was exactly what Danni had done, Chevejon nearly ran out of his building in his shirtsleeves, crossed the Piazza Santo Spirito in a hurried stride, and headed quickly toward the Ponte Santa Trìnita. Across the river, among the crowds of foreigners touring through the afternoon, he pushed his way down the via Porta Rossa to the open expanse of the Piazza della Signoria. Arriving, he paused to catch his breath, then moved through the tables on the terrace with assumed casualness, noting with relief that in this tourist crowd, any Florentines who mattered were, like him, keeping by day to the more obscure parts of town.

But just as Paolo had said, Danni sat at a table in jeans and a T-shirt, reading the *Herald-Tribune*. Chevejon passed directly in front of him, his heart twisting in his chest. Danni looked up without recognition, and as he turned his eyes back to his paper, Chevejon felt a surge of relief and fear. For this—this *sosie de Danni*, as he said to himself, once safely installed at the bar—was uncanny.

Of course, it was not Danni; this man, with his smooth, sallow face, was no more than thirty, an obvious stranger. On the other hand, the resemblance was close to perfect: the high forehead under a sweep of black hair, the deep black eyes, so disarmingly wide-set, the sharp, high cheekbones over sunken, unshaved cheeks. With a little more amusement in the eyes, a little more life to the expression, it could with no doubt whatever be the Danni he had known midway through the growth of their business in Florence. Who was it? Danni's double? Danni's illegitimate son? Danni's brother?

Chevejon took a coffee from Vittorio and drank it in short, thoughtful sips. He paid at the cashier's booth, returned to the bar to leave a lavish tip, guaranteeing Vittorio's discretion, then slowly made his way out of the bar and past the tables on the sunny terrace until he stood, unsure of his exact intention, behind the man. Here he paused, and then found himself pronouncing, quietly, in the little Hebrew he was able to speak: *"Habibi, ma ata oseh can?"*—Buddy, what are you doing here? The man started and began to turn in his seat, but Chevejon, having observed his reaction, had already turned and was walking away.

Danni had never told him he had a brother.

12 As THAT AFTERNOON passed and a slow evening fell over his adopted home from the backlit summer sky—detailed as a Maxfield Parrish, plastic as a Magritte—Peter Chevejon felt the harmony of his year of vacation falling away. Night came, he remained in his office, and at last Paolo and Gianlucca reported by phone that the man was staying at the Excelsior, had spent his afternoon sitting in cafés, had returned to the hotel until dinner and then eaten at the Cibreo, in the front room; whoever he was, this young man was not saving money. But, Chevejon reflected, since General Benami's death and the pillage, the absolute pillage of his collection, Danni's brother must be as rich as he was stupid. While waiting for this report, after much thought, he had placed a few careful telephone calls around Europe. First he put the standard rental ad in the *Herald-Tribune*—"Florence pied à terre available immediately"—the last word conveying urgency. But he did so with a feeling of futility—he doubted Danni was checking the papers. Then Chevejon began calling business contacts—only a few, and only the most trusted. He, who had never before dared question the least of Danni's movements, instituted even this minimal search among the surest of contacts with real reluctance. From Antwerp to Barcelona, no one had seen Danni, heard from him, or heard of him. The last call he made, after long hesitation, was to Paris, and there, the telephone in the apartment on the rue de Fleurus rang with what, to Chevejon, who was hardly given to sympathetic fallacy, seemed a distant, a lost, a mournful sound.

Well. Standing up from the telephone, crossing to the windows of his office above the Piazza Santo Spirito, he shook his broad shoulders, aching from tension. Whatever else was true, this was sure: If Paolo, who had worked for him and Danni for years, mistook this stranger for his employer, then certainly so would dozens of other people in Florence, important people. And this could not be allowed.

Furthermore—he felt increasingly convinced as he reflected—as was often the case in these situations, if no information was available by oblique means, the simplest thing to do was go straight to the source. He crossed the room to the oak display cabinets, plucked a rocks glass from the collection of crystal, and poured a shot of scotch from one of the unlabeled bottles. He drank it, holding it on his tongue for a moment, then tipping his head back with a slight jerk and swallowing. He'd wait until Paolo and Gianlucca next reported back from their positions in the lobby of the Excelsior, then make arrangements for tomorrow. What would be easiest? To approach the man wherever he took his breakfast? No, whatever scene was going to take place could not be in public; he could not risk anyone witnessing Maurizio Tueta, in jeans and a T-shirt, not recognize his partner. To go up to his room first thing in the morning, Paolo and Gianlucca large presences flanking him in his impeccable dark suit? That was more like it. A momentary calm descended on him; then suddenly, his frustration crystallized and, turning, he spoke aloud, surprising himself yet again.

"Why should I have to spend the night wondering what the fuck is going on with this little shit?"

He crossed to a closet to pull out a tie and jacket. Suddenly, to Peter Chevejon, right now, one in the morning on a midsummer's night, seemed the right time to find out what this was all about.

CHAPTER ELEVEN

1 IT HAD BEEN three days since the morning Luke had arrived in the high, early sun of a Florence day filtering through the vaulted ceilings of the Stazione Santa Maria Novella.

He had bought a map and wandered, uncomfortably following the twisting streets, toward the river, looking for the single hotel he knew of in Florence, the one at which his father had always stayed. He found it impossible to ask directions. The map now nearly useless, he picked a street at random and walked through to a little square. Houses with shutters that folded oddly, not on vertical but on horizontal axes, rose around him with an air of patrician decay. In the shade of a small fountain, a group of pigeons moved like a grazing herd of miniature beasts. To one side lay the baroque façade of a very small church. As he turned a corner into a cul-de-sac, a sudden silence fell and a cello, long, low, practicing in duet to an absent partner, sounded mournfully from a third-floor window. Luke listened for a long time, then turned. At the bottom of a street he found the Arno and, after checking the map, followed the bank, for a distance that revealed how lost he had become, to the Hotel Excelsior.

Almost immediately he was mistaken for his brother. And then again, the very next day. Neither encounter led to Chevejon. It was discouraging.

The afternoon of his arrival, after emerging from his hotel, he found an English-language bookstore and bought a *Schaum's Outline* to Italian grammar. He crossed the river and walked aimlessly until he arrived at an open café, surprisingly lively in the afternoon stillness, filled with well-dressed people whose professions and stations he found impossible to surmise. He took a terrace seat and repeated what he had just heard a fellow patron say: *"Un caffè, per favore."*

He turned from the waiter and began to read the *Schaum's Outline* when, from across the square, a figure imposed itself on his attention. Raising his head, he saw that an elegant woman was approaching purposefully, with a smile. Tall, in a black, sleeveless jumpsuit, its simplicity embellished by a flash of diamond and heavy gold around her neck. Speaking in Italian. Volubly. At length and with affection.

He watched. The friendly, animated face. Shocked. And in a pause in her rapid speech, finally he managed to interject in English: "I'm sorry, I don't speak Italian."

"Ah." She stopped short and stared hard at him for a moment. *"Scusi."* Still watching him, she moved off, and Luke, his equanimity lost, put his empty cup on the table and walked quickly away. When he stopped and turned around, he saw that there was simply no chance of finding her again in these tiny, twisting streets.

2 THE SECOND DAY, at a restaurant in Santa Croce, a man broke off from a passing group and headed toward him. He was tall, gray-haired, perhaps in his sixties, dressed in a dark serge suit. As he approached Luke, his handsome face broke out into a smile, his eyes seeming actually to sparkle in the bright sun as he greeted Luke.

"Eccolò, Signore Tueta è ritornato."

Without rising, his heart beginning to pound, Luke hesitated, then spoke in English. "Pardon me, you've mistaken me for someone."

The man stopped in his tracks, evidently shocked. Quickly Luke rose and spoke again.

"Do you speak English?" The man seemed stunned, so he repeated, *"Est-ce que Monsieur parle français?"*

Now the man passed his eyes over Luke's body, from head to toe. When he looked at Luke's face again, he was evidently in control of his shock and spoke with an insolence that seemed, to Luke, deliberate.

"Certainly I speak English." His accent was nearly perfectly British.

"I wonder if you can help me then. I'm trying to find a Mr. Chevejon. Peter Chevejon."

"I don't understand."

Luke began to speak again, but as if having just reached a decision, the man stepped backward again, turned, and began to walk quickly back toward his friends. A stranger, receding into streets only he knew, without a glance back.

The phone book listed no Chevejon, nor Benami, nor Tueta. That was no surprise.

The third day, in a crowded café opposite Michelangelo's David in a large piazza, he was reading a *Herald-Tribune* when behind him sounded a voice in Hebrew: *"Habibi, ma ata oseh can?"* With a start he turned and saw the back of a receding figure in a dark suit.

Five tiny, guttural words, utterly coincidental, but in a second fear lit the space of his awareness, concentrating it, refining it, like a series of tiny, speedy little lights. He called the waiter, settled his bill, and walked quickly back to the Excelsior.

That evening he ordered a bottle of whiskey to be brought up. Then he poured a hefty drink and drank it, standing by the window.

The night air had dried, but long, smudged clouds stained the ink-blue sky. The river was a gash through the city, whose lights, in the humid air, appeared within little blurred halos. For a long suite of minutes, perhaps twenty, he stood drinking purposefully. Then a knock sounded at the door, and, thinking it must be room service, he called out that the door was open. Only after his voice had sounded did he realize he had not ordered anything.

Luke turned now to see three elegant men enter the room: a short, very handsome Asian flanked by two giants. One of them shut the door while the Asian advanced into the room. Too drunk and too shocked to react, he saw that the man was not really Asian, and an intent, even menacing expression was on his face. The two large men arranged themselves on either side of the door. The short man sat down in an armchair, perfectly composed, and spoke in perfect English.

"Excuse us for barging in. We think we have some business with you." He paused before the passivity of Luke's reaction. "You do speak English?"

"Yeah." A bottomless fatigue was pouring over Luke as he realized his success. "Yeah. You would be Peter Chevejon?"

The man's menacing face shifted, almost imperceptibly. Then he nodded and waited wordlessly.

For a time he anxiously examined Chevejon's face, as if for a clue to what he should tell. Then he pronounced an unpremeditated sentence very, very slowly. "I'm afraid I bring you some very bad news."

3 "ACH, NICOLE KILLED." Chevejon made a sound with his tongue against the roof of his mouth, several times, a sound of real pain. "Ach. How could we let such a thing happen?"

He did not ask who did it.

They sat, the nearly empty whiskey bottle on the floor between them. The two giants had left hours before. Day was dawning, and thin sunlight began to illuminate the lamplit room. Chevejon, low in the armchair, stared at the carpet between his feet, his face flattened in an expression of grief, wholly unaware of Luke's scrutiny.

Finally he reached for the bottle, drank, and then hitched himself up. Luke remembered, briefly, the way Nicole's expression, the night he had arrived at the rue de Fleurus, had seemed to fall in and out of the recognition that he was not Danni, like a tired person dozing off and then, suddenly, waking. Chevejon did no such thing; now his face peered at him with the same menacing curiosity it had worn during the night while Luke told his story—a version of his story—up to Nicole's murder.

"What did you do after you found her?" He had sounded more and more American as the night wore on. So, Luke realized, did he—when had he last spoken English at any length? He brought his mind back to the present and answered mechanically.

"Called the police."

"Right away?"

"No." Luke licked his lips. He had never thought ahead to what he would actually say to Chevejon. Now he found his explanation ready and waiting, nestled snugly next to the truth. "I cleaned out the safe and the apartment. I had to destroy some things. Some I hid."

"Why?"

Luke watched him for a moment, then spoke deliberately. "I had some idea what kind of business you and my brother are in. I thought it best that the murder look like a robbery."

The other betrayed nothing. "Where?"

"Where what?"

"Where did you hide the things you hid?"

"In the broiler pan of the oven. Also inside a baguette in the garbage."

Chevejon considered. "They find them?"

"No."

There was a pause. Then Chevejon said, slowly and injecting threat into the words: "If I were inclined to think you were lying, I wouldn't believe that."

"Why?"

"Because those are two of the most obvious hiding places conceivable. The oven and the garbage, for Christ's sake."

Luke felt annoyance—not at being doubted but at being doubted on one of the true parts of his story.

"I'm telling you, they never looked. When the cop in charge found out I was . . . my father's son, he was on the phone to the Israeli Embassy in minutes. And he had proof of my story: There was a security tape from Le Drugstore that had me buying cigarettes there at the time she was killed. I'm telling you, that guy treated me like I had diplomatic immunity. He arranged a fucking *carte de séjour* for me. You ever try to get a residence permit in France? I doubt there's a harder piece of paper in the world to get."

"Okay." Chevejon cut him off. "What did you hide?"

"A few marble pieces. Some jewelry." He hesitated. "A gun."

Chevejon didn't seem to care about the gun. "What'd you tell the police?"

"What I told you. I'd been out to buy American cigarettes up on Saint-Germain, at Le Drugstore. It's the only place open all night. I got back to find the door open. And found her." He stopped and bit his lower lip. He had not mentioned what the barman from Le Fleurus had said before he went up to the apartment. He had not mentioned how he had explained that to the police, by claiming that he had returned to the apartment before going to Le Drugstore; how his resemblance to Danni had hidden Danni's presence from the police. He realized he was biting his lower lip, stopped, reached forward for the bottle, from which Chevejon had been sipping directly, took a sip himself, and continued.

"It was pretty easy to make out that it was a robbery. I mean, it was obviously a rich man's apartment."

The other considered. "She would have come home while you were out."

"Yes."

"Could she have left the door open?"

"I suppose. But I doubt she would have."

"Then whoever it was convinced her to open the door. Thinking, I suppose, that it was you. Is that what you're saying?" Chevejon looked at him sharply. "Did Nicole know the combination to the safe?"

Luke answered readily; this man must not know that it was Danni who killed his girlfriend. "Yes. Danni had given it to her."

Chevejon: "Then what?"

Feeling the man was only temporarily done with this part, Luke took a breath and went on.

"Like I said. The detective arranged a *carte de séjour* for me. And made me stay in France a couple of weeks. They called once or twice with questions. Once they asked me if I knew a Maurizio Tueta; I assumed the gallery had been in that name. I thought they were following me for a while, but then I thought they weren't. The Israeli Embassy got them to keep it all out of the papers. After nothing happened for a few weeks, I left."

"Thinking?"

Pause. "Sorry?"

Patiently, as if he had all the time in the world: "What were you thinking when you left?"

"That I'd come find you. I thought if I hung around long enough, sooner or later you'd find me."

4 CHEVEJON REFLECTED. "Nicole told you a lot."

Shrugging: "I was there a long time. Waiting for Danni." He paused, realizing the inadequacy of his response, and knew he must continue. "I don't think she believed that he was coming back."

A ripple of surprise on the other's face. "Why not?"

Now Luke was surprised. "Well, she hadn't heard from him since he'd left."

Chevejon began to speak, stopped himself, then began again. "Why do you say that? I must have forwarded a dozen letters from Danni since he left."

Luke said, flatly, covering his shock: "She never got them."

A tone of correction. "She *said* she never got them."

"No. She never got them."

A silence. Then: "What was the cop's name?"

"Lecéreur. Jean-Baptiste Lecéreur."

"Any trouble leaving France?"

The sun was up, casting long shadows from the curtains over Chevejon where he sat facing Luke.

"No. I went by train via Nice. Used one of Danni's passports. I found it in the safe. There were others. I burned them."

"You tell the police you were going?"

"No."

"I see." He rose abruptly and put on his jacket, then stood and looked down at Luke.

"You said only two people spoke to you, right?"

"I want to talk about my brother." But Chevejon was not done with the subject.

"One down in *l'altro Arno,* a woman. And one up at Santa Croce, a man. Right?"

"Right."

"Okay, Gianlucca'll take care of that." Chevejon spoke as if to himself.

Luke stood. "I want to talk about my brother."

"Oh, yeah. Well, we'll talk about that, too." He moved toward the door. Then, to Luke again: "I'll be back this evening. Until then you stay in the room."

"Pardon me?" He tried to speak coldly, but Chevejon went on calmly, confidently.

"I can't have you walking around the streets looking like Danni. You've done enough damage as it is. If you leave this room, you'll be stopped."

Luke turned to the window, shrugging. "I'm scared. No kidding."

He could not see, as the other left the room, the expression that, knowing himself unseen, Chevejon allowed to cross his face.

5 | IT WAS eight in the morning. The city sent busy sounds of its awakening through the open window, an ever-richer light flooding the room. Luke opened the curtains and stared out at the day. He inhaled in long breaths to extinguish the tension that filled his body. He turned, paced anxiously through the small suite of rooms, lay down on the bed, then sat up and began, again, to pace.

It was a surprise to him that Chevejon, obviously so smart, and so sly, still missed the obvious: That only Danni could have killed Nicole and why he would have done it. It spoke of a blind spot in this extraordinarily sharp man, and again Luke reflected on the power that his brother must have—or have had—over the people who loved him. Particularly over this one, Luke thought, this powerfully charismatic man. So charismatic that through that long night the temptation to tell Chevejon everything—about Nicole, about the murder, about Jerusalem and about New York—had been so insistent that in a strange way, it had made it easier to lie; Luke's concentration had been so taken up with resisting the other man's charms that he had no time to think about the fact he was lying. Briefly he let the image of Chevejon back into his mind: the strong face under its thick bangs exuding a confidence that was virtually impossible not to trust. It was extraordinary: That you recognized him as a master hustler, that you were scared of him, did nothing to diminish your urge to trust him. To be ascendant over such a man, what could Danni be?

Could he be trusted? Luke yawned, drained now, tiredly recognizing the temptation. Of course he could not be. Still, he was all Luke had.

The twelve hours to Chevejon's return dragged interminably. He ordered breakfast, ate, tried to marshal his thoughts. But he could not concentrate. Now, for the first time, he realized that Chevejon had not told him a thing, not a single thing, about his brother. He had revealed nothing. As if it were a lesson in memorization, he reminded himself that he must not trust Chevejon. And that he must beware of what Chevejon might have in mind for Luke. At this thought, fear surfaced; he closed the bedroom curtains, stretched out on the bed, and fell asleep.

 CHEVEJON spent less time with me during that day, leaving me—to my disappointment—in Giorgio's care. The morning he spent in his office. There was much to think about.

For one thing, he now had two children, not one, to baby-sit. Giorgio was going to have to be put on retainer; he needed both his bodyguards for the boy. Overkill was in order here, for he had to be very, very careful. And as for him, he saw quickly, a different kind of pressure was going to be required. The boy must be afraid, that was sure; he must think that Chevejon was prepared simply to toss him away. Which was easy, because it wasn't far from the truth. He knew the little esteem in which Danni held his family; he did not expect that his partner would object to anything he did to dispose of the absurd threat this boy posed.

But then, before he did dispose of him, he needed better to understand exactly what that threat was. This was not a question that could be posed directly; as with the girl, there was nothing to be gained by directness. So, in fact, he was cornered.

Sitting in his office, unfazed by his lack of sleep, he thought carefully. No, he was not cornered; there was something he could use with the girl. It was about time this cat-and-mouse game with her had its end. And if he could not pose a question directly, he could a threat.

Accordingly, he rose, showered in the little office bathroom, and dressed again in a suit from a small closet. Then he picked me up and, before lunch, took me for a walk through the Accademia.

And, in front of Fra Bartolommeo's *Isaiah and Job,* he stopped his guided tour to tell me what he knew about my father. At least some of what he knew; he made no reference to General Benami.

I listened with mounting anxiety, my eye on the painting, trying not to show surprise. And when he was done, I spoke at once.

"Who is this Maurizio Tueta, then, and what did he want with my father?"

Now Chevejon thought, watching me, perhaps, while he chose a lie. But before he could decide on it, I spoke again: "Maurizio Tueta, that must be a phony name, right? His real name must be Danni Benami."

Now Chevejon was shocked—not that he let me see.

"Why would you think that?"

And now it was my turn to tell him a story.

I told him now of my apprehension and interrogation in Paris. Clearly I had impressed him.

"And you think these people were Israeli?"

I looked away, my neck twisting above the low collar of my dress, then back.

"I thought I recognized they were speaking Hebrew, but it's hard to be sure."

Now it was clear to Chevejon that I knew too much. Knowing the stakes had been seriously raised, he went on. He told me about Yosef Benami. He told me about Yosef Benami and my father. He spoke as if he were a doctor, giving me a prognosis I both expected and feared. But the payoff was big.

First I asked: "This Benami, is that a given name or a Hebrew one?"

He corrected me. "Hebraicized."

"And the original name, was it Neumann?"

Almost showing his shock: "How would you know that?"

But instead of answering, I told him something else.

I told him how I came to Paris and found the address on the rue de Fleurus.

I told him how I went there and saw Danni enter the café Le Fleurus, only it wasn't Danni. I told him how I had watched the man who wasn't Danni and the woman through their weeks together, wondering who they were, wondering what they were doing. How I had just about determined to ask them when I was derailed by the three Israeli men who asked me about Danni Benami. I told him how I had left Paris, through Munich, and run away to Florence.

The most important thing I told Chevejon I didn't even understand. That was when I told him that this couple I had seen in Paris, the man-who-was-not-Danni and the beautiful older woman, were in love.

7

LUKE WOKE in the early evening disoriented, hungover, ravenous. Slowly the events of the night reassembled in his mind. Now the question of what this man had in mind for him seemed much, much more urgent. Showering, he felt aware of the worlds of experience that lay between him and Chevejon and, by extension, his brother. He shaved, studying his face in the mirror; he dressed, then ordered coffee, which he drank with the little whiskey left in the bottle from the night before.

Chevejon was at the door, alone, precisely at eight. He was in a loose sharkskin suit and, shaved and fresh, did not seem just to have woken. He came into the room with his hands in his jacket pockets, nodded to Luke, looked around the room, and said: "Let's get packed. I'm parked illegally."

Luke stood, suddenly very scared.

"What's up?"

"I'm taking you back to my place. It'll be better than being cooped up here; there's a garden and everything."

Luke didn't move, resisting Chevejon's evident hurry.

"What is this, house arrest?"

"Something like that, I suppose." Perhaps noticing now how alarmed the other was becoming, he spoke more slowly. "I can't have you showing yourself around Florence anymore. At least you have to grow a beard. Let's hop up now."

Luke crossed to the window, considering. Below, the two giants stood across the street in their black suits and white shirts, leaning against the low wall next to the river. He turned and began slowly to gather up his things. Unsure of what was best to do, he felt he was no longer in control of his body's movements. While he packed, Chevejon, hands still in his jacket pockets, looked curiously around the room.

"Learning Italian, I see?"

"Uh-huh."

"How do you find it?"

"Good."

"What else do you speak? Hebrew, I suppose." The Americanisms were gone, again, from his speech, replaced by the indeterminate accent of a European who has learned English well.

"And French, German, Russian."

"What is it you do, anyway?"

"I'm a translator." Though the humor of the response was obscurely evident to Luke, he was surprised to see the other's easy, winning smile, so incongruous with the menace of his demeanor.

"Live in Jerusalem?"

"No, no, New York. I grew up there."

"Ah, with your mother."

Luke didn't answer, and silence fell as he packed his bag. After a moment he asked, while packing: "How long have you known my brother?"

"Long time."

"Know him pretty well?"

"I'd say so."

"Doesn't it strike you as strange he never told you he had a brother?"

Chevejon considered, and when he spoke, it was as if to himself. "No. I never told him I have a sister."

Luke felt a pang of regret as they left the room, as if some sort of cere-mony were being neglected. Chevejon insisted on carrying his bag, they walked downstairs to the hotel lobby in silence, and when Luke started to veer off to the cashier's desk, Chevejon stopped him.

"It's taken care of."

The desk staff nodded to Chevejon with apparent recognition, gazed curiously at Luke. Outside, in the warm night, Luke recognized the low, wide body of an American car—monstrous in the small scale of the city—parked in front of a No Parking sign; they approached it and, after Chevejon had thrown Luke's bag into the backseat, climbed in. The car was a convertible, a Chevy from the sixties, in immaculate condition. Chevejon kept the roof up and, making a U-turn out of the square, took a route designed, Luke realized later, to avoid the populated center of town, where evening strollers would be mingling among the slow-moving traffic. The giants, wherever they were, were not visible. After a few minutes of driving in silence, he spoke up.

"Where did you meet my brother?"

Chevejon turned to look at him, then back to his driving. The question, apparently, was a presumption, and for a moment Luke thought the other was not going to answer. Then he shrugged, as if it really didn't matter what he said, and answered in an offhand tone.

"In Istanbul. I was working at the dig in Sardis."

Luke nodded, noting that Chevejon had returned to his American accent. "You're an archaeologist?"

"I was. When we went into business, I left the, uh, academy." At this last word Chevejon's voice took on a fruity, mocking tone.

Luke thought for a while. Obviously the other didn't care for his questions. But then, there was nothing to lose by asking. He said: "I was expecting you to be a little more reticent about your business."

Chevejon shrugged. "You know all about it."

"How do you know I haven't told the police?"

Chevejon didn't turn from his driving, and Luke had the feeling that this man had not slept since they had last met but had been investigating, by whatever means, Luke's authenticity. "Let's not be silly." There was a silence; then he spoke again, surprising Luke.

"How do you like Florence?"

He considered. "It's different. Half of it's a big mall; the other half a little village. Italians are different, man. So friendly."

The other shrugged. "You're coming from Paris. It's another thing altogether down here."

"Well, I like it. I was wishing I'd come here instead of France."

"How's that?"

Luke explained: "When I got out of the army, I went to France."

"What, you went back to Israel for the army?"

"Uh-huh."

"My God. What for?"

Luke didn't answer. They were passing through the residential neighborhood on the north of town where he had walked the day before, having taken a wide berth around the center of the city, and soon Luke understood they were on the road to Fiesole. Then they mounted higher into the hills and turned off onto a narrow road.

Chevejon drew to a stop in front of a tall gate set in a stone wall. The giants were there, and Luke watched them in the light of the head-lamps as they opened the padlocked gate. They drove through and, while the gate was relocked behind them, went up a winding lane through a few turns and up to a small palazzo. Luke could make out, in the moonlight, a sweep of lawn cut out of surrounding olive trees and brush. Then the car pulled onto gravel and stopped in front of the house, where wide-open windows spilled light out into the garden.

Through the soft night full of cicadas, Chevejon carried Luke's bag in. They crossed a marble foyer and climbed a set of winding stairs to the third floor, where Chevejon led him through a massive oak door into a small library. An archway led to a connecting bedroom, beyond the windows of which he could see, past the trees, the lights of Florence. Chevejon flipped on the lights, put Luke's bag on the bed, opened the windows to the night air, and turned to Luke.

"These are Danni's rooms. Bathroom's through the door there. If you want to change, Danni has some clothes in the closet. We'll eat in fifteen minutes."

Luke nodded and said: "I suppose this means that my brother isn't here."

The other looked surprised. "No. Of course not. You didn't think he was, did you?"

"Well, I don't know where he is, do I?"

Annoyance crossed the other's face. "No, I suppose you don't. But when you think of it, if he were here, then I wouldn't be going through this song and dance trying to figure out what to do with you."

Luke watched him for a moment. "Are you going to tell me where he is?"

Chevejon shook his head. "Come back down the stairs when you're ready, I'll be in the living room off the foyer. And Luke, don't shave. Okay?"

8 LUKE PACED the bedroom. There was a single bed, an armoire, and a dresser arranged around a kilim. Nothing on the walls. In the armoire were hung a number of suits, some slacks, some ties. He walked into the bathroom and found a massive

bath resting on brass lion's paws, a pedestal sink, a heavy ceramic toilet, an antique oak medicine chest.

He walked back out and paused for a time in front of the open window. As his eyes adjusted to the light from the floor below, he could see a smooth-cut lawn surrounded by a border of flowers, a marble fountain gurgling in its center. Some notes of music floated up from below.

He turned back to the armoire, took out a pair of dark green cotton slacks, removed his jeans, and put on the slacks, a white poplin shirt, a green paisley tie, a pair of black wing tips, and a dark green sports jacket that clearly was meant to match the slacks. The cuffs and the neck of the shirt were slightly loose, the shoulders of the jacket slightly too large; otherwise, everything fitted. Dressed, he went back through the library and into the hallway, found the stairs, and walked diffidently down and in the direction of the music.

Chevejon was waiting through the open door of the living room. A piano sonata was playing, perhaps Beethoven, Luke wasn't sure. Chevejon handed him something dark in a martini glass, which he called an *aperitivo*. After a few moments he excused himself and went out, leaving Luke alone.

Now he was able to take in the splendid room, with its grand piano, a collection of Turkish prayer rugs scattered on the mosaic floor, its uncannily familiar-looking art on the walls, among which he identified an Ernst and a Picasso sketch. There were, he noticed with interest, no antiquities visible. Soon Chevejon returned and ushered him back through the foyer into a dining room, where they sat at one end of a long table built of wide, ancient planks of lightly stained wood and were served their meal by a startlingly pretty maid.

Dinner ended after midnight, and Chevejon led Luke out of the dining room, across the foyer, and through the living room to a small, paneled study. Luke noticed the grace of Chevejon's movements in his well-cut suit, and the proprietorial eye that he cast, constantly, around his house. Chevejon unfolded a bar from the bookshelves and poured two brandies. These he carried to the table with an ashtray balanced on one and a blue tin of short cigars on the other. Sitting, he offered Luke first a glass, then a cigar, then a light.

They sat in silence for a time, Luke's mind floating on the *aperitivo*, the wine at dinner, and the brandy he was sipping. Somehow he felt himself drawn to this man, feeling a kind of admiration for him in his magnificent, well-ordered house. But why did he need to admire someone who was in effect keeping him prisoner? He pushed the thought away and turned his attention again to Chevejon, who was talking.

 "LET ME TRY to put this together a little more. Your lawyer in Jerusalem—Yerushalmi, right?—said he had instructions from Danni concerning the will. How did he get the instructions?"

Luke noticed that the other was talking, again, like a European, and he felt reinforced in his earlier feeling that this man had spent the day working hard at his investigation. He found himself accenting the American in his speech as he answered.

"He said he notified Danni my father was dead and Danni told him what he wanted."

"And how did he know where to notify Danni?"

"He said he had the address."

Chevejon raised a single eyebrow. "The lawyer had it?"

Luke continued, as if in defense. "Yes. Danni had been back to Jerusalem. Yerushalmi said so."

"I see."

Luke tried to think through the growing haze in his mind.

"Are you saying he hadn't been back?"

"No, he had. But you see him leaving his address?"

"How would I know? I don't know the man."

"Yeah." He sounded, suddenly, American again. "I keep forgetting. So the lawyer wrote to Danni. Where? At the rue de Fleurus?"

"I don't know. I asked Nicole that; she didn't know. Danni was long gone by then. But two things are sure: Danni and my father corresponded from the rue de Fleurus. And Danni's check arrived there."

"But Danni's letters to Nicole didn't."

Luke shrugged. He thought for a moment, then asked: "Why didn't Danni write directly? To Nicole?"

Chevejon was silent, thinking. Then he, too, shrugged, as if just having made a decision. "Standard practice. We didn't want him traceable through a postmark."

"And where were the letters from?"

Chevejon answered quickly this time, dismissively. "Various places. Why are you so sure she never got them?"

"She would have told me."

"You're that sure."

Briefly Luke considered the possibility of her lying. "That sure." Then, in the face of the other's evident skepticism, he went on more forcefully.

"She was very upset. She thought Danni was never coming back. When I got there, she had been waiting for months. She told me a very lot—about herself, about Danni. I don't see her lying."

Was he convinced? "Uh-huh. So who gave you Danni's address in Paris?"

Luke answered readily. "Yerushalmi. The lawyer." Somehow he did not want to mention Dov Sayada; it seemed important that Chevejon think Luke's trip to Paris had been officially sanctioned.

"Why? Wasn't that confidential?"

"The estate's tied up without Danni's signature. Someone had to find him."

Chevejon's reaction to the lie was ambiguous. "Oh? So what are you living on?"

Luke looked at him. "What are you living on?"

There was a silence; then Luke spoke again. "Yerushalmi, as executor, advanced me a portion of my money for expenses."

"I see. So why did you go to the most expensive hotel in Florence?"

Luke shrugged. "I'm a rich man. Or will be."

"When did you last see your brother?"

"When he was eighteen. I was eleven. What's that got to do with it?"

The other spoke carefully, with contempt. "Well, now that you've seen a little of how he lives, doesn't it surprise you that he should have wanted the estate liquidated?"

Luke started to say something, then stopped. "Yes, it does."

"What does that suggest to you?"

Luke asked: "What does it suggest to *you*?"

There was a silence, then it was Chevejon's turn to admit: "I don't know." He went on. "Before I read about it in the papers, I never even knew there was so much money involved."

"Danni knew. He never told you?"

"Danni'd been gone five months when your father died."

"And you're saying that his going away had nothing to do with my father's death?"

"I told you, he left in August. Your father was alive."

"When did he go to Israel?"

Chevejon paused for a long time. "July, I think it was. Or August. Just before he took off."

Luke stood up in frustration and walked to the window. Outside, in the cicada-filled night, the garden lurked in still shadows. Finally he turned.

"Look. What's the point of this? Why don't you want to tell me where he is? Obviously he had an address somewhere. Yerushalmi wrote to him; he wrote back. What does it matter?"

But the other, sitting back in his chair, smoking one of the little cigars from the tin on the table, seemed unmoved. "As far as I'm concerned, Danni doesn't even know your father's dead."

"How can that possibly be? I told you, he wrote to Yerushalmi."

"So you say. But you have to admit, you've lied about so many things, it's hard to know what the truth is."

Chevejon's face was blank, and Luke felt the menace in those words, the menace underlying even his neutral comments. He crossed the room again, sat down, lit one of the cigars, evading the—correct— accusation behind the smoke that billowed and drifted between them.

"Even if he was in fucking Kuwait, it would have been in the papers."

"I doubt that he's in Kuwait. I doubt that he's seeing the papers. And I know that if he knew your father was dead, he'd have come back. To keep you from selling your father's collection, for one."

"Where do you think he is? Where did those letters come from?"

He answered in a steady tone, as if speaking to a child. "As to where he is, I don't know. I maybe have some ideas that would help you find him, but I don't see why I'd want to tell you."

Frustration. "Why?"

"Because you're a liar, one. And two, I don't understand why you're trying to find him."

"I told you—"

"No, you gave me a fucking line." Still, he did not sound angry, and that made him all the more menacing. Luke was silent for a long time, aware of being observed. Finally Chevejon said: "You tell me something, I'll tell you something."

"What?"

"Why you want to find him."

10 A SWIRL OF IMAGES went through Luke's head, too fast to capture, too strong to ignore. Images of the street in the Puces de Clignancourt, of Nicole's bed, of the explosion of bullets in the black street, of Nicole. His mouth went dry. He licked his lips, drank some brandy, drew on the little cigar. They were called, he noticed, Panters, an illustration showing a gold panther climbing a cigar on the little blue tin box. When he spoke, his voice was low and tired.

"I wasn't lying about Yerushalmi. He's my father's oldest friend. They escaped the war together. And he said he had written Danni and Danni had written back."

Chevejon answered quickly. "What made you decide to go to France?"

It was as if Luke weren't in control of his own words. "At first I wanted some kind of revenge. For my brother having made me sell the estate. He knew what that collection was worth. It was like killing him again. My father, I mean. And then I saw that was just an excuse. Really . . . I had nowhere else to go."

"And now?"

For a moment he thought he was going to cry. He said simply: "Now I want revenge *and* I have no place else to go."

There was a silence. Luke braced himself, he was not sure for what. But when Chevejon spoke, it was in the same quiet tone.

"The first letter was from Vienna. The second from southern France. The rest from Italy, small towns in the south."

"Did you read them?"

"No."

"Where's he going?"

"I don't know."

"I think you do."

"Think what you want." Chevejon stood up. "I'm not going to help you hunt Danni down. Besides anything else, you'd just get killed yourself."

Luke looked up at him. "Thanks for caring."

Chevejon didn't smile. "I do care. I care that Nicole was killed and you think your brother did it. I care that you've shown up here, stumbling around, fucking things up. I care that you're wandering around Europe with some illusion in your head that your brother's trying to steal your mess of pottage, commit some bogus kind of symbolic parricide, when *I* know that *he* doesn't even know your father's dead, and if he did, he wouldn't want anything in the first place. You're dangerous. You go off alone, someone's going to get seriously hurt. Maybe me or Danni. With luck, only you. But I can't count on that."

"Then why don't you help me?"

Now he laughed. "Help you? You want me to help you? Why don't you tell me a few true things?"

"Why don't I just leave?"

"Leave anytime you want. I'll take you to the Rome airport right now if you'll understand that if you come back to Europe, you're a dead man."

"And if I won't?"

Chevejon answered without hesitation. "Then you stay right here until you tell me the truth. Don't think I can't make you."

There was a silence, and then Chevejon spoke again. "Look. If you want to find Danni and to untangle this knot of nonsense you've got in your head, I'm about all you've got."

This last part was so true that Luke didn't answer. In the lamplit room, he imagined himself, pale, afraid, drawn. Chevejon, standing, looked as fresh as if he'd just woken up. He said: "That's enough for tonight. Come on, I'll take you upstairs."

They walked together through the living room, Chevejon switching off lights as they went. They climbed the stairs in silence, and at the top, Chevejon asked, as if in passing: "Where's the mail delivered at the rue de Fleurus?"

"To the concierge. Then she puts it under the doors."

"Could anyone get to it before the concierge?"

Luke thought back, then answered slowly. "No, I don't think so."

"So Danni's check came that way?"

"No, that was a courier from the bank. It was a big check. The only reason he left it was he thought I was Danni."

"I see. Good night now."

And in front of the door to his brother's rooms Luke found himself alone.

11   HE WOKE in the late morning, lying on his back in his brother's bed, tired still, a feeling of remorse tugging at his stomach with dull insistence. For a time, lying in the room flooded with light that filtered through the thin curtains, he indulged that feeling of remorse. It was true: He had entirely lost control of his life; he was at Chevejon's mercy. Still, he thought, even if he was powerless, he was learning: Danni, or whoever was pretending to be Danni, was somewhere in Europe. He turned his head to one cheek and gazed at the backlit curtains billowing softly against a warm breeze. For a time he lost himself in the contemplation of the Florentine light. So strange, so unfamiliar, and yet in its very unrecognizability, in its very lack of associations, it seemed to open a vast mental space that all the lights of the past, all the bedrooms of the past, rushed in to fill.

He sat up on the side of the bed, shaking his head. And sitting, he found that after all, a process of crystallization had been taking place while he slept. He saw now that the alternatives, really, were only two: Either the person who had killed Nicole and whom he had killed in the Puces de Clignancourt was not Danni—in which case the murder of Nicole had either to do with Danni and Chevejon's business or with some Israelis who wanted to assassinate Danni. Or, the person writing to Nicole from points always farther south across Europe was not Danni but some impostor—in which case, from Chevejon to the rest of the world, the possibilities were countless. And where, then, was Danni's check? But no sooner had he thought this than a third possibility presented itself: that Chevejon was lying. Lying about forwarding the letters from Danni, for a start. From that premise a thousand different theories were possible.

He rose, lit a cigarette from his almost empty pack, and, in his underwear, walked through to the other room. He sat in a corner of the low chesterfield that, with a light table on which rested a collection of tools—tooth- and paintbrushes, toothpicks, a can of compressed air—was the only furniture in the room. Smoking, he gazed at the books lining the wall in front of him.

These seemed to be exclusively archaeological and art historical references, but as he twisted to follow the shelves around the room's circumference, he saw that this was not actually so. Here, as in Danni's study in Paris, there was a section of Judaica, much more extensive. First he noticed a few volumes of the Anchor Bible. Then a Hebrew Talmud. He rose and, approaching the wall of books, saw that the upper half of shelves was entirely filled with Judaica in Hebrew, Yiddish, German, French, and English, meticulously arranged by subject. Working downward, he found another complete Freud, then a complete works of Joseph Benami in Dov Sayada's Oxford Edition, the Yarmolinsky biography of Benami in the original Knopf edition, and the Greenberg biography in the Hebrew paperback. And the lower half of this bookcase was given over in its entirety to works about the Holocaust: Jean Ancel, Hannah Arendt, Lucy S. Dawidowicz, Martin Gilbert, Raul Hilberg, Henri Michel, David Rousset. In the lowest corner, next to the wall, he found Bergmann and Jucovy's *Generations of the Holocaust;* Judi Benami's collected essays, *Living Death;* Epstein, *Children of the Holocaust;* Keilson, *Sequenteille Traumatisierung bei Kindern;* Steinitz and Szonyi, *Living After the Holocaust;* a number of issues of *Israel Annals of Psychiatry.*

Luke stepped back, stunned. If there was anything that he had imagined himself having in common with this stranger, his brother, it was a complete avoidance of precisely this kind of book, of these ways of thinking. He could not think of a single book of his father's he had read all the way through, and if he had read his mother's work, little of it had made sense.

He picked a book at random, then another from the shelves. Immediately, from the print on the pages, the strangely familiar shape of his brother's handwriting in the marginal notes struck him; he had not known he knew it. These were books that had been studied, marked up, underlined. He replaced them and walked back into the bedroom, then into the bathroom, and turned on the water in the bathtub. While it filled, he stood in front of the mirror, rubbing the palm of a hand over the stubble of his beard, a far more profound desolation than he had felt even at the most lost points of his trip gripping him. It was a farce, he thought, the idea that he was making any progress, any order of his life, by this random stumbling through the lives of people who would have preferred, each and every one of them, that he not exist.

CHAPTER TWELVE

1 LATER, when I was to come to know Peter Chevejon almost as well as I now know Luke, I would understand how strong a psychic muscle he had exercised in order so smoothly to absorb the shock of Luke's advent. For I would come to appreciate that as Chevejon listened to this strange, serious young man, it was dawning on him with dead certainty that this story was, as he heard it, changing his life.

There was real grace in his response, in the rapidity with which he pirouetted to face the reality of what was before him. Being scared—he knew he must leave that to Luke and Natalie.

Perhaps you will say that it was easier for him, that the reality facing us all affected me and Luke more profoundly. Peter Chevejon would not have said that. Not given how Luke and I affected Danni Benami. Not given anything at all that affected Danni Benami.

And Danni, clearly, was implicated, not just psychologically but legally, in this story that between me and Luke was beginning to unfold, to reveal itself, to Chevejon.

He knew, for example, that Luke's account of the night of the murder was an out-and-out fabrication; Chevejon had spent far too much time and energy bypassing the laws of France to think the French police as foolish as the boy made them out to be. Much more had to have happened in Paris that night. And Luke must have told the police much more, enough to make them believe they had a plausible explanation for what had happened. Doing that without implicating Danni, Chevejon thought, was beyond this humorless young man's powers. And so, therefore, he must have implicated Danni. And so the

French police—the Common Market police—must be looking for Danni.

As, surely, were the three men who had chased me out of Paris. Israelis, for God's sake, and he pronounced now, out loud, the word *fuck*.

And if either the police or the three Israelis found Danni before he did, this would be a very terrible thing. And therefore, there was a growing urgency to his using these two children to their best potential. Without letting them become aware of their manipulation.

It was a strange puzzle.

More than a puzzle. A riddle.

The night after his first evening with Luke, waking smoothly from the couple of hours that sufficed for his night's sleep, he lay in the darkness and considered. Immediately he saw that there was not much more he could do, just now, with Danni's strange, angry brother—beyond forcing him to recognize the necessity of staying out of sight until his appearance could be credibly altered. What he could do, however, was encourage this Austrian girl to stop being so coy; she had had time enough for that. That was just as important: Neither one of these children alone could answer his questions, but both together might, without even their knowing it, be able to take him where he needed to go.

If he simply put the two together, would they solve it? Perhaps, he thought, but probably incorrectly, for it was a very complex puzzle and they were very young players. And then there would be no predicting the wrong conclusion at which they would arrive, no controlling their reactions. A third intelligence was needed, one that could draw on what the two knew, without engaging what they feared. That was what he had to be.

Luke. For a moment Chevejon wondered what he would do if his sister, now a woman, were to appear in Florence. Then he dismissed the thought; there was no way anyone from Howell, Michigan, was going to be able to find the person he had become. But if she did, he would have to find it in him, somewhere, to make room for her, too. Adaptability, Chevejon had always known, was key.

But what to do with Luke? The question was far from answered.

And given the threat, clear and ever more immediate, facing him and facing Danni, none of its possible answers was farfetched.

He rose in a fluid movement and stood by the window, a naked witness to the movement of his flowers in the dark night's breeze.

He had not lied when he told Luke he did not know where Danni actually was. But it was only in the most banal of senses that he didn't know; on a profound level he knew much about the trip Danni had embarked upon. As to where Danni physically was, that, Chevejon saw suddenly, was a question only Luke could answer. Not I, Natalie, although I was useful mental leverage, but Luke.

And I cannot emphasize this enough: that he saw this at all tells more about the pure, brute force of this man's mind than anything else. No one else in his position would have seen it, not Luke, not Danni. It was Chevejon's genius to understand that only Luke had the sources to seek it out. Sources to which only Luke had access, those within himself. For where Danni had gone, Chevejon knew, was not governed by a financial itinerary. This was not business, and it was certainly not pleasure. Danni was traveling not just in space but in time, following a psychic itinerary, and the only person in the world who could follow him was this person with access to the same past.

The problem was that he doubted that the boy—so angry, so confused—could pierce through the veil of fear that hid those sources from him. This was his job: to make him find them. And, Chevejon saw, it was really rather a simple formula, one that had served him before. It was a question of opposing that fear with an equal one, on one hand, and then allowing a path out of that corner: the path of trusting Chevejon. Menace and seduction: two muscles Chevejon knew very well how to use.

How much pressure, then, should he apply, and how much support should he offer? Here was where the question, already labyrinthine, became devilish. For just as Chevejon, thanks to my help, had at his disposal more pressure than he had yet chosen to exercise, he also had at his disposal more help than he had yet chosen to offer.

What he had was a notebook—an ancient, faded green high school *carnet de devoirs*. The writing in it was Yiddish, illegible to Chevejon.

Danni had given it to him just before his departure, asking him hurriedly to "be a pal and dump this in the safe, would you?" His voice sounded in Chevejon's ears as he remembered, as if Danni were there in the bedroom with him.

Chevejon did not know what was in the notebook. But he knew, with the same intuition that had guided him this far, that it was centrally involved. And now he asked himself, not for the first time: Should he give it to Luke?

How much would it be useful for him to know, and how much was he going to have to find out by himself? He sighed, ran his hand through his thick hair in a rare gesture of nervousness. For a moment he felt unequal to the task before him.

If Luke found Danni, he would try to kill him.

If he tried to kill Danni, Luke would be killed.

If the police found Danni, their partnership would crumble.

And then he himself would be finished.

He took a breath, deep into his lungs. Luke, source of threat, holder of solution, had to understand; he had to, and Chevejon had to make him. And to understand, he had to grow up. This night, watching his garden of shadows shifting in the night breeze above Florence, Chevejon could not see how to do it. Then he shook off his discouragement.

What mattered was that the boy talked. But first he would make the girl tell what she had to tell; it was time. He dressed and quietly slipped out of the bedroom. There were still hours till he could decently wake me at my *pensione,* and he had planning to do.

2

I DID NOT UNDERSTAND the source of Chevejon's emotion during the conversation that ensued between us that morning, some six hours after he had awoken himself and a few moments after he had woken me. But I did not need to know its source to feel its urgency.

He woke me in the hot shade of my room, his eyes on my T-shirt and underpants, on my exposed legs, and waited for me in the breakfast room while I dressed. Over breakfast, by a window of sun—past midsummer, a goldening heat—he kept his counsel until I had finished a coffee. Then, although I was eating, he lit a cigar. And when he spoke, it was in a way very different from any of the voices in the repertoire he had used with me before.

"Now, darling, this has been very much fun. Very much. If it were up to me, I'd spend my life looking at Florence in your company. You're lovely, you're curious, you're smart. And you're a liar, which makes you my perfect companion, I think you know that."

I watched him. "I know that a liar's your perfect companion, if that's what you mean."

But he only nodded. "Of course it's what I mean, and it's good that you know it. But you see, my darling, that's where what you know ends. You are, forgive me, very young. You know, forgive me, very little. I'd like to give you an example."

I stopped eating. "Go ahead."

Smiling kindly, as if to soften his words, he began to speak. And at first I did not understand what he was saying.

"You and I are very similar people. I know you don't believe that. But look at it this way: We both know a lot about guilt. Is that not right? That the sources of our guilt are so very different—which I dispute—really doesn't matter. What's really different is our response. You're afraid; I'm not. And that's important to you, although you don't realize it. Because you need help, and I'm in a position to give it."

Now he wasn't smiling. And I did understand him. He went on, dead seriously. "I need you to return to me, not to Danni but to me, what you took from your father's house. You need me to find out what it means."

And I answered: "Bullshit. You'll take what you need and forget me. I'm just the Austrian."

Perhaps I had a sheltered life. I did not expect what I heard him say, next, in a whisper.

"Ah, the monstrous Austrian, born in nineteen-fucking-sixty-seven, my God. Darling, I've known Nazis, Argentinian juntaists, ex-Stalinists, Colombian drug lords. I've done business with Baby Doc Duvalier. You, who have committed the unpardonable crime of having had your ski vacations and college paid for by a Nazi father, you know the way you feel? When I was your age, we called it liberalism. You think that your guilt is in your birth makes it that much harder to bear? Bullshit. You just don't want to face facts. You're afraid. Just like you're afraid to trust me."

"Right. Trust you. You think I'm a fucking idiot?"

"You want to learn about guilt, ask a criminal."

Now I stopped. For a long moment. And then asked: "What do you want from me?"

"I want what you took from your father's house."

"And then you put me on a train to Vienna, you and your big, stupid guard."

"Wrong. That's where you're wrong. For one thing, Giorgio's not stupid at all. No one who works for me is. You give me those things, then we deal with the reality before us. That's what adults do. And I see you through to the point that you ask me to leave you alone. Not a second before you ask me."

I watched him, not moving. And he met my gaze.

"You see, I was right: You don't understand. Listen carefully, I'm going to tell you what's going on. And I'm going to say it only once."

He dropped his voice to a whisper again.

"We're in an alternate reality, you see? You're not stupid, you see what's going on. Want me to spell it out for you? Danni Benami and I are c-r-i-m-i-n-a-l-s. Smugglers. We're that 'murky' world you read about in magazines. We contravene the laws of governments and morality; we steal ancient artifacts and buy illegal art and then sell it to the highest bidder. Sometimes—often—we hurt people to make it work. Sometimes people die. We do it for money.

"You beginning to get it? This isn't your little Europe; it's mine. We do business here, and what matters is green. Welcome. Stay as long as you want. Guilt doesn't matter here. Now do you understand?"

I nodded, my mouth dry, my lips open; I swallowed, but he did not let me speak.

"You're going to say it's a different kind of guilt. You're right: It's more refreshing. And it's more original. Because this is Europe, Natalie, Europe. You think you're special, think again. What do you think that guy was doing under Mussolini"—he motioned to the elderly busboy clearing tables—"fighting fascism? I admit, it's possible.

But it's not fucking likely, darling, and it's a hell of a lot less likely as you travel north. Fuck Austria—I mean, France, I mean, Belgium. This is Europe. Everyone's guilty."

3 EVERYONE'S GUILTY.
I don't know if I can explain to you, you in that other world, what it meant to hear this. How tempting it was to believe it. And how impossible.

And I don't know if I can explain to you how hard it was, what Chevejon was asking of me. Let me try.

Did you ever, when you were a child, stand on a cliff above a lake and will yourself to jump? You know there is no danger. That when you find the will to step into the air, your body will writhe to its balance, that the water will crash around your face in a brilliant flash of green, and that laughing, you'll rise to the surface in a tunnel of bubbles exploding against the sun. Yet with all you know, with all you want to jump, before the act itself a paralysis overtakes you.

It is not the height, it is not the cold of the water; these are there but are not what stops you. It's the consciousness that before you is a decision, and trivial or not, once taken, it cannot be revoked.

There are other things like this. Other decisions. Such as to tell someone the truth.

We left the *pensione* in silence, walked into the Boboli Gardens, and sat on a bench. There was the hot, radiating light of the morning on my skin. I felt thirsty, then dizzy. And then I told Chevejon about my father.

This is what I told Chevejon. That I knew all the rationalizations, all the justifications, even the very true things about the hell that was the war for us—the executioners—us, too. It is a very particular suffering I described to him. One for which commiseration universally is—must be—denied. For which justification must not be uttered, excuses not made, and guilt—above all, guilt—never denied.

I told him that he was not a known Nazi, not a towering figure of evil. He was an officer in Hitler's bureaucracy, only marginally involved—in his duties—with the Final Solution, responsible for processing Jewish emigrants from Vienna.

This is what I told Chevejon. That all my life I had known about my father. I had known during my idyllic childhood on Frederickstrasse, my summers in Majorca, my ski vacations in Gstaad. But I had known something else, too.

I had known that under the Nazi oppression my father had also arranged the escape of hundreds of Viennese Jews, at enormous personal risk. That working with a Jewish secret agent, he had used his contacts in the Italian Army and in Greece to forge a secret route out of Europe to Palestine, and scores of these people's descendants now owed their life to my father. And that so great was this Israeli's debt to my father that he had come from Jerusalem to testify when my father was tried at Nuremberg.

Tried at Nuremberg. My father. You: Try that. Try saying to yourself: "My father was tried at Nuremberg." See how it feels.

I told Chevejon that when Maurizio Tueta—Danni Benami—came to our house in Vienna, all that I knew came tumbling down. And that when, on his orders, I climbed to our attic, what I found there made everything that was most familiar in my life—my father, my sprawling home—strange; all that I knew, a question.

Perhaps degrees of guilt do not apply, I don't know. But I did know that heroes did not appropriate Jewish households during the war.

It was a question that only Danni himself could answer.

If I could find him.

It was like a sentence of exile.

This is what I told Peter Chevejon. That I had taken from my father's house a pile of exit permits from Nazi Vienna, the first one of which had been for Joseph Benami's father. And that I had taken, from the hiding place in the attic, the gold menorah and the Torah.

And this is what I did not tell him. That when I found those objects in my dear attic, my world became a world of pain. Pain that I cannot ask you to recognize, you in that other world who either have suffered a pain that makes mine nothing, nothing at all, or simply enjoy a factitious righteousness that can take no account of my pain.

I question that righteousness. I question that righteousness. But I did not tell him that, for where the victim's legacy—like the victor's—

is a proclamation of righteousness, the part of the executioner's heir is silence, only silence.

Instead I started to cry, so bitter did I feel, so bitter was the loss of my life, my whole life, in the accusation of those objects. I did not want to cry in front of Chevejon, but I did, for a long time, the sun drying the tears on my blouse as I sat in the noonday silence with that man, and he did not touch me, and he did not speak, and he waited while for my childhood, for my father, I wept. So much fucking talk. Only that crying was true.

When I was done, Chevejon asked me: Danni told you where to find those things in your attic? I answered yes. He asked me: How did he know they were there? I answered that I did not know. He thought for a long time, as if there were something important about this, but he couldn't put his finger on what it was. Then I told him that it was all in the left-luggage office of the Gare de l'Est. I said: "I'll have to go up to Paris to get it."

"What?" He drew himself from his reverie and answered abstract-edly: "No, don't bother. I'll have someone pick it up tomorrow. Just tell me what the suitcase looks like."

"Don't you need the receipt?"

"The what? Oh—" His eyes focused on me now, he smiled and explained patiently. "Oh, no, don't bother about that. Not at all."

And then he told me, softly, calling me darling, that I had done the right thing, that I had done the brave thing, and that he was going to take care of me.

 NOW IT WAS Luke's turn. After he left me, late that morning, back at my room, Chevejon, walking back to his office in Santo Spirito, thought with satisfaction: Now it is Luke's turn.

But his satisfaction was short-lived. For as he walked, another feeling began to present itself, a growing exhaustion beginning to assail him. Exhaustion before the pure strength of the emotions playing around him in these two children. He felt raw from the constant of his respon-sibility for them. It was good that the girl had spoken so openly, but to open those same floodgates in Luke, he thought, was going to expose him to much, much more than he cared to confront.

He climbed the steps to his office, suddenly listless, and sat heavily at his desk, face in hands. For a time he rested like this. Then he shook his head, as if to clear it, and picked up the phone to dial Paris. First, he thought, let's get Natalie's bag. Then we'll see what Luke has to say.

CHAPTER THIRTEEN

1 OVER THE next day or two Chevejon gave the maid and gardener a paid vacation. The house empty, he occupied himself with the practicalities of his life with Luke. He washed up the lunch and dinner dishes himself, working with smooth competence, planned meals, sending Gianlucca into town with shopping lists, spent hours in the garden, carting compost, weeding, and tending his flowers. Mornings he visited me at my *pensione*, leaving Luke to Paolo's care. By the second day, he noticed, Paolo was passing the time conjugating verbs for Luke, which Chevejon found an interesting way to go about learning Italian. But then, the boy had the Italian grammar also and seemed to spend a lot of time reading through it.

That really wasn't what he wanted. He wanted Luke to watch, and think, and wonder. And get ready to talk. So he asked Paolo to leave him alone. He wanted the boy to be scared. Meanwhile, he waited to get Natalie's suitcase from France. Then he would know what to ask Luke.

In the event, it was the day before my suitcase arrived from Paris that he found himself talking to Luke again.

Chevejon was out in the garden in the baking sun, deadheading the season's first growth of roses, when he realized that Luke was watching him from the kitchen door. He greeted him with smooth amiability and, when he did not go away, rose, joined him in the kitchen, and made coffee.

They sat in the heat of the afternoon at an iron table in the garden and smoked. Around them sounded the lazy buzz of bees from the flower beds, the coos of doves from the roof of the palazzo, and the distant chirp of birds in the branches of the trees above. Now, for the first time, Luke asked where the maid was and seemed disappointed at the news that she was gone.

Chevejon laughed and spoke with the American intonation of his English. "Now you have only me to look at."

"She was a whole lot prettier."

Chevejon laughed again. "True. But it would have gotten harder and harder to explain why this guy had come to Florence and never left the grounds of my house."

"So am I never to leave?"

Chevejon stopped laughing. He thought for a moment before answering. "Let's see where we're at in a few weeks. Anyway, first you have to stop looking so exactly like Danni. That's for my sake, but also for yours. And for his. You must see that."

Luke's reply was slow in coming. "I suppose."

"But more important," Chevejon went on, plunging in, "more important, I think you have to figure out where you're going."

Luke looked at him, evidently responsive to this change in tone and, Chevejon noted with approval, suspending judgment long enough to hear him out.

"Which means?"

"Which means, where you're going." In the swimming heat of the afternoon, Chevejon's own voice sounded to him as if it were coming from far away. "I mean, I don't know what Danni would want me to do with you, though I don't guess it's anything you'd like. You wait here long enough, I guess he'll come back. But that could be a very long time. I don't know any more than Nicole did where he is, but her getting murdered would seem to me to indicate a certain urgency is in order to find him. So we're going to have to figure out where to look. And whatever you think of me, you're going to have to help."

Luke answered dryly. "Don't you think, in that connection, we might think about who killed Nicole?"

"Well, I don't know—do I?—since you haven't told me how things really went that night. But it seems clear that whoever it was, he was able to make Nicole believe it was you returning. Now look"—speaking over Luke's objections—"you don't have to tell me what happened. But just think for a minute: Is it possible that someone could have done that, made her believe it was you coming in? Is there something in what you haven't told me that would make such an idea plausible?"

Luke halted in his protestation, drew a breath, exhaled through pursed lips. "Yes. I even thought that maybe it was Israelis."

"Israelis?"

"I mean, with my father dead and Danni being a deserter . . . Did you ever think that Danni might have been more than a smuggler?"

Chevejon nodded and smiled. "Yeah. I mean, yeah, I see what you're getting at. But no, he wasn't a spy. Not a chance."

He expected remonstrance and was surprised by Luke's response, which was a shrug and, in a resigned tone: "You know, you're so fucking sure of so many things, it's really rather hard to believe you don't know where Danni is."

2 NOW IT WAS Chevejon's turn to shrug. "Yeah, well, I see what you mean." He spoke with sincerity, and Luke stared at him anew. There was nothing, not a hint of a shadow in an eye, that indicated he was lying—in spite of Luke's conviction that he was. "Danni never told anyone where he was going even when he traveled on business, and this isn't business."

"Surely there are people you can call."

"I've called them. I'm telling you, this isn't business, and outside of business, Nicole was the only friend he had."

Luke thought for a moment, weariness assailing him. "So you can't tell me anything about where he is. Then what am I doing here?"

The other answered calmly. "What you're doing here is what you're told. Otherwise I'll kill you, so that's simple. But as to my not being able to tell you anything, I didn't say that. I can't tell you where he is, but I can help you figure out, maybe, where to look."

"How? What can you tell me that you're not—"

But Chevejon interrupted him. "Let's see how. Until your beard comes in, and we can get you some new clothes and maybe some glasses, you're stuck here. That's not so bad: You don't really have anywhere else to go, and you have to admit, there are worse places to be stuck. Also, if you left France without telling the police, then I'd think some new papers would be a good idea. So I can help you with all that." He paused now—Luke thought, for effect—and then spoke carefully. "As for what I can tell you, I hope you're sure you've told me everything I ought to know before you expect me to open my fucking heart to you. Otherwise, I would say, that wouldn't really be fair, would it?"

3 FAIR OR NOT, what Luke could tell, he couldn't. What was he to say? Listen, Chevejon. Nicole and I fell in love. So Danni killed her when he came back to Paris, then he tried to kill me, but I killed him first, and now there is some impostor traveling through Europe, posting bogus letters for you to forward, and I have to find him. Or: I killed whoever killed Nicole in Paris, Chevejon, and now if I don't find Danni, I'm going to have to kill myself. Luke didn't see either of those flying too high as stories to tell his host, and besides, fairness didn't seem a concept that one would apply too readily in one's dealings with this dangerous man. Who was actually keeping him prisoner. So he kept his own counsel.

He kept his own counsel, and the afternoon passed without any further talk, as did the evening, and as the hours passed, Luke watched his brother's partner with an appraising eye. Silence, he knew, was only a delaying tactic; it got him nowhere and could not go on indefinitely. Anyway, he wasn't really inclined to be silent. Whatever Chevejon was, he was all Luke had, and even if he weren't, there was something about this man that belonged to a world Luke had never known. Behind the charm, behind the charisma, the perfect house, there was a self-reliance that, if Chevejon were not a criminal, could have been called integrity. Luke knew not only that he was going to find it increasingly hard to resist talking to this man but that it was not necessarily in his interest to do so.

And so when, the next day, he found himself again seated across from him at the wrought-iron table in the garden, the heat of the afternoon rising steadily, the pulsing hot sky around them resounding with silence, he asked simply: "So where do we start?"

The other answered readily. "With who murdered Nicole, I would think."

"Let's see then. I know! Someone kills the girlfriend of a smuggler, a thief, and a forger. How about a business associate?"

"No way." It was astounding to Chevejon how Americanized his speech had become, and in such a short time. Some of these expressions he hadn't even thought of for ten years and more. He adjusted his tone. "I don't deny that there might be a certain level of violence intrinsic to our work. But if there's a person in the world besides us who knows that Maurizio Tueta and Daniel Benami are the same person, I tell you, there's just no way."

"You all are that good, huh?"

"Oh, sure." Chevejon, surprised, forgot his determination to modulate his accent. "Oh, sure, we're that good."

"So how'd you let Nicole be killed?"

"That's just it, Luke. That's just what I'm trying to figure out."

Luke watched the other in silence for a moment, trying to frame a response. But Chevejon spoke first.

"Why did you never look for Danni before?"

"Is this going to help us figure out who killed Nicole?"

In the garden the summer afternoon had turned into evening like a perfect peach ripening. A rich golden sunlight filtered through the trees, bathing the pair at the little iron table in ever more acutely angled light and lengthening shadow.

"I think so."

Luke lit another little cigar, the flame of his match nearly invisible in the hot light. He thought: I'm going to smoke this guy out of house and home. But how am I supposed to buy more if I can't go out? Then he understood that the thought was a way of avoiding the question before him, and he answered.

"I never knew he was alive. In my family they acted like he was dead."

"I guess . . ." Chevejon, too, lit a cigar. "I guess your old man was . . . mortified. By Danni."

"No, not really ashamed. It wasn't in his . . . emotional vocabulary. *Pissed off* is more the term I'd use." He considered for a moment, undecided, then went on.

"I think he'd given up, my father, really expecting my brother to behave in any way predictable. To him, not wanting to die for Israel, it was unthinkable. When you think what that country had saved him from, you can understand why. He'd lived through the Holocaust. His wife had been four years in the camps. And he couldn't grasp that we didn't live under the same threat, under the same necessity. He thought it was a failure of imagination, or a moral failure on our part, and if he told us enough times, we'd understand. But he didn't get it. He never got it that we *did* understand, only we weren't having it."

Chevejon scrambled to catch up; he had not been expecting such a voluble response from this normally dour young man. He wondered briefly what was making him talk so freely; certainly it was not his, Chevejon's, manipulation. It was a decision Luke had made on his own, and he found himself feeling new respect for Danni's brother. He said: "Why not?"

"Why not? Ever seen the Gaza Beach Internment Camp? Or Ketsiot? Or Far'ah? Ever seen the border guards in East Jerusalem? Or West Bank fundamentalists—the Kahane Chai types? Then you get this shit about Germans and Nazis, fuck that. You show a Star of David and a swastika in Jericho, no one'll notice the difference, and that's a travesty, a travesty of what the Holocaust means. You don't have to have been in Auschwitz to make that judgment. Read Camus. You see?"

Chevejon nodded. "I see. But there is a difference."

"Sure, I know that, you know that, but you ask a sixteen-year-old Palestinian who's lived his whole life in a tent city on the Gaza Strip for some historical perspective—why should he? Why should he? I was in action in Menachem Begin's army, for Christ's sake. If I hadn't gotten a transfer I'd have been at Shatilla. And I'll tell you what: The distinction got pretty dim to me, too."

"I also see that the Holocaust happened."

"That's not in dispute. What's in dispute is the proper reaction, now, in 1989. Look, I'm not going to argue Israeli politics with you. Israel exists. I don't care how that happened; that's all history, blame the fucking Sykes-Picot Agreement, I don't care. It exists at the expense of a terribly oppressed minority. Whether that came from defensive wars makes no difference. And to excuse a police state because of the Final Solution is bullshit; the precise opposite should be happening. Instead the army bulldozes an Arab's house in Jericho, they blame it on Auschwitz, then they build a nuclear reactor in South Africa, and excuse that one with Majdanek."

A silence. Then Luke, more calmly: "Look. I don't say there's not a proper reaction to the Holocaust; there is. There is, and it should inform every fucking minute of our lives. Every minute. But it's not self-righteousness—not even righteousness at all. Not anymore. Israel's changed, the world's changed, and what was simple for my father in 1942 isn't simple anymore—if it was ever simple in the first place, which I doubt. You may say I don't have the right to judge, and I'm sure you're right. My mother was in the camps. You think I don't wish I could kill—kill—every German who had anything to do with that? I'd do it this minute. But I just don't believe that the Holocaust was ever about 'them and us,' you know? It was always about *us*, all of *us*, and if there was ever any doubt about that, then the Israeli occupation's made it crystal fucking clear."

"But other Israelis do. Understand your father. I mean, young ones." Chevejon sounded sincerely curious.

Luke nodded, calming somewhat. "Well, there's a heavy Holocaust indoctrination—from grade school through the army, national holidays, memorials, TV shows. Masada, Yad Vashem, it's all the fucking same there, and it never stops. Even then there are plenty of people who, as they say, 'go down.' New York, South Africa, Australia. Plenty. There were plenty of people who refused to serve in Lebanon or the territories. God, I wish I had."

He stopped, staring into distance, smoking. Then he said: "Me, I grew up in New York, and Danni . . . I don't get the impression he was easily indoctrinated."

4 CHEVEJON half closed his lids against the setting sun, a million spikes of light emanating from the golden ball. There was something forbidden in listening to what Luke was saying, something disloyal to Danni in discussing, with this brother of his, his character. And yet the mental picture that composed itself before Chevejon's closed eyes was clear. The choice the two brothers had to make. Its historic ambiguity, but more important, its symbolic obliquity before their father's past. Perhaps even more important, he saw that all Luke was saying was a view formed diametrically in opposition to what he had been taught, as an Israeli, as a Jew. Antiauthoritarian opinions, Chevejon knew, like all original thought, carry their own attrition: They are hard to hold, confusing, and threatening. Finally he said, "I don't think it was the question of dying for his country that tripped up Danni. I think it was a question of killing."

He was surprised by how quickly Luke looked up at him, the eagerness of his answer.

"Is that so? Is that so?" He thought for a time, then went on. "I suppose my old man expected Danni to have the pioneer spirit. Only everything had been pioneered already. He was harder on my brother than on me."

"How's that?" Chevejon found himself unable to resist asking.

"Oh, for one thing, I was out of the country by the time I was twelve. My mother was determined I would be an American, or a European, rather than an Israeli. God, by the time we left, she hated Israel. So I really grew up in New York. Going to a French school, and when I went to see my dad in the summers, it was as likely to be in Paris, or in Oxford, or in Berkeley, as anywhere else. I think my dad saw me as some kind of Eurotrash, you know, not much to expect from me. But Danni, he was a sabra. A real first-generation Israeli, pride of the country. You see, for my dad it was a new kind of Jew. The first kind never to be ashamed, never to be humiliated, never to feel left out. To be purely proud. Do you see?"

Chevejon nodded. All this was familiar to him, not so much from what Danni had told him but from what he had inferred. So much so that it was like checking off, in Luke's version, the points of an itinerary he had already, years before, traveled with Danni. "That's why your dad made him go into the army."

"Right. My mom wanted him to go to medical school. That would have deferred him. But Danni didn't want to go to medical school, for one thing. For the other, there was no arguing with my father. Israelis, man, without the army, you don't exist."

Chevejon gazed at him. "But you didn't have to go."

"No. I was American. And by then an only son—as far as the army was concerned anyway. No one gave a fuck what I did. No one expected to fight a full-scale war in Lebanon either."

He insisted, but gently. "That's funny, isn't it? Because Danni deserted, and you went."

"I went." There was a silence, and Chevejon decided to save that one for a little later; right now, he obscurely felt, he was chasing another point.

"So they treated Danni like he was dead, and you didn't ask any questions."

Luke looked up. "So?"

Chevejon shrugged. "So nothing."

"No, you're saying that I should have done something different."

"I'm not saying anything."

"Didn't Danni abandon his family? You're not saying he wanted to be in touch with my parents."

"No, not as far as I know." There was a silence, while Chevejon accused himself of cowardice. Finally he said: "Look, there's a differ-ence. Danni was exiled so thoroughly it's almost biblical. Talk about Isaac and Ishmael, man. Or look at it this way: The patria wouldn't let him in, and the pater didn't want him. You see what I'm saying?"

"Yeah, a cute pun."

"No, excuse me, but that was your age speaking—I mean, your youth. If you think it's a coincidence those two words are the same, then I'll tell you, you're a long way from finding your brother in any but the most banal of senses." Chevejon regretted this speech the moment it was out of his mouth, not because of the likelihood of Luke's taking offense but because it was too close to the truth; he hadn't expected to hear himself talking this way. But the boy's honesty demanded response.

But Luke only regarded him curiously. "Okay. So what?"

Chevejon liked that. He, too, he thought, had never minded taking correction.

"So you've told me about the patria. Now tell me about your father."

5   LUKE CLOSED his eyes while a slow wave poured through him as those words echoed across the summer back to Paris, the words Nicole had pronounced. For a time he was silent, his answer from those months ago sounding in his mind. Then he shook his head, opened his eyes, and answered: "Go the fuck upstairs.

There're two biographies and his complete works in Danni's library."

Chevejon frowned. "No. I want to hear you tell it."

And Luke, watching the other man's face squinting in the sun, wondered why he was asking this.

"If you want to make small talk, can't it be about something else?"

"It's not small talk. It's important. Now stop wasting my time, and get on with it."

"Or what, you'll kill me?"

Chevejon laughed. "Right. Or I'll kill you."

6 AND SO Luke told him. Not the story of the man he knew, that towering will, that overpowering force who had shadowed his whole life, but the other story. The story from the biographies, from the newspapers, the mythology. A story of heroism and righteousness.

He told him about Reuben Neumann, son of a professor of German literature, growing up in Vienna. A normal boy, with one oddity. In his perfectly adjusted family, thoroughly at home in one of the epicenters of prewar European civilization, he was a Zionist.

It wasn't that hard to understand why—not on the surface level. Hitler was appointed Reich chancellor in 1933, several years after the successful publication of *Mein Kampf.* The very near past showed an unbroken European tradition of anti-Semitism, leading to the very present. And Vienna had always been a center of anti-Jewish activity; the Christian Socialist party, model for Hitler's National Socialists, had provided the city with a mayor as early as 1896. It was easy for the boy, as for many Jews, to find his way to the Zionist movement; its executive office was also in Vienna. To Neumann, that office offered the single solution to a persecution that seemed to him unalterable; Palestine, the only opportunity to act positively.

And yet that kind of logic never accounts for a person; it's good for tendentious biographies and propaganda, but not for much else. People never act from purely political motives any more than they do purely from moral ones, so Luke knew. Beyond the official biography, Neumann hated his father as much as his fatherland. What profoundly motivated that hatred, Luke could only guess. But it took the form of hating his father's kind of assimilated Judaism, hating his acceptance of the petty humiliations of daily life for a Jew in thirties Vienna. His father's embrace of the language and literature of Goethe, of Schiller was part and parcel, to the young man, of his unwillingness to confront the realities of anti-Semitism, as was his deep attachment to the city of Vienna. And at the heart of his decision to run away, perhaps, was his absolute inability to bear the conventions of an Austrian upbringing: the discipline, the authoritarian paternalism, the formal obedience. Palestine, with its pioneer counterculturalism, its refusal of convention, was a liberation from a moldering, moribund Europe. But it was more. When, at sixteen years old, Neumann ran away to Palestine and changed his name to Benami—Son of My People—he did not so much leave his father as, in the guise of the fledgling kibbutz in the Yizreel Valley, exchange him for another.

By 1938, the Anschluss, Benami was twenty-one, a member of the Haganah, wavering on the brink of a more radical military allegiance in Palestine, the Irgun, the Stern Group. Corresponding with his father, he followed closely the chronology of oppression in Vienna: the deportation of Zionist officers to Dachau following the Anschluss in March; the useless conference at Évian-les-Bains in July, *Kristallnacht* in November. Exit permits were available, and he urged his father to come to Palestine; his mother, two sisters—one married, with a daughter of her own—and a brother made up the family.

His father refused: refused either to believe the glaring writing on the wall or to use his relative wealth to escape the Jewish community. The world was not going to permit, he wrote, the Nazis to continue much longer; no one would say that he was part of the Jews' abandonment of the country he sincerely, entirely considered his fatherland. Vienna—Wien. Few of us will ever experience the attachment these people had to that mythical prewar city.

By 1939, when Benami's father was expelled from his opulent house on Frederickstrasse and sent with his family to find lodgings as best as he could in the "open" Jewish ghetto, the Haganah-run illegal immigration operation, the Mosad le-Aliya Bet, was operating in Vienna, in cooperation with the Eichmann-sponsored Stern Bureau. Benami, with his "Aryan" good looks, his extraordinary courage, his unquestioned dedication, his fluent German, and his familiarity with Vienna, was an obvious choice to join this effort. Accordingly, in this year he traveled on forged documents to Vienna and began his rescue work.

The work was slow and difficult. Jewish refugees from all Europe were gathered in Vienna, facing two choices: deportation or the increasingly difficult path of emigration, which in its turn led to the nightmare of refugee life in some country that had neither use nor desire for them. Until late 1941 Benami lived as an Aryan in Vienna, searching, cajoling, bribing, buying the exit permits, more valuable than gold, shipping human bodies across Yugoslavia, down the Danube, by any means possible to waiting Greek boats for illegal passage to Palestine.

His family, he knew, were steps away in the ghetto, but he dared not see them. Occasionally other Mossad agents brought him news of them. It was not good news: If they had escaped deportation so far, it could not last much longer, and in Vienna, where Jewish soup kitchens were feeding 85 percent of the surviving Jewish population, deportation could hardly be any worse than escaping deportation. Slowly, as his two years of hazardous service progressed, Benami grew more and more desperate: Permits were impossibly pricey, the money from the American Joint Distribution Committee, the London Council for German Jewry, and the American Friends Service Committee bought less and less. He resented, was embarrassed by the degree to which Viennese Jews relied on help from elsewhere in the Diaspora. The Jews of the Yishuv, of Palestine, had to contribute more, he believed; the judgment of history would be harsh. And the final deportation of Viennese Jewry was obviously, ominously approaching. This is when something happened—something that would make Benami famous.

Now Luke told Chevejon what happened, based, as the biographies reported it, on Benami's testimony at Nuremberg. For apart from his testimony at Nuremberg, Benami had refused, his whole life, to speak of it, as did his German counterpart, as did Yerushalmi. And there were no other witnesses.

Benami testified at Nuremberg that late in 1941 he had been summoned to the office of a Nazi functionary, one Obersturmbann-führer Hoestermann. The *Obersturmbannführer* felt oppressed: by his role in the Nazi party, by the increasingly dismal prospects of the Jews. He had been a Lutheran before the war. He wanted to help. On his desk were four hundred precious exit permits. There were more where they came from, too. Hoestermann asked only to help; his concern was only for posterity.

Benami admitted that he hesitated. Could it be this easy? Was it a trap? He talked with Hoestermann all that day and into the night, and in the end he concluded that he had found a righteous Austrian. And from what the Nazi said about plans for the deportation of Viennese Jews, he concluded that there was no time to lose: They must find a new route of escape. Hoestermann had good connections: in the Italian Army, where anti-Semitism was far less prevalent than in Austria and prominent Jews had been early in the Fascist party, as well as in Athens, where anti-Semitism was resented almost as deeply as was the German occupation.

Accordingly, with Hoestermann's help, and working with another Haganah member, Avishai Yerushalmi, Benami testified that he had arranged the escape route for which he would later be so celebrated, the Italian Passage: across the Swiss border, down the length of Italy, from Brindisi across the Ionian, the Aegean, to Greece. Here Hoestermann had connections with the Italian Consulate in Salonika, which was actively helping Jews escape the German-occupied zone. And with their help, he was able to arrange sailings from a tiny Greek island, only loosely held with second-rate forces by the Germans.

As to the exact route and the island at which it ended, Benami refused at Nuremberg to say—as did Hoestermann, as did Yerushalmi—and no biographer had ever been able to find out. Too many people had risked their lives, he said. People had betrayed their families, broken laws, and even been killed along the passage, and now, the war over, the world owed them their secrecy. It was an argument that convinced his judges.

In any case, from here Greek fishing boats brought them, a few dozen at a time, to the beaches of Tel Aviv and Haifa. The operation ran for five months, and only twenty of the first four hundred were lost.

And perhaps the operation would have continued. But in the fall of 1942, in October, the final deportation of the Jews of Vienna took place, including the deportation of "privileged" native Viennese Jews to Theresienstadt, and among them the Neumann family. Benami himself was arrested by the SS and would have been deported had not Hoestermann intervened. The last people to use the Italian Passage were Benami and Yerushalmi themselves, running on forged documents from the SS. Hoestermann provided them with a safe hiding place in Florence, where they spent some months, waiting for passage from Brindisi. It was, oddly enough, an essential period for Benami's intellectual life, for here the themes of his first, seminal work, *Sacrifice and Symbolism*, were born, in this city to which Benami would return again and again throughout his life. When word came that passage was arranged, they ran again, passing through the Greek island they would never name and arriving in Palestine some weeks later.

7   WHEN HE FINISHED, the afternoon heat had peaked and the sun had sunk to the lowest point on the horizon, leaving the garden in soft shadow while lighting the sky a brilliant blue.

Chevejon, watching the boy watching nothing, wondered how much Luke believed the story he had just told. Could this be all there was? The weight of being the son of a hero, did that account for everything in this bitter youth? He felt not, and for a time he wondered what question would unlock the passage to that true reason. He rose, carried their cups through the garden door to the kitchen, and began cutting tomatoes for their evening meal. When, after a time, he felt Luke arrive at the open door and lean there, smoking, he said: "Tell me something. Why do you think the escape route's such a big secret?"

Luke reacted with surprising energy. "I don't know. I've always wondered about that. Guy once wrote in *Ma'ariv* that it was to protect contacts between Ben-Gurion's party and the Nazis, and man, he was crucified. Or maybe the Austrian guy was not quite as . . . idealistic as my dad made out at Nuremberg. Maybe money changed hands. Or Christ, maybe they saw Yasir Arafat and Shimon Peres out fishing widemouth bass on their way to Cyprus, who the fuck knows? I really don't know."

"Didn't you ever ask your father?"

"Sure, every morning at eight and ten o'clock. No, man, you never asked my father anything. No one did."

"I see. And tell me this: Why did you never look for Danni before? I mean, didn't you think his deserting might have indicated a certain, say, common point of view with you?"

Luke answered readily. "I know. I've been through all this before. But no matter what you think, I'm old enough not to waste time regretting . . . regretting not having done what I was incapable of doing when I was younger."

Chevejon turned from his task, then back. "That's a good policy."

A pause; then, as if unable to stop speaking, Luke went on. "After the army for a long time I was . . . not in my right mind."

"That's my next question. Why'd you go into the army? You aren't exactly what I'd call a patriot."

"I don't know." It was easy, somehow, to talk to someone who was concentrating on cooking. "I graduated from high school in New York. I was supposed to spend the summer in Switzerland with my father, then go to college. I knew my dad was going to spend the summer talking me into enlisting; man, I can't tell you what kind of pressure he could generate. I don't know. Just going seemed easier."

"And how was it?"

"How was what?"

"The army?"

Luke shrugged and looked away. Neither said anything for a long time; then Luke wandered back to his seat at the little garden table. The sun, a low red orb, hung heavily out of sight behind Florence, leaving the garden in a shadowy haze, swimming with bees and little swirling clouds of mosquitoes. After a time Chevejon emerged from the kitchen carrying two glasses of wine and took his seat at the table. They lit cigars, and without any forethought, Luke found himself speaking again.

"At the end of basic training my mother killed herself. Everyone knew she was going to; now I see she was just staying alive until I was grown up. At the time the . . . causality seemed different. I went back to New York; then the war broke out. I was under orders then, so I either had to go back or desert.

"They sent me to Beirut. My status was as an only son, so I had to volunteer for any active service, and still, I was supposed to be in the rear lines. But somehow we ended up in a refugee camp. A mop-up: A rocket launcher had started firing from this little tent city. No one expected it to be there. I mean, we were advancing north and suddenly shells started flying in from the east."

He paused for a moment, his cigar burning itself out between his fingers. "We were detailed to guard prisoners, so half of us went after the rocket launcher. My sergeant made a mistake, sent me with them. By the time we got there, a tank brigade had come back south, silenced the launcher, and secured the camp. So we started to go back to our prisoners. Only suddenly, in the middle of this camp that had now been occupied twice, this kid steps out of a house with a fucking Kalashnikov."

Luke stopped; there was silence. Finally Chevejon spoke. "So you shot him."

"So I shot him. You know how many bullets it took? One. I was carrying this Galil with these monstrous tracer shells. I hit him low, in the pelvis, but you could shoot a horse in the leg with those shells and still just about kill him dead. This kid was so surprised. He must have thought he was Sylvester Stallone. You ever kill anyone?"

There was a pause, while Luke regarded the other intently. Then Chevejon nodded his head, softly, once.

Silence. Luke, and perhaps Chevejon, too, aware that a communication had occurred.

"It's no damn fun, is it?"

"Some people get off on it."

"Them it would be fun to kill. Ironic, huh?"

Luke rose, took a step or two into the garden, and crouched on the lawn, fingering a dandelion between his feet. An enormous silence reigned under the sky, now entirely backlit by an absent sun, the garden around them swimming in the soft shadows of a summer dusk.

"And then?"

"And then the war was over, and my dad helped get me into Nachal, the agricultural service, and I spent two years on the West Bank guarding kids planting string beans on occupied land. God, what a fucking hole. By the time they were harvested, those beans must have cost an American dollar apiece, and they weren't even that good. When I got out, I went to France. Got a degree, trained at the UN in Geneva, got assigned to New York. End of story." He tugged at the dandelion, pulled it up without the roots.

Where Luke crouched there on the lawn, Chevejon could barely see him in the failing light. There was a stillness, a perfect silence, and he felt he had to break it.

"Until your father died."

"Until my fucking father died."

"Then the story begins."

Luke looked up at him, a shadowy figure at the white iron table, then away—it seemed to Chevejon—in sudden contempt. "Yeah. You could say so."

8

"AND SO here we are."

Chevejon watched the young man across the long dining table. They had eaten, practically in silence, while through the open kitchen door all light drained, slowly, out of the sky and the night came in.

Unmoved, apparently, by all he had told, Luke was gazing dourly into the night, a forgotten cigar turning to ash between two fingers. For a moment Chevejon allowed his eyes to rest on the other's face.

He could see now how different he was from Danni. But it was uncanny, the deep genetic resemblance that united them. It brought up something like affection in him, and since it was an affection he had never felt for anyone other than Danni, it felt oddly out of place. The father, from the pictures he had seen, had been of a wholly other type: an imposing man with a head of thick white hair sweeping across his forehead, a handsome, almost Teutonic face. The look the brothers shared, Chevejon thought, their asymmetric dark faces, their high, wide-set eyes, their thin, sharp jawlines—it must all have come from their mother. A brooding dark woman was the impression he had, with two almost identical sons. Danni's face, though, was transformed by the mirth that seemed, always, to illuminate his eyes. That must have come from the father. This one had only hurt in its place.

Remembering his cigar, Luke lifted it to his lips, burned his fingers on the tiny coal, moved it quickly to the ashtray beside him, eyes focused on it as he crushed it out, spoke slowly.

"We don't seem to be making much progress on who killed Nicole."

Chevejon answered, tossing the tin of Panters across the table. "We will. What was she like?"

"Nicole? You never met her?"

"Never. Just a couple phone conversations."

"Well, she's hard to describe. She was lovely. A woman . . ." Embarrassed, he turned away. "She loved Danni. She thought he was never coming back. She thought she had . . . let him down. No, more: She thought she had failed him."

Chevejon didn't understand that, but he did think he understood something else, suddenly: how the two had ended up in love, Nicole and Danni's brother. United by his absence. Had they really been in love? He wondered, and then he thought of how, one day, Luke would have to wonder the same thing. For a long moment he considered the ramifications of this insight. Then he said instead: "Failed him how?"

"Oh . . . it would be long to explain. She knew he was changing when he went to see my father. She didn't change with him. That's the simple version."

"And is it true? I mean, was she right?"

Luke answered slowly. "I don't know. I think so."

"That the only reason?"

"Reason what?"

"That you two fell in love."

Now Luke stopped, shocked.

"What makes you say that?"

Chevejon didn't think that he needed to explain. "Never mind that. Answer my question."

Luke paused, staring at him. His face had fallen, hard. Then he answered, as if automatically, as if he had no choice. "I don't know. She took me in. She felt sorry for me."

"Uh-huh." The answer, Chevejon felt, was revealing. Nothing was dead in this young man, none of the sorrows and guilt he had ever felt. What was required to lay some of them, at least, to rest? He asked: "You never thought Nicole might have killed herself?"

"Never. Besides that she'd never have done that, the thing was too staged. The open door. The open safe. And the only thing missing being the check."

Chevejon started to ask, What check? and stopped himself just in time. Luke seemed wholly unaware of having revealed a new detail. He said suddenly instead, in a calm, matter-of-fact voice: "Your thinking, then, goes something like this: Danni comes home. Finds Nicole in love with his kid brother appeared like magic from the past. Shoots her dead. Takes his inheritance check. Then what? I guess, goes back to his travels, writing these bogus letters to convince me and you he'd never been to Paris."

The other looked up at him, as if resigned to his odd omniscience, a prisoner's attitude before an interrogator.

"More or less."

Chevejon continued, unfazed. "Seems to me if he was going to start murdering people, he'd have wanted to get you, too."

Luke looked away and answered without looking at Chevejon. "Maybe he meant to."

"Well, look. You told me you knew Nicole would never have killed herself. What if I tell you I know Danni'd never have even thought of killing her, no matter what she did?"

He answered slowly. "I guess I'd have to believe you."

"Then where's that leave us?"

"I don't know. With Israeli intelligence?"

"Right. So how's that one go . . ."

THEY ROSE, cleared the dinner plates together, then walked through the living room into the den. Chevejon brought out a bottle of cognac this time, a half-full bottle whose label was blank save for a penciled number. He poured two glasses and, tasting his, hoped that Danni's brother could appreciate what he was about to drink; for himself, the deep, sweet heat rolling from his tongue to his throat could be compared only with the sun that evening, the moment before it fell beyond Florence.

Outside the window, night was fully there, only the slightest wash of blue showing above the shadowless earth. Hitching himself up in his chair, Luke turned to Chevejon and said, as if their conversation had never been interrupted: "I guess the Israeli intelligence theory isn't that believable."

Chevejon, thinking about Natalie's inquisitors in Paris, answered absently. "Israelis, maybe. Intelligence, not to me, I admit. Though who knows about these things?"

"So we're back to Danni."

"No, no, not me. We're back to someone, we just don't know who.

Not yet. The key, I would say, is what happened to Danni's letters. You're sure there's no one you haven't told me about."

Luke shook his head. He was silent for a moment. Then he asked, as if collecting on the debt imposed by his recent confession: "You say you don't know where my brother is. Is that the same as saying you don't know where he went?"

Chevejon answered carefully. "Not quite the same."

"So? Do you know where he went?" There was a great demand in the question.

"I'm beginning to, maybe."

"And are you going to tell me?"

The boy, Chevejon realized with surprise, was getting angry again. But still, he didn't answer right away.

He looked out at the grays of the garden lying beyond the window in the night, then let the focus of his eye change and saw their reflection in the windowpanes. Two men, one younger, one older, sitting in a book-lined room over snifters of cognac. How was he to tell this boy, he wondered, that it was only now, as he told Chevejon his reason for being there, this night that Chevejon was beginning fully to understand Danni's reasons for leaving a year before? How was he to tell him when the young man didn't understand even his own reasons for looking for his brother? And how could he tell him that if it were to have any meaning whatsoever, he would have to discover it for himself?

He asked suddenly: "Did you like your father?"

Luke answered quickly. "Of course not. Are you crazy?"

"And Danni? Did he?"

"Well, I'd infer maybe—wouldn't you?—that he maybe didn't feel too fucking tight with him. I mean, the desertion, the name change, the secret life . . . call me overanalytic, but I discern a trend."

"So it's hard to have a hero for a father."

"Oh, bullshit, fuck heroes." Luke was getting very drunk now, but he didn't care. "Haven't you been listening? Heroes, that's for Yad Vashem and their bogus, kitsch memorials. Ben-Gurion, the Yishuv, they did fuck-all during the war. The money, the time they put into rescuing real people, it was nothing. They knew perfectly well that the Holocaust was going to be the ultimate moral Balfour Declaration and that the survivors were going to people the country, like it or not, 'cause they'd have nowhere else to go. Just about every chance they had to make a meaningful rescue effort, they either passed up or fucked up."

Chevejon listened and then thought, and then asked, in the suddenly still room: "But your father did. He saved hundreds of people."

Luke snorted. "Yeah, right. Why don't you write a new biography? Or better yet, cut the crap and write a hagiography. It fucking amazes me, sometimes I think I'm the only person who ever noticed: My father, he imported cannon fodder for the War of Independence. The Italian Passage didn't bring a soul over twenty-five into the country, and it didn't bring any women. Know how many of the soldiers who died in the '48 war were camp survivors? One in three. Know why? They didn't fucking speak Hebrew; there was nothing to do with them but put them at the front."

Now Chevejon thought for a long time, as if slowly, infinitesimally absorbing each of those words. Then he said, from the depth of his reverie: "Then tell me this: Why do you think your brother went back to see your father? After all those years."

Luke was still mad. "Who cares?"

"I see." Chevejon sipped his cognac, gazing over the rim of the snifter. "Well, you give some thought to that, why don't you?"

"Thanks." Luke stood up suddenly. "Thanks a lot, man. Just what I need, right now: a Zen master to guide me. Got a koan I can go meditate on in the moonlight?" He put out his cigar and crossed the small room to the window.

And as he watched the young man's back, outlined against the blue of night, Chevejon thought.

Where was Danni? The names of the physical locations were yet to come, but they would be easy to find. It scared him. For he saw that on this trip of Danni's there had been no place for Chevejon; this was not a trip through space, but through time, a time predating their partnership. A time neither of them had thought ever to visit again. It scared him as he realized that such a trip might be in his future, too. On this summer's night Peter Chevejon realized that as things had changed, so radically and so suddenly, those years before, when he had met Danni, now this advent of Danni's past heralded another upheaval, equally unexpected, equally profound. And with all his ability to adapt, Chevejon found himself deeply sad, for all that was coming so inexorably to an end. He had not thought to have to face such change again.

He detached his mind from himself and brought it to bear again on the other. This young man, all was changing for him, too, and Chevejon saw more clearly than ever before it was not up to him to tell him where his brother was, even if he could. It was like giving the tour of Florence to one of his student girlfriends: You could lecture them all day on Brunelleschi, but it was not until stumbling, stupid drunk one night, they came upon their first original view of the Duomo in the splendor of its creation, that they stopped having fun in a foreign city and began to be in Florence. For most of them it never happened. With these thoughts in mind, after a very long time he lifted his face to Danni's brother's back and said quietly and as if apologetically: "You don't get it, do you? *You're* the one telling *me* where Danni went."

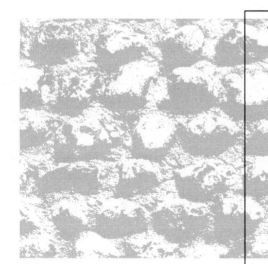

PART THREE

*It is only to the free man
that the truth can come,
and to be free, there cannot be
the cultivation of memory,
which is righteousness.*

—Krishnamurti

CHAPTER FOURTEEN

1 AT THE VERY LEAST, it was a truce.

As if each had realized the enormity of the transformation that was about to take place, and in this period of forced idleness, while Luke's beard grew in, each preferred to take refuge in a time that was rapidly becoming the past. All changes are sad, even those that are for the better, and each welcomed the chance to put off, for as long as he could, the one that was about to occur.

For Luke, the days passed with the ever-repeating rhythm of the southern sun: a suite of gemlike August days, each a span of languid, constantly shifting light, followed by kind southern nights.

Not that anything was forgotten. A continuum existed, intact, between the winter dawn in New York and the generous Italian summer. But in that never-shifting heat, the present seemed almost irrelevant, and Luke's thoughts receded to another level. A deeper level than the logical figuring of where Danni might be. A more intuitive level than the ways and means of Nicole's murder. A level whose progress he felt, rather than knew, and for which he had no name.

Meanwhile, as the wordless days passed, Luke was teaching himself to ride the massive Triumph motorbike he had found in the palazzo's old stables, at the far end of the garden. He presumed that this was Danni's old bike, the one that had roared up and down the rue Gabrielle, announcing his arrivals and departures to Nicole. It revealed something about Danni and his partner that the bike was kept in working order. It revealed something else that it was stored next to a small gate in the stable's back wall, which was common to the wall enclosing the grounds, and let out to a path in the surrounding woods. And yet something else again that the key to that gate was hidden in a drawer in the escritoire in Chevejon's study.

It told that if these gentlemen were confident, they were also careful.

Perhaps it told something about Luke also: that he had searched Chevejon's escritoire with sufficient care to find the well-hidden key. And promptly appropriated it.

So Luke passed his time, waiting for his beard to grow, waiting for his chance to escape. In the meantime, he spent his days sequestered in Danni's room, reading. Following a path that was progressively defining itself, as the French say, *à son insu,* in a part of his mind.

Much later he would come to feel a nostalgia for this period of inaction, which, in the end, turned out to be so brief.

2 BRIEFER YET was any period of peace for Chevejon. For him, only a bittersweet feeling would characterize his memory of this time. It was true that he found in the presence of this strange double of his friend an odd satisfaction. As if, in Luke's person, were not—of course—Danni but the stuff of Danni. A physical similarity as strong as their temperamental difference and with the same past. As the days passed, Chevejon found that he felt oddly eased of the pain of missing his friend by this person who was not his friend. As the days passed, he found himself thinking more and more of his sister in Howell, Michigan.

He still went to his office at Santo Spirito each day, working on the reconstruction of a set of fragments he had acquired from a site in Iraq known only to a group of Kurds, who, in turn, were known only to Danni. The Kurds, Danni had told him with a wry expression, were armed with Israeli surplus, Galils and captured Kalashnikovs, bought with their profits from the dig.

The slide of his mind, however, into that blank abyss of concentration, so familiar to him, was now marred. Business had been virtually at a standstill since Danni had left; now he ignored even those occasional offers phoned in by American dealers he knew, too far away to know of the hiatus of his operation.

But Paolo was there, and Gianlucca was there, still on payroll, as was his enormous network of contacts throughout Europe still available, by telephone. And so, all the while he worked, or cooked, or gardened, or sat by the window of his study on the road to Fiesole in the evenings, drinking cognac in silence with Luke, the engines of his subterranean connections, if not those of his subtle mind, worked surely on the questions before him.

Meanwhile, there was me, Natalie, to take care of, a responsibility, now that there was nothing more I could tell him, that was purely pleasant. For both of us. The important thing, Chevejon knew, was that I wait. The impending arrival of my suitcase was a more delicate task than he had foreseen, for now he was afraid that it might just possibly be under Israeli surveillance. Who knew? Really, he felt it reasonable to overestimate the forces that might be involved and to orchestrate a much more careful removal of that suitcase from the Gare de l'Est than might, to another, have seemed necessary.

3

IT TOOK two full weeks to extract my suitcase from the left-luggage office in Paris. Chevejon was at the airport when it finally arrived, early one morning, carried by a friend of Paolo's, who met his sometime employer with a respectful handshake and a Romany greeting. He bought the man a brandy and a coffee at the little airport café, observing curiously this distant presence who, on Paolo's recommendation, had carried out a few simple but potentially dangerous transactions for him over the years in Paris. Chevejon liked his look: his dark Gypsy face with a black mustache, his quick, funny speech; perhaps, he thought, this Philippe could be relied on for more complex tasks in the future. Then he dismissed the man to his return flight and drove into Santo Spirito.

A smell of fresh water filled the empty square with its running gutters. Alone in his office, he opened the suitcase: a woolen skirt; a cardigan, soft and worn and carrying Natalie's perfume; a small framed photograph of Nijinsky—God, she was planning on a long trip, this girl. Underneath a pair of wool socks he found what he was looking for: the gold menorah, a magnificent object; the family Torah; and a stack of ancient documents. These he placed on his coffee table and perched before them on the couch.

First he examined the menorah. Pink gold, surely Portuguese, as was the workmanship: fine-cast Hebrew letters lining the base, winding foliation mounting the individual arms. Leaning back, he considered it from a distance: seventeenth century, he felt sure, a museum piece, an exotic Sephardi object for an Ashkenazi Viennese home.

He turned to the Torah, a thick leather-bound and gold-embossed book of fine paper, resembling modern supercalendered but of a hand process, holding the colors of the Hebrew initial caps brilliantly. Too brilliantly, he suddenly thought. He rose and crossed to his desk drawer, returned with a loupe, and, stooping, examined an open page. Right, the initial caps had been, at least once, professionally restored, though the restoration was a good century old itself.

Now he opened the book and saw, on the first page, a list of Yiddish words, written with a thick-nibbed fountain pen. Each followed by a date. Clearly the words were names, the numbers birth dates; the dates went back to 1750. He went back to the beginning and counted the names with dates since 1880: thirty-five. He knew, because Danni had told him, that only Benami had survived. Thirty-four people. The last date recorded was 1937. One by one, he sounded out the Hebrew characters: Rachel. He pronounced it to himself with the guttural Hebrew *ch,* Rachel. A cousin of Benami's? She would have been, what, fifty-two now? She must have been—what?—four or five at her death?

Finally he turned to the last item: a heavy pile of papers, tied in a very tight knot with ancient waxed twine, now shrunken and brittle with age. He untied them carefully, looked at the top one, and was shocked again: In an entry marked "Name," he read "Julius Michael Neumann," a familiar name, though he did not at once grasp why. But his blood quickened as his eye traveled to a stamped photo that showed an aging face, and he realized that this could only be Danni's grandfather.

Now he sat back and looked at the page as a whole. At its head, in the Gothic type of the Nazi bureaucracy: "Exit permission is granted to the bearer," then the statistics of the man: Profession: Professor; Sex: Male; Age: 59; Address: Frederickstrasse 29, Wien; Race: Jewish. Chevejon turned the page and found himself looking at Benami's mother, then brother, then sisters. The second sister had a different name, Weissmann, but another line gave her maiden name, Neumann. He turned again and found David Weissmann, clearly her husband, then turned again and was shocked again: Here he saw Rachel Weiss-

mann, born 1937, aged five. For a moment he felt he was hallucinat-
ing, so clearly did he see Danni, and Luke, in the girl's face.

There were some four hundred of the exit permits, all numbered
sequentially, from 3576A to 3978A: dozens of families, grandparents,
children, young couples, teenagers. Some showed the effects of the
years of war—the date was early spring of 1942—some showed still the
health of affluence.

All were signed and dated, in the bottom right-hand corner,
Nicholas Hoestermann, Zentralstelle für jüdische Auswanderung.

4   CHEVEJON ROSE. He noticed his hands were shaking—a
     thing he could not remember happening in years. He
     breathed in, and then out, but the cascade of suspicions
through his mind was unstoppable. He walked to the bookshelves,
poured a drink—a large one—and lit a cigar. Then from the window
he gazed down at the square below, the dappled afternoon light
reflecting in a checkered pattern from the façade of Santo Spirito.

Finally he turned to the phone and dialed the number of my room
at my *pensione*. When I answered, he talked with what Luke would
have recognized as forced casualness.

"Natalie. Good morning. Tell me, what is your address in Vienna?"

As I spoke, his eyes closed

"Frederickstrasse 29."

He was hardly even surprised.

"Thank you, darling. Now, I have your suitcase here. Would you
like to step over?"

5   THIS CHEVEJON KNEW: that Yossi Benami, returned to
     Vienna as an agent of the Haganah, had entered into a
     famous partnership with an Obersturmbannführer Hoester-
mann to arrange the rescue of some four hundred Viennese Jews. That
the exit permits now in his possession were Hoestermann's A copies,
office copies, of the permits. And that this partnership had been at the

origin of Benami's fame and had saved Hoestermann from a war crimes conviction.

And this he believed: that Obersturmbannführer Hoestermann had taken over the house of Yossi Benami's father—Julius Neumann—in Vienna when the Neumann family was evicted. That before they left, someone in the family had built a secret hiding place in the attic and placed the family's most precious possessions there. That Hoestermann had never known these possessions were there. But that somehow Danni Benami had.

But the consequences of these facts—of these beliefs—were only more questions.

How had it happened that Benami should have become the partner of precisely the man who had evicted his family from their home?

Why was it that all the Neumanns should have perished in Theresienstadt when he had in his very room exit permits for the entire family?

How had Danni known to tell Natalie about the hiding place in the attic of Frederickstrasse 29?

All of that had to be deciphered before he could come to the final, most important question: Danni Benami, descending the length of Europe in a southerly fugue—what in God's name was he looking for?

That, it would seem, was a complete mental inventory. Except that he did not feel it was complete. There was something else. At the window his mind traversed all that he had realized since he opened Natalie's suitcase; until, arriving finally at his first shock at opening the exit permits, he heard Luke's voice snorting in contempt, and an electric jolt seemed to pass through his limbs.

My father, he imported cannon fodder for the War of Independence. The Italian Passage didn't bring a soul over twenty-five into the country, and it didn't bring any women.

A long pause in Chevejon's consciousness now. A long space for a brute functioning of his brain, in which, beyond his immediate consciousness, many ideas began their slow dance of gravitating into place.

Had he remained undisturbed, where would this process have concluded?

In the event, he was interrupted by a ringing of his doorbell that made him start: Its insistence struck him as hysterical.

And frightening.

6   WHEN HE HAD CALLED, that morning, asking my address in Vienna, I knew immediately he had the suitcase from Paris. And I knew that he immediately had understood what those objects meant, what they must mean. My heart paused and twisted in my chest; I felt a foreboding at once familiar and strange. After a moment I identified its familiarity: It was how I had felt when I was forced onto the train from Paris to Vienna, with no assurance of being able to get off before I arrived. I pronounced my address slowly, and there was a silence. Then he told me to come over.

It was when I stepped outside, the big bodyguard beside me, that I saw the three men from Paris.

I stopped still, and Giorgio looked at me in surprise, then followed my gaze. I needed to tell him nothing: He understood and, taking me by the arm, turned me and hurried me up the street.

Things started happening very fast now.

When we arrived at Chevejon's office, Giorgio pushed me up the stairs, walking backward behind me. At the office door he stopped, watching down the stairs, and I, as if his partner rather than his prisoner, leaned on the doorbell until Chevejon opened the outside door, punching the code in the lock. Wordless, he took in the scene; then Chevejon swung the door open and pushed me into the antechamber. Giorgio glanced back, then settled against the wall at the top of the stairs.

"It's three men. They were waiting for her in the piazza. I didn't want to lead them here, but I'm outclassed."

Chevejon nodded. "*Sta bene cosi.* You did good. Stay where you are. They won't come up."

Inside he ushered me to the window. The three men were spread out, two by the fountain, one next to the café, the only life in the late-morning square. He looked at me with eyebrows raised. I nodded. "That's them."

"The same ones as in Paris?"

I nodded again. The one by the fountain was the man in glasses who'd caught me on the rue de Rennes.

Now Chevejon nodded. He paused to think. Then, moving quickly and apparently calmly, he crossed the room and opened a safe in his desk, under the big canvas that could not possibly be a Botticelli. He put in the pile of documents, the menorah, the Torah, slammed the door, and spun the lock, then went to the window again. Still watching, he picked up the phone, punched some numbers, then spoke. "Cinzia. Chevejon. You rehearsing? Good, do me a favor, will you? Open the back door. *Grazie, bella,* see you in a sec."

I made a sound now: I was beginning to feel that I didn't exist, and the pounding in my chest was unbearable. He looked up and, seeing how scared I was, suddenly smiled his wide smile. "I'm sorry. I should have told you: This is easy. It's not like the movies, I promise you. Just come with me."

7 NOW HE TOOK ME through the vestibule, setting his locks and alarms carefully on both doors, then into the hallway, where the bodyguard was waiting. He said something in quick Italian, too quick for me to catch, and we went down the stairs, first Giorgio, then Chevejon, then I, my mind dizzy with fear, the two men moving quickly and silently. At the ground level Giorgio stood in front of the closed door; then Chevejon moved next to him and motioned me behind him. I swung around the newel-post of the staircase, and then Chevejon was pushing me down a corridor, away from the front door, and Giorgio was following, walking backward. It was dark now, and Chevejon was telling me just to keep going. I walked blindly perhaps six steps, then a door swung open on light more blinding yet than the darkness. Chevejon kept pushing, and I stepped onto what I slowly realized was the stage of an empty theater.

A woman stood behind the door. She kissed Chevejon without a word; then we filed past a costumed cast, standing in silence. Chevejon jumped down first, lifted me down—he was surprisingly strong—and we hurried up the aisle, through a darkened lobby. Now we waited while the woman caught up. She opened the front door, I started to follow Chevejon out, but he turned, closing the door on my brief glimpse of the street.

"Wait."

We waited in the lobby for what seemed like a half hour, but was really minutes, Giorgio's broad back against me, his hand inside his leather jacket. Then I heard a car in the street, Giorgio peeked out, then opened the door wide to the sunlit day.

Chevejon sat at the wheel of a long convertible, its engine running. For a moment I had the horrible feeling that Giorgio was going to climb in and they were going to speed off, leaving me. A horrible feeling, a metallic feeling of abandonment in which my father and his past seemed to swirl like an orchestra of plaintive music; for a moment I felt frozen to the ground. Then I was in the air, Giorgio carrying me as if I weighed nothing; he deposited me in the passenger seat, and Chevejon was speaking to him as if I weren't even there.

"Excellent work, Giorgio. Call up to Fiesole, tell them to get the kid out of the way. Then get your bike and come up to Fiesole, okay? Oh, get her things from the *pensione,* bring everything up. Here"—he reached into his pocket and tossed the bodyguard his wallet—"settle the bill."

Then we were moving through cool air, across a bridge, through the center of Florence, and uphill into countryside. I looked behind; the road was empty. Chevejon pulled into a driveway, stopped to open a high gate, brought the car through, closed the gate, and drove up to what seemed to be a small palace. He parked, pulling to a stop on gravel, and came around to open my door. His voice seemed loud in the sudden silence.

"You okay? Don't worry, we're safe here. This is where I live. Come." He helped me out—unnecessarily, for I was beginning to feel normal again—and started to escort me up a gravel path to the front door.

Two men, two massive men, immaculately dressed in loose-cut black suits, were approaching. "Here's Paolo and Gianlucca. Ciao, gentlemen, what's up?" I had time to notice the men were looking scared and to notice the incongruousness of that expression before Chevejon, dwarfed in front of them. Then one of them spoke.

"Chevejon. The kid. He's gone."

. . .

Standing in front of the door, the two men still speaking, excusing themselves, but Chevejon was thinking too fast to listen or even to be angry. And then he was talking.

"Okay, enough. Go down to town. Luke's down there. I want you to find him, I don't give a fuck how. Check the English bookstore on Tornabuoni; look out for the motorcycle; check the train station and travel agents. Stick to this side of the river; the only place he won't be is Santo Spirito. And the second you find him, first call me up at Santo Spirito, then get him the fuck back up here, and don't let him go again."

The two bodyguards took off at a run to their car, and Chevejon went inside with me. Inside I asked a bit fatuously: What was going on? Who was Luke? Why would those men try to kill him? Chevejon answered, in rapid Italian, as if he were thinking out loud: "He's the guy you saw in Paris. They're going to think he's Danni. That's who they're after; they never really wanted you in the first place."

I asked, guiltily: "Did I lead them here?"

Now he switched to German, as if just becoming conscious that he was speaking to me. "No, no, it was my fault, not yours. Some so-called friend of ours must have talked."

"What do they want from him?"

He answered tersely. "The papers you stole from your father."

There was a noise outside, Giorgio arriving on his motorbike, my bag tied on the back, and Chevejon went on. "There's no time to explain now. Wait." He ran up the marble stairs, then down again in a moment, carrying a set of keys.

"Come." He led me outside, untied my bag from the back of the bike, and threw it into his car. Then he gave the keys to Giorgio and spoke hurriedly. "Got my wallet?" He took it, emptied it of cash, and gave Giorgio the money and a bank card. "Listen now: Take my car, take her to Capri. Stop in Rome, get some money out of a bank machine—a lot of money, everything it'll give you. You remember how to get to my house? Here are the keys; stay there till you hear from me. If you need more money, call—make sure she's comfortable."

Then, to me: "Listen, darling. You know me a little now, can you trust me? Tell me the truth."

I thought, biting my lip, then nodded.

"Good girl. Now go with Giorgio. He's taking you to my house in Capri; it's nice, it's safe. You'll be fine there. I'll be in touch soon, and I'll explain everything. Can you do that?"

I nodded again, and then I was in the car with Giorgio, following Chevejon on the motorbike through the gate. On the main road we diverged, and I was alone with Giorgio, roaring toward the highway south.

CHAPTER FIFTEEN

1 IT HAD not been difficult for Luke to get out.

As the weeks progressed and his beard came in, he had felt his relationship with his captors develop and mellow. There was a sense with the four men—the bodyguards, Luke, and Chevejon—of fraternity. And so the morning that Chevejon was dealing with Natalie and her three pursuers in Florence, up in the palazzo in Fiesole he was able to take his leave.

The opportunity was well timed. Luke's beard was in, low and thick, obscuring his lower face. A haircut and horn-rim glasses, both supplied by Chevejon, made him virtually unrecognizable as Danni's brother. That much, Luke felt, was all he owed Chevejon for his troubles. Now it was time for him to see where he could get with the questions before him.

They were very different from those that faced Chevejon; posed a different existential threat—or so Luke thought. For with all that he had told Chevejon, one thing he had managed to keep to himself, and that was the murder he had committed in the Puces de Clignancourt. And before Chevejon should find out that his partner was dead, Luke thought it wise to leave this safe place.

Indeed, a part of Luke's mind had, since the very beginning, been planning his escape. He knew where he needed to go, and he was foolish enough to think that Chevejon could not take him there.

In fact, of course, he was shortly to find that, to the contrary, he could not get there alone.

.   .   .

So it was that on that morning he was able to elude the increasingly casual attention of Paolo and Gianlucca and leave from the villa's garden door on Danni's old motorcycle. It was easy: After Chevejon had left for town, Paolo for his post at the front gate, and Gianlucca for his post by the front door, Luke climbed out the window of Danni's bedroom and dropped to the lawn. He skirted the house to the gravel walk, followed it past the sunny beds of roses and behind the compost heap to the stables. After opening the little gate with the stolen key, he pushed the Triumph out into the shadow of the woods. On the narrow path there he mounted the bike, turned on the ignition without start-ing the motor—though he doubted that he could be heard—and clutched and geared down with his left foot. Then he let the bike, gathering speed, roll silently down the path to where it met with the main road before he let out the clutch, jumped the engine into life, and gathered speed toward town.

2   THE INVENTORY of what Luke knew, what he believed, and what he failed to understand—the inventory that now led him to run from Chevejon's kind captivity—was a very differ-ent one from Chevejon's, and the actions he planned to take were very much less direct.

His facts were, to say the least, evanescent—far too much so, he thought, after all his months of searching. What he had were nothing more than scrawls of his brother's hand scattered through his books, hints at a process of thought—nearly nothing.

And yet Luke did not think it was nothing. He thought, rather, that this process, centering on his father's writing, was at the origin of Danni's fugue; he clutched at the slim hope of following it. Perhaps that hope came from the fact that these scrawls, this trace of a process of thought, were all he had.

Danni's careful notes in the margins of his father's books charted a course through the library that Luke would never have otherwise found. The key had been in starting at the beginning, with his father's first book. From there a number of paths diverged. From *Sacrifice and Symbolism*, the first title in the thick, cloth-bound Oxford Complete

Works, Luke followed his brother along one trail to his mother's work, not *Living Death,* but to articles in psychiatric and academic journals. From here Luke followed his brother through histories of the Holocaust, through Ka-Tzetznik and Tom Segev. And by now Luke was familiar with his brother's thought, familiar enough to realize that what Danni was finding in this complex reading was a sophisticated, convincing, and—Luke thought—heartfelt refutation of his father's major statement of Jewish philosophy, *Sacrifice and Symbolism* itself.

But as to what fault Danni found in his father's central book, Luke was unclear. In what appeared to be a kind of ideational shorthand, Danni's notes referred, again and again, to Caravaggio, as if the painter's name were synonymous with "sacrifice." Benami, however, as far as Luke could see, made no reference to Caravaggio in his own work, and so this key term in Danni's notes remained elusive.

Tantalizingly so. For although Luke was unfamiliar with the painter—he confused him with de la Tour—somehow the association seemed apt. A vague recollection suggested that the painting Danni had in mind was on the cover of a paperback edition of Benami's book. That edition was not in Danni's library, and, stuck in Fiesole, Luke had no way to be sure.

And this provided him with his purpose—one of his purposes—for escaping today from Peter Chevejon's house.

3 Now, having parked the Triumph and entered the English-language bookstore on the via Tornabuoni, Luke made for the Penguin paperback shelves. Balzac, Barthes, Beckett, Behan, Bell, Belloc, Benami. The name appeared three times on the top shelf in black nonfiction spines, mixed in with the orange-colored fiction books. Standing on tiptoe, he pulled down the first volume. This was *A Brief History of Jerusalem,* and pictured, on the front, the view of the Jaffa Gate he had watched, that winter, from his father's study. The second was *The City and the King* and featured an aerial photo of the Western Wall. The third was *Sacrifice and Symbolism,* and on it, in brilliant color, was a painting.

The image flooded him with a feeling of familiarity, as if he had once known it well and forgotten it. In vivid colors and exquisite detail, a boy's face, twisted in pain, crying out in fright. His eyes were dark and sullen and looking at nothing, as if the source of his torture were out of his field of vision, like an animal at slaughter. Now, as his eye traveled away from the face, Luke saw that a massive, wrinkled hand held the boy at the neck. But whoever owned the hand was not included in this reproduction, evidently a detail; everything in the reproduction's composition indicated that it was part of a wider tableau. He flipped the book, looking for a picture credit, and found it finally on the back: Uffizi Gallery, Florence.

Checking his watch again, he found it just after noon. He had another errand in mind for the afternoon. Still, he thought, there was time enough if he hurried, and after replacing two of the books, he bought the third. He stuffed it into his back pocket as he strode quickly out of the store.

He left the motorbike where he'd parked it and hurried down the via Porta Rossa. The crowds here were almost exclusively foreigners; it was high season, and, as Chevejon had said, every Florentine who didn't depend on tourist trade had already left. Chevejon himself, Luke knew, would have left by now for his house on Capri had Luke not been there. Feeling trapped, he made his slow way into the Piazza Signoria, passed the Rivoire, crossed the open square, and entered the doors of the Uffizi.

It was a hopeless task, pushing through the crowds to look for the painting. People appeared to be actually waiting in line before the canvases. Voices from all over the world swirling around him, he pushed through, running his eyes over the portions of the walls he could see.

And then, in the last rooms of the museum, he found it.

4 THE SCARED, suffering face, stretched in a dumb, sullen cry of pain, belonged to a naked boy being held in a horizontal position by one powerful, gnarled hand of an ancient man. The man's other hand held a knife, halted on its descent toward the boy's neck by another boy, this one thin, with golden, curly locks, an angel, clearly. The old man's attention was engaged by the angel, who pointed across the canvas at an eager-looking ram, his horned face watching the scene with curiosity and compassion. Behind them stretched away an Etruscan countryside, a castle on a hill in the distance. A tour guide started to move in front of him, Luke held out a hand to stop him and, pushing him gently to the side, stepped forward and read the ID of the painting, and as he did so, a quick movement rippled over his scalp. The painting was by Caravaggio and titled *Sacrificio di Isaaco.*

5

THE TOUR GROUP between him and the canvas now, Luke moved on blindly and was pushed, by the flow of the crowds, out onto the loggia, where a little cafeteria served food at tables in the shadows of umbrellas. He elbowed his way to the stone rail at the edge and for a time stood in the sunlight above the teeming piazza, watching the line at the entrance of the Uffizi, the crowds around Michelangelo's *David,* the packed terrace of the Rivoire.

The heat, wet and stale, seemed to emanate visibly from the people below. Sweating, he wiped a hand across his forehead, then on the seat of his jeans, and felt the hardness of the Penguin paperback in his back pocket.

For a moment he did not remember what it was. When it came to him, he withdrew the book and held it against the stone railing. He lit one of Chevejon's Panters, then opened it to the first page. At first, in the brilliant light's obliteration, he could barely see the type. He turned, shadowing the book against the sun with one hand, and read the dedication, evidently written for this edition, for he had not seen it in the Oxford edition in Danni's rooms:

> To the people of Italy, without whose heroic help thousands like me would have perished in the death camps of the Third Reich.

And in the introduction:

> In the summer of 1942 my flight from occupied Vienna to the shores of Palestine brought me across Italy—a country still far removed from the programmatic genocide of the Nazis, where refugees like myself received considerable help not only from Italian Jewry, but from the Fascist army itself—to the city of Florence.

In that year my own father was to disappear into the massive death machine where ultimately my entire family was to perish. Yet whether it was the natural insouciance of youth or the kind peace of the Florentine summer, the fact of the War Against the Jews—a fact with which I had been living, day and night, for two years of underground service in Vienna—seemed to recede as, waiting for arrangements for my escape to be completed, I hid in that beautiful city. Until, one morning in the Uffizi galleries, I came face-to-face with the painting reprinted on this book's front cover: Caravaggio's depiction of the Sacrifice of Isaac.

Many things were to happen between that day and the writing of this book: I was to escape, eventually, to Palestine; World War II was to be fought to its end; the War of Independence was yet before me; and the foundation of the State of Israel was yet to take place. But now, looking back, I see clearly that it was that day, standing before Caravaggio's depiction of my own God, that I first realized the enormity of the disaster that threatened not only the Jews of Europe but Western civilization itself.

For what Caravaggio painted was not an isolated moment in Jewish history but a turning point for humankind. He painted the moment when God, giving Abraham a ram instead of a human—a symbolic sacrifice instead of a murder—taught the power of symbolism to Abraham, and through him, to the Judeo-Christian future, of which it is the originating moment. From that moment on, that power—of symbolism—would be held ascendant over the primitive power of sacrifice and that ascendancy would define the thin bridge of civilization that unites our present to Abraham's past.

On that day in the middle of World War II I saw that the ascendancy of symbolism over sacrifice, of reconciliation over aggression, was being challenged in a way unprecedented in history—a way that neither Caravaggio nor even Abraham could ever have imagined— by Hitler's Third Reich. And although I had just finished two difficult, dangerous years of fighting the Nazi threat, it was not until I stood in Florence before Caravaggio's vision of *the central revolution in human values that is Judaism: a father and a son being brought to peace by their God*—on that summer day in Florence, while far to the north the Holocaust raged and reached its tentacles of death ever across Europe—that I, who was beginning to realize that I had lost my father, became aware of the meaning of my people's history. With that awareness came my understanding of the threat that history was posing to the Jews, to their history, and to their very contribution to humanity.

There my adult life began.

Luke closed the book suddenly, abrupt waves of shock again rippling from his back, up his neck, and across his scalp.

He had been right to find this painting that sat at the center of his father's life, at the center of his brother's fugue. But in the heat and bright, bright light, that didn't matter. All that mattered was his sudden realization. That his father had not just been in Florence before him, but been here—right here—before the painting he had seen. Perhaps right here on the loggia of the Uffizi, right where he was standing.

And that if he had first found, then lost his long-lost brother, he had also found his father again.

6 AT THE COUNTER of the Rivoire he drank a whiskey and a coffee, then checked the time again and hurried across the piazza. The errand he had in mind for the afternoon was now all the more important. On the via Lamberti, he entered the Alitalia ticket office, whose address he had found earlier in Chevejon's telephone book. He paid for and pocketed a ticket that was waiting there for him. He left again, retraced his steps to the via Tornabuoni and the bike. Now his step slowed: There were hours to pass before his late-afternoon flight, and he did not intend to return to Fiesole.

The afternoon closing had begun. Luke crossed Tornabuoni and the crowded center of the city, then walked northeast, the hills of Fiesole appearing between houses on his left, the crowds thinning again to nothing in this neighborhood, which held nothing for tourists. In the thick heat his step on the hard stone began to ache; he was sweating. A street ended in a small children's park; he entered and sat heavily on a bench. The park was deserted. Closing his eyes, he tipped his face up into the sky. Against his closed eyelids the sun appeared in a distance of swimming red. Like this, he rested a moment.

And now, as if his mind were following rules known only to itself, he found himself gazing at a boy's face, a boy dying. First it appeared to him in the black and white of his memory of the war. The Palestinian youth as Luke's bullet, striking his pelvis, bore him against the stone wall of the little building he sprang out of, his face an almost comic picture of surprise, then shock, and then a strange look that was nearly sheepishness, as his body left his control and began to fall to the ground.

But then, as sleep took over, the scene narrowed and the boy's face, now in vivid color, filled Luke's eye. He saw that the boy's mouth was open in a cry of bitter distress, his eyes dark and sullen and looking at nothing, as if the source of his torture were out of his field of vision, like an animal at slaughter, his mouth open in plaint against the unjustness of pressure that was bearing down on his neck from a massive, wrinkled hand, the unjustness that he could not move, that he could not breathe, that he was dying, slowly and inexorably, thirsty and suffocating, dying.

The vividness of the image nearly woke him from his descent into sleep, but only nearly, although his face was flushing with blood and sweat was beading on his forehead. Slowly the image faded. Now he was dreaming that space and time were nothing, for he was showing his father the apartment on the rue de Fleurus, guiding him with a proud commentary through the collection of objects in the living room, to Danni's study, through Nicole's bedroom. At first there was a sense of tremendous pleasure, even revenge, in showing his father that Danni lived so well, with a woman as lovely and good as Nicole. Then guilt began to grow in his chest as he realized there was something false about what he was telling him, false because Nicole was not a Jew, because the apartment was in France, because under these circumstances Danni's happiness, to his father, was nothing.

He woke heavily, sweating, startled, when a nanny entered the park with a baby and a girl. The girl, perhaps three, ran toward the swings, moving in short skips, her thick brown ponytail bouncing behind her. When she saw Luke, she stopped in her tracks to stare at him with somber brown eyes. The nanny, occupied with the baby in her arms, who was staring up into her face and cooing, did not notice. But when she looked up, first at the girl and then at Luke, she stood and called: "Leila. *Vieni qui. Siediti accanto a Jacopo.*" Still, the girl, her wondering eyes locked in place, did not move, and Luke rose, walked slowly across the gravel ground of the park—as if he were being ejected—and directed himself back to town.

Now the streets, labyrinthine, were filled with passersby, each generating a heat that Luke could nearly feel; now his mind, dulled and confused with his half sleep, seemed to cringe from contact with this strange city. He hurried past the Piazza della Signoria and to the Triumph, dimly he was aware that he had a plane to catch. But as he drew near, he came to a stop.

Paolo, his vast bulk perched sidesaddle on the bike, waited there, anxiously looking around him.

Luke froze for a moment, then stepped into a doorway. Christ, how had Paolo found the bike? He rested for a moment, sweating in the heat, then turned and stepped onto the sidewalk again, meaning to retreat up the street.

But as he stepped down from the doorway, he found himself facing the chest—immovable—of Gianlucca's white cotton shirt, which was slowly replaced in his view by Gianlucca's broad face, as he lifted Luke in his arms and carried him toward Paolo and the bike, muttering: "What's the matter with you? You trying to get us all fucking killed?"

Walking between the two now, arms linked in Florentine fashion, they escorted him to a phone booth, where Paolo placed a hurried call to Chevejon, and then to a car, in which Gianlucca drove him back to Fiesole while Paolo went back for the motorbike.

It had been a brief escape.

7 CHEVEJON, by the time Paolo notified him of Luke's apprehension that afternoon, had had plenty of time to think.

Returning to his office through the theater, he'd stationed himself by one of the big windows and watched, without pause, the square below. The three Israelis—Larry, Curly, and Moe; he'd already assigned names to each, surprised by the American reference from his childhood when it came to his mind—had been conducting an evidently practiced surveillance, each holding a spot for twenty minutes or so, then in turn shifting casually to another, putting on sunglasses and taking them off, taking turns leaving the piazza and coming into the building to wait inside the little entrance downstairs. Chevejon did not think it likely that Luke would come to Santo Spirito; eluding Chevejon, rather than meeting him, was obviously the boy's intention. Still, he had not been willing to leave the window, just in case, and standing there, he'd had plenty of time to think.

What he thought had not been pleasant.

First had been a rush of emotion: What a fool he'd been to let Luke get out. How had he done it? He chastised himself for some time, bitterly. Only as the recrimination faded did it begin to occur to him that there was something strange about the depth of his feeling. That his normal, manipulative attitude toward the people around him—all except Danni—was not serving him, neither in his relationship with Luke nor, in its own way, with Natalie; the very fact he hadn't slept with her proved that. Christ, he thought, next I'll be buying Christmas baskets for Gianluc's family, for Christ's sake. The thought made him laugh unexpectedly, and as his mirth subsided, he realized that he had been, these past weeks, happy.

And now his thoughts took on a smooth rhythm, flowing quietly as he watched out the window while the square darkened with shadow.

He realized that Luke had changed everything, not only in the routines of his life, not only in the way of conducting business, but in his emotional makeup. All that he felt for Danni, he saw, had spilled over into what he had come to feel for Luke, for his suffering, his lost journey through life, launched by the same past that had launched Danni on his so different journey. Despite himself, he had come to feel a deep sympathy with the boy. Despite himself, he had fallen, as he had once so long ago with Danni, in love.

He knew he had been right to hold Luke under virtual house arrest in Fiesole, right to keep him safe while he tried to arrange a zone of safety for him, for Danni, and for himself. But it had been house arrest; Luke's escape proved that. Now he thought that if he could just find the boy again—and if he could get these three motherfuckers downstairs out of the way—it would be time to let him go.

If he wanted to go.

Whatever that might mean to them all.

As for the three stooges, there was an impasse. It would require very particular circumstances for him to take care of them, and the air of smooth professionalism that attended the Israelis' surveillance made him doubt that he and Paolo and Gianlucca, even with their extensive practice, were equal to the task; there was a big difference between operating in a criminal world where such skills were a matter of adaptation and the state-trained craft of these men. Certainly, in the open square, filled with early-evening crowds, there was nothing he could do save assassinate them, and he did not want to assassinate them.

This scared him and led his mind on an unwelcome tour of the possible dangers that presented themselves to him, to Luke, and to Natalie. Not to mention Danni. And following these thoughts, by the time the phone rang, he had become seriously worried that Luke would be stupid enough actually to come here. He picked it up, listened, then spoke with evident relief.

"*Bene,* take him up to Fiesole, and sit on his head till I get there. Okay. . . . Good, Paolo, see you in a while."

Now Chevejon forced his mind sharply to the present. That was one problem solved. Now there was another. It would be easy enough to leave Santo Spirito altogether; these men must still think Natalie was up in the office, and there was no way they were going to recognize Chevejon. Still, he felt obscurely that there was something these three could teach him, if he was careful enough. He crossed now, for the first time, from the window to the liquor cabinet, poured a drink, and lit a cigar. He stood thinking for some time. Then he tossed off the drink and let himself out of the office, moving quickly.

That way there was no time to be scared.

In the square, squinting in the late, low sun, Chevejon found he had been right: These men paid him not the slightest attention. That gave him the advantage, and walking slowly, he crossed to the one he had named Moe. A tall man, in glasses, with the look of a Jewish intellectual, but Chevejon felt there was a powerful body under his cheap suit and saw, in the absolute lack of humor in the face, a real determination. A few steps away from the man now, walking casually, he paused. Was he doing the right thing? He wasn't sure, and there was no more time to wonder, for the man was already looking at him. He forced himself to smile and talk conversationally.

"You're wasting your time, you know. Natalie's been gone for hours. What, you think I'm a total idiot waiting up there with her?"

The man reached a hand automatically inside his jacket, and Chevejon now bent his arms at the elbow to show his hands very clearly. In the periphery of his vision he saw the other two approaching at a rapid step.

"Oh, my, I wouldn't do that." He stepped forward now and lowered his voice. "Shoot an Italian citizen in front of his office? God, I can see it now: 'Israeli Hit in Florence.' And then, you'll be the one to explain it all to the minister of state, a close personal friend of mine as it happens. Tell me, what you going to say?"

Silence. The other two had approached now, and standing in the middle of their loose triangle, Chevejon worked at controlling his breath. He allowed a practiced pause, then went on, his voice dropping and growing more earnest.

"I got what you're looking for right upstairs in my safe—no, don't get any ideas; it would take dynamite to get it out of there. You want it, you're going to have to negotiate for it. Otherwise we may have to kill each other, and we don't want that, do we?"

That was all he had to say. In the silence he reflected painfully: He had nothing more to say, and it didn't seem to have worked.

Or was it all? Without thinking, he was talking again, calmly, conversationally, as if there were no hurry in the world. "And you know what? You know the funny thing? Danni Benami's not even in Florence. His brother is, but so what? God, imagine this one: 'Israeli Tourist Killed by Shin Bet Agents in Florence.' Subhead: 'Mistook Him for His Brother.' How're your bosses going to like that one?"

That worked. At last. There was a visible hesitation on Moe's face now. He removed his hand from inside his jacket and looked down at Chevejon. Then, finally, he spoke. "Who the hell are you?"

Chevejon answered readily. "I'm all you got, gentlemen. Natalie's gone, Danni's gone, and his brother is safely stowed away, just like your little Nazi documents. So why don't we step over to that café and have a nice drink together?"

8   AT THE CAFÉ they sat around a table in the dusky evening, the Israelis silent over coffees, Chevejon talking quietly in English. "Look. I know who you are; I know what you want. Either you're independents, or you're working for the government of a small Mediterranean country where Hebrew is spoken. It really doesn't matter, does it?" He paused, and Moe gave a short nod that showed not agreement but attention.

"Good. Now listen. First of all, you're not going to find Danni Benami. Because why? Because no one knows where he is. The general didn't know; Luke doesn't know; your German friend Hoestermann certainly doesn't know. Why? Because I don't know." He paused, watching. Now there was no nod, but he felt fairly certain that their silence was confirmation that Hoestermann had been the one who told them to look for his daughter in Paris. That made sense to him. He went on.

"Anyway, it doesn't matter: Danni doesn't have what you're looking for. I have it. Natalie—shall we say?—entrusted it to me. And it still doesn't matter because Natalie only had the A copies. They're worthless without the Bs, right? One copy for the Reich, one for the emigrants themselves; without both, you have no proof. Right?"

No more nods from Moe, but now he spoke. "Where are the Bs?"

Now Chevejon laughed; he loved a bluff. "Well, my friends, working on the theory that the whole reason you're here is that Danni stole them from his father in Jerusalem, let's see, late last summer it would be, then I can tell you this: They're totally unretrievable, in a safe deposit in another country. And that safe deposit, there's not a fucking soul in the whole wide world"—he said it slowly: whole . . . wide . . . world—"who knows where it is but me. And there is no way in hell"— again: no . . . way . . . in . . . hell—"that I'm going to tell you. So what you want to do, *chaverim?*"

·   ·   ·

A long silence. Then Moe, with deep distaste: "So you speak Hebrew? *Lech tizdayen*, you bastard, fuck you. What do *you* want to do?"

Chevejon's smile faded, and Moe was clearly surprised by the expression he saw in its place. But the tone was still conversational.

"This is what you do: Go the fuck home. Tell your . . . employers that what they want, I want, too. Tell them to have a nice little meeting, maybe some tea, and think it all over. I'll be letting you know what my terms are for an exchange of the documents, but they might want to think of what guarantees they can offer me of a pardon for Danni Benami. *Beseder?*"

A long pause. Then Moe: "I'll tell them."

Chevejon nodded now. "Good, fuck off then. There's a two A.M. train to Paris. My men will be waiting to see you on it."

The three rose and stepped away from the table before Chevejon called them back.

"One more thing. Tell your little Nazi friend"—and suddenly a surge of adrenaline flooded his stomach—"that Luke and Danni get either title to Frederickstrasse 29 or fair market value. Whichever they want. Otherwise no fucking deal."

He watched the look of confusion on Moe's face for a long moment, wondering what the other understood. Then he spoke for a last time.

"Don't worry." He spoke slowly, emphasizing the name in its German pronunciation. "Hoestermann will understand."

They left; he stayed. For another drink, a large one. Then, reminding himself to tell Paolo to go watch the station, he rose and walked to his car.

9   UP IN FIESOLE, Luke had passed the remains of the evening in Danni's rooms, Paolo at the hallway door, Gianlucca in the garden under the window. On the way up in the car Paolo had been sulking; neither had seemed inclined to give him dinner, and a growing hunger was growling in his stomach, alongside an increasing trepidation about what Chevejon planned, on his arrival, to do. Toward seven he heard Chevejon's car coming to a stop on the gravel parking

area; an hour passed; then Paolo opened the door and, with a motion of his head, ordered him downstairs.

The four of them ate silently at the wooden kitchen table, a hurried dinner of pasta and bread. Finished, Chevejon rose and gestured for Luke to come with him. Gianlucca followed, through the living room, and only when Luke was sitting in his armchair did Chevejon nod for the bodyguard to leave. He shut the door behind him with a marked slam. Now Luke found himself gazing nervously around while Chevejon poured himself a drink. After the noises of the hot town Luke found it ominously quiet in the low room above the garden. He was scared, but still, after a time, he moved to the fold-out bar by the escritoire and helped himself to a shot of scotch.

A long silence reigned, a silence that seemed to Luke more threatening than whatever punishment Chevejon might have in store. But the conversation that ensued was entirely different from the one he had so nervously anticipated. When Chevejon, glass in hand, finally spoke it was in a neutral tone.

"So. You've had enough of my hospitality. Ungrateful of you to leave without telling me your plan. Perhaps you'll be kind enough to let me know now what you have in mind?"

Luke rose, refilled his glass, and crossed to the window. There was a long pause, and then he turned to Chevejon.

"I'm going to Paris. I missed my plane tonight, but there's another tomorrow. I intend to be on it."

Chevejon nodded, thoughtfully, and Luke went on. "If you and your goons want to stop me, you better be prepared to go all the way."

Now Chevejon raised an eyebrow, smiling slightly. "You think of those boys as goons, do you?"

"I do."

"Well, you're not alone. But you do them an injustice." He thought for a moment, no longer smiling. "Paris. You think Danni's there."

"No." Luke was surprised. "Why do you say that?"

"Well . . ." He shifted in his chair and lit a Panter, exhaling a cloud of smoke toward the open window. "I spoke to a colleague yesterday. A French guy, he's been in 'Fort Worth, Texas,' for the past few weeks." He pronounced it, as a European would, with an exaggerated American accent. "You wouldn't believe how much business there is to do in 'Fort Worth, Texas.' Anyway, he just got back to Paris, and he told me he saw Danni there earlier this summer. At the Cygane, up in the north of Paris." He rose, poured another drink, then turned, his face suddenly impassive, and spoke in a different tone.

"Or was it you he saw?"

10

LUKE ANSWERED SLOWLY. "It was me."

"How did you know about the Cygane?"

"I didn't. That is, Nicole had told me about it. Danni had taken her there once, when they first met. But I was there by pure coincidence."

"When?"

"I don't remember. One night."

"Before Nicole died?"

"After."

"The same night there was a murder in the Puces de Clignancourt?"

Luke crossed the room from the windows, sat down. This was not the conversation he had expected, not at all. And knowing it was a waste of time, he answered automatically. "What murder?"

Chevejon's face softened slightly. "Come on, Luke. There are places you just can't go impersonating Danni Benami and wearing a gun without a lot of people noticing it. The Cygane is way the hell up there—maybe even top of the list."

Luke thought, then answered. "Your friend also tell you who tried to kill me up there?"

"Who *what*?" Chevejon stiffened, adopting yet a new tone.

"Tried to kill me. Shot me in the leg, in fact." He raised his trouser leg and showed Chevejon the scar.

Chevejon rose, examined the scar in silence, then returned to his chair and spoke in a voice that was nearly aggrieved.

"Why didn't you tell me about this?"

Luke shrugged, unapologetic, and there was a silence while Chevejon thought. Then he said: "So someone shot you. You had a gun? You shot back?"

"There was a gun in Danni's place. The same one used on Nicole.

It's an ambush trick: You hold a flashlight away from your body—when they shoot at the light, the flash of the shot gives you your target."

"Bullshit. Even I wouldn't fall for that."

"No." Luke continued earnestly. "You'd shoot two feet to the right, then two feet to the left before you shot at the light. But if I held it first to my chest, then stepped to the left, you wouldn't hit it till your third shot."

Chevejon paused, staring at Luke.

"You hit him?"

"Yes." Thinking: Five times.

"You see who it was?"

"No." Silence. "I knew who it was."

Another silence. Then Chevejon, in a flat voice: "And then?"

Luke got up, paced to the window and back, absently stroking his bearded cheek. He knew now that there was no point any longer in lying. "I was sick for a while after from the injury. I think it got infected. And then, when I was feeling better, a letter came for Nicole. From Danni. True, I had only your postmark. I didn't know when it had been mailed originally. But if he was in Europe, like you say, it still must have been written after I . . . after the night in the Puces."

A silence. Then Chevejon: "You're an asshole. You should have told me."

Luke started to reply, then stopped. "I'm sorry."

Chevejon nodded and spoke in something more like the tone Luke had become used to.

"So then you knew it wasn't Danni?"

"No, not at all. Anyone could have written the letter." Luke's voice rose at the end of the sentence.

"You have it? I can tell you."

"No, no. Of course not. I burned it."

The other looked disappointed, and in the silence that followed, Luke reflected that the longer he knew him, the more emotion Chevejon's face registered. Or was Luke just learning better to read the face? Now he spoke apologetically. "I didn't want the police to find it."

Chevejon nodded, his eyes focused inward. "That was, I guess, early July. The last letter he sent."

"What was the postmark?"

Chevejon hesitated, then looked up. "Athens." And, as if sharing Luke's thoughts, said: "I apologize also."

Luke spoke quickly. "Ah, there you have it, Athens. Home away from home for every intelligence agent in the world. Anything can fucking happen in Athens. Don't tell me if it was Danni's handwriting, I couldn't care less."

Chevejon spoke dryly. "Well then, I guess you just got it all worked out." He thought for a moment, his face abstracting again, then asked: "So what's up with Paris?"

"I want to know why none of Danni's letters arrived but the last one."

He expected remonstrance, but Chevejon nodded intelligently and spoke as if Luke's departure were a fait accompli. "I wouldn't be contacting the police if I were you."

"Why?"

"Because if they think it was Danni killed up there, they must have looked for you, and they found you gone. I doubt they'd leave you that . . . liberty again."

Luke's heart fell. "They identified him?"

"I don't know yet. But they questioned everyone at the Cygane that night, and the investigating officer was your old friend Jean-Baptiste."

"How do you know?"

Chevejon answered impatiently. "I told you. I spoke to a friend."

Luke turned his palms to the ceiling, and Chevejon smiled. "It wasn't Danni you killed."

"Then who? Who?" Even with this new element, Luke realized, the conversation was taking a well-worn path.

"I don't know, Luke."

"It's fucking absurd." Luke stood up. "Let's say, let's just say that it's out of the question that Danni comes back to Paris, finds me and Nicole there, *shoots* Nicole, then tries to kill me. You say it's impossible, fine, it's impossible. But just tell me what's wrong with this: an Israeli deserter, traveling right around the Arab world, and you say he can't have been involved in anything more illegal than tomb robbing. Someone kills his girlfriend, then tries to kill him—at least, they think they're trying to kill him—the first time he turns up in Paris after his father dies, his powerful, establishment father, who's the only thing been protecting him for years."

"Absolutely not."

"Chevejon, for all you know, you're part of his cover."

"Absolutely not."

Luke's voice rose. "You really know him that well? You really think *anyone* knows *anyone* that well?"

Chevejon nodded, once. "Absolutely."

11 SILENCE. Then Luke: "Then where does that leave us?"

"With someone else."

"Well." Luke sighed, reached over for one of Chevejon's Panters, lit it, and exhaled. "Well, then it seems that the only question I can maybe answer is what happened to Danni's letters."

The other nodded. "Good. What's your plan?"

"Go to Paris, speak to the concierge at the rue de Fleurus."

"Yeah. Only I'd start at the post office."

"Why?" Luke was surprised.

"See if there was a change of address put in there. In Nicole's name. That's the way I would have done it."

Luke pondered, smoking. "Then she'd never have gotten any mail at all."

"No. Whoever was doing it could have taken out the letters he wanted, then redelivered the others the next morning. Or that night. You said the concierge just put them under the door. They just had to leave them by her door. Or put them directly under the apartment door."

"Right." Luke looked at his feet, thinking, then after a time looked up again. "So you're not going to stop me?"

"From going to Paris?" Now Chevejon rose, strolled to the window, and looked out for a time. Was he taking stock of what he knew? Or of what he felt? He turned back and spoke slowly. "No. Only I could have someone do this for you. Then you wouldn't have to go." Luke shook his head once, determined, and Chevejon nodded. "No, I'm not going to stop you."

"Why?"

He answered in a patient, pleasant voice. "Because then you wouldn't find what you're looking for."

There was a long pause while Chevejon sipped at his drink. Then Luke spoke: "Surely it's occurred to you that *I* killed Nicole."

"But you didn't."

Addressing his back, insistently: "But it makes perfect sense that I would have."

"But you didn't. So it doesn't make sense of anything." Watching, Luke was surprised to see the other's handsome face suddenly tired. "I *know*, Luke. Proof is for the police, and look how far they get." He stood up now. "I'm older than you, and I know you. So let's not waste time. Hop up now. One of my goons"—he gave Luke a look of reproach—"will take you down to the train station and get some passport photos taken; there's a booth there. Let's hurry; someone'll have to take them down to Rome and be back tomorrow. You're making a lot of work."

Luke interrupted. "Why?"

"Well, what passport you planning to travel on? Your own? Let's get moving now; you can pack in the morning, and if the new passport's back from Rome, I'll put you on the afternoon flight to Paris."

He stopped suddenly, keeping Luke fixed in an absent gaze. Then he said, slowly, "I don't know if you're going to be able to find your brother, Luke. It's up to you. But I'll tell you something: You'd better do some serious thinking before you do. 'Cause if you don't, as sure as the sun's coming up tomorrow, if you find him, when Danni understands the crazy bullshit you have in your head, he will kill you."

CHAPTER SIXTEEN

1 | LUKE STOOD, the next afternoon, gazing around the rooms of his brother's domain, now stripped of his, Luke's, passage. Chevejon had treated his trip as a short time away, a quick flight to Paris and back. Now, poised to leave, his suitcase packed, Luke did not believe he was to return. *En passage.* The expression, as it entered his mind, implied a short passage between two points. But applied to himself, he thought, it defined a state of being, well known and possibly permanent.

Downstairs in his study Chevejon stood weighing a thick notebook he had brought from his office safe. Outside the window the late sun threw its long light over the garden, raising its shapes and hues in a clarity that seemed, for the briefest moment, to resonate in Chevejon's thoughts.

He was not sure what was in this notebook, but he knew that it had sent Danni traveling. And he was fairly sure it would show Luke where his brother had gone. What Luke would do with that knowledge—that question was what caused him to weigh the wisdom of giving him the notebook.

And then, with a long, low sigh, he admitted that the decision before him was not fact but faith and that it had already been made.

As they drove to the airport, the Florentine sky dull over them, talking calmly, Luke realized that Chevejon, too, was one of those people for whom crossing borders represented nothing. He sank, silent, deeper into his seat.

Chevejon parked illegally in front of the small terminal and walked

Luke inside. Luke checked his bag with a feeling of unreality; then they crossed to the espresso bar. At the counter, over coffee, Chevejon took a thick envelope out of his breast pocket and gave it to Luke. When he began to talk, his voice, in the noises of the airport, seemed to be coming from far away.

"Here's an old driver's license of Danni's; you'll need it at the post office. The name's Maurizio Tueta, of course. They give you any trouble, tell them you lost your current one and just brought this for ID; it's just the goddamn post office. But don't use it unless you have to; the police have to be on to the name. Also, there's my phone number in there; memorize it and get rid of it. If I'm not there, Paolo or Gianlucca'll man the phone. Finally the passport. It's Teabag, can you do the accent? Let's see, London SWI, a little ritzy."

"Sure." Switching his voice and forcing himself to smile: "I'm brilliant at accents."

"Good." Chevejon smiled. "Very good. Memorize the name and the stats on the plane. Don't use the passport you took from Danni. You got it?"

"Yes." The conversation, amid the neon lights of the little airport, the rising sound of an engine outdoors, began to seem unreal.

"Okay." Chevejon finished his coffee, twirling the cup in his fingers before the last sip, and stepped away from the counter. Standing slightly away from Luke, he reached into his overcoat and withdrew a package. Speaking slowly, he said: "Take good care of this, will you? I think it's valuable."

Luke took it. "What is it?"

"I'm not sure, Luke." Chevejon hesitated, then went on. "I can't read it myself; it's Yiddish. Danni left it for me to keep in the safe while he was away. I think maybe it'll help you."

Aware that something important had just happened, Luke put it in an inside pocket of his jacket.

"Now, one last thing." Luke looked up, and Chevejon was holding a key ring. "Just hold on to this, okay?"

"Okay." Luke answered readily. "What is it?"

"Safe-deposit key. You might not need it, but just hold on to it. Okay?"

Luke started to answer, but Chevejon had stepped toward him.

"I'll expect to hear from you tomorrow night at the latest." He leaned forward and kissed Luke on both cheeks, smiled, and began to walk away across the lobby.

"Chevejon." Luke spoke above the whine of a plane landing, and the other stopped and turned. "How do I know you aren't behind all this?"

He answered calmly, without hesitation, as if making a logical point in a long, abstract discussion. "I'm not going to try to convince you, Luke. You're just going to have to wait till you know." With a smile he began to turn, then stopped again and spoke. "You will know. Just wait. I promise you'll know. Hurry, your flight's boarding." And now, with a wave, he stood to watch as Luke walked away.

2 ANDREW KLAVAN, born December 16, 1958. Five feet ten, 165 pounds, black hair, black eyes, a thick black beard. Luke memorized the identity of the passport's onetime owner. Memorized Chevejon's number. Burned the scrap of paper in the ashtray. Leaned his forehead against the plastic window and felt the plane's steep ascent from the lights of Florence level off into the black of night, loneliness gripping him like a disease. He wondered how he, such a practiced traveler, had come to feel such an emotion. He wondered, and now Chevejon's house presented itself as somewhere he had felt intensely at home.

In time he sighed, sat back, lit a Panter. The interior lights came on; the flight leveled into its short cruise. He felt in the seat pocket in front of him for something to read and, with a small shock of surprise, remembered the package Chevejon had given him.

Now he paused for a pronounced time before bringing it out from his jacket pocket. He held it unopened for some time, then ripped open the paper and took out a vaguely familiar schoolboy's notebook, its thin cardboard cover worn nearly velvet with age. On the cover, the spaces for the owner's name and address were blank, save for the number 1. Lifting it to his nose, he breathed a dry, dusty smell. Finally he opened it, and a sheaf of photographs fell out, revealing, on the first page, a date: April 12, 1940, followed by a closely written page of Yiddish text. And a slow-dawning understanding came over Luke that he was holding in his hands the first—the missing—volume of his father's diary.

And it seemed suddenly the most natural thing in the world. Deep in his eye he saw the space for the two missing volumes in his father's desk in Jerusalem. And deep in his ear he heard Nicole talking about the package that had arrived, after his trip to Jerusalem, for Danni, from his father.

So this was the first volume. Where was the second?

Luke flipped through the ancient notebook gingerly, page after page of his father's minuscule Yiddish script. A wave passed over him at its familiarity, a strong and deliberate bolt through his midriff. Then, turning to the first page, he began to read.

3 THE HIGH-ALTITUDE cruise ended nearly immediately, as if the plane had followed the contours of a tall, flat mountain and were now following the northern face abruptly down. He passed customs on the British passport, carrying his bag in one hand and the open notebook in the other, found a taxi, and, in the car's interior light, read through the ride into Paris from Charles de Gaulle Airport.

He read over a late supper in a café on the way to the hotel Paolo had booked, hardly noticing the rhythm of slurred, low-voiced French around him, as if after voluble Italy, the whole country spoke in secrets.

And arriving at his hotel—the Lutetia, he later noted wryly—he left his case packed on the bed and lay next to it, reading far into the night. When he awoke, late the next morning, lying fully dressed on the bed with the book next to him, he began to read again.

As if he could see the big, muscled hand—smooth, hairless, and young—that had written these characters on this page. Feel the warmth of it on the page that he held between his own thin hands.

As if time were nothing, traveling even less.

As if in this book lay the key to the riddle of his existence. Mystic instructions, like all he had read in Danni's study, about what he had come to this city to do.

4 THE STORY the diary told was a familiar one. Benami had started it, clearly, just before his departure from Palestine to Vienna in 1940. The years between 1940 and 1942 were covered in a dozen pages: tiny, obviously coded notations, two or three sometimes covering a period of months, interspersed with descriptions of Viennese streets, as if his father had been developing a detailed mental map of the city.

It was at the end of the period in Vienna, 1942, that the entries grew longer, when Benami began his own escape from Vienna; perhaps, Luke thought, his father had known that if he were caught now, it would not matter what kind of incriminating evidence he carried on him, and his diary was now also a testament. Indulging real detail, it told of his preparations for departure, his crossing of borders, and, Luke read with growing shock, his arrival, in April 1942, in Paris.

And then Luke learned that his father had covered in reverse the distance that Luke had just traveled in a one-hour flight on an Alitalia twin-engine jet. It had taken his father, in the spring of 1942, months.

For he learned, to his great surprise, that in April 1942, forty-seven years before Luke arrived, Yosef Benami was here. In Paris. About to leave for Florence, in flight, on foot. Now, lying on his bed in the Lutetia, he read with growing amazement the story of that trip. Crossing the border at Ventimiglia, aided by a sympathetic guard; making his way south, Genoa, La Spezia—the stops on the train Luke traveled a half century later—Pisa, Firenze, all under the deepening Italian sun.

Benami, followed by Yerushalmi, spent some months in Florence, fed and supported by a convent that had served also as a station in the Italian Passage, waiting for the way south, which had been disrupted by the attention of Hoestermann's superiors, to open again. When it did, he continued, Rome, Naples, moving cautiously, as summer heightened, toward the sea.

Strangely the diary painted that summer of 1942 in terms of a long holiday. Benami, released from his secret life in Vienna, wrote more as a tourist than a refugee. Strong, healthy, wandering from town to town under the warmth of a sun he had never even imagined. Learning Italian with a linguist's rapid ease, finding food and support in nearly every village. Then he crossed to Brindisi and found passage to Athens on a Greek fishing boat.

In Athens, Benami and Yerushalmi were supplied with false Turkish papers by the police, for the Turks were welcoming all with any claim to citizenship, and in late July the two were passed from fisherman to fisherman, island-hopping toward Turkey. As such they were the final two to use the Italian Passage to Palestine.

And here the diary ended. Luke closed the book, early on a Paris dawn, and turned his face out to the drizzling street.

From the biographies Luke knew that Turkish refugee records indicated that the crossing to Turkey never took place, and an anonymous interview with a prominent intelligence agent held that in August 1942 Benami and Yerushalmi embarked from a Cycladic island in a small boat piloted by a fisherman in the employ of the Mosad le-Aliya Bet. From there, the biographies theorized, they would have followed the Turkish coast east, then cruised the waters north of Cyprus until they were picked up by an Aliya Bet refugee ship and landed on the coast of Tel Aviv.

Perhaps so. Neither was ever willing to say where they had gone from there.

The only person who could say, Luke knew, was the person in possession of volume two. Danni.

5 LUKE EMERGED from the Lutetia in the August morning. Walked north toward the Seine in the hot, sun-flooded streets, transformed by tourists. At the rue de Rivoli he bought the Vintage paperback of his father's biography, and carried it to the Café de la Paix, where under a terrace umbrella he opened the thick volume to the first section of pictures.

Here were his grandparents, an aged couple in archaic European clothes of black, his grandfather with a wide handlebar mustache. Here was his father as a child, a studio sitting with hand-painted color tints, a smiling, fat boy in a sailor suit. Then again, a uniformed schoolchild on a Vienna street, carrying a leather satchel. Then again, in the second section of photos, in the khaki of a soldier, a powerful young man with an open, smiling face under a British Army-issue beret.

His mother at twenty: dark, her short black hair framing an intent expression. There was a deep blankness in her eyes, her face and body bone-thin, still, from the camps.

The whole family on the steps of the Israel Museum: his mother now a beautiful, delicate woman in her late thirties, her face shaded under the brim of a wide hat. His brother, awkward at fifteen, his dark eyes deep in his long face. Himself, smiling incongruously at the camera, showing a missing tooth in a smooth face, full with baby fat. And his father, towering above them all, his thick white hair sweeping back from a sunburned forehead, a short nonfilter cigarette hanging in the corner of his smiling mouth.

But of his father, a child abandoned in Europe at war, he found nothing.

He returned to the Lutetia to sleep and dreamed for the first time since he had arrived at Chevejon's from the Hotel Excelsior. In his dream he walked on the Place Pigalle, where an aging Arab whore stopped him and, peering anxiously into his eyes, asked: *"Toi, où en es-tu avec ton père?"*

Upon his waking, the summer sun pulsing in the hotel room's blinds, his mind searched automatically for a satisfactory translation of the idiom. "How far have you come with your father? Where have you gotten to with your father? Where are you at with your father?"

He thought, Why had his dream confused the question, substituting *père* for the real question, *Où en es-tu avec ton frère?*

He rose, lit a Panter, stood naked at the window, the deserted air of the long vacation hovering above the street below.

He left the hotel, drank a marc de Champagne with his coffee, walked aimlessly for some time in the hot streets crowded with tourists, too nervous to eat. Finally, just before lunch, he presented himself at a window of the Saint-Germain post office. Inquired politely whether the forwarding order he had left for his and his wife's mail had expired. The clerk, presented with Maurizio Tueta's driver's license, disappeared into a back room and returned, a long quarter hour later, with a computer printout. She explained, in the pointless loquacity of French bureaucracy, that he had failed to renew the change of address in mid-July and that the mail would have then reverted to his former address. While she talked, Luke read the forwarding address on the printout. He thanked her, accepted a new forwarding form, and walked out, pocketing the driver's license, his heart beating lightly in his chest.

It was that simple.

6 *Quinze, rue de l'Abbé Grégoire, sixième étage, numéro douze.* Virtually around the corner from the rue de Fleurus.

In the still of lunchtime, Luke found himself in front of an impassive prewar building, its porte cochère open to what little breeze the hot afternoon held. The concierge was evidently lunching beyond an open window; sounds of plates and a smell of roast meat drifted faintly out to him. The street was empty. He ducked under the window, entered the courtyard, then passed through a set of glass doors to a small caged elevator around which curled dirty wooden stairs. These he mounted, walking quietly into the darkness of the stairwell, to the top floor of *chambres de bonne* each opening off a narrow hallway.

At the top he waited, catching his breath. The landing was deserted, the door to number 12 locked. Next to this door, he saw, was a communal bathroom. He hesitated for some minutes, as if unwilling to admit that he knew what he was about to do.

But he did know. It was as if every student girl in every *chambre de bonne* he'd ever visited had prepared him for this moment. It was as if someone had taken him by the arm and told him precisely what was to be done. He tried to remember when he had felt this way before. Then he remembered the night in the Puces de Clignancourt.

He took a deep breath and went into the bathroom, skirting the Turkish toilet and stained sink. At the window he opened the dirty glass sash and looked out. The bathroom, like the rooms themselves, stood out from the steeply sloping roof, above a wide tin rain gutter.

From somewhere below he heard a female voice singing an aria from *The Magic Flute.* His thoughts quick, disconnected, distant like those of another person. With a quick grunt he pulled himself up onto the window ledge, crouched down, and extended a foot gingerly down to the tin rain gutter. It held, and he stepped sideways out from the bathroom window, leaning against the roof, and made his way to the room next door along the gutter, the dizzying height unseen beneath his feet.

The window was not locked. He pushed it open and fell through, breaking his fall with the hard slap of his hands against the floor. He rose quickly, shut the window, then sat on the floor, breathing very hard.

A tiny room with a narrow bed, a desk, a tiny, closed closet. The floor was bare linoleum, stained, the bed unmade. On the desk was a hot plate, a dirty frying pan, and a plate containing the remnants of an egg and a baguette. As he watched, a round roach made its way over the plate. Luke rose, walked to the closet, and opened it to a couple of dark suits, neither any good cut, both new.

In the bottom of the closet there were a few dirty shirts, stained at the underarms and smelling of old sweat. A small suitcase contained underclothes, a pair of Adidas.

On the bed were crumpled sheets and a thin blanket. A tiny refrigerator on the floor next to the bed held a carton of milk, nearly solid with age, some more eggs, butter, and the rest of the baguette, rock hard. There was also a tin of instant coffee.

In the desk drawer: a pen, an empty French notebook, some yellow metro tickets. And ten envelopes addressed to Nicole Japrisot in what he now knew to be Peter Chevejon's hand.

 "WAS THERE anything inside?"

"Nothing. Just your forwarding envelopes. Empty."

A long silence traveled across the phone line.

Worry was a new emotion to Chevejon. He had felt it now for the two days since Luke had left for Paris. It did not abate when Luke finally called, late the night after his visit to the apartment in the rue de l'Abbé Grégoire, from a telephone booth, as instructed. Nor did it while he drove into Florence to call Luke back from a public phone in a café.

Chevejon knew that whatever happened now would be his fault, and he wondered with real remorse if he had done it all wrong.

A thin rain was falling over all Europe, that summer of 1989, as August approached its peak and a late summer storm flattened ripening fields from Aberdeen to Barcelona. A thin rain was falling on the deserted Piazza Santo Spirito outside the café where, at the end of a zinc counter next to the telephone, Chevejon stood over an empty glass, feeling dread. Dread of the distance between himself and Danni's brother in a telephone booth on the Boulevard Saint-Germain. Dread of the swelling summer, whose consequences he felt no longer able to control. He wished the boy would come home. He said: "Fuck. So what then?"

"So I left." Faint over the line, the voice sounded barely familiar. "Obviously there'd been no one there for a long time, and . . . at least at the time it seemed obvious to me . . . that whoever lived there— Danni, or whoever—was long dead."

"In the Puces, you mean."

"Uh-huh." Luke was perhaps waiting for a reaction, Chevejon thought, but he said nothing, and after a moment the other went on.

"Chevejon, there's something else. What you gave me, it's my father's diary. Did you know that?"

Pause. Then, hesitantly: "I didn't *know*. I guessed."

"Well, you guessed right. And you know what? It tells the route of the fucking Italian Passage—some of it at least. That's my point: He started in Vienna, then went to Paris, then to the south of France, and then he pretty much walked across Italy. And then I remembered what you said about the postmarks of Danni's letters. And then it seemed to me . . ."

He trailed off. And Chevejon, the phone cradled between his shoulder and ear, pronounced Luke's thought clearly into the phone, as if Luke were not going to have the nerve.

"It seems to you that Danni's letters were following the same path."

"Right." The voice at the other end of the line began to rise now in pitch. "See? Makes no sense. Where did Danni think he was going? Who would have wanted to take Nicole's mail?"

Chevejon made no answer for a moment. For the first question he wondered briefly if Luke had realized that wherever Danni had been going, for the past twelve months, for the past twelve years, Luke had already succeeded in following him as far south as Florence. But it was a point he did not pursue, for as his mind went forward to the second question, suddenly little electric flashes of realization were coming over him. He spoke without thinking. "Maybe it wasn't her mail they wanted. Maybe it was his. Maybe they wanted the check."

"Huh? You mean Danni's check? Why? You can't steal a personal check. Anyway, it never came by mail. It came by courier."

"Well then." Chevejon felt sweat break out on his forehead. "Well then, that explains a lot."

8   OUTSIDE, in the black, nearly deserted Boulevard Saint-Germain, the rain increased in pitch against the telephone booth. Somehow, Luke realized, the intimacy of the telephone conversation, the isolation of the booth in the falling rain, the passing cars on the avenue splashing by, bouncing their lights off the glistening black of the road, were causing him to trust Chevejon too much. And still he went on.

"Explains what?"

The other started to speak, then stopped, and Luke felt his unwillingness to answer—a not unfamiliar feeling, from Chevejon. "Let's see. Let's see what I can find out. What about the diary? How far does it take your father?"

"It ends when he leaves Italy. The rest must be in the second volume. That Danni was in Athens would seem to indicate the diary led him there next—if there's any reason to think that Danni would be following my father's escape in the first place. What, does he think there's some buried treasure my father was hiding on the way? While he's running from the fucking Nazi army?"

Pause. Then Luke: "The biography says they went through Greece. But that's unverified. The only person who would know is Yerushalmi."

"Who?"

"Yerushalmi, my dad's lawyer. But I'll be damned if anyone can get him to say anything."

There was a long silence while the line filled with static. Finally Chevejon's voice came back.

"So what next?"

"I don't know." For a moment Luke listened to the scratchy silence on the line.

Then Chevejon: "Tell me this, would anyone else have any idea where they embarked from?"

Thinking, Luke went on slowly.

"Maybe Dov would have an idea. If I could only fucking reach him."

"Dov?"

"Sayada. David Sayada. He was my father's prize graduate student. Then became his assistant. I've known him all my life. In fact, it was Dov who gave me Danni's address in the first place."

CHEVEJON'S HEART came to life again in his chest.

"I thought you said it was the lawyer."

"What lawyer?"

"What's his name. Yerushalmi. Who gave you the address."

"Did I?" It was a lie Luke had long since forgotten. "No, it was Dov. What's your point?"

Chevejon took an instant to master himself, then went on in what he hoped was an offhand voice. "This Dov character, would he have seen your father's diary?"

"Maybe. Only maybe." Luke paused. "I don't know how much he was actually in my father's confidence. My father didn't treat him what you'd call well. He was a bastard, you know. I mean, he entirely left Dov out of the will. Not for money, I mean. For his papers. His research. Everyone just assumed that all that was for Dov. Dov's been preparing himself for years to carry on my father's work. But there wasn't a word about it." Luke paused while deep in his memory, Hela's voice sounded: *"Dov was more of a son to your father than Danni ever was."* Then he went on, in a tone of reminiscence.

"I called Dov when I was in France, but his wife said he was in Warsaw on research. In fact, I called again, and there was no answer at all. I wonder if he's there now."

"Yeah, well, that's easy to check. Just call him." Chevejon paused, then went on, trying for a casual tone; his gift for dissimulation seemed, for the first time ever, to have deserted him, and with what he thought he had just learned, he suddenly wanted Luke close to him, under Paolo's and Gianlucca's protection. But there was something else to accomplish in Paris, something he had hoped to avoid, and in a moment he had decided that he must trust Luke to it. "Listen, Luke, I'll tell you what you have to do now."

"Go ahead."

After a long pause Chevejon went ahead hesitantly, as if not sure about what he was saying.

"Look, in Châtelet, on the fountain, there's a Crédit Lyonnais. I want you to go up there and to use Danni's driver's license to get into the safe-deposit room. Box five-nine-eight. Account number four-two-one-one-seven-zero-zero. Now listen carefully, Luke. You should find a pile of documents inside. They're Third Reich exit permits, and there should be about four hundred. Now there'll be a photocopy machine at the bank. Copy the first, say, seven; they should be numbers three-five-seven-six B through three-five-eight-three B. Make sure the numbers match exactly. Then put them all back, lock up, and call me from the hotel with the copies."

He stopped when Luke interrupted him. "Chevejon?"

"Yes?"

"What the fuck are you talking about, man?"

Chevejon sighed. "I know it sounds strange. Just do it, okay?"

Luke shrugged. "Whatever you say."

"And, Luke? When you leave the bank, I want you to make sure no one's watching you. You know how to do that? Find a big, empty space to walk across, and keep looking behind. And when you're sure, dead sure that no one's behind you, drop the safe-deposit key in the Seine."

 A GRAY PARIS MORNING, summer rain dripping from the sky, misting on the hot sidewalks. Stores closed for the long holiday, tourists having taken over the streets like a parody of

'68 radicals. At Châtelet, Luke, bleary-eyed from a nervous, sleepless night, presented himself at the Crédit Lyonnais and was escorted to the safe-deposit box.

Inside he found an Italian birth certificate for Maurizio Tueta, an expired Lebanese passport dating from 1973, and a few short stacks of Krugerrands. Underneath was a thick pile of yellowing papers, clearly what Chevejon was looking for. He lifted them out and had began untying the thick string that held them when a voice from the doorway distracted him.

"Monsieur Tueta?"

Luke's heart leaped into action as he looked up at a suited figure.

"*Je vous en prie,* monsieur, the manager asks if you will stop by his office on your way out?"

Now Luke breathed again. "*Désolé,* monsieur, would you tell the manager that I'm in a terrible hurry, and won't he call me?"

"He's been trying to call you for weeks: Your taxes are past due, and we haven't heard a word from Madame Japrisot."

"Ah, of course. We're under construction. We're at a hotel."

"Which hotel?" There was something strangely insistent in the man's manner, and with Danni's safe-deposit box open before him, Luke answered nervously, without thinking.

"The Lutetia. He can call this afternoon."

The man left, and too nervous to think now, Luke quickly matched the numbers Chevejon had given him without looking at what he was copying, replaced the originals, and hurried out of the bank.

11 IN THE EVENING, over the pay phone at the café in Florence to a phone booth in Paris, Chevejon asked immediately about the bank, and Luke realized he had almost completely forgotten about the photocopies. Letting the receiver hang in the booth, he hurriedly patted himself down and found them finally, folded in a back pocket of his jeans. As he unfolded them, Chevejon asked: "What did you do with the key?"

Luke answered absently: "I FedExed it to Thomas Hoving."

"Luke."

The papers were unfolded now. "I dumped it down a sewer last night. First I crossed Trocadéro at around eleven. No one was following me."

"Good." Chevejon sounded satisfied. "Now tell me what you got."

"Let's see, here . . ." Luke smoothed the papers down and looked at the first. "This would appear to be an *Auswanderungsvisum* . . . to travel from Vienna dated 1942. 'Permission is granted to the bearer, a Julius Neumann . . .' Wait a minute." He stopped now for a second. Then: "Jesus Christ, Chevejon, this is for my grandfather."

"Read me the number."

"Three-five-seven-six B."

A pause. Then Chevejon: "Fuck, Luke, I'm sorry. All that was for nothing."

But Luke wasn't listening. "This is crazy."

"I know, I don't understand. I thought I did. But I don't."

But Luke was still talking. "This is insane. This guy is nineteen years old. In 1942? My grandfather must have been sixty."

 12 THERE WAS a long pause on the line while a slow movement passed over Chevejon's scalp, like a passing breeze. Finally he managed to speak.

"What's the next one?"

Luke's faraway voice answered wonderingly. "Neumann again, Moses. Male, twenty-two years old."

Chevejon, at the café bar, counted on his fingers: Malke, Moses, five letters. "Next?"

"Neumann, Shalom, male, twenty. Neumann, Yudel, male, eighteen. Now Weissman, Samuel, male, seventeen."

Chevejon interrupted. "Skip the next. Then what is there?"

A pause. Then: "Weissman again, Moishe, male, twenty-five."

Chevejon felt a sinking in his stomach. Moishe, Rachel: six letters. Rachel had been five; to get twenty-five, add a two. Forgeries. Beyond his abstraction, he heard Luke speaking.

"Chevejon? These are fucking Nazi exit permits. What the fuck is going on here?"

But a deep nausea was rising in Chevejon, filling him so that he could do nothing but force himself to swallow. Finally he managed to talk.

"Luke." His voice was hoarse. "Now listen, burn those fucking things now. I want you to come back to Florence. Tonight."

"No." Chevejon was surprised by the rapidity of the boy's answer. "Explain right now, damn it, Chevejon, or you won't see me again."

A long silence. Then Chevejon spoke.

"Remember what you told me? All young men, no women? These are the exit permits your father used on the Italian Passage. The ones you've got there are the bearer's copies. They've all been altered. Forgeries. I've got the originals here; I'll tell you some other time how I got them. Luke. The first six were for your father's family."

Silence. While slowly the truth dawned on Luke.

"Ah, my God. Cannon fodder."

13

CHEVEJON SPOKE now with urgency.

"I don't want you to do anything. You understand me?"

He could practically see the boy shrug. "No."

"Look, when can you get back down to Florence? What about the night train to Marseilles?"

"Not a fucking chance in hell I'm taking that train again. There'll be flights tomorrow. Why?"

"It's time to move, fast. I'm going to Capri. I have a place there. I go every year this time. You come with me. Florence is a fucking zoo in August, and if Danni comes back, he'll look for me there first. So let's go? Tomorrow."

"What's the hurry?"

"No hurry. But you've done about all you can in Paris, and . . ." He paused, but finding no reasonable lie why Luke should come back, he admitted the truth. "Look, I don't like you there. There're two murder investigations you're connected with, for Christ's sake. And sooner or later the police are going to come looking for a Maurizio Tueta in Florence. You should be out of Paris. I should be out of Florence. We should both be on Capri."

There was a silence, during which he knew he had failed to convince the boy. Then the other spoke slowly. "Let me check out the plane times in the morning. Let me call you tomorrow."

"You have to call me in Capri. I'm going down tonight. You should be coming with me."

"I'm okay, I swear it. I'll call tomorrow."

"You have to call from a public phone."

"I know."

"Well . . ." Chevejon knew Luke would not call. He could, he reflected, have the boy kept under observation, and he would arrange that directly with Paolo, but so what? Was he prepared to have him abducted across an international border? Doing so with a human, he supposed, was not much harder than with an object. But it was a different order of crime, one with which he was unfamiliar. Reluctantly: "Okay then. Tomorrow, in Capri. You have a pen? Write down the number. And Luke, memorize it, then burn it. Okay?"

There was a click; then a long, low buzz sounded in Luke's ear. The night dark with rain seemed to close in around the glass booth.

CHAPTER SEVENTEEN

1 IN FLORENCE, against the dripping rain, Chevejon left the café, drawing the collar of his raincoat up as he stepped into the silent street. He crossed the piazza to his office, climbed the stairs slowly, the cigar still burning in a corner of his mouth, navigated the security system and, inside at last, sat heavily at his desk.

He was, he felt, halfway there.

Only he hadn't expected to dread arrival so.

From outside, streetlamps dimly lit the dark room, an occasional passing car throwing a slow-moving yellow light across the ceiling in a diffuse arc. Chevejon turned on the desk lamp, shrugged his coat onto the back of the chair, and, squatting, opened the safe and withdrew a small leather notebook. He crossed to the phone by the Le Corbusier couch, sat, and dialed a long series of numbers from the leather book. He waited, staring at nothing, and when he spoke, it was in a perfectly modulated, entirely expressionless tone.

"Armand. Chevejon. Sorry to wake you." Pause. Then: "No, Maurizio's still away. I'm calling about a—a different kind of job. . . . Okay." He waited for a few moments—perhaps the other was changing phones—then spoke again. "Ready? I need you to find a man in Jerusalem. Name's David Sayada. A professor at the Hebrew University. I believe he lives in General Benami's old house—you can find it? . . . Good. I need a description—an exact description. When he was last seen in Jerusalem. Exactly when. And no one is to know you're looking."

There was a silence, then: "No, I can't do that. I'll talk to Maurizio when he gets back. But I can give you five thousand for this. Dollars." Listened. "Okay. I'll be on Capri. Soon as possible, please."

He hung up and sat staring straight ahead, his left arm flat on the arm of the couch, his right in his lap, his face entirely devoid of expression. Then he leaned forward and dialed a short number from memory.

"Paolo. *Mi dispiace svegliarti così.* I'm sorry to wake you up like this. Your man in Paris, Philippe—can you get him to baby-sit Luke?" Listened. Then: "Good. Get him on it, will you? He's at the Lutetia. Look, don't touch—you know? And call us every time he wipes his ass. Paolo? Do it tonight."

2   DAWN FOUND Luke looking out the open window of his upper-story room in the Lutetia, drunk. Next to him on the floor were a bottle of brandy, a box of cigars, and his copy of *Sacrifice and Symbolism.* He had read all night.

All night in front of the open window, the street below deserted, its trees mad, leafed objects in shades of black, rustling in a wet wind that pushed smudged clouds across the sky. So bright was the light that it cast shadows, and Luke, drunk, for a moment could not understand if it was night or day. Then a cloud passed, and a harvest moon appeared low over the city, a pregnant, fat orb radiating a moist duotone clarity against the ink-black distance of clouded sky, and he knew it was still night.

Luke was not used, as was Chevejon, to thinking in terms of puzzles. Had he been, he would have seen that he had just acquired a decisive piece of his own and that, with the pieces previously acquired, he was in a position to fill in a large amount of detail.

A large amount of detail to add to the picture he had built from pieces of Danni's notations in his father's writing. To add to what he had learned from his discovery of the Caravaggio; from Benami's own introduction to the paperback edition of his book.

Without thinking in this metaphor, however, Luke was still conscious of having immeasurably expanded his understanding of where his brother was. And that understanding expressed itself to him as a sudden contempt for his father's high, confident intellectualism.

You had, he saw, to have the exit permits to arrive where Danni had arrived—and where he had brought Luke. You had to have proof. With the proof, everything changed.

Then, in his grand, his eloquent voice, this man who had sacrificed his father to historical necessity confronted the terrible image of Abraham, unwillingly pausing in the thrust of his knife before God, and failed to understand.

A misunderstanding that, with all Luke now knew, explained everything.

3 ON CAPRI Chevejon—who did think in terms of puzzles— was advancing in a different direction, but with equal results. Late the previous evening, while Luke was beginning his night of reading, he left his dinner table, where Natalie and six guests sat over coffee and fruit, when the phone rang and ran up the stairs to his bedroom. When he arrived, the answering machine had already picked up, and standing in the doorway of the dark room, he listened to the accented voice.

"Chevejon. Armand in Jerusalem. Your man is six-oh, or just about, black hair, black eyes, medium build. Hair curly, no distinctions particularly, looks Jewish. He's been out of the country since round about last April. Funny, because his son was born last month, and he never came back. You know, he's some kind of war hero? Military intelligence, an officer. No one seems to know where he is; you find out, I'd say stay the fuck away. Let me know if Maurizio's interested in my mosaics. Money by Geneva, please, as usual."

The machine clicked off, and Chevejon thoughtfully closed the bedroom door, removed the tape from the machine, which he smoothly dropped into a cassette recorder next to the phone, and started erasing the message. Then he picked up the phone again and dialed a Paris number from memory. He waited for a time, then spoke in French.

"Jean-Michele, Chevejon. *Comment va ton pote à* 'Fort Worth, Texas?'" He listened, then whistled. "*Épatant. Superbe.* I congratulate you. Now listen, I have a hard one for you. Ready? That man in the Puces de Clignancourt, can you find something out about him? I need a description and in particular to know this: What kind of papers was he carrying? *Eh, oui,* passport especially." He listened. Then: "I know it's expensive. Spend what you have to. You know I'm good for it."

Pause. "Jean-Michel, do this for me, will you?"

Pause. Then, coldly: "*Comme tu veux, eh?*"

He hung up and, standing, looked across the room and to the window, where the lights within reflected his presence back to himself. His annoyance faded quickly as, his heart alive, he realized how close he was. And for a moment he experienced a familiar satisfaction.

It was, he thought, as he erased the message with well-practiced movements, remarkably like reconstructing a set of fragments. Step after little step, a shape began to emerge and revealed insights about its past. And also remarkably like his work, luck had played a tremendous role; as so often, the key fragment had lain buried not in logical juxta-position but senselessly far from where he was digging, and he had unearthed it by the purest chance. Once put in place, however, it made sense of the whole piece.

Only unlike his work, as he began to understand, there was no plea-sure. In its place was a deep, and growing, dread.

4   AND AT THAT MOMENT LUKE, far across Europe, next to the window of his unlighted hotel room, felt dread also.

Watching that huge moon pouring its light into the black street, by now, from a practically cloudless sky. A not more than three-quarters full moon, and waxing toward an orange harvest moon, an end-of-summer moon.

In its impassive light falling over all Europe, Luke felt the vast distances around him, from Vienna to here, from here to Athens, all lying under that indifferent light.

They were, he realized, the measure of the borders of the Third Reich.

And here, in its epicenter, in this city where his father and brother had launched their journeys south, his journey was, after all this time, finally beginning, as he understood his father's sacrifice.

In war-torn Vienna perhaps it had not seemed such. Perhaps he had seen himself as declining to save rather than deciding to murder.

Murder was everywhere. It had the omnipresent efficiency of work in the rhythm of their lives; it was installed in statu quo. Brown-shirted boys passing on patrol; the direct step of ubiquitous Wehrmacht soldiers; the incessant passage of matériel toward the raging front in the east.

East—their east was so different from Benami's, the direction from which rolled the empty cattle cars into West Bahnhof, witnessed not only in Vienna but in Paris, London, Moscow, and Washington. Witnessed, and ignored.

And Luke's father, twenty-three, come from Palestine to Vienna, this city that he had hated even when it had been his home.

Somehow he had procured the power over four hundred lives, lives given up by the world entire.

Only they were for the wrong lives.

These beaten people—where was the place for them in Palestine, that arid, hard, struggling country? The Yishuv had been open to German Jewry in the Haavara agreement, in 1933, and true, not all the country was kibbutznikim. A mercantile, cosmopolitan Jewish life had never left Jerusalem. But the German Jews of the Haavara had had money to bring, to invest in new lives. Now in Vienna there was no money left; the taxes, the confiscations had taken it all, and there was no one in Palestine who could possibly take in these penniless, half-starved city folk but the kibbutzim.

Could these people learn to live in Palestine? A few years ago, perhaps: A few years ago they were such a different community of dignified, proud people, leading lives of assumed equality in prewar Vienna. But now the remnants of that community were half ghosts, malnourished, unrecognizable as the people who had once been seamlessly part of this city, of this continent. And if some of the few he recognized in his rare visits to the ghetto were dignified, gentle, and very occasionally heroic, most were bitter, selfish, terrified; some were dishonest, some had gone mad. All were unhealthy, and that they were alive at all attested to the fact that the entirety of the lower classes had already been deported.

The privileged remnants now occupying the informal ghetto had not yet been to the camps, and still months would be needed, and money, just to nurse them back to a semblance of humanity. Many would leave, and many more would be dead weight in a new country that was hoarding its every resource for its own coming war.

No one should ever have to make such a choice. No one should ever have to be judged for the forgery that Benami now committed. In a mad world Luke's father made a mad choice. It was the only choice.

Now Luke flipped forward, as if through the family photos he had found in his father's biography, and saw that it was only years later, in the relative peace of Palestine, that anyone had even been interested in the fate of such Jews. Only years later, as Benami began, in the expanding Israeli administration, to reap the fruits of his service to the country, during the war and since, and to grow in the public eye, had anyone even thought to write about what he had done in Vienna.

And only many years later, with war reparations flowing from Bonn to Jerusalem, with the completion of the farcical denazification that cold war politics had dictated, and all but the most prominent SS officers welcomed from Washington to Paris, had Benami come to understand how few were those who could any longer grasp the decision he had been forced to make. When Kastner was tried, and the strong sense of self-recrimination within Israel bemoaned how little this community—not yet a country—had done during the war for the Jews it claimed to represent, Benami was shocked. But he was not entirely surprised—to understand how few were those who understood. Very few understood how little could be done, on what Ka-Tzetnik called "the other planet." How few particularly, he saw with a politician's instinct, were those among the people currently in power.

Only those who had been there on that other planet could understand that if it was a decision of sacrifice, nothing could be more anodyne in this quotidian theater of death. Even the Austrian middle and lower classes, the people providing the Wehrmacht with cannon fodder, knew more of bereavement, of suffering, than the world across the ocean. Even they knew more of what it was to be helpless.

It was ironic to Luke, insofar as he was able to isolate its irony. Those others, those who would not understand the choice that Benami had to make, had the distinction of being first-generation Israelis. Even Ben-Gurion, Moshe Dayan, Shimon Peres, Mapai loyalists like himself, never had been on that other planet, as accident caused him to be.

.   .   .

As for the rest of the world, a world that year after year knew General Yosef Benami better and better, they could never understand the choice he had had to make—whom to sacrifice and on whom to bestow the chance of survival—and could never know of it. Benami had, he knew, to make sure of that.

The rest of the world. That included his own children.

Although for them, the sacrifice had never ended.

Danni had understood that. Now Luke understood, too.

Although in a way, Luke thought, he had always understood.

He crouched now in front of the window and shut his eyes tight, as if by pure physical will he could avoid what was coming. But the logical progression of his mind overflowed the dike of his fear like a rising tide, and vividly Luke heard his mother's voice: *"Your son is gone. Your son is gone. Where is the fucking symbolism?"*

Only this time—had he drunk too much?—it seemed to him that "Your son is gone" was a mistranslation. Or a misremembrance. This time it seemed to him that she had said, in the hysteria of learning that Danni was missing, was "You've killed your son."

First it was Benami's father, and then, one by one, his wife and his sons. All sacrificed, not, as Benami saw in Caravaggio's Isaac, to a God sending angels, but worse: to an idea, to a country, a country of soldiers.

Luke crouched lower, his head between his arms, his eyes tightly shut, as realization—realization that came suddenly, like an answer from another person—dawned, dawned as if somebody had taken him by the arm and were whispering in his ear: Danni, too, had always understood.

Even as a child, before he had learned anything about his father, Danni understood the weight of his father's hand on his neck. Even as a child, Danni had always been more comfortable with the victim than with the powerful. Benami had liked to say that Danni was happier with the help than with the masters, so little time did he spend in the New City and so well did he know the Old. Why not? He had grown up on the streets of the Old City, talking Arabic to shopkeepers, playing with Arab children on his explorations of the Wall.

These elegant, often educated people whose lives had been rendered passive by the many, many governments around them, from Jerusalem to Damascus, Riyadh to Moscow and Washington. They taught him everything.

Because the people to whom Danni was supposed to belong had also, until 1948, been forgotten from Moscow to Washington. And now they, too, had turned executioner. And they let fall over the Palestinian Arabs whom Danni knew so well exactly the same pressure that Benami had always exerted over his son. These people around him, these Arabs, they did not feel like the enemy. They felt like himself.

There was a brief hope when his mother tried to keep him from the army. His father prevailed.

It was as if his entire life he had gone with his father's hand on the back of his neck, pinching, pushing. What was right, what was wrong? All he felt were friends on one side, fellow victims; the pinching, the pushing on the other.

Then it was the war, and his call-up code came crackling over the radio in his father's house. From on the stairs his little brother was watching. An argument was raging, and Danni realized he was being sent to the front. He watched his parents with strange detachment. He was not afraid of what was going to be done to him. He was afraid of what they were going to make him do.

What they made him do, he did. Perhaps, Luke thought, he, too, had been shocked by how easy it was to do. Danni did it, and then Danni ran. And within weeks, as his first ship drew out of Beirut into the shimmering blue of the Mediterranean sea, he felt, for the first time in his life, freedom.

As his father once, a child of sixteen, had felt freedom when he ran away to Palestine.

As Luke was beginning to feel now.

He had not known that freedom would feel this harsh.

5 LUKE RETURNED to himself, a small degree or two. He was crouching by the window, staring unseeing at a massive moon stepping across the night. And his heart in his chest

seemed to ache, liquid and heavy, like a balloon filled with blood, for his brother.

Ten years passed for Danni, the ten years of which Nicole had told him and that Luke suddenly, vividly understood. Ten years in which Danni came to dominate a risky, difficult world—perhaps a world less complex than his father's Vienna, but one that was certainly as dangerous. Ten years of Nicole, centering his life, providing a reason for it. And ten years of his mind alive, growing.

By the end the terms of his father's ideology were no longer so frightening to Danni. Perhaps he could see them now as inevitable to his age, his time in history, what his father had had to survive. It didn't matter: After ten years of living, of reading, of growing, and, above all, ten years of Nicole, Danni was no longer afraid. And with this reading, this growing, came the most fundamental of an adult's curiosities, the urge to go back.

He was lucky to reach that point before his father died. And yet, returning to Israel fifteen years older than when he ran away, Danni found his father offering nothing more than what he had offered those years before. Only now the more closely he examined the product, the more it struck him as suspect. Very much as, with what he had learned those many years past, he recognized the splendid Derwatt hanging in his father's living room as a fake.

Perhaps it was not an accident, the career he had chosen; perhaps the eye that so efficiently determined an object's veracity or falseness had first, as a child in Jerusalem, been honed on his father.

And Luke saw that Danni, with his fine eye, had identified the fault lines of his father's story, and with the machinery at his disposal—whether it was his own skill at spotting a fake or the wide contacts in the sub rosa world that extended across Europe—he searched to find what they so imperfectly hid. How had he come upon the doctored exit permits he had obtained and locked in the Crédit Lyonnais safe-deposit vault? It did not matter. Perhaps he had stolen them from his father; perhaps he had acquired them another way. In any case they were only half the proof.

The other half could be provided in three ways, and Luke enumerated them now as if he could hear Danni's thoughts: He needed the original exit permits; or failing that, a provincial record; or failing that, a witness. Evidently Danni had not found the original permits; evidently he had turned his attention to the other two, and to pursue them, he had to go traveling. Good, he was familiar with traveling, with hunting through space for hidden objects. And this was an easier trip than most, for his father's diary provided the route.

Perhaps he hoped to find the person who had done the forgery; perhaps he hoped to find proof abandoned with the German retreat, or Greek police records, or even witnesses on the island of embarkation.

Proof that would justify the other half of what he already knew.

That proof, in the end, had been left, in that mad underworld, for Chevejon to acquire instead. Where had he found it? Luke shook his head; he would never figure that out. And it didn't matter.

6 FOR EVEN WITHOUT that proof Danni already knew. Luke was sure of that, and with a little flash of insight, he understood that in all that he had realized, Chevejon had been his guide: Chevejon had brought him to his brother, precisely and definitely and in the only sense that mattered. For Chevejon had directed his attention to the past and brought him to Danni's library, and there the books on his shelves, underlined, notated, told the whole story. Not just the complete Benami, and the Gilbert and Dawidowicz and the whole bibliography of the Holocaust, but also the seditious works. Arendt, critically examining the Eichmann trial; Ka-Tzetnik, transcending the Jewish victimization for the human guilt; Segev, indicting Israeli righteousness with his skeptical insight into Benami's own generation of leaders. The *Israel Annals of Psychiatry* and then the books of Judi Benami. And then Freud.

All leading to the Caravaggio.

The Caravaggio had shown Danni—and Danni had shown Luke— everything. It was there, Luke now saw, so long after first being exposed to it, that Danni had understood—first intuitively, immediately, before the enormity of the canvas; then deliberately, and coldly, and surely, working with the massive library of references that had been at his father's disposal—the lie on which his father had built his life.

No one could ever judge Benami for the decision he had made in

Vienna in the winter of 1942—Luke knew that immediately. Could anyone judge him for the mistake he made, months later, in the Florence spring, before Caravaggio's *Sacrificio di Isaaco* hanging in the Uffizi?

His sons could. For Benami had been wrong. None of his deeply felt, world-celebrated intellectual work, the work of his life, had been in the Caravaggio he saw, in Florence, escaping the Nazis after sacrificing his father. Where Benami had seen symbolism about the Jews, Caravaggio had painted moving flesh, immediately rendered in a timeless, inexistent countryside. Where Benami had seen duty, Caravaggio had painted passion, a father intent on murdering his son. The Caravaggio was not about sacrifice; it was about murder, and the meaning of the murder he had just committed—not the actual meaning, so conveniently occulted in his public career, but the psychic meaning so silenced by the weight of his work—he had spent his life trying to hide.

It was only possible to hide from if you saw God in the picture. But Caravaggio had painted only three men in the picture, and an animal, and God simply was not there.

Without God, in Abraham's intent determination, there was not obedience, but passion. Without God, Abraham was not fated to sacrifice his son, but determined to. Without God, what the angel brought was not liberation, but imposition.

Now from deep in his memory came the sight of one of Danni's scrawled notes in his father's book: "Who is testing whom?" And he understood now what Caravaggio had understood, what Danni had understood, and what his father, fanatically, had spent his life trying not to know. God was not testing Abraham, but Abraham God. No one was being sacrificed, and no one was going to. God was not in Caravaggio's *Sacrifice of Isaac;* the angel was an idealized Renaissance device, the painter's nod to his patrons.

He could not have been there. For God had not been in Vienna with Benami or with Danni in the Golan—nor had he in West Beirut with Luke or in the Puces de Clignancourt. None of the three had felt obedience, and all, Luke knew, had felt passion.

God had ordered none of them to kill, for God did not believe in them anymore.

.   .   .

Two last facts came to Luke in his clarity, just as dawn broke, just before he passed out.

Chevejon, Luke saw, was right: Danni did not know his father was dead.

He couldn't know. Not only because the fact of his father's death demanded too much of Danni for him to stay away. Demanded that he see to the estate, fantastic objects, the responsibility of whose wardship Danni would have felt deeply. He couldn't know because knowing rendered his trip pointless.

Because the father Danni was searching for was gone. Gone the man who had oppressed him, tormented him, gone. Never to hate, never to hurt. And never to participate in the real drama, the psychic drama that Caravaggio painted, where God provides the ram and, in a cosmic, quantum flash of psychic growth, hate comes to master its own terms.

Now, as he began to pass out in the blind, drunken reality of the dawn, Luke felt Danni's loss with an intensity impossible to assume, loss unimaginable, for the father he had so very nearly found.

And as he tumbled, facefirst into a pane of the long window, the window gashing his cheek as it shattered, then slamming shut so that he struck its woodwork as he fell, Luke knew how to find his brother.

7 IN THE MORNING Chevejon woke seriously worried. Days had passed with no word from Luke. He knew where he was—Paolo's friends kept him thoroughly in sight—but he could no longer imagine what Luke was doing, alone in deserted Paris at the height of the tourist season. On the deck of his house above the sea, lounging in shorts and an open shirt, he asked himself once again whether he had done the right thing.

He worried that he had relied too much on the boy's intelligence, on his capacity for growth. Most people, Chevejon knew, were uninterested in—incapable of—growth.

He considered going up to Paris—no matter the risk—to find out firsthand what was going on. And had all but decided to do so when he thought he would try to call.

He passed through a wide set of sliding doors into the shaded interior of the house, stopped to pick up a cigar and a lighter, then sat by the telephone, and, ignoring the danger of what he was doing, called *renseignements* in Paris and dialed the Lutetia.

Luke answered, a sleepy *"Oui?"* Responding, Chevejon glanced at his watch; it was nearly eleven. He asked if Luke wanted to order coffee and call back. But Luke, clearing his throat, answered no. Chevejon heard him lighting a match, drawing in smoke, then, when he judged Luke's cigar was lit, spoke.

"So what's up, *habibi*?"

A pause. Then, in a very gravelly voice: "I'm not sure, Chevejon. I'm not sure. How did you find me?"

"I can find you, anyone can find you. I hope you know what you're doing."

A pause. "I'm not sure I can say that I do."

Surprised. At the rawness of the voice, at its honesty. To gain time, he said: "You call Israel yet?"

"No." And as if in excuse: "I'm afraid I've been drunk quite a bit."

"Bastard. And I'm waiting for you to call." He heard Luke not laugh but smile.

"I'll bet you are. Who you waiting with? How old is she?"

Chevejon's laugh, quieter. Then Luke: "Thank you, Chevejon. For everything."

Chevejon stood up, the phone to his ear, and turned toward the doors. Outside, over the deck, the brilliant blue sea stretched away under a cloudless sky. He said, softly: "You know where you're going?"

Luke answered slowly. "Not yet. Not yet, Peter. Almost."

Surprised by the sound of his first name. Wondering: What has the boy understood? Thinking: There's nothing else I can do. Saying, before Luke had a chance to say any more: "You always know where to find me, Luke. For anything. Anytime."

And then it was over. And there was nothing left to do but hope. For Luke, for Danni, and for himself.

CHAPTER EIGHTEEN

1 LUKE HUNG UP, and for a moment tears welled in his eyes. He shook them off, then stood up from the bed where he had been sitting to talk with Chevejon. Something was wrong; the bed was perfectly made. For a moment he paused, confused. A horn sounded through the open window, and he looked over. There an armchair was lying, turned over on the floor, next to a three-quarters-empty brandy bottle, a spilled ashtray, a book. A pane in the high window was smashed, and there was the stain of dried blood on the carpet. His head began to spin; he reached up with a hand and felt a gash scabbing high on his left cheek. He crouched quickly and vomited.

After a time he rose and stepped backward from the splash of thin liquid and, spitting, stumbled to the bathroom. In the mirror he saw his face, bloodless, a deep cut on his cheekbone. He stripped and climbed into the shower, slowly realizing how drunk he had been—drunk enough to pass out and topple the chair over.

It was pure luck, he thought, that he had fallen backward into the room rather than forward out the window.

And it was pure luck that he remembered what he had learned during the night.

When he climbed out of the shower, he felt a wrench in his knee and limped back into the room; evidently he had hurt his knee, too, in the fall.

Now he checked his pockets and found everything there: the passport Chevejon had given him, the thick wad of bills he carried in his wallet. He rested for a while. Hungover as he was, each step of his thought the night before was crystal clear, and his decision was certain.

He was in plenty of time. He had to pack. He had to burn the photocopies from the bank. Then he had to call Yerushalmi, and then he had to buy a ticket to Athens. He had no doubt now that Yerushalmi would tell him where to go. Luke could make him.

But something was wrong again, and for a long moment, in his hangover, he stood in the center of the room trying to understand what. Finally he crossed to the window and, with a flash of adrenaline through his body, understood: Six blue-and-white police cars were drawing up in the street, sirens wailing. And someone was pounding, pounding at his door.

2 ON CAPRI, Chevejon, naked, was reading in his living room, early light spilling through the wide doors to the ocean. The phone rang; he picked it up quickly and, after answering in Italian, continued in French.

"*Oui. Oui. Ainsi, celui qu'on a trouvé*—the man they found, was an Israeli? What name?" He listened for a time, then nodded. "Who the fuck is Daniel Benami?" A pause, then: "If the driver's license is French, how do they know he's an Israeli?" Pause. "*Ah oui,* I guess I have heard of Benami, the old guy." Silence. Then: "Yes, I believe I know who it is. Guess what: The police got it wrong. No"—laughs— "no cash value, I'm afraid. *Merci à toi,* Jean-Michel. We owe you a lot for this."

Smiling, he hung up. Then his smile slowly faded on his handsome face, suddenly so tired. The French police had found a corpse in the Puces de Clignancourt bearing Maurizio Tueta's driver's license. From Luke they had known who Tueta really was and had identified the corpse as Danni.

Imaginative, Chevejon thought, but wrong. Now he knew everything. Now he knew the whole stupid, bumbling tragedy.

He hoped Luke had done as well.

3 FOR LONG SECONDS Luke froze. Then he stepped to the little hotel-room desk, crumpled the photocopies, and put a match to them while the pounding went on. Only when they were well ablaze did he step, resigned, to the door.

But, rather than the police, a man was there, panting, sweating. He was tall, with a black mustache and black eyes in a dark face. Without a word he took Luke by the wrist and pulled him out of the room, then down the hallway away from the elevators toward a red light marking the fire exit. Only when they were in the stairwell, running now downstairs, did he speak.

"*Sh'suis* Philippe, I work for Paolo Cavalari. He told me to keep you out of trouble. *Salope,* I guess I fucked this one up."

His voice resonated above their footsteps, running down the stairs two at a time. Luke had nearly to shout to make himself heard.

"You been watching me?"

"Every step, *mon petit lapin.*"

The stairs ended, Philippe pushed through a pair of metal swinging doors, and they were in a vast stainless steel kitchen. Holding Luke's wrist again, Philippe ran the length of it past the startled staff, through a laundry room, and then to a doorway beyond which Luke could see the sun reflecting from the surface of orange plastic Dumpsters. A maid waited there; when she saw them, she stepped out into the street, then back, holding one hand up: Stop.

Panting, Luke looked up at his rescuer. "How'd you manage all this?"

"Romany house staff. I had the room next to you. I hear those cops, I think, Jesus. Thank the Lord Paolo told me to be ready for something like this. God, you can't get paid enough for this. How'd you let them get you?"

Luke thought now. "I don't know. No one knows where I am. I sure as hell didn't tell . . . oh, God." He looked up again, his face stricken with remorse. "The bank manager. Oh, God, I screwed up."

But now the maid was gesturing to them, and Philippe began pushing him toward the door.

"What's done is done. Keep going."

They edged out the door, crouching behind the foul-smelling Dumpsters. Philippe stepped into the street, paused for a moment, reached into his back pocket, then stepped out of sight. Luke heard a shout, and Philippe came back, gesturing for him to follow. He stepped onto the sidewalk, past the body of a uniformed policeman, facedown, as a Renault van drew up and stopped, the driver reaching back to swing open the passenger door. Philippe beside him, the van drew away slowly, turned a corner, then another, and finally accelerated down the Boulevard Raspail.

Now Philippe spoke, first in a language Luke didn't recognize to the driver, then in French to Luke. "Okay?"

Luke nodded. *"Merci à toi."*

"Pas de quoi. Paolo said to put you on a train to Rome and to tell you to change there for Capri. That good for you?"

Luke thought. He had left everything he owned, save his wallet and passports, in the Lutetia. His credit cards couldn't possibly be used now, and he realized with some shock that if the police had found him at the Lutetia, then they could trace Chevejon's call. He could not go to his bank; he could not call Chevejon, and he could not go to Capri. But he had some cash. He said: "You got any money you can give me?"

"Umm . . ." The other reached into his pocket and counted. "I got about forty thousand, but I haven't paid the hotel yet. Paolo good for this?"

Luke nodded. "Make it the airport then."

4 THE MORNING FLIGHT got Luke to Rome by lunchtime. He had slept, but the hangover was thick in his blood. At the airport he changed Philippe's francs, bought a map, had a coffee and a brandy, then found a taxi and asked for a hotel. The driver took him to the Campo dei Fiori. Here, before the stores closed, he found a drugstore, bought a razor and some shaving cream. Along the way to the hotel, he passed a post office and made a mental note of where it was.

He woke that afternoon to the peal of bells in the silent city, high above a narrow street. He showered, dressed in his dirty clothes, and stuck the razor and tube of shaving cream into a pocket. Then, after consulting the window and finding the street again alive, he descended to the lobby and checked out of the hotel.

In a café, nearly weak with hunger, he ate something. Then he retraced his steps to the post office. A clerk directed him to a booth; he sat, consulted the list of dialing codes posted there, and dialed. There was a short delay, some rings, and then a female voice: *"Ken?"* He spoke, and the Hebrew words, once so pregnant to him, filled his ears without feeling. He waited again, breathing deeply, looking at nothing. When Yerushalmi answered, he spoke, without thinking.

"Avi," Luke said, "it's Julius."

"Julie, *baruch ha shem*, where are you? I've been worried to death about you, absolutely to death."

Luke tried to sound unconcerned. "Why would you be worried about me?"

"Why? I've had calls from the French police, from the American police. You disappear off the face of the earth, I haven't heard from you but for a phone call months ago, and you ask why I'm worried? Do you know about your brother?"

"What about him?"

"Julie, for God's sake, the French police say he was murdered in Paris. Did you know that?"

Luke hesitated. Then: "Are they sure it's him?"

"They seem sure. They found ID on him."

"What name?"

"His name. No, a pseudonym." The old man was nearly shouting, but Luke interrupted.

"What nationality?"

"French. For God's sake, Julie, where are you? What are you doing? Is Dov Sayada with you?"

"Dov?" Luke's voice rose in surprise. "Why should Dov be with me?"

"I can't explain that now. Hela's out of her mind. He went to Warsaw in April; no one's seen him since."

"Surely the . . . government knows something?"

There was a pause; then the old man went on in a quieter tone. "Hela thinks he's with you. Where are you, Julie? What's going on?"

Luke, too, let his pitch drop. "Avi, I have a lot to tell you. But first you have to tell me something."

"Tell you what?"

"You have to promise to tell me."

"I don't make promises."

"Where did you leave for Palestine from? With my father."

A silence. As if the old man were not even surprised by the question. "In '42? From Greece."

"No, that's not good enough. Which island?"

Now Yerushalmi was silent for a long time. "Julie? Don't ask me that. I can't answer." For a moment the scratchy voice filled with something genuine. Now Luke paused, took a breath, exhaled it halfway, and then spoke.

"Avi, I have the exit permits. The first one's for my grandfather. But the guy in it is nineteen years old. And either you tell me what island you left from, or I take it all to the closest *New York Times* bureau this fucking second."

"Jules? I'm warning you, Julie, don't go down that road. You won't like what you find."

"I found it already, Avi."

A long silence. Then: "You give me no choice. But you have to promise me something. You have to promise to come back here. Straight back. On the next flight. From wherever you are."

Luke answered immediately. "I promise."

"Swear on your father's name. No, on your mother's."

"I swear on my mother's name."

A silence. Then, in a voice that sounded very old: "Astipálaia. In the Cyclades."

Luke let out a long, long sigh.

And hung up the phone.

And walked into the street and hailed a cab. For the train station.

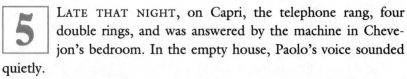

LATE THAT NIGHT, on Capri, the telephone rang, four double rings, and was answered by the machine in Chevejon's bedroom. In the empty house, Paolo's voice sounded quietly.

"Chevejon. The kid is gone. Philippe calls this morning, says the police found him at the Lutetia—don't worry, he got the kid out. Says he put Luke on a plane for Rome. I shoot down there, pick him up at the airport, follow him in a taxi to the Campo. He goes to a hotel, takes a nap, goes to the post office, then to the train station again. Buys a ticket, for Christ's sake, to Ancona. Ancona! I saw him go, then came up to Florence to close up the house and get my car. If I don't hear from you tomorrow, I'll go to Ancona. So call me. Ciao."

There was a click, a pause, and the machine cycled around to wait for the next call.

6 | IN THE VERY EARLY MORNING Chevejon returned to his house, a woman in an evening gown on his arm. Inside the door they embraced slowly, his hands traveling lightly from her neck, over her exposed back and down. Finally the two went upstairs, and he showed her to the bathroom.

While she was in the bathroom, he checked on Natalie, sleeping soundlessly in a guest bedroom. In his bedroom the answering machine was blinking steadily. He closed the door and listened to the message from Paolo. Ancona. His finger was on the button to erase the message when a beep announced that there was a second message waiting; he paused as Luke's voice sounded in the answering machine's speaker. Luke's voice? Slowly, wonderingly, Chevejon absorbed the fact that only one voice on earth called him Pete; that this gravelly, used voice, extraordinarily familiar, and stretched now with an anxiety that grabbed him in the pit of the stomach as soon as he heard it, was not Luke's at all.

"Hey, Pete man, sorry to break security but I need some help pretty bad. First thing is, can you send someone to Paris to check on Nicole? Haven't gotten a letter in months; I called the rue de Fleurus; no one's ever there. You find her, check with her that she's coming down here, and if she's not planning on it, see if you can convince her to, will you? I'm in Greece, an island called Astipálaia. I'd go to Paris myself but I'm afraid to budge in case Nicole's en route, and I can't miss her.

"Second, I have a man coming to see you from here, Petros Martinides—we owe him fifteen K in American dollars. He's got some documents and some photocopies—I'll explain later—but they're important: They prove a forgery I've been trying to figure out, and if they get out it's front-page news. Could you get them all in a safe-deposit box, somewhere new, under a clean name? Better make copies, too, and put them in another box under another identity. Okay? And Pete? You can't be too careful on this.

"God, I can't wait to get out of here. My liver's the size of a fucking cow's, no kidding—there's one plane and two boats a week to this hole, and in between waiting for them there's nothing to do but drink. Soon as Nicole comes I'm out of here. If it's soon enough, we'll come straight to Capri. Then I'll tell you a crazy story. See you, man."

The machine clicked, and Chevejon's shock faded. Moving automatically, he erased the messages. Luke to Ancona. Danni in Greece. Dimly he registered that Danni must be getting nervous indeed to break security twice: once to call Nicole, then a second time to call Capri directly. Then, his shock having passed, Chevejon turned suddenly and ran downstairs to the living room. Ancona. After a short, frantic search, he found a *Blue Guide to Northern Italy* on the bookshelf. Hurriedly he leafed through the index, turned to a page, and read intently for a moment. Then he shut the book and stood stockstill, savoring the sentence he had just read: "Ferries to Yugoslavia (Zadar, Polo, Split, Dubrovnik), Greece (Piraeus), and Turkey."

Perhaps it was irrational, but a long, luxurious feeling of relief, of deep physical comfort, passed over him. Perhaps he was drunk; his eyes filled, suddenly, with tears. He picked up the phone and made a call, speaking very briefly.

"Paolo. *Va bene.* You did fine. Find out what ferry he takes, and make sure to get its arrival time in Piraeus. Then you can let him go."

Then he climbed up the stairs to meet the woman coming down the hall.

7 DAYBREAK. The morning hot, a thick fog hanging over the port-side town in the wake of the receding storm. Luke woke in his shabby single room in the Grand Hotel Palace. Before breakfast he walked to the port, gray with dirty white surf throwing spume up over the concrete quai. Moored Yugoslavian container ships, an oil tanker, Greek ferries sitting in berth. Fleets of fishing boats, idle, lashed together in the rising sea.

No ferries were sailing. Luke ate at a fishermen's restaurant, wandered through the wet town, bought three tin boxes of Panters, all he could afford, then went back to the hotel. Someone had left a *Blue Guide to Scotland* in a drawer, an English edition, and he read the historical introduction without attention, missing sentences, repeating paragraphs.

In the evening, skipping supper, he flipped on the TV, watched a dubbed version of an American show, then a game show whose rules he could not follow but which obliged the losers—all women—to do a striptease, exposing their uniformly massive breasts to the sound of Brazilian music. A tremendous, tired desire swept through him, unwanted, uncontrollable.

He rose, walked to the little bathroom, and, standing before the cracked mirror, shaved his beard with the razor he bought in Rome. Gingerly around the scab on his cheek. His face, pale and thin, emerging under his dark, sunken eyes.

In the morning the sea was calm. The harbor lay under a muffling blanket of dirty white fog, thick like the floor of clouds below a plane, a wall of nothingness, hollow and strange. Luke, clean-shaven now, limping slightly, climbed the gangway to the Greek ferry, bought a ticket. He had just enough money left for the second ferry, to Astipálaia. Passengers were to embark in an hour, weather permitting.

He went to drink coffee in a port-side café. As he sat at a little table, there was fear again, fighting against his courage of the night before.

He told himself, There is no proof; there have been no answers. Still, he did not know who killed Nicole; still, he did not know whom he killed in the Puces de Clignancourt.

But he no longer felt as if he didn't know. For there, where all along he had been looking for proof, he had found something else, something resembling *belief.* Belief that where he had been, his brother had been there before him; belief that, united by a common past, they had come to the same present.

But what is belief? His decision was weak in him as minutes passed, the whole elaborate construction of his thought trembling, then falling. And when the dust cleared, there was nothing but thin intuition, a thread of conviction, and he knew that whatever he might find at the other end, he must have the courage to follow it.

Or perhaps it was not courage; perhaps he knew it was just too late to do anything else.

Which also is a kind of courage.

8   CHEVEJON was in his living room. The woman had left before dawn, Natalie still slept. He was naked, standing by the windows giving onto the deck, where a cloudless sky was rising over the sea. On the coffee table behind him sat a laptop computer and a small printer. There were words on the screen and sheets of paper scattered on the table.

For a time, smoking, he indulged a vast feeling of satisfaction. Then his mind turned it all over, this double mystery, one more time.

Half he had to tell Danni; this half he had already written in a long letter on the laptop computer, where it waited to be printed.

For the other half he was going to send Natalie. She would tell it better than he, if less directly. Because less directly. She would take them, Danni, and Luke, too, along the same path of discovery he had so laboriously traversed. And Luke, in turn, as he came to understand, would tell her. By the time the two reached Danni, they both would understand nearly everything, and Danni would tell them the rest.

Now his heart skipped as he thought what a double messenger of death Luke was to be. He would have to tell Danni of his father's death and of Nicole's. He thought again: Whose job was that? He decided again: It was Luke's.

It was business between brothers.

Now he turned, opened the sliding doors, and stepped onto the balcony into the fresh light of dawn, descending from the sky recently washed by the summer storm. He wondered what Natalie would tell Luke. Would Luke understand?

But it had to be. It was inevitable. He had kept his two wards apart for so long. Now it was time for them to meet. She would tell him a story about herself, and Luke would hear, as Chevejon had, a story about Danni.

And Luke would tell her a story about himself, and she would hear a story about her father.

And between them they would find the truth.

And that truth? Chevejon switched focus. Perhaps the details of what he imagined were in error. In essence, though, he knew it was close to the truth. Perhaps very close.

In the sun-flooded living room of his house on Capri, he imagined the scene, nearly fifty years before, in Nazi Vienna when a man had presented himself at the office of Obersturmbannführer Hoestermann at the Jewish Emigration Bureau. And slowly Hoestermann had begun to understand that this man, no matter how well he spoke German, was not Viennese but from the Jewish government of Palestine.

Chevejon could imagine the terrible story Benami had told Hoestermann. The story of a massive war effort, at the height of its extension. Where did Hoestermann think it was going to go? Every resource was strained, and yet, in the center of this overdriven machine, an enormous force of bureaucracy and manpower, of essential resources, was being directed into a mad scheme of genocide. With America in the war, was Hoestermann prepared to cast his lot with the Thousand-Year Reich?

The man—Benami—suggested that it was not necessary to.

Benami had it in mind to offer him insurance.

He knew his man. From the biographies Chevejon knew that their fathers had been acquainted. Benami's uncle had once held an interest in Hoestermann's family business before he was, under the Nuremberg Laws, forced to divest. Benami and Hoestermann himself had many years ago briefly been in gymnasium together. They had played tennis. Chevejon wondered: What would he have told the Nazi—or, better yet, what would Danni have said?

The answer came smoothly to his mind. He would have said that he knew the pressures that Hoestermann was under. That he understood, and could not criticize the Nazi's self-protection under this dismantling of all reason in his country. The two men, however, could understand each other; they both came from that same country in the past.

But Hoestermann had to understand, too. What was done today would not be seen in the same light in a very possible tomorrow. What would a Western war crimes tribunal make of Hoestermann's very address, the former residence of the late Julius Neumann, perished in a concentration camp? A record of these things was kept, he must inform the *Obersturmbannführer,* in Jerusalem, and in a very possible future Jerusalem would head a sovereign state. If that were not enough, the *Obersturmbannführer* should know that there was other proof available, proof of which only he knew.

Benami did not name that proof, no doubt because, Chevejon slowly realized, Benami did not want to have to explain later how he knew about it. He did not want to have to explain that he had seen his father in Vienna, and his father had told him of the hiding place in the attic of Frederickstrasse 29 and of the family heirlooms he had hidden there. But he was able to convince Hoestermann that the proof existed. And the future would perhaps, he told Hoestermann, view the present differently if he were to produce that proof.

Anything could happen. Hoestermann should know that; he, too, had been there watching while the world went mad.

Perhaps Hoestermann had answered, sitting back at his desk in a black uniform: I could make one call and have you deported.

And perhaps Benami had responded, You could. Or you could provide me with every blank exit permit you can get your hands on, and ensure that I survive the war, and then be assured that the address of Frederickstrasse 29 be removed from any archive and any mind.

Perhaps Hoestermann had understood that this was not the first time that Nazis and Jews in Palestine had negotiated with the lives of Jews. He had argued, perhaps, over the number of permits. Perhaps he had insisted on a promise of testimony in the event of a war crimes tribunal's being convoked if the Wehrmacht lost the war. Or perhaps it was after the war, when he had learned the full extent of Benami's use of those exit permits, that he had insisted on Benami's coming to Nuremberg. Certainly, by then Hoestermann could have understood the exposure with which he threatened the Israeli.

What mattered was that a deal had been struck.

It was the kind of deal Chevejon understood.

What had gone wrong? Perhaps, when Benami received the first permits, he discovered to his horror that they were not only not blank but made out for his own family, a small goodwill gesture from the

Obersturmbannführer. Furiously he had demanded new ones. But what does it matter? Hoestermann had asked. Jews are Jews. They're all going to die the same way. Anyway, it couldn't be done: A blank exit permit is more than any money can buy; the Reich keeps an exact copy of every one granted, and only the B copy can leave his office.

So Benami took them.

Forgery was a skill the illegal emigration effort had mastered long ago. It was a skill they needed now. Because Palestine did not need these people for whom Hoestermann had provided the permits.

So Benami arranged the forgery that saved four hundred other Viennese Jews. Young, strong men needed for the coming War of Independence.

And sent four hundred others to their death.

How long, Chevejon wondered, had it taken Benami to understand that in this imperative there could be no exemption for himself? How long did he resist understanding? And did he see that, in the eyes of the world, to exempt his own father from those he was about to sacrifice would double its inhumanity and compound his crime?

He included his family. He had to. Unencumbered by the baggage— moral and historical—that Luke and Danni brought to this question, Chevejon saw that Benami was right to include his family, given his mad premise. Was Chevejon prepared to doubt that premise? He was not sure that he was qualified to. He was not sure it was his to judge.

Perhaps no one could; a mad premise in a mad world.

Chevejon, at least, would not. A sense of humanity, he knew, was not always appropriate; certainly it was rarely profitable. In Benami's case, he saw clearly, it had been neither—though the profit, in that terrible decision, had been measured in lives rather than money. As for whatever morality was involved—and Chevejon suspected that the term was, as so often, irrelevant—he doubted that anyone at all had the business to judge. Certainly nothing in Chevejon's not inconsiderable experience of evil qualified him to do so. Perhaps, even, to sacrifice his own humanity was the only fitting thing for Benami to do in that mad world of evil.

But that was not important. The important thing was the consequences of Benami's sacrifice, consequences that stretched across time and damned this boy and this girl: damned them to relive their fathers' impossible choices, damned them to leave their fathers and, alone in the world, understand something that should never, ever be understood by anyone.

And Chevejon knew, if accounts ever came due—and he knew with certainty, after his own criminal, immoral, often rapacious passage through Europe, that they did not—then it was not Benami and Hoestermann but their children who were having to pay. Who were paying, and had long been paying, not fifty years ago but today.

But Benami had not thought of this when he sacrificed his family. As far as he knew, only three people would ever know of what he had done: Benami, Hoestermann, and Yerushalmi. Everyone else who might have understood was dead. And the three were tied together for life in silence.

Until one late summer's day, nearly fifty years later, when Hoestermann had called from Frederickstrasse to Hamevasser Street in Jerusalem. To tell General Benami that his son had been there, demanding to see the A copies of the exit permits. Chevejon imagined the scene vividly. For God's sake, Hoestermann, you kept them? You sold me the insurance, General; why should I not keep the policy? No, Hoestermann had no definitive proof it was Benami's son; the man had used a pseudonym. But he was mortally certain he was right. Did my son see the permits? Not in my house, General, not in my house.

Hoestermann had held firm, good; Benami waited. He thought that he would hear from his son. True, he had given his son his diaries, and in them Danni had learned of the family objects hidden in the attic of Frederickstrasse 29. But that alone proved nothing. Still, when he didn't hear from his son, Benami began to consider his alternatives. Perhaps that was when he reinherited his elder son. Perhaps that was when he began to plan.

And then, in the spring, Hoestermann called again, with a further complicating factor—a dangerous one this time. The permits were gone, as was his daughter; the general's son must have gotten to her. She is young, impressionable, stubborn; no, he does not know where she is. Yes, she has his son's address. His pseudonym, too.

Now Chevejon laughed, almost happily. Where was Benami to turn? Where? Why not to his trusted assistant, a reservist in military intelligence? He was not to use his official apparatus, this was a private matter; still, it was a matter of serious importance to the state. Dov Sayada was an insider; he would grasp this matter in its moral and political dimensions alike. And Dov, with his lifelong courtship of the great Benami, asked nothing better than to be trusted to help.

He picked a team of three colleagues, of whom one had contacts in Danni's sub rosa world of business. Then Benami had told him not to hurt his son and to tell him, when they found him, that he was to be reinherited, to receive half of his father's vast collection of artwork, artifacts, and documents, with its vast value. Now Chevejon, his own perfect audience, shook his head in wonder. That Benami had thought Danni, because he was so good at selling, could also be bought.

They had not found Danni. Three of them had found Natalie but had not been able to hold her. One of them had found Nicole. And it was that one whom, after he killed Nicole, Luke had killed.

But now Chevejon was getting into what, awake all night, he had been writing on his laptop computer. Natalie was going to tell Luke all this, and Luke and Natalie were going to tell Danni. Together, each with his and her own misunderstood half of the story, they would tell the whole story to Danni. And Danni would, as Chevejon had, understand.

But now, before going on, he had work to do.

9   CHEVEJON ROSE, climbed the stairs, dressed in his darkened bedroom, and then walked into Natalie's room. An open window let in the wind off the sea. She slept in great peace, the sheet flung off in the sunlit room, exposing her slim body in its underclothes. Chevejon covered her with the sheet before he woke her.

"Darling. Hop up now, get dressed and packed. It's time for you to go."

She—I—woke immediately, straight into full comprehension.

"I told you. I told you you would kick me out."

"Kick you out? No." Chevejon laughed kindly. "I thought you wanted to find Danni Benami? Anyway, things are going to get pretty hectic here for a few days, and I do believe I will be obliged to go away for a time. No, I'm not kicking you out. I'm sending you to safety."

While I dressed and packed, he returned to the living room and, sitting in front of the computer, gazed blankly at the screen.

He knew, with deep certainty, that it could only be this way. If this story, this miserable interlude in their lives, was to be more than just a mystery, an international thriller, then these three people had to follow its story to the end, by themselves. All he could tell them—and he could tell them nearly all the answers—was meaningless, nothing, if they did not find it out by themselves. Then it would be not a solution but a reconciliation. Then it would bring them not just to the answers but to a peace, of sorts. And then all these deaths, from Nicole to Judi Benami, perhaps even to Rachel Weissmann, would be reduced, the tiniest bit, in their terrible meaninglessness.

Although that was an unusually dishonest thought for Chevejon, who was not in the habit of fooling himself. For he did not believe— none of us did—that their meaninglessness could ever be reduced at all.

10 WHEN, WARM WITH SLEEP, I descended into the brilliant morning sunlight from the sea, Chevejon, looking up at me from his computer, said: "Listen, darling. The police will be here soon, and it's time for you to go. Gianlucca's coming to take you to the airport."

I asked: "And are you going to tell me where I'm going?"

He answered, turning his attention back to the computer screen, "To Greece. Go have breakfast, quick now."

What he had written during the night was a reconstruction that again was as much imagination as fact. But the imagination did not matter, and the facts were clear.

He had imagined a man who, a year before, had seen himself displaced by Danni. A man whose years of service, of admiration, of loyalty, devotion to Benami were shunted aside by Danni. Danni, suddenly returned from years of exile to claim his place as Benami's son. But to David Sayada—Dov—this weak claim, the accident of his birth, Danni had long since forfeited. Forfeited by cowardice, by stupidity, by dishonesty, by fear.

For Dov had learned, from Benami himself—as Chevejon had learned from listening to Luke—that the strength of that long-since forfeited claim was, to Benami, stronger than his own years of loyalty. He, Dov Sayada, a highly placed officer in military intelligence, he who had fought, murdered, sacrificed his most basic humanity for the country that Benami valued above all things, he was to be displaced by this traitor.

Yes, Dov would find Danni for Benami. Yes, he was going to prevent Benami's past from being discovered by his son.

But when Danni came to Jerusalem, and left, and Dov saw Benami one day wrap the original of his coveted diary—the diary that by all between them had been implicitly promised to Dov for years—and send it to an address in Paris, something deep within him had shifted. Now he was still going to find Danni. But when he did, he was going to kill him.

It was an agenda born the moment he heard that Danni was to be reinherited, a plan put into action the moment he learned that his mentor was dead. For the agenda it did not matter that Benami was gone; now, alone, Dov held the strings of this operation, which was no less important because the man it was to protect was dead. As for the plan, it came to him complete, entire, in a single flash.

It was perfect: Once Hoestermann had his documents back, no one was ever going to look for Danni again; the less they heard from him, the better. Perhaps Dov would even keep the documents; then any proof affecting Benami's memory would be hidden forever.

Or perhaps the thought crossed his mind that, the exit permits in hand, he could crucify the dead man, destroy him.

The inheritance, it should have been all Dov's: not the money but the diaries, the letters, the lifetime of work that he had been meant, for so long, to carry on. Well, he could not have those. No. But he could have the money, and he could have ultimate arbitration over his deceitful mentor's place in history. That, at least, he would have.

It was no less than his due.

. . .

Carefully and thoroughly, without Danni or Chevejon's even guessing of his existence, this man had planned to undo their lives, they who were so fanatically careful. Perhaps he had listened in at Benami's door while Danni was there; perhaps he had understood the old man's heart after Danni had left.

Whichever it was, Dov had understood that Danni in the last months of his father's life, in going to Vienna to see Nicholas Hoestermann, had again performed an act of parricide, an act of state treason.

It had been easy to locate him: Benami had given him the Paris address and the pseudonym, and a simple plan had allowed Dov to trace Danni's progress. Well before Benami's death, before Luke had even left New York, Dov flew to Paris, rented the maid's room. Then he filed the change of address order, using a forged document, perhaps a driver's license, this time in the name of Maurizio Tueta.

Perhaps it didn't happen exactly like that, but Chevejon knew it was as close as made any difference.

And then Benami had died, and Dov's plan took on a life of its own. The day after the death he flew from Jerusalem to Paris, perhaps under the guise of his academic research. He knew Yerushalmi had telegraphed Danni. He telegraphed back, in Danni's name, claiming half the inheritance in cash. Luck was on his side in a way he didn't appreciate: Chevejon, no longer manning the office telephone but relaxing in Fiesole, traveling in Europe, had not received Nicole's call about the telegram. It was his mistake, but there was no time for remorse.

Perhaps Dov had a moment of pause when Luke offered him Benami's papers. Or perhaps by then it was too late. It was all in motion already. When he had offered Danni's address to Luke, and it became clear that the boy had no intention of finding his brother, that was a major hurdle cleared. He even tried to convince the boy that he had to go to Paris. But Luke was too apathetic, too uninterested. Too spiritless even to think of fighting the bogus directive to liquidate the estate. Good, very good. And when he came to understand how far Danni was traveling, and why he was going so far, it was a godsend. All Dov had to do was wait for the check to arrive. In perfect confidence that Danni, an exile, a traitor, and a criminal to boot, would have no recourse against his plan.

. . .

Now Chevejon's face shifted, nearly imperceptibly. Dov hadn't expected that the check would come by courier. And he hadn't expected Danni to return to Paris.

At first it seemed a major setback. But then Dov saw that there was something wrong. Slowly, following Nicole and Danni from a distance, he came to see that it was not Danni but Luke who had come to Paris. Danni's letters continued to arrive from ever farther south, and Dov saw that Luke had lied to him about his intention to return to New York.

When had it occurred to him? When had he realized the perfect confluence of events? He had to get into the apartment to get Danni's check, and he had to get Luke to leave. Killing Nicole was not the slightest obstacle—this man, state-trained, had a part of his brain where his murders sat in perfect self-sufficiency, hardly touching the rest of his life. And if Nicole died, the only possible suspect was Luke—the only one possible. The French police would take care of Luke, and Dov had only to go south to find Danni. Once Danni was dead, his already shadowy identity was up for grabs, and everything Dov wanted, deserved, was his. All he needed was to get Danni's check.

How ironic that he, a hero, should have to take on the identity of a deserter to get what was rightfully his.

In any case, now there was another imperative. With Luke in Nicole's very bed, who knew what the boy would manage to discover?

He killed Nicole.

Confident that the dark would make him enough like Luke to pass unnoticed, he'd waited until Luke went out and mounted the stairs at 6, rue de Fleurus.

And in the bargain he took the check.

Here Chevejon paused in his reading—rather, his rereading—of what he had written. For the first time he fully comprehended the enormity of the tragedy. Nicole killed by this stupid, bumbling thief, after they had so carefully protected her, for so many years, from the slightest hint of danger. And he would have killed Luke. Now Chevejon thanked God for Luke's own stupidity, those years before, in deciding to return to Israel, to the army. For Dov would have killed Luke had not Luke already learned himself how to kill.

What happened? Slowly, watching from a distance in Paris, Dov had come to understand that the police were not accusing Luke.

By every means they should have: to the bartender, all dagos looked alike, and when he passed by the café heading up the stairs, the bartender should have seen a dark-haired Jew and assumed it was Luke.

Of course, Chevejon knew, what Dov hadn't counted on was that Luke—convinced that Danni had killed Nicole—had been clever enough to account for that possibility in his alibi and that the videotape in Le Drugstore on Saint-Germain should have confirmed it. That left the police looking for someone else, someone no one had seen enter the building late that night.

And now Dov began to see that the State Department was involved, the Israeli Embassy. He had not only misjudged Luke's ability to protect himself but also underestimated the interests that would come into play to protect the boy.

There had been no choice; he would now have to kill Luke. Another irony: The Israeli Embassy, unaware of the forces at play, was protecting Luke, and Dov would have to act against his own government's interest to do what needed to be done.

For days he followed him around Paris. Once he thought the boy had recognized him and had run from him in the Tuileries. Then he'd tried to make his move in Les Halles, but he'd lost Luke in the crowds. When, finally, he followed Luke into the Puces de Clignancourt, he thought that his chance was there. Perhaps he leg-shot the boy on purpose, to hobble him, to take him somewhere else to kill him. No matter. Because after the first shot the boy had scrambled into a doorway, and while Dov tried to adjust to this fact, a massive white light had suddenly flooded the street. He shot at it with animal instinct and textbook aim—left, right, and center—but he hit nothing but the light, and that on his third shot, and then five lead bullets drilled into his body, stopping all thought, and he folded, like a split bag of sand, into the street.

.   .   .

Had his face not been nearly drained of blood, Chevejon would have smiled. At the chance perfection of it all. At Luke's good luck—even when he understood nothing. Perhaps, he thought, this boy is Danni's brother in a way more profound than his looks; Danni had always been an intensely lucky person. Perhaps, he thought, as he recovered from the grim story he had just told himself, this boy had a future.

Certainly, it had been smart of Luke to come to Florence. As it had been, he thought, of Natalie.

What had not been smart was for Dov's partners, directed now, probably, by Hoestermann, to continue the search. In his position, Chevejon thought, he would have sat back and waited. Because now, with Benami dead, the stakes had changed, and the truth had moved to a different order of meaning. And because now everyone was compromised: Luke by murder; Natalie by theft.

As for Danni, he had always been compromised. By his very existence.

That was what Chevejon was thinking as he sat back from the computer screen and hit the print command. Briefly he wondered how Luke had found out where he was going. In his place, Chevejon would have called Yerushalmi and bribed him with his possession of the exit permits. Perhaps Luke had done the same.

But it didn't matter now. As the printer started to hum, Chevejon began to talk, through the open kitchen door, to me.

I was, he told me, to go with Gianlucca to the airport, from where I was to fly to Athens and then to find a taxi to Piraeus. He told me to find where the 6:00 P.M. ferry from Ancona was docking and wait there.

The man I was looking for would arrive on that boat. Only it was not the man I saw in Vienna; it was the one I saw in Paris, and his name was Luke Benami. Yes, he was the brother. Be careful, though. He might be wearing a beard and glasses; probably he'll have shaved it off. I was to bring him this money, and I was to go with him wherever he was going. There I'd find Danni Benami. And only when I got there was I to give Danni this envelope.

He gave me some money, a lot of money in Italian and American bills. Then he gave some messages that he had not wanted to put in print.

I was to tell Danni that he, Chevejon, had in all probability been arrested but that he'd be out soon. That when he was out he'd let Danni know by the normal method via the *Herald-Tribune* classifieds. That Danni shouldn't call or write until then, and on no account was he to come back to Europe. That the only person who could tell where they were was Yerushalmi and Yerushalmi would not talk; he was making sure of that. Then, worriedly, he asked me: "Have you had enough to eat? You have a long day ahead of you."

Now, as we waited for Gianlucca, Chevejon turned to the computer screen again. On it was the text of a letter, addressed to Monsieur l'Inspecteur Jean-Baptiste Lecéreur, Préfecture de Police, Paris, and cc'd to Avishai Yerushalmi, Bank Leumi, Jerusalem. He reminded himself to tell Gianlucca to send the two copies:

> Monsieur:
> The person you have been looking for concerning the murder of Miss Nicole Japrisot is named David Sayada. He himself was the victim of the shooting, this summer, in the vicinity of the Clignancourt flea market. His wife can be found on Hamevasser Street, in Jerusalem: you'll locate her with ease by addressing yourself to a Mr. Yerushalmi, with whom you are no doubt already acquainted.

He finished reading, considered for a moment, then continued writing:

> I very much hope to have the occasion to explain these killings to you and will do so as soon as you are able to provide sure guarantees of amnesty and safety for my colleague—whom I do not believe I need name—both from your department in France and from the government of Israel. Mr. Yerushalmi should be in touch with David Sayada's office at the Department of Military Intelligence to know the exact terms of the guarantee I require. And you can contact me by being in touch with the Italian police, who will doubtless have me in custody by the time you read this.

Chevejon reread the telegram. He paused. Then, after a minute, he moved the computer's cursor to the sentence that read "amnesty and safety for my colleague." He put the cursor between "my" and "colleague" and inserted the word *two*. Then added an *s* to "colleague." Then he hit the print command.

Now it was time to get ready for the police; his address in Capri was no secret, and it could not be long until the French police, having traced his calls to Luke's room at the Lutetia, sent their Italian counterparts to find him. Interesting, he had never actually been arrested before. And he was confident that he wouldn't be in jail for very long.

Still, as he heard the key turn in the front door, heralding Gianlucca's arrival, for a sudden moment he asked himself: Could he have it all wrong? Could there be forces in play that he had simply not understood?

For a long moment he wondered. Then he shook his head and stood.

The truth, Luke would find it on the Greek island at the end of his trip. He would find it, and he would tell it. It would be hard news of which he would be the messenger, but he was the right person to tell it, the only person. Chevejon, here in Capri, felt suddenly confident that they would come through this okay. All four of them.

11 IN ANCONA a foghorn sounded, and Luke, at his café table, started from his reverie. He found himself calm.

He crossed to the port and boarded the ship. Found a seat on the steerage deck, smoked. He wanted a drink, badly, but there was no money even to eat. A time passed; then, with a shuddering lurch and the deep boom of a foghorn, the ship went into motion.

He looked back, just in time to see Italy disappear as the boat, gliding smoothly above the deep churn of its engines, moved steadily into the thick blind of white.

1 IN THE BLINDING HEAT of a late-summer afternoon, my bag in my hand, I stood at the dock in Piraeus, watching the Ancona ferry disembark.

Around me a hot crowd of young people traveling, families gathered around their bags, and freight—a Jansport backpack next to a boxed Trinitron next to a roped leather trunk dating from the last war. The crowd was bisected by a line of trucks idling in a fog of exhaust, their loud engines mixing with a dozen languages being spoken at once. From the ferry gangway came other trucks, and along their side, a stream of passengers, identical to the people around me, as if the one group were pointlessly replacing the other.

That was where I saw Luke. Limping slightly in the slow-moving line of disembarking passengers, distinguished by a high red cut on his pale face.

I followed him to the ticket office, then to another dock, where he boarded another ferry. I boarded, too, without a ticket, then at the purser's office, bought passage to the last port of call.

By the time I finished, I could feel the boat's engines churning away in reverse. Then, as I arrived on deck at the bow rail, the engines shifted, and we began the long, slow curve from our berthing into the Ionian Sea.

That was when I saw him again. Looking up to my left. His beaked nose in profile, his face pale below his eyes, yet burned above, as if he had just shaved off his beard, with a thick, red scab on one cheek.

2 AFTER A TIME he turned, absently, to look down at me, at the woman at his side. He stared for an uncomfortable time, his eyes traveling over my breasts, suddenly so exposed under the thin white shirt, at the fall of my stomach, at my round hips and the expanse of burned skin exposed under my skirt. Then he looked away again.

For a long time, as he gazed out to sea, I watched his profile. Then, reaching into my pocket, I produced Chevejon's money.

My voice faint in the dome of sea and sky, I spoke, as I had with his brother, in French.

"This is from Chevejon. He told me to give you this and to go with you wherever you're going."

He turned now, sharply, and looked at the money for a long time without taking it. Then he looked at me, and evidently my French accent had betrayed me because he spoke in German.

"*Weiso wußste er daß ich nach Griechenland kam?*—how did Chevejon know I was coming to Greece?"

"*Ich weiß nicht.*"

"Are you coming from Florence now?"

"*Ja. Nein.* From Capri. I was in Florence." I looked into his face, searching for my words. And at last I said simply: "*Mein Name ist Natalie Hoestermann.*"

He nodded, slowly, his eyes abstracting, then coming sharply back to focus. "Hoestermann. Then this has to do with my brother."

"*Nicht genau*—not exactly." We watched each other. Then I tried again. "Yes, in a way. I met him once, in Vienna. A year ago." I wondered how to make clear my sense of our connection and found only facts that I myself did not understand.

"He came looking for some documents my father possessed." I could not name the documents; I could not bring the words out.

But it didn't matter. While I spoke, Luke's eyes had again abstracted, and when he refocused on me, the connection was made.

"Of course. But you did not give them to him."

"Not at first." I watched him anxiously for a moment. "Then I tried to bring them to him."

He was smiling now. "Let me guess. You found Chevejon."

I nodded, not smiling.

"And Chevejon took you in. And then sent you here."

"Yes."

He turned now to the sea and laughed, a long, low laugh that brought tears to the corner of his eyes. Finished, he lit a cigar, wiping the back of a hand across his eyes.

"Chevejon said you would know where your brother was."

"Did he?" He seemed about to laugh again, but then it died on his face. "Then I guess we're both still guided by Chevejon's omniscience. Let's hope he's right."

"Is he? Is he right?"

Now it was Luke's turn to answer that he didn't know. He thought for a time, smoking, then said: "And tell me this. What did Chevejon say my brother was doing, wherever he is?"

"He didn't say." I paused, then went on. "But I already knew. He's looking for proof. Of what my father did. Is that not right?"

A pause. "No, not exactly. He has proof of what your father did already. What he's looking for now is proof of what my father did."

I blanked. "You mean *my* father."

And he shook his head, decisively. "No. I mean mine."

3　WITH CHEVEJON'S MONEY, Luke bought bottles of iced retsina for both of us and food for himself. We went back to our solitary post at the railings while he ate, hungrily. His clothes were very dirty, and I offered him an oversized T-shirt in which I had slept the night before.

And then, as if neither of us had any doubt in the world as to the necessity of what we were doing, we began to talk.

And this is what Luke told me.

He told me how he lost his father in the bitter rain of a Jerusalem winter and found his brother in the blossoming of a Paris spring.

How, looking for the brother he had murdered, he traveled south through the blooming of a European spring, from Paris to hot Italy, and there he found the father he had lost.

And how, guided by a dead father looking for a murdered son, he traveled over the Adriatic to the Ionian and on into the always strengthening sun. Always more south, always more summer, and always, always more lost.

4 IT WAS AS IF our stories were to take exactly the time of the boat's passage, the time allotted, no more and no less. It was as if we understood, each in the same way, exactly where the stories were heading. The day passed, and then the night, and then the morning. Naxos, then Amorgos drew close. And then they passed, great bulks sleeping in the sun on the rippling surface of blue as the ship drew nearer to its final call.

It was as if the whole summer we had neither of us been lost, neither of us driven blindly across Europe under the weight of our fathers' guilts, but traveling surely to this point where, talking and listening, we were able to take each other there.

5 LATE the next morning we stood at the rail on the bow of the boat—the sun nearly straight overhead—as the passengers crowded below to disembark on the last stop of this long trip, the port of Astipálaia with its white houses and red roofs slowly approaching on the blinding bright sea. In my hand was the letter from Chevejon to Danni. I gave it to Luke, and he stood weighing it in his hands.

"And so do you think we will be able to deliver this?"

I didn't answer, watching him. I knew the answer, but instead I asked, without thinking: "Luke. Why did you trust me?"

Surprised, he looked down at my face, and in his look I felt I could see the same look his brother had given me, a year before, in my father's study in Vienna. And then for a moment I nearly hated him, firm in his righteousness, righteous in his suffering. I said, bitterly: "Your brother didn't understand either."

But I was wrong. Glancing toward me, then returning his eyes back to the port, where the shapes of moored boats next to the pier were beginning to come clear, he answered, for the first time using the familiar: "*Ich habe geglaubt Du würdest mich dorthin bringen.* I felt you were going to take me there."

"*Aber mich? Warum denn mich?* Why me?"

And he answered, in a low voice, as if speaking only to himself: "*Ist das nicht offesichtlich?* Isn't it obvious? You're the only one who could understand."

For a long time we stood watching the approaching port. Then he went on.

"Chevejon was right: It all matters. Who killed Nicole, what your father did, what my father did. But it matters only in the most banal of senses. I'm not interested in judging my father. Less so yours. I've sat my shiva for them. Don't you see? There's no reparation payable for crimes of existence. Whom would we pay it to? What could it be?" He paused for a long time, then went on in the intonation of a question more than a statement.

"*Nein.* We've both of us traveled a long way to be free of our fathers. Mine is gone; yours will be, too, soon. I've finished my mourning." He looked at me briefly now, and in that brief look a whole new world was born for me. "And so have you."

He turned away again as the ferry crossed the small harbor and approached its berth with reversing engines, showing his profile against the sky of blinding blue. An eagle nose above a thin cheek with a night's growth of beard, sunken eyes looking through dark lenses at the shore.

I followed his gaze and saw, on the dock, a man in black glasses under a shock of jet black hair. In a white suit. His whole being concentrated on the boat that he thought, he prayed, carried his lover. Perhaps he waited for this boat every day. Perhaps he had been waiting for weeks.

It was still far too far to see if it was him. And there was no proof. There was only Luke's belief, a thin faith that the path he had traveled could not be his alone, but it was also mine, and it was also his brother's. And if it were him, I thought with a shock, then there would be no conclusion when the boat docked, but an opening up of a whole new world of pain for this suffering man.

And I thought, What a long, long way Luke has traveled to bring his double news of death.

Crowds had engulfed the man on the dock now, and though he craned his neck to watch the approaching boat, he was all but hidden from our view. And now, my first words in freedom, I returned to Luke's question. Above the rising roar of the engines in reverse, above the cries of circling gulls and the shouts of the crew, I spoke into the brilliant sunlight in a voice that was so nearly lost in the din that I had nearly to shout to make myself heard.

"Und Du? Der Mann der dort steht, weißt Du jetzt wer er ist?"

"And you? That man there, do you know now who he is?"

"Ja," Luke answered, shouting too now, above the noises of arrival, looking straight ahead into the light, his face pale and set as if his mind, too, were not on the end of his long journey but on the terrible task that was before him. Still, as he shouted, his voice carried not only sadness but also triumph away into the deep groans of the boat settling into its berth, the noise of all the gangways coming alive and the passengers disembarking into the suddenly living harbor. "Ja. Das ist mein Bruder."

AFTERWORD

In all fiction that relies on historical reality, there is the risk of trivializing great and tragic events by misusing them as background to personal stories, of misrepresenting the actual in a dramatization of the possible, and of passing facile judgment rather than dramatizing moral complexity. I hope I have been successful in avoiding these three pitfalls, but certainly I have taken great care neither to falsify history nor to oversimplify contemporary politics.

That the two central Israeli characters of this novel, for example, have left that country no more implies a fundamental anti-Zionism than the fact that the sons of some leading Zionists never went to Israel, or the sons of others have left. To Israelis of Luke and Danni Benami's generation, the existence of a Jewish state is a fact rather than, as for the country's founders, a question. The question, for many of this generation, is no longer whether Israel has a right to exist—that is a given—but how it will continue to do so: at the expense of its Palestinian minority or with a settlement of that minority's national aspirations? Nor are the many historical complexities behind the present dilemma—the fact that the territories were occupied in defensive wars, the manipulation of the Palestinians by other Arab governments, etc.—of relevance as pressing as the question of what effect the occupation has on Israeli society. It's worth noting that, as this novel goes to press, the grounds of these questions have shifted dramatically from the fictional setting in 1989, and the onus of opposing territorial concession and Palestinian autonomy has shifted from the Israeli government to the right-wing religious fundamentalists, both Muslim and Jewish, each less concerned with historical justification than with a purely religious imperative, and each posing an unprecedented threat to peace.

As for the novel's re-creation of the past, none of the characters of this story existed; none of their stories is true. But all of their fictional stories are dwarfed by comparison to the real stories that serve as their background. At no point have I invented a historical situation or moral quandary that did not face, to quote Raul Hilberg, the "perpetrators, victims, and bystanders" during the war and since.

Jews were the prime object of the Nazi policy of genocide and made up the overwhelming numbers of victims of Nazi atrocity; that we know well. But fifty years after, we are coming to understand what Camus knew during the war: that the Allied governments and their citizens as well as the Axis countries—Jews, Israelis, and Germans alike—all contributed to each of Hilberg's three categories, and most liberally to the last. Readers interested in exploring the ample historical documentation and moral analysis of these questions and events are referred, among the plentiful historical and analytic sources, to Tom Segev's *The Seventh Million: The Israelis and the Holocaust* (particularly the sections on the Kastner trial); Dina Porat's *Trapped Leadership*; *Born Guilty: Children of Nazi Families*, by Peter Sichrovsky; *Testimony: Crises of Witnessing in Literature, Psychoanalysis, and History* by Shoshana Felman and Dori Laub, M.D. (particularly Felman's essays on Camus's *The Plague* and *The Fall*); Claude Lanzmann's *Shoah*; and finally, and most important, the masterful work about Viennese Jewry during and after the war by Axel Corti, *Where To and Back*, consisting of three films: *God Does Not Believe in Us Anymore, Santa Fe*, and *Welcome in Vienna*.

NEIL GORDON was born in South Africa, grew up in the United States, and has lived in Scotland, Israel, and France. He was educated at the University of Michigan and Yale University, where he received a Ph.D. in French. Until recently on staff at *The New York Review of Books,* he is currently managing editor of *The Reader's Catalog* and a book-review editor at *The Boston Review.* He lives in New York with his wife and two children.

ABOUT THE TYPE

This book was set in Galliard, a typeface designed by
Matthew Carter for the Merganthaler Linotype Company
in 1978. Galliard is based on the sixteenth-century
typefaces of Robert Granjon.